Waterbaby

a novel

Cris Mazza

Soft Skull Press

Published by Soft Skull Press
New York, NY
www.softskull.com

cover design: Edmund Tse
interior design: David Barnett

Library of Congress Cataloging-in-Publication Data

Mazza, Cris.
  Waterbaby : a novel / Cris Mazza.
    p. cm.
  ISBN-13: 978-1-933368-84-9
  ISBN-10: 1-933368-84-5
  I. Title.

PS3563.A988W38 2007
813'.54—dc22

2007028184

Preamble

She'd been feeling a seizure coming on for several weeks, and for the first time in twenty-five years. The quarter-century anniversary of the convulsion named Denny.

Retired at 43, now pushing 49, making (or earning) money had been an efficient distraction for twenty years. Surely enough time had gone by to make Denny no longer a factor. Besides, there were too many others that conceivably could spin her into a convulsion. Since retiring, ordinarily, she dodged the news—not conducive to essential tranquility—but had been unable to evade elections auctioned to the highest paid attorney, terrorist sharks concealing themselves in the surf off playground beaches, passenger jets used as guided missiles, and junk mail bacteria. Meanwhile her life-saving brother became even more renowned, her as-of-last-week ex-roommate held her belongings hostage, and a whole family on the next block was massacred by an estranged adopted son. Perhaps non sequiturs—wasn't everything?—but good enough excuses for Tam to stop trying to dilute her eddying brain waves just with new age muzak—instead head off to Maine and attempt to discover if her great-great grandmother was a shipwrecked baby.

Before leaving for Maine, living temporarily in an empty bungalow after Meryl kicked her out, Tam had sent the news article about the family massacre to her sister, Martha. Father, mother, adult child, uncle, aunt-by-marriage, grandparents, tied up, throats cut. The defense attorney maintained that the young man suffered from "a form of epilepsy called rage syndrome." Martha, in return mail, sent two things. One a newspaper clipping about their brother, with a post-it sticky and Martha's round girly writing: "Gary's a hero again—this one has been on my desk a while, I kept forgetting to send it to you!"

3

August 3, 2001

Abandoning his own chances in the Mission Beach Triathlon, sports-writer Gary Marr-Burgess, 46, stopped his race during the rough-water portion of the three-part race to assist a struggling fellow-swimmer. A certified Water Safety Instructor (WSI), and a member of the Red Cross canine search-and-rescue team, Marr-Burgess returned to the beach with Jason Udall, 32, eight minutes after the start of the race. With the eerie sound of screams from the 75-year-old Bellmont Park roller coaster in the background, Marr-Burgess emerged from the 4-foot surf carrying Udall. "He'd swallowed a mouthful and was sputtering when I passed him," Marr-Burgess said after paramedics took Udall by stretcher to Mission Bay Hospital. "I turned and saw him go down." Marr-Burgess's mother, Emily Marr-Burgess, 71, on the beach as a race spectator, said, "This is what he's been trained for, since he was four or five years old." She added that Marr-Burgess had been the youngest person in county history to achieve the difficult WSI certification when he was 13. Udall was listed in good condition and is expected to be released from the hospital tomorrow. Marr-Burgess is the author of TRIATHLETE IN TRAINING, RESISTANCE TRAINING IN WATER, *and* NEVER TOO OLD, THE 40-SOMETHING'S GUIDE TO SPORTS CONDITIONING.

The other piece of paper also had a post-it sticky, "From my new computer!" On first glance, it looked like one of Martha's children's school history reports. But it was a segment of the genealogy project Martha had been pursuing since she was 16.

In 1866, Jaruel Marr became the keeper of the Hendricks Head light on the Island of Southport in Sheepscot Bay, the coast of Maine. [Note: boring to start with dates and names. Punch this up a little. Ask Gary for help!] *Born April 3, 1829, Jaruel was of the appropriate age to serve in the Civil War. There, as a private, he was injured and also taken as a Prisoner of War. Another prisoner, Doctor Wolcott, caring for the sick and wounded, inspired Jaruel, who never forgot him. Thus Jaruel's first born child after the war was named Wolcott. Jaruel was a carpenter who built his own house on Marr Point on the island of Southport, where he also was the lighthouse keeper for 29 years. He died of apoplexy* [Note: Tam, don't get excited, I don't think it's the same thing] *in March of 1907.*

Jaruel and his wife, Catherine, had six children (listed below). This is strange because, according to the Boothbay Register (article dated April 24, 1997), Jaruel Marr only had five children. (. . . "five living children" it says.) The Register was attempting to debunk a story in a 1945 book about New England lighthouses that claimed Jaruel Marr, the Hendricks Head keeper, had rescued a shipwrecked baby in 1875. According to that story (a story repeated in a Navy newspaper in 1955) a March blizzard took Sheepscot Bay by surprise. In the 19th century, most terror came at the hands of the weather. Since any ship off the coast might seek a harbor refuge during a storm, Jaruel lit the tower lantern at Hendricks Head. [Note: the rest I'm quoting directly from the 1955 Navy newspaper, until I can put it into my own words. I'm not supposed to speculate and I'm not sure if I wander into speculation when I start putting it into my own words. Gary, help!]

"After lighting the lantern, Marr and his wife, wrapped in heavy woolens, stamped their feet and slapped their arms to keep warm in the captain's walk of the lighthouse. As they shivered with cold, they suddenly saw through the dense snowstorm the faint outline of a ship coming up Sheepscot Bay." [Note: remember they say "coming up" because Sheepscot Bay is also called Sheepscot River,

not sure if it's really a bay or a river.] *"Apparently the captain of the ship did not see the lighted lantern of Hendricks Head. Before he could prevent a disaster, his ship crashed on rocks near Cuckolds, about a mile away at the tip of Southport."* [Note: imagine the story of how Cuckolds was named!] *"Marr rushed down the lighthouse stairway and out onto the rocky shore to see if he could launch his dory and possibly make a rescue. Only when he saw that the rocky shore was being swept by ten to fifteen-foot breakers did he realize that no dory or human being could long survive in the angry sea. To brighten the fading hopes of the persons aboard this wreck, Keeper Marr and his wife built a huge bonfire on a high rock as a signal that the ship had been sighted."* [Note: the 1945 book containing this story claimed the bonfire was to guide the ship in, but the ship soon went under.] *"Next, Keeper Marr surveyed the shore to see if any wreckage was coming in. He observed a large bundle drifting. Heavy seas mercilessly pounded the badly damaged ship. Gigantic waves swept wildly over persons clinging to the rigging. The cold sea water and zero temperature soon froze helpless human beings to the ratlines of the ship's shrouds."* [Note: find out, ask Mom, is a shroud actually part of a ship, or was this a gruesome metaphor?] *"Then Marr ran to his boathouse and grabbed his boathook and some line. Mrs. Marr securely fastened one end of the line around his waist. The pair ran along the shore to a small beach where the bundle was rapidly coming ashore. Wading into the furious surf, Marr finally made fast his boathook to one of the fastenings of the bundle. As he did, a huge wave tossed him and the bundle toward the beach. Marr lost his grip on the boathook, but seized one of the bundle's fastenings and dragged it out of reach of the next breaker."* [Note: question: when I rewrite, I'll have him riding the bundle in like a boogie board? That would be simile, not speculation, right Gary?] *"After getting his breath, Marr discovered that he had retrieved two featherbeds from the angry waters of Sheepscot Bay. Then he cut the fastenings and found to his amazement a wooden box, and from the box came the screams of a baby."* [Note: this article I copied was by George W. Grupp from the Navy Times in 1955. Find out the correct format to give credit.]

At the very end of the Grupp article it says that Jaruel found a locket in the box where the baby's mother had put a message, placing her daughter in the hands of God. This account also reported that since Jaruel and Catherine had recently lost a baby, they adopted the ship-wrecked girl. [Note: this source says their only child!! But see birth dates below.]

Getting back to the 1997 Boothbay Register, in the local history column, a Maine historian who wants tourists to only be interested in "true history" has claimed all versions of this story can easily be proven un̲true by the names and birthdates of fi̲v̲e̲ "living children." (Those five births probably found in local archives by the historian.)

However, m̲y̲ research shows Jaruel Marr and his wife Catherine had si̲x̲ children, as shown in this segment of my genealogical list:

Eugene Clarence, b. May 10, 1854

Cedelia Ann, b. November 20, 1856

Mabel Verona, b. September 23, 1860

Wolcott Garrett, b. December 15, 1866

*Mary Catherine, b. January 20, 1868 and died June 16, 1899

Lowell Herbert, b. May 11, 1872

Can a mysterious new member of our family be proven ?

*This is the one the historian in Boothbay didn't list!

[Note: Tam, want to take a trip to Maine and check on some stuff for me? Call me and I'll give more details, but you can probably guess from the above what it is.]

No comment from Martha on the epileptic's rampage.

Go To Ground

There had been times when Tam sat on the sofa with Meryl in the evening, like a family, the TV on but neither really watching. The History Channel, Outdoor Network, Travel Network, Home and Garden, channels with soft PBS-style voice-over and serene music. Classical music, New Age, Peruvian flute-and-drum, harps and wooden recorders, slow old-fashioned gospel, anything ancient (except bagpipes) could forestall epileptic seizures. The soundtracks and gauzy voices seemed to affect Meryl as well. A couple of times, Meryl had been sitting there one minute, picking her fingernails or staring at the ceiling as though following a fly, then seemed to liquefy and, uninvited, lay her head in Tam's lap. That's where Meryl was the time she said, "What should I do about Kixy? The Master Earthdog title could cap her career."

Meryl bred cairn terriers—the kind of dog at one time made famous by *The Wizard of Oz*. Beauty alone was not enough for an individual animal to make its mark in the legacy of the breed; dog breed championships were not as valuable without also attaining performance titles. Dogs, in their short lives, could quickly amass titles and honors. While continuing to bring home ribbons and trophies and get listed in the top rankings of their breed, they could also produce offspring who likewise garnered accolades and distinction, which the parent dog could claim and list with their own lifetime achievements. All in eight to ten years.

Meryl was never going to be important, in the larger scheme of things. Tam just needed a place to live while she sat on her early retirement package, her portfolio, and the proceeds from the sale of her condo, and contemplated where she would go and what she would do. Who she would be. What new distraction to throw in the way of possibly imminent treacherous brain waves. Meryl had advertised for a roommate. A housemate, to help her meet the mortgage payments on the new property that her fanatical dog-showing hobby had induced her to buy. Pups and stud service alone couldn't meet the demands of Meryl's expenses. Tam had actually been the broker who'd liquidated bonds left to Meryl by her mother, which Meryl needed for a downpayment. Then—no longer Meryl's broker, since Meryl had no portfolio and Tam retired—the offer to use Meryl's place as a wayfarer's stopover (or halfway house) seemed a sensible decision. Tam didn't have a dog. Her brother did. Her famous hero brother.

But Tam had lived with Meryl longer than she'd thought she would. Three years. "I think I've found something to do, and I'm good at it," she'd written to Martha, across the top of a xeroxed page from the *Cairn Terrier Reporter*, a photo of herself handling one of Meryl's dogs to a terrier group win.

Martha had replied pleasantly, "The dog's so cute! We're thinking of getting a puppy for the kids. Gary thinks a lab would be best."

It was Martha, not Gary, who sent Gary's books to Tam. In the weekend-athlete training manuals he wrote, every photo of a conditioning exercise or rough water swimming technique included his black lab, and in the margins he had sidebar tips called "The Coach Says" with a cartoon character of a dog standing in swim trunks at the edge of a pool, or in racing pants riding a bicycle. Gary's dog's name was Coach.

Tam had at first said no to helping Meryl show her dogs. She'd said, "My brother has a lab with some kind of rescue dog certification, and the dog's practically . . . I don't know . . . some kind of star."

"And this has something to do with showing my dogs?"

"It'll look like I'm copying."

"*Copying?* What're you, 10 years old?"

"Make that 12. Sometimes I wonder if I ever stopped being 12. Then I wonder if I ever got over being 22. Two times my life stopped. 12 and 22—"

"Wow, I didn't know dog-showing could open a closet of such *drama.*"

"Sorry."

"You're such a brooder. Your brother probably doesn't think for two seconds about what you do. He needs to come rescue you from drowning in your self pity. I just thought you should get involved in something, and I could use a, you know, *partner . . .* "

Tam started showing dogs for Meryl. It was soon apparent that even when Meryl showed a dog in the same class—Meryl handling the dog she hoped would win, Tam showing another dog just to help raise the number of entries—Tam was the one who took the class, took the points. Tam had the right poise, the right amount of apparent aplomb to allow the dog at the end of the lead to radiate its aggressive terrier attitude, its spirit and animation. She didn't have to wave a liver treat or stay in constant amusing motion to help the dog stay focused, alert, showing off its sturdy body and acute senses. Other people began to hire her to show their dogs. She put championships on dachshunds, Welsh corgis, French bulldogs. It was only in the past year Tam and Meryl had started doing earthdog tests to add performance titles to the dogs' distinction.

A cairn was a go-to-ground terrier, originally bred to go into the tunneled dens of vermin quarry, anything from rats to badgers. In actual use of terriers on farms, the quarry was brought out of the den dead. That's how you knew if your terrier was a good one. In sanctioned earthdog tests, a judge had to determine that the dog was "working the quarry," which meant barking, digging and scratching at the caged rats placed behind a barrier in a den at the end of the tunnel. But not killing. No quarry was allowed to be harmed, and the securely-housed rats had to have food and water available to them at all times throughout the test, even when they would have likely preferred to run away.

Sometimes Tam fed the dogs, or helped bathe and groom them. She helped clean the runs. The dogs were all the same color, same size. She didn't adopt one to share her cereal bowl or sleep on her pillow. She couldn't even tell them apart.

So, that night, with Meryl's head on her lap, when Meryl had said, "Poor Kixy, how can we help her get her Master Earthdog title?" Tam shrugged without answering.

"We'd go down in history for having the first Champion Master Earthdog bitch. When she has a litter, they'll go for two thousand apiece, maybe three."

Tam kept her head up in these situations, so she couldn't see Meryl's face. Her leg muscles twitched. On the TV, some kind of documentary where a disembodied camera sailed through an old castle, something Martha might tape and show her kids. Tam concentrated on the music. Piano, with a flute. So she wouldn't look completely indifferent, she asked, "How do you know she'd be the first?"

"OK, maybe the first best-in-show bitch to do it. People hardly ever do it with bitches because if they're any good, so much of their career is spent having their litters."

"What's her problem?"

"She doesn't want to work with another dog, and at master level they have to work in brace. She backs off. But think how it could be if she won Westminster *and* was a Master Earthdog. She'd be the toast of New York, just like your brother's Lab." Her head still in Tam's lap, Meryl rolled to her back and stretched her arms up, barely missing whacking Tam in the chin. "And if she doesn't like rats, she can go to ground looking for other things. They said the terrorists go to ground after an attack. How about Kixy searches for terrorists with your hero brother? What a hoot!"

Of course by this time Gary and Coach had already been to New York, last year, with the canine search-and-rescue team. Previously, they'd been to an avalanche and Oklahoma City. On network news, Gary—his thick steel-colored hair standing straight up, dark growth on his gaunt cheeks, and blotches like make-up under his eyes—was kneeling, an arm around his dog whose black coat was snowy with pulverized concrete, as he explained via remote to Tom Brokaw how the dogs are trained. "Every time he finds the scent of a living human being, he gets rewarded with his favorite toy. The dogs are conditioned, through training, to crave that toy," Gary had said. "He *wants* to find someone," Gary stressed. "He can't get the reward if he doesn't. If there's no one to find, he'll work and work all day, but with no reward. The dogs get as discouraged as we do, their spirits take a hit, too. That's why these have to be special dogs to start with, with lots of heart." Coach and the other search-and-rescue dogs had all gotten medals of heroism from the N.Y. Fire Department, and they'd all been allowed to hold their new reward toy during the presentation—tennis balls with stars-and-stripes tails attached. Martha had sent Tam a video that their mother had taped of the ceremony. "Such a good boy," their mother's voice murmured on the tape when it was Coach's turn to receive his medal.

"Get up," Tam said, which is something she hadn't said the other two occasions Meryl's body had drooped like softened wax until her head came to rest on Tam's lap. "So how can we help her—Kixy?"

Meryl rose like a young storm-drenched tree, drying slowly and slowly unbending until it was upright again. And like a tree shaking its branches, she ran her fingers through her brambled hair. "I don't know . . . but she sure doesn't like working in brace. Except . . . "

"What doesn't she like about working in brace?"

"That she doesn't know the other dog. Especially if it's a male. She's submissive."

"What if it was a dog she already knows and has practiced with?"

"Well . . . there's this rule, their brace partner should be unfamiliar."

"Oh."

"Actually," Meryl removed her earrings, perched her bare feet on the edge of the coffee table, her toenails painted pink. "What the rule says is that the dogs paired as partners shouldn't have the same *owner*. They could even be littermates if they didn't have the same owner."

The castle on TV had an old-fashioned moat, with a pair of swans sailing past ancient stone walls. "So, aren't there any dogs in Earthdog who she already knows?"

"Yeah, but *I* own them."

"Oh." Tam leaned forward to reach the TV remote. "Why not . . ." She switched to CNN, then to the Weather Channel.

"Go on."

"What if one of the other dogs that she already knows was mine?"

"Not a bad idea." Meryl slipped the remote from Tam's hand and put the TV on mute. "But how could we be sure Kixy would be paired with *your* dog?"

"The odds have to be made better. There would have to be at least two other entries that are dogs she knows that also have a different owner."

"Okay, what if *Kixy* were yours. Then *I'll* enter two or three other dogs. We'll change just Kixy's ownership. And then change it back again, after." Meryl picked at the polish on one of her toes. "Or after she's finished, we can share her. Co-own. Make her the first piece of our partnership." She sat up and took a deep breath. "Should we do it?"

"If you want to."

"Tam, do *you* want it?"

"I don't know. I'm doing pretty well as a handler. I was thinking of getting licensed, maybe become a breed judge—"

"Tam, I'm serious, I need you to tell me if we should do this." Meryl leaned forward as though examining her feet. Her hair closed off her face like a curtain. "I thought you used to be competitive. I thought that's what you were about, once. I want this so *bad*."

"Well . . . Since it isn't breaking any actual rules," Tam said, "what could they say?"

What they said was, "You're disqualified."

But first: They'd driven south four hundred miles, advancing another week toward the end of winter for each hundred miles, so that the earthdog test in February in southern Indiana was during that region's first light of early spring. In addition, Meryl hoped no one there would know them.

Working together on a hundred-yard approach, no one could tell the bitch, Kixy, was deferring to her cousin bracemate as they searched for the scented trail ranging twenty feet from the obscured mouth of the den. Neither dog was waylaid by the false den, but both had to decisively indicate the actual den before the test's next phase when they would, one at a time, enter the tunnel to find the quarry. Instincts aflame, Kixy's bracemate clawed at the dirt, barking with his muzzle thrust into the den's bushy camouflage, tail vibrating rigidly upright. The bitch backed off, looked over her shoulder for a second, and Meryl shouted the command, "Look!" even though Meryl's dog was already looking—*Tam* was supposed to be Kixy's owner. But no one seemed to notice. When Kixy finally leaned forward and sniffed the den, the judge gave the signal

CRIS MAZZA

that Kixy should be removed so the first dog who found the den could go to
ground.

Honoring while her cousin worked the tunnel in search of the quarry
was easy enough for the tentative bitch. The question was would Kixy
then take her turn while the other dog was told to wait, or would she
continue to yield to him? She had ninety seconds to get past the constric-
tion point narrowing the earth tunnel to six inches, to avoid the false exits
and empty decoy nests and reach the quarry behind a barrier at the end
of a twice-bent thirty-foot tunnel. As soon as she meekly scratched at the
barrier hiding the quarry, and sustained her work long enough to qualify,
an interminable two minutes, the judge signaled for the final act of the
test—for the handler to open the trap door and remove the dog from the
den without being bitten. Hardly a hazard, as Kixy went limp as soon
as Tam slid a hand under her ribcage and lifted her. Meryl left her dog
still tied to his stake and snatched Kixy from Tam, whereupon the bitch
showed the most enthusiasm she had all day, wiggling and licking Meryl's
face while Meryl declared, "I knew you could do it!" Tam, holding the
empty leash, watched another exhibitor say something to the judge.

Both dogs were disqualified, the judge said, because Meryl and Tam
had concealed that the dogs were housemates who'd even, possibly, been
trained together. "Another pairing would've been possible," the judge
said, "and you could've asked to be re-paired."

Meryl sobbed, still clutching the bitch to her chest.

"Everyone wants to win," the judge said. "Just learn a lesson and do
the next test within the spirit of the regulations."

Meryl held the dog up in front of her face—a suspect hiding under a
tented jacket or behind a briefcase—and turned away. She was probably
going to go immediately, get away from the judge, the other people, but
Tam was standing right there behind her. Meryl paused in front of Tam,
her savage whisper came from behind the dog, "*Do* something." When
Tam didn't do anything, Meryl's voice hissed again, "This is destroying
who I am, don't you understand that? You've never wanted *anything*
enough." Then she dodged around Tam and took off, half running, down
a path through spring mud and the skeletons of last fall's goldenrod and

15

Queen Anne's lace, toward the truck, more than a football field away in a dirt parking lot with only ten or twelve other vehicles.

Tam shut her eyes against the warnings. The pre-seizure aura. Floating blank spots and faint buzzing, numb feet, cold spine, hot chest, tingling fingertips . . . And . . . *Denny.*

Counted her heartbeat, ran a finger lightly, slowly over her wrist and inner arm. When she opened her eyes, she directed her gaze to bare branches rattling like windchimes in trees surrounding the open field, and above them perfect popcorn clouds not blocking genial February sunshine. Shrill barking of penned dogs and yammer of voices fading behind the twitter of field and song sparrows, a low call of a dove, invisible in a hedgerow beneath the trees.

Spasm at least postponed, Tam, balancing her head carefully on her shoulders, collected the dog Meryl had left tied at his honoring post, picked up his crate and brought him back to the truck. She went back for their two folding chairs and Kixy's crate. She went back for their cooler and training bag. She walked with eyes fixed well ahead of her boots, not looking up nor down, not at anything nor anyone. Each time Tam opened the back of the truck to stow their equipment, she heard Meryl wailing. Meryl was a heaving mound on the front seat. The dog was wandering loose in the cargo section.

When Tam was finished and got into the passenger side, Meryl unfolded herself, flinging her bush of hair away from her sticky face, kneeled sideways on the seat and tried to put her forehead down on Tam's shoulder but Tam edged just out of reach. So, head merely hanging between them, Meryl grabbed Tam's arm and said, "That bitch Marti Perkins, I never thought she'd stoop to this."

"As opposed to what *we* stooped to," Tam muttered. Just before her last seizure, in college, the night after the last time she'd seen Denny, there was also only one person crying. That time it was Tam.

It seems bad, but you'll forget in no time, Tam, by this time next month, look forward and see yourself in a year.

"What're you talking about?" Meryl scooted closer, fingers still digging into Tam's arm. Tam had crushed herself against the door. When Meryl again tried to collapse against her, Tam got back out of the truck, went around to the driver's side, got in and started the truck.

A half hour later, Meryl sat up, again swept her hair back, sniffled fiercely and said, "You don't even *care*. You don't know what it's like to *want* something. Now you've ruined my entire reputation. I needed a sympathetic, understanding partner and you've ruined my life. What'll I do now?"

"Show your dogs, without thinking about the consequences of what you do and say, like always."

"You cold bitch." Meryl said it, and then she screamed it. "Cold bitch!"

At a gas station north of Indianapolis, Meryl took the truck and left while Tam was in the restroom. It took Tam more than twelve hours to get to where a bus stopped, wait for the next scheduled pick-up, then take a cab from the downtown Greyhound terminal in Chicago to the Metra station, and walk from the village station to Meryl's house.

When she arrived, around 6 the next morning, Tam had already been evicted. A note on the front door said so. All the bolts were thrown, every door, every shade pulled, the phones unplugged. But none of Tam's belongings were stacked outside.

Tam never cried anymore. The heated passion of it, the contorted pushing and squeezing all occurring somewhere in the skull, were too close to a convulsion.

But this time she tried. First on the scratchy plaid bedspread that smelled of dust and disinfectant and cigarette smoke in what used to be a small country-road motel now surrounded by the suburbs of Chicago, four-lane boulevards, box stores and town houses; tried again, three days later, curled on a battered striped sofa that smelled of permanent-wave and faintly sweaty perfume—part of the "furnished" in the furnished bungalow she found for rent in an old residential area of a suburban town that used to be a train-stop village. The pulpy sofa in the mildewy bungalow sat facing a maple-lined sidewalk, cracked from too many winters and too many roots, bumping along in front of other shabby too-small-to-sell houses—old people hanging on to their last days of independence in the homes where they raised their children, immigrant families, single parents, and rentals, like Tam's, where she tried, again, to cry. Perhaps she'd forgotten how. The heat of her folded body aroused the odor in the lumpy cushions. The pulse of each huff of breath was counted off by the rhythm of a dripping faucet in the kitchen. Her eyes, aflame with dryness, stared at the floor where a ladybug, surviving winter indoors, struggled through the crushed shag pile of the bluish-green carpet someone must have been so proud of twenty years ago.

Twenty years ago Tam was five years out of college—five years past *you'll forget in no time*, five years after her body thrashed out a bloody confirmation that she was unfit to procreate. During those five years she saw neither her mother nor Gary, not since the day both, for some reason, had been unable to attend the graduation ceremony that Tam had subsequently decided not to participate in anyway, still feeling weak from the bloody seizure. Twenty years ago, five years out of college, she still wasted five minutes, ten, a half-hour once or twice a day thinking about the swim coach for whom she had swum no laps but had helped mismanage his budget, and had also felt the cool silk of his hairless body beside her. Twenty years ago, when her eyes burned from staring into numbers floating on a computer screen, she still thought about the burn of chlorine, of oxygen-inflamed lungs, the sear of peak-performance muscle. Twenty years ago she still hadn't been in the water since junior high when she'd been diagnosed. Twenty years ago, making over seventy-five thousand a year investing other people's money, she didn't even go on top of the water on any of her clients' sailboats in Lake Michigan. But other than no longer living in the tenth floor condo near Chicago's Gold Coast, which had not doubled but tripled in value by the time she sold it four years ago, how was *now* any different, twenty years later and still unable to cry on a former hair-stylist's sofa in a slightly leaning bungalow that still vaguely smelled of the onions someone had fried twenty years ago?

If she could cry now, what would she have been crying for? Not for Meryl. Not for leaving the dogs. She'd never listened when Meryl yapped about their pedigrees and conformation. She took a walk on the lumpy sidewalk, found some old postcards at the white elephant store in town and wrote a short note to Martha on the doddering coffee table in front of the smelly sofa: why there would be no more e-mail for a while.

Martha had always corresponded voraciously. Not just e-mail, but fat envelopes filled with clippings, sometimes photos, occasionally a portion of her genealogy project, folded inside greeting cards their mother made with digitized images of her own watercolor paintings of lighthouses. So it didn't take long for her to reply.

Dear Tam,

How horrible for you that your roommate would treat you so badly. Can't you get a lawyer or something to make her give you your things? Don't worry about sounding like whining, writing about it is good therapy. Why not start a journal? Gary's writing a new book— it's about Mom! He's calling it WaterWings, or Wings of Water. He says he hasn't decided which. He's shown me some of it, and it's helping me do Mom's portion of my family history, which G calls my book, but that's not what it is. After all the hunting and investigation, you have to put it down on paper, in regular writing, but it's just for the family, not a book like G's. I'm starting to do it, after all these years of research. So Mike's buying me a new computer and the old one goes to the kids. You can see what I've got so far on Mom, all taken (stolen) from G's book-in-progress (he said I could). I gave your new address to Mom. She still worries about you.

Hey, guess what—I found a copy of The Water Babies at an outlet bookstore. Remember, Mom used to read it to us.

—M

There was a snapshot of Martha's boys on a beach in huge swim trunks down to their knees, wet wrinkles plastered to their skinny legs, gigantic diver masks covering most of their faces. And a paragraph on a separate paper:

From 1942-1946 Emily Marr smoked, drank beer at the USO with officers-in-training from Harvard ("90-day wonders"), worked as a bowling alley pin-setter, dove from the 3-meter springboard, swam on the freestyle relay team, hitchhiked all over New England to go skiing, had summer jobs as a life guard at pools or beaches and as the sailing counselor at Girl Scout camp, and sailed her own one-person skiff all over Sheepscot Bay from the Yacht Club in Southport Maine.

One of Tam's doctors had told her she might someday be able to recognize pre-seizure, or aura stage, symptoms. Perhaps sound fading and returning, floating white spots, buzzing or ringing in her ears. She researched methods to forestall or prevent the actual convulsion stage of an epileptic seizure. Someone—maybe Martha, or maybe it was something Gary had said to Martha—had once recommended water therapy. Did they mean one of those sensory deprivation chambers that were supposed to recreate the womb, 98.6 degrees and just the right percentage of saline? Or a little contraption that tinkled water over stones all day? Or an actual session in a pool with a therapist leading dance-like exercises or the old-lady-style breaststroke? Tam never asked. She hadn't even gotten into the pool with Denny. Mixing water and epilepsy had long been a quagmire she couldn't see through.

The first dozen years of her life, she'd ridden a crest of seemingly inherited supremacy in water. In water, her too-broad-for-a-girl shoulders didn't slouch to hide being too-tall-for-her-age. Her muscled back surged in rhythm with barely a splash. As a swimmer, her greasy or stupidly bowl-cut hair was hidden in a racer's cap, cutting through an aqua clear pool. A seizure in water was not only a danger to her brain cells, it could cripple her distinction, her pedigree. It already had.

Austerity was an effective tranquilizer. She'd known it before getting sidetracked in meaningless dog games. So now, in the nearly-empty bungalow, Tam had everything she needed, the items that had been in her day pack and purse. Check book, credit cards, ear muffs and scarf, three of her atmosphere tapes—*Woodland Voices*, *Call of the Loon*, and *Frogs and Crickets*. Also her cassette headset, reading glasses, and cellphone. No need to hook up a phone in the rental house. No need to obtain anything but throw-away stuff for this temporary stopover. The white elephant store provided a pillow, a blanket, a saucepan, a cereal bowl, a juice glass, a spoon. Walking to town, to the eight-cornered town center where the white elephant store squatted across the street from the train station, took two hours every morning, stretched out if she sat in the library and scanned sports or gossip magazines. Before leaving the library, she paused, with a long glance, at the row of computers, public access to the internet. Would Denny have a website? Would it be dangerous to look at it? Gary had a professional one built by his publisher, and last summer he'd made a family site where they could all post their news and projects. The most mediocre, ordinary website, just basic clip art for icons. So far a few photos—of Gary and his dog at the award ceremony, her mother in a bathing suit on the beach holding a pair of scuba fins, her mother's watercolors, a badly scanned copy of the dog show picture she'd sent to Martha, and an icon that would start a herky-jerky version of Gary's network interview. The area he'd designated *Martha's Family History*, for Martha's genealogy project, was still blank except for Martha's posted note: *I'm not ready yet !*

Welcome to
The Marr-Burgess Family Website

your hosts:

Gary Marr-Burgess (author, triathlete, sports therapy, adventurer, **martyr**)

Martha Marr-Burgess Richter (historian, chronicler and keeper of the family tree)

Tamara Burgess (mystery woman who would emigrate from California)

Emily Marr-Burgess (athlete, cook, counselor, coach, artist, freespirit)

 Sample Gary's books

 See What Tam's Been Up to Since She Retired

 Gary's Latest Triathlon Results

 Message from Gary

 Gary & Coach, Search & Rescue

 Message from Martha

 Read Portions of Martha's Family History

 Message from Mom

 Mom's Watercolors

 Message from Tam

On the way home, Tam looked in the candy store and dress shop windows, at the grocery store picked up apples, bran muffins, and pot pies, bought decaffeinated coffee and a newspaper at the train station. Routine, a slow plodding routine, a trivial one, suitable for a retired person, likewise was a calmative.

She didn't miss Meryl or the constant yapping of the terriers. She didn't miss her computer. She'd used it to make pedigrees for Meryl, check stock quotes, visit internet dog-showing bulletin boards for insights into the politics of winning or losing, and to e-mail—not just with Martha but her growing list of clients, who would wonder at her disappearance. Well, the dog games were over, the newspaper had the stock prices from yesterday's closing, and when answers to her letters to Martha came in eight days instead of one, she realized she didn't require the response any faster than that. The cell phone, if turned off, didn't ring. The display showed no missed calls or voice mail from Meryl, or anyone else. Except one, once, from her mother. And four days later, a notecard, her mother's writing filling every available space.

> Dear Tam, my bridge group was just here and I made that lemon cake you always wanted for your birthday. Tomorrow's watercolor class is meeting at the Point Loma Lighthouse, but I've already painted that one so many times! This card is the last one I did on the scanner, Egg Rock Light in Massachusetts. Now I'm painting lighthouses that no longer exist! This one has a good story, I'll give you a copy of what I found on the internet. You'll see Gary and Coach have some doubles in history. (There's a double for you too—a woman keeper named Abbie Burgess. No relation to Dad, just a funny coincidence. Martha will also send you something interesting about a legend at Hendricks Head.)
>
> I'm glad you're out of that place and away from that woman and her dogs. You can afford a place of your own, your own dogs if you want. Gary would help you find a dog. Maybe you'd like to learn search-and-rescue, or pet therapy in hospitals. He says there are so many

worthwhile things you can do. He came over last night with clams he dug yesterday. He found the clam beds while training. He says Coach digs in the mud for the clams too! He'll take me out next time to raise the limit, and we'll have Martha and Mike and the kids over for a feast. Wish you could come home and see everyone. Then maybe you could talk to Gary. He doesn't say anything, but he's been having a hard time ever since going to New York last year.

Love you, Mom

A folded paper, in the notecard's envelope, had pages printed from the internet.

Egg Rock is an unprotected cliff over the Atlantic. The location is frequently buffeted by ferocious gales and waves, and is usually entirely icebound in winter. Egg Rock was one of many places along the New England coast where there were reported sea serpent sightings. A chronicler of the 17th century, Obadiah Turner, reported that the local natives had spotted the serpent. "And ye Indians," wrote Turner, "doe say they have manie times seene a wonderful big serpent lying on ye water, and reaching from Nahantus to ye greate rocke wich we call Birdes Egg Rocke."

The first keeper at Egg Rock was George B. Taylor, who lived at the lighthouse with his wife, five children, a few barnyard animals, and Milo, a Newfoundland-St. Bernard mix. One day Taylor was shooting water-fowl on the island, with Milo accompanying him. The keeper shot a loon which fell to the ocean. The bird was wounded, and Milo swam in pursuit, but every time Milo got close to the loon, the bird took off again. The chase continued until Milo disappeared, and the dog wasn't seen again that day. The next day, Milo was discovered swimming back to his home from Nahant, a mile away.

Milo became famous for rescuing several children around Egg Rock. Sir Edwin Henry Landseer painted a portrait of Milo with Keeper Taylor's son, Fred, nestled between the dog's paws. The painting, titled "Saved," became well known across America.

http://www.sentinelpublications.com/abbie.htm
Matinicus Rock's Twin Lights
© Elinor De Wire, 2000

Abbie Burgess was a young girl who became famous for keeping the lights burning at Maine's Matinicus Rock. Her father, Samuel Burgess, was the lightkeeper there in the 1850s. He had to be away much of the time, so he left the lights in Abbie's care. She was only 14 years old when she first began tending the lights!

Matinicus Rock is 22 miles from the mainland and is surrounded by other dangerous rocks.

The light station there was very important for vessels heading into Maine's Penobscot Bay.

Each day Abbie had to clean the lamps, trim their wicks, refill them with oil, and polish the silver reflectors. The oil in the lamps was usually whale oil, and it smelled rotten when it burned and also smoked, so she had to spend many hours cleaning the surrounding glass. In winter the oil had to be heated in the house before being taken into the tower. Otherwise, it congealed in the cold air and wouldn't pour. The tall pedestal for the lamps also had to be cared for. Its brass needed to be polished, and the little chariot wheels that turned the lamps to make them flash needed to be oiled so they would roll easier. Keeping the lights involved caring for twenty-eight oil lamps—fourteen in each tower. She held a lantern in her right hand to help her see the work she needed to do. Abbie always wore a dress, for women were not permitted to wear pants in those days.

Abbie became famous when she kept the lights burning during a bad storm in January, 1856. Her father had rowed to Matinicus Island, seven miles from the rock, for supplies and medicine for her mother. Abbie tended the lights during his absence, took care of her sick mother, and looked after her little sisters. Abbie's father was gone nearly a month and could not get back to Matinicus Rock because the sea was so rough after the storm.

When Abbie's father gave up his job as lightkeeper at Matinicus Rock in 1860, he left Abbie behind to teach the new keeper about the station. Abbie soon fell in love with the keeper's son, Isaac Grant. They married and became the assistant keepers at Matinicus Rock. Four children were born to them during their time on Matinicus. In 1872, Abbie and Isaac moved to White-head Lighthouse where Abbie served as assistant keeper to her husband until 1890.

Tam walked to the window that looked out to the patch of scrubby lawn and cracked sidewalk. The grass was winter-dormant, yellowish. It had not been cut before the first snowfall, and had last fall's leaves matted in the weedy-looking mess. A line on either side of her front yard was still evident where each neighbor had done their final mowing and raking some time last November. A stick fell from one of the trees on the parkway.

Her mother's kinship with lighthouses had been the focal point of family trips, during her father's four-week vacations. Coastal Oregon and California, portions of the Circle Tour around the Great Lakes, Key West, Cape Hatteras, Cape Cod, and up the New England coast to Maine—Whaleback, Nubble, Cuckolds, Goat Island, and of course, Hendricks Head in Southport. They didn't go east every year, and Tam couldn't remember visiting New England before she was ten. The last trip to Southport was the summer Tam turned 13, nine months after she'd sat in a doctor's office while the doctor, with a hand on her head, recommended to her mother that Tam never again go swimming alone or even take a bath by herself.

She'd had a grand mal seizure at swim practice the day before. One minute posting her best time ever. Then, like a flip of a switch, she was in an emergency room, her ribcage feeling like someone had jumped up and down on her back, her tongue mashed and bruised, but not sliced enough to require stitching. She couldn't say, "What's going on, where am I?" but could mumble, "Mom?" Her mother wasn't there yet. She arrived soon after. Tam could hear her voice in the hall outside the ER. Then she was beside Tam, hovering over her, smoothing the sheet, brushing hair off Tam's brow, smiling her upside-down smile. "Gracious sakes," her mother said.

When her mother left for a moment, and someone pulled a curtain, Tam could hear her mother saying, "A grand mal seizure, out of the blue? What caused it?"

Gary.

She could remember. Coach had run a drill of one-on-one races, and there were an odd number of girls, so he put Tam up against Gary. "A faster swimmer beside you can push your time," he'd said. But *she* had been the faster swimmer, pushing Gary's time. She was winning. You're not supposed to know you're winning because you're not supposed to be looking, but she did, tipped her head back while getting a breath, so she knew, she was ahead, more than half a body-length. He was three years older than her, and a boy, but her reaction off the block had always been better, her flip-turn always smoother. So they were on the last lap, the last length of pool, with the fire in the lungs, the word *kick* pulsing through her brain until she forgot what she was saying, a meaningless chant, water thudding against her capped ears becoming some kind of pulsing roar. But still, she was ahead. Until.

A sudden electric shock, too quick for her to recoil. His hand on her leg, on her calf, near her ankle. And she was submerged. Going down. Fast, like a waterbaby from the old fairy tale, growing gills. But she had no gills.

A man was talking, his voice growing louder, approaching. "Seizures can be caused by neurological or brain injury of any sort, but usually, with an otherwise healthy patient, we often won't be able to determine a cause. Epilepsy may not present its recognizable symptoms until adolescence. A seizure may seem out-of-the-blue, but there may have been other signs no one recognized."

So this might explain the few times Tam had found herself sitting on the bathroom floor, or lying on the rug in her room. She'd assumed she'd been so tired she fell asleep for a second, the way public announcement warnings said you could fall asleep while driving and she'd wondered, how do you fall asleep while *doing* something? No, she hadn't fallen asleep while swimming, but the startling impact of Gary's hand on her leg, his locked grip, her abrupt plunge from the surface, her gasp of alarm may have plugged her airways with water, shut off the oxygen to her brain— even if the convulsion was already there, waiting to happen, wouldn't what *he'd* done be enough of a goad to kick-start it?

"She had quite a bit of fluid in her lungs, because of it occurring in a pool," the doctor said as he and her mother parted the curtains and came to stand on either side of the gurney.

"Gary. Grabbed my leg," Tam mumbled.

"I know. He pulled you out. Lucky for us he was right there,"

"No, before. He grabbed my leg. Pulled me under."

"I think you're mixing up time, honey. He pulled you out."

"You're a lucky girl," the doctor had said, holding her wrist with thumb and two fingers, looking at his watch like he was late for another patient.

Tam didn't see Gary that night because they had kept her in the hospital. The next day, in another doctor's office, her mother had said,

"She's on a swim team, so she's rarely in the water alone. Even doing their laps, at least her brother would still be there."

"Well, that might work," the doctor replied. Tam was facing sideways between her mother and the doctor. "Family is always best, people who understand your condition."

"And her brother's already certified as a Water Safety Instructor. He's the one who pulled her out when this happened."

"I hope you take him out for an ice cream sundae, his quick action might have prevented brain damage, or worse." His hand was hot on the top of her head. "Are you an Olympian in training, Tamara?" The doctor's hand squeezed a little, then patted her, before he took it away to write something in her chart.

"I was winning." Tam was surprised she'd said it. Maybe she did have brain damage. She rubbed her sore tongue along her teeth.

The doctor went on with some sort of prepared speech. "So we're pretty sure from these tests that Tamara didn't have a brain trauma. If it had been an injury or circumstance at birth, the symptoms would've shown up long before now. So we call it congenital, something she's born with, but it's often a hereditary condition. Are any of your relatives epileptic? Your own parents? Your husband? His parents?"

"Not that we know of," her mother said, then smiled at Tam. Her mother wore red lipstick, the only make-up she used, and when she smiled the corners of her mouth tucked down. But it could never be mistaken for a frown. It was always there, easy to find, when Tam's head broke out of the water and her arms hooked over the lip of the pool after a race. But this wasn't winning a race. Why was she smiling now?

There was an article in the newspaper three days later. "Hero Boy Saves Drowning Sister." After introducing Gary and his status as a "developing Olympic swimmer," and that he was a Water Safety Instructor, and how many laps per day he swam, and what that equaled in miles, the story gave Tam's name, and that she'd suffered an epileptic seizure in the pool, but didn't bother to mention it was a race, and she'd been winning. Who had called the newspaper? Her mother cut out and saved the article. She went to the post office and made copies, shiny and smelly enough to make Tam want to faint, but she couldn't say so. Her mom sent copies to relatives and gave them to friends, saying "Gary's our hero," or "Gary saved Tam." She didn't mention that Tam was now an epileptic—the article took care of spreading that news—or that her days as a swimmer were threatened. Or that she'd been winning the race.

In the La Costa Swim Club, Tam was number one in her age group at both freestyle and butterfly and anchored the 4x100 and 4x200 mixed and freestyle relays. Every day their mother picked up Martha from elementary school and Tam from junior high to take them to swim practice. Gary rode his bike from high school and was always already in the pool doing laps by the time Tam and Martha were suited up. For two weeks after her seizure, Tam had sat in the car during club practices, claiming a lingering wooziness.

"It's probably your medicine," her mother said, reaching sideways as she drove to put a palm on Tam's forehead.

"Aren't you going to swim the meet this weekend?" Martha had asked from the back seat.

"Maybe," Tam had said, and whispered, "not."

She didn't swim the meet. The day before, Gary asked if she was swimming it.

"What do you care," Tam said, "you wouldn't have to go up against me."

"What that supposed to mean?"

"You know. I was winning. You pulled me under."

"Like shit. You came into my lane. I wanted to teach you— I didn't mean to— Hell, I *saved* you."

"I'll bet you made sure you won first."

"You're full of shit, Tam. You know, you were peeing in the pool. *I* didn't make you do that. I could see this yellow cloud—*ouch*." Tam had kicked him. "What the hell's the matter with you? You *are* brain-damaged."

That night she told her mother she was quitting the team.

She'd waited until Martha was in bed then went in her pajamas to where her mother was balancing the checkbook in a pool of light at her desk. Her father was an engineer on an offshore oil rig, three weeks on, one week at home. During his week at home they often had friends over in the evening for dinner and cards, or the whole family went to the movies on a weeknight. It was difficult to contact him on the rig—in the 70's and no cell phones—so he hadn't yet been told about the seizure. Tam wondered if he would find out about the seizure when her mother showed him the news article.

"I'll tell the coach you're taking a sabbatical," her mother had said, again with the palm on Tam's forehead.

During the rest of junior high, Tam might have gone back to swimming, but the longer she waited for the things she was waiting for—for Gary to admit she was winning and say he was sorry, and for her mother to encourage her to swim again—the more impossible it seemed to go back. Martha had begged repeatedly for Tam to rejoin the team, in the dark of their shared bedroom before they went to sleep. And once Gary had complained that without her the team's chicks were all rocks, his word for bad swimmers. But why had her mother not told her, cajoling but tenacious, adamant in her confidence and reassurance, that there was no danger, that Tam could do anything? Tam waited.

Two times, such clear memories, Tam thought it would happen. Quiet moments, once while they stood side-by-side at the sink washing dishes after dinner. Her mother was scouring the cast iron frying pan where she'd cooked meatballs before making spaghetti sauce. She handed the pan to Tam, and said, as she always had, "Heavy."

"Okay, I've got it." The window above the sink was dark, and Tam could see herself looking straight ahead as though gazing out, and her mother looking down, into the sink.

As Tam dried and put the pan onto a towel on the sinkshelf, before her mother handed her the salad bowl, her mother could've said, "It's easy to stay in shape at your age. I'm sure the coach still has a spot for you on the team."

The other time, Tam was reading *The Pearl* for English class on the floor in the living room. Her mother had been sitting with the newspaper, in a chair above where Tam lay reading on the floor. Her mother folded the paper softly, then turned off the light—the only light in the room.

"Hey mom, the light?"

"Sorry." The light didn't come back on right away. Tam's heart leaped, the same kind of surge after the voice said *take your mark*. In the dark, before reaching for the light, her mother could have said, "State semis are coming up next month, it's not too late." Or even, "I'm sad that you're throwing away something I thought you loved."

Maybe it was only later that it seemed it could have, *should have* come that night.

That afternoon, Gary'd had a bad workout and Martha had weighed in under her optimal. So their mother talked to Gary and Martha about their training and the competitions—they were her children, they were learning to compete in the real world, they got discouraged, this is what a mother did. But this time she tried to do it when Tam was somewhere else—still reading in the living room, after the light went back on and her mother left her chair. That was probably why her mom had turned the light out in the first place, thinking about what she needed to go say to Gary and Martha, forgetting Tam was there at her feet, reading on the floor in the same pool of light. That's also why Tam thought the suggestion, *her* guidance, would come that same evening. Her mother unusually quiet. Gathering her thoughts, and waiting.

They did it in Gary's room. As Tam passed in the hall, she knew their positions. Her mother seated on the edge of the bed, Martha close beside her, their backs to the door. Gary at his desk. Then Tam stopped before going into her room, the room she shared with Martha. She lurked in the hall. She couldn't hear every word. Gary's voice cracked once. He emphasized *five seconds*. Their mother's voice hummed longer sentences. A serene melody, never sharp, never berating. Tam didn't have to be in there to know, the refrain was always *You can and you will*. It didn't matter the specifics. She would point out that Gary had had those five seconds yesterday and the day before that and every day before. And that Martha could make up in endurance what she may have lost in muscle, that she would certainly put on a growth spurt next year, and they would go have a protein milkshake before bed.

You can and you will. Never a demand, not an order, a charge, or requirement. It was her blessing. A sanctification. A gift. *You can and you will*.

The first time, Tam had been 6 or 7, learning the flip turn for when her race would double from fifty meters to a hundred. She was scraping her shins on the concrete pool edge, spraining her toes on the underwater tiles, slowing down to feel with her hand before flipping, involuntarily lifting her head to see where she was. Finally she'd erupted out of the pool, spitting water, maybe crying but it was hard to tell with her rage and water streaming from her head as she stomped past the coach toward the empty bleachers to tell her mother "I can't and I won't!" The coach had followed her, but it was her mother who put a towel around Tam, wiped her face with the ends, smiled upside-down but turned Tam back around toward the pool, two hands on her shoulders. "You can and you will."

But when Tam was 12 and had quit the swim team, she became a shadow slipping into her room as Martha and their mother came out of Gary's room, heading to the kitchen for the protein milkshake. By the time Martha came in to go to bed, Tam was already under her covers, breathing slowly, her face to the wall.

It was hard to fool Martha. "Tam, I know you're awake."

"So what. I'm going to sleep."

"Are you mad?"

"What would I be mad at?"

"You seem mad." Martha turned the light on.

"It doesn't matter what I am because it won't change anything now. Everything's already changed."

"What?" Martha was only 9. She only understood mad or not mad; nervous before a meet and content afterwards; sick for a day then not sick any more.

Tam sat up. "Maybe I'm adopted!"

"Why?"

"Who else around here has seizures?"

"Mom says you'll be okay, that you'll be like normal."

33

"*You're* like normal. You're swimming in the state semis."

"You could too."

"I can't. I have *seizures*, dummy."

Martha left her jeans, underwear and t-shirt on the floor beside her bed. "Gary or me can pull you out."

"I don't want Gary touching me ever again. And you couldn't pull me out."

"But what if you *didn't* have a seizure and won the freestyle?"

"Yeah, I'll win the freestyle with everyone standing around the edge with hooks and nets, ready to yank me out before I pee in the pool."

Martha dove into her nightgown, squirmed under the material for a second then came out the other end. "Did Mom say you shouldn't swim?"

Tam pulled her knees to her chin, tucked her head down. "She didn't say I *could*."

"She said you'll be normal."

"A normal lardbutt. Maybe she's afraid I'll pee in the pool in front of everyone. Or maybe she doesn't care, since she's got you and Gary to cheer for. She doesn't know who was winning."

"What do you mean?"

Tam looked up. Martha was kneeling on her bed. She had her little 2-pound barbells in each hand. She kept them under the bed and did 50 reps of three different exercises every night. Tam's five-pound weights were still under her bed.

"Gary will *never* admit he pulled me under when I was winning. That's one thing. But does Mom think I'll drown if Gary isn't there? Or why should she care if I'm adopted anyway?"

Martha started her reps, both dumbbells held at arm's length on either side, slowly raised over her head. She had long blond hair, even though she had to stuff it into a racing cap for practice and meets. Tam's hair was dark, and short, so at least the cap wasn't all lumpy and hot with tighter places pressing into her skull. Not that it mattered anymore, now that she knew why her skull didn't want to be pressed into.

"All she cares about is that he saved me. Gary got the glory, and all I got was . . . who-cares-if-she-quits-the-team-she-can't-swim-anyway."

Martha lowered the dumbbells to the mattress on either side of herself, her thin arms like two broken wings. "Are you crying?"

"I can't cry anymore. I might spazz out." Tam flopped back onto her stomach and pulled her covers up over her face.

Martha finished her reps in silence. Her pinprick bedlight didn't go off for another half hour. It was Martha, the next day or the day after, who went looking for and found a photo of their mother, very pregnant, with Gary as a toddler beside her, holding the seam of her maternity pedal-pushers in one fist, sucking his finger.

"See, here you are," Martha said, putting the photo down on top of the book Tam was reading at her desk. "In mom's stomach."

Tam let the photo sit there for a second, then picked it up, handed it back to Martha without looking at her, but said, "Show it to Gary. He should know what a dork he was."

Then in June, just before she finished junior high, before they went to Maine, and despite the medication, Tam had a second seizure.

She didn't realize it until she found herself on the floor of a restroom, at school. She'd asked to leave class because she'd been feeling lightheaded and unable to hear the teacher, as though he was talking in the background of some other noise. She couldn't even remember if she asked for a hall pass or just walked out, causing everyone to stare after her as she left without permission. Had the teacher sent someone to follow her? Had whoever it was come into the restroom after she'd gone down? Had her A-line dress been up around her waist, exposing not only the puddle of pee spreading around her, but also her drenched underwear and undershirt, the thing she wore because she didn't need a bra yet? And if she'd been having her period, then that elastic belt would've shown, with the clips holding the pad, maybe the bloody pad itself. All this besides her eyes becoming just the whites, like huge moon-marbles with gross red veins. Her tongue might have been sticking out, thick and round, like a moron, not to mention her arms and legs thrashing and kicking in ways she'd never done at the few junior high dances when she'd been asked out to the dance floor, and even then knots of girls giggled at how Tam jerked her body to Iron Butterfly.

But when Tam came back to herself, in the puddle on the dirty tile floor, staring at the white receptacle where you were supposed to put used Kotex, she was alone. There was a bump on her temple, but the skin wasn't broken. Again, her tongue was mashed and bruised, but not cut. The bottom of her skirt and her underwear were wet, though, so she couldn't go back to class. And she didn't know what time it was. She stayed in the stall, sitting on the toilet. Groups of laughing, prattling girls came in and left, came in and left. "Who's that sitting on the pot!" someone yelled. One banged on the door, but Tam sat like a stone, holding her head; sometimes she thought she was going to sleep, and a few times she might have.

Tam had started taking the bus from school, after telling her mother she was quitting the team. She usually walked a half mile home from the bus stop, and the house would still be empty, her mother still at team practice with Gary and Martha. That day the buses were gone by the time Tam came from the restroom. She walked the four miles home, stopping frequently to sit with her head on her knees, counting to sixty over and over. She still made it home before swim practice was over.

So . . . she knew the truth about her first seizure when she was still 12. She wouldn't go through her life believing Gary caused the seizure, and she knew that seizures in water could kill her, if somebody, like Gary, wasn't there to pull her out. But she also knew: That Gary had grabbed her leg during a race—what else could that mean, he was trying to pull her back, pull her under. And she knew she had been winning. She had been good. But Gary had to hit the lip *first*, before checking to see if his opponent was drowning. Granted, she knew that you don't discern anything when you're kicking the last twenty yards, you don't see, you just drive toward the edge. But she knew when he grabbed her leg, she suddenly went dead in the water. How could Gary not notice that? And she knew: even though her mother had no knowledge of the second seizure, she still hadn't ever been able to say "you can overcome this, Tam, you can go on swimming," even while bragging about Gary being a lifesaver. Tam didn't ever want him saving her ever again. And in the water a seizure would disable her beyond her own ability to come back to herself. If it happened again in water—where she had been graceful, fast, streamlined, and buoyant, but instead became an undulating octopus of twisting, lurching limbs, with pee gushing out and water gushing in and flooding her unsinkable lungs—how much more horrible could it be? The sparkling aquamarine water was now full of darkness and direction-lessness and danger. And Gary. It was partly because the call of encour-agement from her mother never came, but she also resolved that night, she would not put herself in a position where he might have to save her again; she would not go back into the water.

A few weeks into Tam's transient residence at the bungalow, she cut out the article about the family that was found murdered two blocks over.

> Seven members of an extended family were brutally murdered last night in their southwest suburban Maple River residence. Dead are Peter Nicholas, Jr., 49, his wife Meta, 45, their adult son Stephanos, 25, Dimitri Nicholas, 38, his wife Sandra, 34, Aileen Nicholas, 72, and Peter Nicholas Sr., 75. All were tied, hand and foot, and had their throats slashed. Police arrested Danny Nicholas, 19, adopted son of Peter Nicholas Jr. and his wife. Danny Nicholas, who police found sleeping in the garage, was taken into custody without incident. He will be arraigned today. Neighbors said the adopted Nicholas had been estranged from the family and was drifting throughout the Midwest, last known to be employed by a downstate cement company. Investigators believe Danny Nicholas announced a visit to his adoptive parents before arriving, and that relatives had gathered for the occasion. A court-appointed attorney has indicated there will be a plea of diminished capacity due to a form of epilepsy called rage syndrome, usually associated with certain breeds of dogs.

She had sent the article to Martha who answered with the clipping about Gary's pre-ground-zero rough-water heroism, and her rendition of the legend of the shipwrecked baby at Hendricks Head.

Tam used the computers at the library to buy a train ticket online: Chicago to Boston via New York, then Boston to Portland. She bought a suitcase in the white elephant store on the way home, bought a laptop in the office supply store, instructed the post office to hold her mail and wait for a forwarding address, charged up her cellphone, packed what she needed. The next day she took the Metra downtown to the Amtrak station. That was so easy, these links, these tasks, these steps. But then, sitting in the plush seat, in a private little box of a room where she could also sleep, she had three days with no list of next-in-line duties to keep her on autopilot. When the train was still moving down the South Shore, she took out her cellphone.

After her own years in college, swimming competitively and studying British history, Martha had worked for a few years in marketing and publicity for an opera company. Since then, for the past ten years, what Martha did was have children and take them to music lessons and karate and art classes at the museum. She also did her genealogy thing, a kind of research hobby, born of doing a gravestone rubbing of an Earl of Mar on a high school trip to England. A few years ago, Tam had stopped calling Martha and started using e-mail—she'd told Martha it would be more convenient for her because Martha could read and answer her messages when she had time, instead of being interrupted by the telephone when she was busy with something else. Something else: cooking dinner, helping with homework, supervising piano practice, running a Cub Scout meeting, playing Chutes 'n' Ladders, mediating fights, reading bedtime stories. The truth was, every time Tam tried to talk to Martha on the phone, Martha's kids would be in the background, sometimes interrupting to ask questions—which Martha always answered, never telling them not to butt-in—but often it was Martha who interrupted Tam to praise one of the kids for a somersault or a picture he'd colored, to ask what they were building with their Legos, to laugh at how they'd dressed their stuffed bears. It always ended up with Tam holding the phone and listening to Martha spend time with her kids.

This time, 10 a.m. in California, the kids should be in school.

"Tam!" Martha's voice snapped out of its business-like salutation. "Is everything all right?"

"Sure, yes. How're you?"

"Grand, as mom used to say. Hectic and busy, barely a moment to spare. I think I left half a cup of coffee somewhere. I'll try to find it while we chat. So what really happened with that dog woman? Did she trick you into cheating?"

"Trick me? Unfortunately, no. I tricked myself. I think competition is as bad for me as relationships. I make the same kinds of bad choices."

"You used to do OK with competition in swim meets. Remember when—"

"Anyway, I just wanted to ask you about Southport. About what I would do for you there? The research you need?"

"Really? You would really go? Hey, but if you're up for a trip, how about Scotland instead?"

"What? Um . . . what? I thought you needed Maine."

It looked like no one was working at the steelmills—had they been abandoned since she retired? Tam didn't know. Wisps came from some of the smokestacks.

"Just kidding. But not really." Martha laughed. "I found something exciting and wish I could verify it. We might be related to Robert the Bruce. To his sister."

"I've heard of him."

"Yeah, in the movie where the Scottish clans fight against England. There's my coffee! But, Tam, it could be what you're looking for."

"What *I'm* looking for? Your coffee?" Tam paused but didn't laugh, although Martha did, again. "No caffeine for me," Tam said. "It doesn't fit into my eternal search for serenity."

Martha was still laughing until she took a loud sip. "No, I mean, you know those lineages in Great Britain and how inbred they were, cousins marrying and whatnot, there was that bleeding disorder in the British royal family, or was that the Tsar's family . . ." Martha was shuffling papers. Then it sounded as though she was blowing to cool her coffee, but the coffee, sitting waiting for Martha to find it, wouldn't still be hot.

"But maybe the Bruce lineage had epilepsy. We'd finally know where it came from."

"Where *it* came from or where *I* came from?"

"You know where you came from. I mean all this neurological stuff in our family."

"My epilepsy is now *our* neurological stuff?" Here and there, between rusty forsaken industrial infrastructure lining the channels off the lake, old men stood next to thirty-year-old station wagons, fishing. There was no ice. Occasionally a stand of last season's tall reeds, now browned, and a few Canada geese, backgrounded by yet another looming corroded factory that may or may not still be making rebar or wire or sheet metal. "I don't want to go to Scotland," Tam added during a short silence. She heard the cold blade in her voice. Tried to shift it: "Airplanes, even before the terrorist thing, I was always afraid, you know, low oxygen, re-circulating everyone's breath. What if I flipped during a flight?"

"You haven't had a seizure in how long? Why are you still so . . . I don't know . . ."

"You're the one trying to find epilepsy in Robert the Bruce."

"I thought it would be a way to get you interested. Damn, I can't find that thing I was working on. About mom. I wanted to tell you—"

"I *am* interested—in Maine, that shipwrecked baby story. I haven't had a chance to tell you yet. I'm . . . I'm actually on a train, on my way there."

"You're kidding! Why didn't you say so?"

"Okay, I'm telling you. So what if epilepsy came from that shipwrecked baby?"

"Did you read my history thing? I know it's not finished, but . . . did you read it?"

"How else would I know about the baby? And you asked me to go find out if she's our great grandmother."

"No, I didn't. Where'd you get that? I guess I should've been clearer." Again Martha's breath, like wind through a window crack. A soft thumping. Was she rearranging the furniture? "That baby, even if the story's true, isn't our relative." More shuffling papers. Another sip. "I wouldn't mind knowing how much of the legend *is* true . . . it would be a great part of our family history . . . but just a . . . side story. *Hey*, so this is where Derek's book report was hiding."

"Have you grown an extra arm?" Tam cooled her hand against the window then pressed her palm on her forehead where a dull headache simmered.

"Huh? Oh! Mike got me a hands-free phone. A headset. I look like a pilot. You'd be surprised how much I can get done while on the phone."

"You mean by not really paying attention to the conversation?"

"Sorry, the house is a mess and Derek had to leave without his homework. I'll have to drive it over to his school. But I'm paying attention. You're actually on your way to *Maine*. I didn't expect you'd take me seriously and leave before we talked about it. There *are* some things I wanted to check on there. But I didn't mean the legend. Even if it happened that way, that shipwrecked baby wouldn't be a Marr descendant, and we don't come down from her."

"How do you know?"

"I can't believe you thought— I'm sorry, I must not have written it right. Our descendant is our great-grand*father*. I mean, Marr . . . Mom's family's name had to come down through *men*, for one thing. For another, it didn't take sophisticated genealogy research to know who our great-grandfather is."

Tam shut her eyes, considered saying maybe Derek should learn a lesson by having to turn his homework in late. Considered reminding Martha about the time they'd run a mile home—crying, holding each other's arms—because they'd forgotten their workbooks on their speech therapy day. They'd both lisped like snakes. Tam's former colleagues at the brokerage house had commented on how she enunciated every consonant so clearly.

Through the phone, the sound of running water. Then it stopped, and Martha asked, "You still there?"

"Where would I go? I'm sitting on a train."

"Are you mad?"

"No." She hadn't had her new great-grandmother long enough to grieve over the loss. "So . . . it's okay . . . you had other things to fact-check in Maine?"

"Yes. And now I remember . . ." A click, a series of beeps as though Martha were dialing a different phone, then a low hum. "That legend also uncovered another mystery—*not* the mystery of the shipwrecked baby, but, you know . . . Wait, I'll start over. I found out about the legend from the *Boothbay Register*, but in the article, it was exciting to see that the reporter, who wanted to prove that the story's just a myth, only found documentation for five children in that generation, but our family records show *six*. The one the reporter didn't find was Mary Catherine. That was what . . ." A pause, a silence without any other noise except the ongoing hum. Or was that in Tam's head? Had Martha forgotten she was talking on the phone?

"And you thought this Mary Catherine was the shipwrecked baby?"

"No, she's not the shipwrecked baby because, first, *my* records show Mary Catherine was born several years before they say the shipwreck happened. Second, it wouldn't have been a secret. I mean, Nana would've been the baby's niece, she would know if her aunt had been a shipwrecked baby. And the story has too many holes in it, like it says the Marrs lost a baby just before the shipwreck, but there's no dead baby, as least not one I found in family records and genealogists aren't supposed to *create* family history with fantasy or speculation, we're supposed to use documented evidence."

The cellphone was getting hot against Tam's ear. Whenever that happened, she thought of the microwaves, or whatever they were, going into her brain. "I thought you said you wanted to find out if the shipwrecked baby was a member of our family."

"Did I? I guess I phrased it all wrong. It's such a great story, isn't it? Maybe I just thought it would get you interested in the family history. Sure, I'd like to know if it's true. But I'm more interested in the stuff I *know* is real, like that Mary Catherine's birth records might be *missing*— why is that? She's also the only one to die young. She was born, survived the winters and harsh life, grew up and . . . then died . . ."

"You mean, without having children?"

"That's not what I was thinking, but it's what women did then, Tam."

"I didn't know they'd stopped."

"You know what I mean." Another series of beeps.

"What're you doing?"

"You can hear that? I was rewarming my coffee in the microwave."

"Okay. So what if our great-grandfather, what's his name . . ." With one hand, Tam took a folder out of her day pack, the one where she'd kept all the clippings, letters, photos and articles she'd gotten in the mail the past few weeks at the rental house.

"Wolcott. The underlined one." Martha sipped. "Yuck, this is awful."

"Okay, so the shipwrecked baby was there, but she's just a guest in their house, they're not related. So what if our great-grandfather Wolcott got this shipwrecked girl pregnant, and she died in childbirth, and *that* baby lived, and so we're—"

"Tam, come on, that's ridiculous. That would make Nana the ship-wrecked baby's *daughter*. I think Nana knew who her own mother was, and her mother didn't die young like Mary Catherine—"

"Yes, absurd, I know. I'm not good at these stories."

"That's the point, Tam, genealogy isn't supposed to be made-up guesses."

"Okay . . . I can just try to find out if the legend is true anyway. And . . . whatever else you need . . ." The train had to go slowly where rows of drab little brick houses had the track practically in their shabby front yards. "It's something to do."

"Mom wants you to come home."

"To talk to Gary." Tam opened the folder on her tray table, then closed it again.

"That's not the only reason." Dishes clinked.

"That's what she said." She opened the folder again and sorted through it. Photos and newspaper article in one stack, the family history in another, the stories of Egg Rock and Abbie Burgess went with the photos and clipping, her mother's notecard by itself.

43

"Is that really why you're going to Maine? To get even farther away?"

Tam paused with Martha's quarter-page summary of their mother's college years. "You asked me to go."

"Okay, stay a week, check Mary Catherine's birth records for me, find out if they're really missing or if that historian was just incompetent, then why don't you come home."

The paragraph about their mother went on the family history stack. "I'll send you an address. Or I'll find phone jacks. We can go back to e-mail."

"Okay. I'm working on stuff about mom." Water ran again. "Did you know grandpa wanted her to be a dentist and take over his practice? Before women were even allowed in dental school? She was in junior high. She told him no thanks, she wanted to be an athlete and was going to swim the English channel!"

Tam pressed her forehead against the window, looking down at the gravel and trash sliding past. The train wasn't going very fast. Tires, beer cans, grocery sacks, weirdly crinkled up pieces of metal, a Frisbee. "Martha, I can't hear you. I think we're going into a dead cell area."

"I'll send you the part about Robert the Bruce. The stuff about mom isn't written out yet. Obviously I need help with my writing." More dishes clinking. "I wish Gary would help me. But he has his own troubles—"

"This is breaking up. I'll let you know where I end up."

Down Maine

Tam opened her laptop. She had always avoided looking at the pulsating light of a computer screen while seated in a moving vehicle. How much closer to emulating, or inviting, a seizure could any behavior be? Perhaps this recent prolonged pre-aura stage had damaged her judgment, why else would she be on a train to Maine? A lot of other decisions she'd bungled lately. So she watched her fingers on the keys, then looked up at the compose-message window.

> Dear Martha,
>
> We just hung up. I'll make sure we can use e-mail while I'm in Maine. I know how bad I am on the phone. I just don't want to hear about G.
> How did we stop talking—I mean more than chit-chat? What was the last *important* thing I told you? Maybe it means telling you about the thing with Meryl proves how insignificant it is. I never told you that I had a few more seizures. The second one, only six months after the first, and that's one reason I never went back to swimming. Then there was another, 8 years later. That one was embroiled with a man—I never told you about him either. It feels like I have so many losses and regrets and don't know how to fix them, but maybe

After gazing vaguely out the window at a blur of brown-stubble farm fields, still months away from their lusty verdant display, she opened another compose-message window. The message to Martha disappeared behind a blank one. Her fingers were still on the keys. Then they began clicking. Slow at first, and erratic. But some momentum and a regular rhythm did develop.

Dear Denny,

Do you still think best in water? I wish I'd jumped in, one of those days you were thinking. I think I almost did. It might've changed everything . . .

You never saw me foam at the mouth that night, then you never saw me again. But you're still with me, in the grand mal aura stage—either it induces memories of you, or else stray memories of you jarred loose by accident (or incident) cause the aura . . . So far I've staved off the next big one. But, over the years when I've dreamed of you, who's to say I haven't gone through the rigid stage and woken with just a slight headache, just a little confused

Like a child blinking hard and wishing she could make the message to Denny disappear and the letter to Martha reappear on top—Tam deleted what was there and started over.

Martha, Meryl told me I never wanted anything enough. How wrong she was. But for a long time, what I've wanted hasn't been something I *never* had.

The person I didn't tell you about was Gary's swim coach. Would've been my coach too, I suppose.

Maybe all I want now is to figure out the stuff I still need to figure out. I can tell myself, make a list. But everything is all mixed together, they won't list out straight.

Who said when you have no one you still have family? It's just one of those things "they" say. Who are "they," the ones who say everything? Is it genealogists? You should've made a pedigree instead of a family tree. With a f-tree, you start with one person and list all the offspring, and for each of those you list all their offspring, and the same for each of those, more and more branches, until you get to us, just little twigs way out there. But on a pedigree you start with yourself and branch backwards to your two parents and backwards again to the parents of each parent, then the parents of each grandparent. You don't list any brothers or sisters, it's like everyone on the pedigree is an only child. I have software to make pedigrees.

A new compose-message was grayish white, the *To*, *From* and *Subject* lines blank. Knowing that was exactly the kind of mindset she should be striving for, she nonetheless began filling in the spaces.

Dear Mom,

Thank you for the lighthouse rescue stories. Funny about Abbie Burgess being a lightkeeper. I am actually on my way to Maine. Why do they call it Down Maine or Up Maine? I forget what the difference was. Whichever, I'm on my way, sent by Martha to discover something about our lineage. Maybe there was an epileptic in the lighthouse keeper's family? Maybe I'm off to rescue her standing, her legacy.

When she opened another compose-message window, she made the window smaller, so the top of the message underneath still showed, just the name of the e-mail software and the name of the message recipient in a blue horizontal stripe, *Eudora – Emily Marr-Burgess*. The window on top of that said *Eudora – No recipient, no subject*. It stayed that way, even after Tam started typing.

Gary,

People would accuse me of living in the past, but you know what happened. No, you didn't cause the seizure,

I've known that a long time, but it didn't mean I wanted you as my rescuer. Why did you have to pull me out and make yourself the big hero? Did that start you on your life's path? What path did it give me? I was winning, you tried to pull me back. Then there was another chance for me to be who I thought I was going to be—with Denny. Why couldn't you just leave us alone? Not everything's a race, and not every race is with *you.*

When she reduced the other two message windows, the top blue stripe of all four showed, with the windows overlapping and cascading, like file folders with variably spaced index tabs.

Eudora – No recipient, no subject.

Eudora – Emily Marr-Burgess.

Eudora – Martha Marr Richter.

Eudora – Dennis Clarkson, no address.

Anyway Denny, I have no idea why I'm dredging all this up on my way to Maine. Traveling north and feeling like I'm sinking, no wonder they call it Down Maine. But why am I spiraling? And why now? I had a successful career and have no need to worry about an income for the rest of my life (I hope). I haven't had a seizure in 25 years. (But the last one was a monument. Too bad you weren't there so you could carry it with you forever too.) Maybe I just have nothing to do now. No goals, nothing to accomplish, no one to impress, voluntarily finished, and it causes one to do a lot of nostalgic retrospect— about the stuff I didn't (couldn't) do. This must be why 40-somethings suddenly get involved in organizing their high school reunions. I've ignored every wistfully cheerful where-are-you? e-mail. Would a reunion with you even be possible?

But I've successfully not thought about you, and I plan to go back to not thinking about you. It's just that you were the occasion for my last seizure, an anniversary in a couple of months. Did you think it was a false alarm—that there never was a zygote? What if I told you, after you decided to abort everything, *I* was the one aborting—it came out all over the floor with my piss that night

Another blink of her eyes and touch of a finger, she pulled the bottom message to the front, *No recipient, no subject.*

So Gary, have you ever wondered why Martha is the only one of us to provide more branches for the family tree? I have *my* reasons, which you could never know. Maybe yours are fear of eclipsing yourself in everybody's eyes with a clone of yourself.

I'll bet you think I should've thanked you for arranging to put me together with Denny. As though you were paying indemnity to me, for ending my swimming career. I never told Mom. She would've thought you were being so good. Looking out for me. Rescuing me from seizure-inducing brooding. Why couldn't you just leave me and Denny alone? Why couldn't you just be satisfied being the center of Mom's universe? She's still so proud of you and yet still always worried about you, and acts as though the rest of us should be as well. No thanks

Then she closed her e-mail program. When the software asked if she would like to send the unsent messages, she chose no. When it asked if she would like to save and queue the unsent messages, she selected no. She lowered the screen of the laptop. The bluish light bled around the edges, glowing less and less as the screen neared the keyboard, until there was just a thin beam, a laser, a pallid sunset, that went out when the laptop made its satisfying and conclusive click.

49

Lately, any time Denny came percolating back, she did wonder if thoughts of him *were* the aura stage—as though Denny resided in the defective spot in her brain, and an impending seizure sent out memories of him like the smell of embers about to combust.

The aura stage was also sometimes marked by an inability to concentrate. The inability to answer a simple question while going through the steps of turning off a computer, to sort the mail while ordering a sandwich for lunch. An incapacity to focus, sort, pin down scattered, seemingly unrelated pieces of anxiety. Questions like *what am I worried about?* or *isn't there something wrong?* repeatedly coming to the surface or running across the bottom of her mind's TV screen like a weather warning.

As frivolous as cheating at a dog show was in a world rebelling against fear, what it said about Tam might be snarled with other implications she couldn't quite identify, and she just didn't know if the most significant events of her life were related only by chronology or a true cause-effect progression. The aura seemed to repeat an assortment of images as though they were still happening: Gary pounding on the door to the swim team office where she and Denny were holed up. Her father dying before he could be called as an informant witness against his employer. Her mother's voice, only the slightest of tremors, this time no red lipstick on her mouth, "He was under a lot of stress, his heart . . ." coming just weeks before Denny ended their workstudy scam for fear she'd be expelled right before her graduation—then ended everything else between them as well. Denny, sitting on the mattress, turned away and bent slightly, his long swimmer's torso and broad swimmer's shoulders all she could see, his voice saying, "I'm a bum." And, "Someday you'll see. It seems bad, but . . . in the big picture . . ." Later, rising from the rigid stage, aware of her surroundings but still immobile, her body contorted around and under a desk in the swim team office, blood-streaked urine pooled around her, already drying in her hair, blood caked in her clothes, and the foamy saliva likewise tinged with blood, already dry on her face and neck where she could smell it even before she was able to move. A welt on her wrist from flailing against a wooden chair. Her tongue swollen in her mouth. A pencil broken in half, splinters in her palm. Looking up at the bottom-side of the chair where she'd sat on Denny's lap, kissing, his hand in her skirt, surrounded by glossy action shots of the star athletes of a swimming powerhouse university, future Olympians or world class swimmers, frozen in a butterfly's lunge or the air-intake stroke in free-style, one arm poised in an arc over a capped, goggled head, droplets of diamonds outlining the power of the thrust. One of them was Gary. She wasn't even sure which one. One of them was Denny. That one she took, when she left, clutched under a towel emblazoned with the university mascot that she used to cover her soiled clothes.

The first time she approached that office was near the end of her freshman year of college. Even though she was going to ignore Gary's "favor," a note on her pillow, which meant he'd come into her room, she nevertheless ended up at the coach's door the next day.

> *Tam, since your not doing athletics, thought you might like to stay close, this looks like a good way, a job as administrative assistant for the swim coach, go see him tomorrow.*

The misuse of *your* evidently not sufficient to prevent him from getting a sportswriting job upon his graduation with a degree in athletic conditioning. Gary's dominance on the swim team wasn't enough to get his victories into the local city paper, and the student body cared only for football. He had completed his last season on the college swim squad, hadn't ever made an Olympic team, his eyes suspiciously red after the last meet. Their parents spoke with him, alone in the den, for over an hour. Tam had never asked what his plans were, now that his competition days were (seemingly) over; it was okay that nobody noticed she hadn't said anything directly to Gary in at least three years. It was Gary's last semester. They'd ended up at the same university for that one year, but Tam disappeared into a freshman class of 10,000.

Denny sat behind a desk that had not stacks but piles of paper covering it—as though a trashcan had been emptied in a ring around a small clear spot where his coffee cup and a chart of the most recent set of his swimmers' lap times shared the spotlight of his ancient-looking gooseneck lamp. The office door was split, so the upper half could be open and the lower half closed.

His hair was only about a half inch long, not the usual fashion of the time, but he explained—not that day, but soon afterwards—that he shaved his head for swim season every year, so the swimmers wouldn't feel alone in their abject unstylishness. His eyebrows looked shaped too, but Tam never noticed them grow or change—thin for a man, rakishly angled, matching his tight, dimpled grin, his high cheekbones, his slightly aquiline nose.

After she'd said her name and that she understood he was looking for an administrative assistant, he said "Gary's little sister" once. Only once. They looked at each other. Tam, still on the other side of the cut-in-half door, deciding whether or not to act on her impulse to turn sharply and walk away.

He never broke eye contact. As though waiting for a sign from her. How long did the moment last? Ten seconds or three minutes? His eyes didn't crinkle when he smiled, but darkened or brightened. Darkened and brightened at the same time. Slanted late-afternoon winter sunlight after a storm. A storm that had never broken. The calm after an averted storm. As though the smile was a laugh. As though it was her own smile.

He said, "Come on in." She tried the doorknob. "Reach over." He stood behind the paper-strewn desk. "Only the outside doorknob is locked." He was wearing blue shorts, as most of the athletic personnel did, with their uniform white golf shirts, school name and their particular sport in blue embroidery over the pocket. His legs were shaved. It was a few years after Mark Spitz's hairy chest with his medals spread across it adorned posters—by the late 70's, swimmers shaved, and Denny had been one of the first.

The rest of the office was a second desk, piled with boxes, and a work table, likewise heaped. By the end of the month, when she'd organized the little room, she knew that the boxes held a variety of odd items no one could explain, like eight track cassettes of The Doors, Henry Mancini, and Christmas music, a textbook for a political science course, a cheer-leader pompom, and one size ten Converse All Star basketball shoe. But the desks and boxes were also occupied by old telephones, an already out-of-date electric typewriter, six or seven coffee cups (some with mold growing at the bottom), numerous rusty and broken trophies, wooden clipboards, boxed stopwatches requisitioned ten years ago and never used, copies of every school newspaper with a swim meet report, official time and placement results from meets—some in loose-leaf notebooks, others stacked or packed indiscriminately—and multiple bound copies of the university code of conduct for athletes for every year starting five years before and going back at least a dozen more years, from long before Denny was the swim coach. She giggled, almost chortled, sometimes had to sit right down on the floor—a strange sensation, déja vu to nothing—as Denny made up stories about the former swim coach and how he might've used some of the mysterious junk she continued to find stashed in file cabinets and desk drawers. The barbecue tools, the Russian-to-English flashcards, the marching band hat.

By the end of May she'd learned to deal with an athletic program budget, to requisition equipment or have bills for services paid, had found desk organizers and a few trash cans and cleared Denny's desk of papers, acquired a new desk lamp, clipboards, a set of metal shelves, and a new coffee maker (Denny had been sending her for tiny paper cups of coffee from a machine that dispensed lukewarm colored water for 25 cents). The end of May was Gary's graduation and she sat in the bleachers of the WPA-built football stadium with her mother, father and Martha (and a horde of other families) to watch the processional march of five thou-sand black-robed graduates, most of whom had decorated their caps with balloons or flowers, even an umbrella, or objects indicating their major—a model of an atom, a papier mache trumpet—to identify them-selves in the crowd. Gary had a contraption built over his hat with two bright yellow swim fins and a spray of blue and white crepe paper like a splash of water. Martha, using binoculars, described the mortarboard-art aloud. Then, before Gary joined them afterwards, Tam left, saying she had to go to work.

"On *Saturday?*" Martha asked.

Denny had asked her to help him with a personal project. "I have to visit my parents and need a buffer zone," he'd said on Friday.

Denny's car, a VW convertible, was too loud for conversation, for guessing where they were going, for laughing at the hint he gave before starting the engine, "Did I forget to tell you? In addition to ten hours a week, part of your job is to help me use my monthly pass at Club Dread. Not a free pass either, it says in the fine print, what you don't pay in time you'll give up in personal dignity." It was the way he said it, mock seriously from behind aviator sunglasses, with his geeky short hair, buckling himself into a light blue Volkswagen, putting down the vinyl top. And, beyond geeky, wearing pennyloafers without socks. Men wouldn't commonly put bare feet into leather shoes until the late 80's or 90's. She'd been jolted the first time she saw a man in boat shoes with no socks, the first time since Denny, and jolted in a different way than the beginning-of-summer smile she felt herself wearing in 1975 as she watched his bare ankles and loafers working the gas, brake and clutch of the Volkswagen.

"They always want me to be a guest at their beloved tennis club," he'd said when they arrived in the parking lot. Not an exclusive country club, it was an anyone-can-join pay-to-use facility, kin to a YMCA. "My parents call it *The Club,*" Denny said. "Maybe that's the explanation— they've been pounded over the head until they're retarded."

"Come on, they can't be that bad."

"Just wait."

Tennis courts, indoor racquetball and handball courts, men's and women's locker rooms, and a pool. Denny and Tam went through the building, past the two locker rooms without pausing at either one, and out the back doors onto the pool deck that was surrounded by a chain link fence and boxwood hedges clipped to the height of the fence. The pool was Olympic sized, with set-aside times for those wanting to swim laps, the rest called "splash-n-dive" on the posted schedule. A few women lay in recliners, one with her face covered by a book, the other on her stomach, head buried in her arms. In the pool, two people, standing in waist-deep water. The tiled sides and bottom were traditional aqua, the water surface glinting, throwing sun spots into Tam's eyes. She fumbled for her sunglasses. The man's hair was shockingly white, combed straight back in a poofy bouffant, country singer style, completely unmussed by his entry into the water. Broad-shouldered with the beginning of a paunch, abundant gray hair on his chest. The woman wore a one-piece suit with a little skirt that the water held up like the petals of a flower around her waist. On her head a cap with multi-colored flowers growing all over it, which matched the petals of the swimsuit skirt. The water so clear, the lane lines were crisp and distinct beneath the people's feet. The woman pointed her foot and ran her toe over the smooth black stripe. Above the water, the woman and man were beaming, even laughing aloud, as they tossed a beach ball back and forth, laughing louder if they caught the ball the same time it splatted on the calm water in front of them.

"What indescribable fun," Denny murmured. Tam might've been about to stifle a giggle, when he added, "Ever wish you were adopted?"

Tam looked down, removed her sunglasses to clean them on her shirt. She was wearing the flared green slacks, sandals and pullover top she'd worn to the graduation. The polyester top only smeared the glasses. She already knew it would. The slacks hugged her butt. She knew that too. She heard Denny, as though in the distance, introducing her, calling her *my student assistant*.

"Come on in, the water's fine!" the man called in a baritone sing-song, as though parodying something. The woman laughed as if she'd learned how somewhere, maybe for a play.

"Okay," Denny murmured, kicking off his shoes. "Time for us to get in there and look like we're frolicking with as much delight and glee. Or die trying."

Tam dropped her sunglasses, bent to pick them up. Wondering if she was having trouble catching her breath. Maybe it took forever for her to gasp, "What?"

He was stepping out of his shorts. "They expect us to play with them."

"*Us?*"

55

Underneath his shorts, a school-logo speedo from the university swim team. "I thought you wouldn't mind playing along, once you got here. They're so stupid it could almost be funny." He removed his shirt. It was the first time she saw his chest. The ideal swimmer's inverted triangle, the ultimate swimmer's washboard, hairless, the color of light wood, not tanned to leather. But she noticed his anatomy like a fact, one she wouldn't appreciate or relish until a later day when she would ask him how he could wear the tiny, revealing speedo in front of his mother.

Her mouth was dry. She put her sunglasses back on. "You expected me to be wearing a suit under my clothes, all the time, like an extra skin?"

"I'm sorry. I forgot, most people don't."

By this time she was smiling again, because he was standing with his back to the pool, facing her, blocking her view of the beach ball game that continued above the surface of the rippled, glinting water. And he was holding her hands.

Aviator glasses on top of his peach fuzz head, his eyes at once earnest and amused, his cheeks slightly flushed, his lips halfway pursed, fighting an outright laugh.

Tam said, "You look like a pro athlete who can't do his skit on *Saturday Night Live* without cracking up."

"That's exactly what this is. See how you understand already? Please, Tam, I need you. Just take off your sandals and roll up your pants and—"

"No."

"—sit on the deck—"

"No." She stopped smiling. He was still holding her hands, tugging her toward the edge of the pool. "My pants will get wet."

"—splash your feet —"

"No." She tried to twist her hands free but he held fast.

"—pretend you've been in a dungeon for ten years and this is the first time you've seen sunlight and touched water."

"Denny, I can't—"

"*Please.* Just consider it part of your job, to ensure my mental health."

They stood frozen for a second, and he must've sensed something. He dropped her hands, used both of his to lift her sunglasses. "Tam? Anyone home?" The splashing and laughing in the pool had also stopped. When she turned and left, she left her sunglasses in his hands.

But not for long. She only sat in the warm, dusty-smelling VW for a few minutes before he got into the driver's side, dressed again in his shorts, golf shirt and loafers. She hadn't been crying. She turned to him so he could see that.

"I'm sorry," he said. "Does this have something to do with over-stepping my boundaries as your employer?"

"No." The word just landed between them like a stone. He wasn't facing at her, which was unusual. He seemed like a guy on a bad date, wishing he could disappear, so she added. "Please don't ever think— Don't think that."

He looked at her, but didn't speak. He looked miserable.

"Just a bad combination of things, for me," she said. "I don't swim anymore."

"I knew that. Gary said—"

"I don't mean competitive, I mean ever."

"I never considered anything about this to be *swimming*. Gary said—"

"Nothing he's ever said about me counts—for *any*thing. Don't even tell me, I don't want to know how he described it."

"How he described what?"

She looked at her hands, folded properly in her lap. "I have epilepsy. I don't ever go into the water. I have to be careful. I keep things at an even keel. Sometimes I even wonder if all the laughing I've done lately with you— Well, anyway, they don't let me take meds anymore because it's been too long since the last seizure. But that also means I could have another grand mal at any time. Not a pretty sight. You would run away screaming."

"I don't scream." Finally, he almost smiled.

"Okay, the man's version of screaming."

"So, does water cause seizures?"

"No, but if I seized in water, after all the ugly part, I would probably drown. Didn't Gary . . ." She looked away, her eyes smarting, as though she *had* gone in.

"You said I'm supposed to forget anything he said." The smile that was not quite there was pulling at his mouth.

"Didn't he tell you, if I swim when he's not there, there'll be no one to save me?"

"How about me?"

"How can you always be there? Gary, unfortunately, will always be my brother."

The bewilderment was in the half-smile he finally showed. "So you won't even get your feet wet? You get upset if—"

"Besides not wanting to drown . . . not that way . . . not *any* way, but not *that* way. Besides that . . . if I went into a pool now, it would mean it doesn't matter that my mom never gave me her . . . this pep talk I thought she'd . . . I thought she'd tell me I could do it." Tam squeezed her folded hands tighter together, staring down at them again. "By the time I had my second seizure, I knew I couldn't, but . . . I still wanted her to *tell* me I could. And . . . but . . . I wonder now if I'd gone back, even without her encouragement, would *I* look like the hero then? Did I lose that chance? I don't know . . . and, anyway . . . I've lost my touch, lost my edge, lost my place. I certainly wouldn't be able to beat Gary now."

"Why doesn't this make sense to me?"

"I know, it's all gotten a little mixed up. It doesn't make sense to me either, but I just . . . I don't know. I'm sorry I got upset."

"But Tam, I mean it's illogical. I understand that a seizure in water is life-threatening, but now you want your mom to suggest you put yourself in danger, and you seem to want to have nothing to do with Gary, and if you can't beat him, you won't swim at all, but you think he's the only one who can save you?"

"I meant that's what *he* would say. Because of how my mom made . . . I mean, *my* downfall became *his* glory." She held a deep breath, released it, then untangled her fingers and let her hands lie flat, one on each thigh. "But, my mom . . . if she *had* ever told me I could overcome anything and swim again—and win again—I wouldn't blame her for putting me at risk. She didn't know. But no, I probably still wouldn't swim. I can't risk . . ."

". . . Gary being right?"

"You'd better be kidding."

"Have you had a lot of seizures?"

"One was too many. But I've had two. I was 12."

"And you haven't been in a pool since?"

"No. See? It worked." She smiled, brighter than she felt, but to help him. "Faulty logic—B follows A, therefore A caused B. Anyway, maybe too much chlorine *would* cause a seizure. That pool was *too* damn clear."

Denny became Denny again, his face bright, his world bursting with amusement. "Are you kidding? My mom probably rented a lab and did a complete water chemistry analysis before she let my dad sign the membership check. Believe me, there's not a single, lonely germ in that pool, or *she* wouldn't be in there. You wanna know how nuts about germs she is?"

"How nuts is she?"

"I wasn't allowed to buy ice cream from a neighborhood truck because she said it was dirty."

"Did she mean the foreign-looking man driving the truck?"

"Hell no, in those days it was a white guy with a complete white suit and black bow tie! But she did tell me to always wash my hands after touching the stairway banister at my grade school. That just happened to be when the school was becoming . . . mixed, she called it."

"Wow. Where's she from?"

"Didn't you hear her accent?"

"No, she didn't say anything, just laughed. And your dad, what is he, some sort of actor?"

"Yeah. Acting like life is grand, he's seizing-the-day," Denny used an imitation of his father's ornate style. "He used to do community theater and put on that bogus voice so often it stuck, just like my mom told me if I made a pig face too much my face would freeze that way."

59

Tam was giggling. Denny's hand was on her leg. Then he took her hand and laced her fingers with his. "I'm sorry," he said. "We should've had a talk about our families before I sprang mine on you. But I knew you were . . ."

"Knew I was what?"

"I knew something was up with you and Gary."

"I haven't even told you everything yet. But . . . you're the first person I've told about my seizures, except doctors."

"It's proper to tell your boss." He glanced down at their joined hands, looked up again, grinning.

But she never told Denny much more about her brother. Most of the time Gary seemed more vanished than a ghost hovering between them—except once, later, when Gary made himself impossible to ignore. *Does* she know why Denny ended it? The reasons, or real reason, almost seemed irrelevant, after the abrupt—and bloody—ending. It *had* been a baby, she was sure, and the seizure had ended that.

She didn't hang the picture of Denny in her apartment when she got settled in Chicago, nor in her business suite, nor in the condo she eventually bought. She wanted to, or thought she did, but when she took it out and looked at it under fluorescent lights, the flicker, the buzz, the glare on the frame made her drop the picture and close her eyes, calm her heartbeat, count slow deep breaths and soothe the menacing hum between her ears. The first, solid evidence that Denny would forever be linked with the aura stage. She put the picture away. Into the box that included her swimming trophies and scrapbooks which had been forwarded to Chicago by her mother for some unrevealed reason. That box now sitting in Meryl's basement.

On a train to Maine via Boston, alone in a pair of seats, iridescent laptop on the tray table in front of her, it had to be more of the pre-aura stage to now be recalling Meryl's head in her rigid lap practically the same moment she's allowed herself a rare idyllic memory of Denny, his hand on her leg, the feather-light kiss after he took her sunglasses out of his golf shirt pocket and tried to put them on her face and instead poked the ear pieces into her ears. A memory (until a second ago) without the agitation, the white-out confusion of losing her feet, losing her sense of direction, losing her discretion, losing her*self.* Or was it just normal chagrin? The same kind she'd drearily felt after her few lonely trysts over the past years—dry sexual snarls with other stockbrokers, (never colleagues).

Dear Martha,

I'm still on the train writing this. We have to be getting close to Portland. It seems I've been on this train for days and days.

Remember how we used to talk in the dark (and get in trouble) when we were supposed to go to sleep. Then there was a time when you were still too young, or I thought so, and I didn't talk to you as much. I wonder, did we ever get over that?

Anyway, I'll rent a car in Portland and continue on to Southport. I'll go straight out there. I'll let Southport be my *first* impression of Maine. I barely remember it.
T.

Their last family trip to Southport, the summer after Tam's first two seizures, no one acknowledged the change in her. It was still tailor-made recreation for her family: dinghies that Gary and Martha rowed in Sheepscot Bay among tiny islands dotted with crabs and bright yellow shells. A 200-year-old graveyard where Martha did her first rubbings. A tidal basin that glistened with bare mud on low tide where Gary found lobster floats and tangled pieces of net, and where legend said the tide came in so quickly that treasure-hunters could be trapped and swept out to sea. Gary and their father went out with a lobster fisherman in his boat. That night they gathered around a boiling bucket set over a fire to eat lobster and the steamed periwinkles Martha had collected. Tam accompanied Martha and their mother to visit the lighthouse where her grandmother had been born, her mother's old family summer cottage, and the general store with one lane of candlepin bowling where their mother had spent rainy summer afternoons during her own girlhood vacations to the family cottage. And Tam was also on shore, with her mother, when Gary insisted there be photographs to mark his swim in the frigid water beside the lone pier of the Southport Yacht Club. There were no yachts, just a dozen or more rowboats and outboard dories of various colors tied to a floating dock that could rise and fall with the tide. The dock was attached to a ramp at the end of the short pier. Martha got into her suit, then squealed when she tested the water with one foot, "Like *ice*, it's *ice* water, Tam!" Gary, in just his speedo, ran down the ramp, hopped to the floating dock, then jumped in from a corner where there were no rowboats. He surfaced shouting, "*Oh, oh, oh!*" Martha waded in, still shrieking, screaming louder when Gary splashed her. Gary swam freestyle laps along the side of the floating dock, outside the boats, but couldn't do a racing flip-turn because there was nothing to turn against. Just the little boats bobbing. It took Martha forever to get into water up to her waist. "Here I go, here I go!" she shrieked, leaned forward and swam a few strokes, came up laughing, or still screeching, or both. She swam again, farther, where only her head came out of the water the next time she stood up.

Tam's mother was taking pictures. Tam stood beside her on dark, wet rocks, exposed by the low tide, beside some pylons from another small wharf piled with lobster pots. The blue sky and cotton-candy clouds and single-sail boats in the harbor didn't disclose the 50-degree water temperature. Gary's and Martha's shouts seemed solitary in a silent landscape postcard. Still looking through the viewfinder, her mother said, "Tam? You can go in if you want. Gary and Martha are out there, and I'm right here."

"Not now," Tam had said. What more had she been waiting for?

In a few moments, her mother handed Tam the camera, stripped off her shorts and sweatshirt and waded into the water.

She rented a car in Portland and continued north up the turnpike, got off Route 1 at Bath, didn't stop to use the restroom at the last modern-looking gas station in Boothbay, drove south into Boothbay Harbor, to the road that crossed the bridge to Southport. She stopped, just off the road before the bridge, to re-study a map she'd pored over the night before. Like many of the jagged peninsulas and off-shore islands off the coast of Maine, Southport stretched south, not east, into the Atlantic. The lighthouse was on a spit called Hendricks Head that itself extended off a larger point called Dogfish Head. The whole island of Southport was roughly the shape of a face, with the chin pointing south. Dogfish Head was an ear on the west side of the face. Hendricks Head was the somewhat pointed lobe of that ear, extending just slightly southwest. The lighthouse, on the end, would be facing south, but toward the open Atlantic. Tam wanted to know, for some reason, what direction she would be facing if she stood there, on the tip of land in front of the lighthouse, and gazed out to sea.

You know what you're going to look like, she told herself. Because she was still wearing her traveling jumper. On planes and trains, long trips in public conveyances, she always wore the jumper. Shin-length housedress style with no waist, it just hung from her shoulders, a loose A-line with a simple white T-shirt underneath—if she had a seizure, she wouldn't strangle in straps, buttons and zippers, her clothing would already be loose, no need for any strangers to be undressing her. But as she drove into the little cluster that was West Southport—general store, post office, graveyard, meeting house and grade school, all surrounding a flagpole in a crude travel circle, instinctively choosing the spur that would go south-west, toward the lighthouse—she thought she would probably look like a stressed Bostonian office worker who'd run from her cubicle, jumped in a car and driven two hours to find corny solace from big city life at a lonely lighthouse outpost. Or like novels Martha sent her—Tam called them *pastoral feminism*—where a woman "recovering" from divorce or some such trauma goes off to live alone in the woods, her shapeless housedress flapping around her legs as she walks beside a lake and gazes off into the hazy scenery.

Suddenly there it was, the lighthouse, still a way off, on a point of land visible across a rocky lagoon of angry, choppy water separated from the road only by a small crescent of sandy shoreline. Just past this beach, the pavement turned right, away from the shore, and a dirt road angled off left, leading onto the point toward the lighthouse. But the dirt path was chained closed, a sign planted in the still winter-bare coastal shrubs, "The Lighthouse is Private Property." So Tam backed up, parked in front of the beach, dug a sweater out of her suitcase, and got out into the gusting wind. She edged around the posts holding the chain, and walked up the path toward the lighthouse, her skirt whipping against her bare legs, like a scene in a movie, a woman clutching a cardigan around her upper body, her loose corduroy dress flapping like a flag, her shoulder-length hair lifted and streaming behind her, then across her face, likely waiting for, even expecting, the improbable appearance of some particular man.

One hand holding the sweater tight and hugging her body, the other grasping and gathering the flying hair, holding it atop her head, she stood facing the lighthouse in lucid gold twilight, with the day's overcast broken open and puffs of clouds fleeing the setting sun. There was no vegetation on the tip of the point except scrubby yellow grass, most of it flattened from winter winds combing the spit of land. Behind where the grass fell away, the lighthouse was surrounded on three sides by outcropping rocks, sloping downhill to meet the agitated ocean. Choppy rollers splashed against the dark, slippery-looking crags that were embedded here and there with pieces of driftwood, lobster pot floats, frayed sections of rope. In the roiled water offshore, a few more lobster floats bobbed, and further out, off the southwestern spit of land, a red buoy careened, warning larger vessels to come no closer. A few gulls called—behind her on the rocky lagoon beach. The wind parting grass and the flapping cloth of her clothes were the only other sounds.

The house's roof was red shingles, but patched here and there with yellow lichens, glowing gold in the westerly sun. The light tower was not the classic round turret, but square, with a bird's nest walkway around the glass-encased lamp—the east-facing glass red, the western side clear.

From the porch of the house, a boardwalk extended southwesterly past the light tower to a smaller structure, the size of a small room, on stilts on the rocks as near to the water as a structure could endure without being pounded to splinters by storms. From a 2x4 extending even farther from the raised room, a bell hung, strangely unmoved by the stiff wind. On this western side of the house, some of the pieces of shale had been used to build a low rock wall, extending the amount of level grassy space around the house, dividing it from the rugged shoreline, perhaps a line of demarcation where the highest tides brought the splash of waves. The wall was splattered heavily with the same yellow lichens, turning vivid firelight orange in the sunset.

The house had modern windows, and had obviously been painted more than once in the seven decades since it was home to a lightkeeper. It was high enough on the spit of land that only a monumental storm-of-the-century could have built waves that could touch it. But a hundred years of saltspray and wind, rain, snow, hail, and sunshine gave all the structures the sturdy, seafaring look they deserved. Tints of discoloration bled from windows in the tower. A wooden deck and a glassed-in sunporch had been added for the house's service as a summer home, but the picket fence looked like it had always been there—protecting a backyard that was just above the rocks on the south-facing tip of the point, where the many children of the keeper would've played during the few months of summer weather. For anyone standing on the rocks outside the picket fence, the ocean was a wide-angle view on three sides, sweeping from the rocky cove on the east side of the lighthouse, open ocean straight ahead, then to the west where Sheepscot Bay moved into the shipping inlet servicing the port of Wiscasset several miles north up the tidal river. Across Sheepscot Bay there were other spits and peninsulas of land, and islands, hazy from distance.

Tam had circled the lighthouse once by now, staying about thirty yards out from the house, sometimes walking on the highest rocks, sometimes on the edges of the grass, outside the picket fence. Still holding her blowing hair, still clutching the sweater closed, she stepped onto each rock to test the surface, keeping her head up, eyes bare against the cold wind, squinting toward the sun to the distant ledges of the jagged peninsula across the bay, where the shipwreck might've taken place in a March storm, with winds blasting harder than this wind, and cold more frigid than this cold, plus the blinding veil of snow.

The wooden ship would have cracked like an egg. As seawater surged into and over the hull and deck, the foam and spray would start to add layers of ice to ropes, masts, the rigging where people were climbing, trying to stay out of the sea. The baby's mother had worked quickly, though, at the first signs of distress. She had a fierce maternal drive to act, had to know the ship was doomed, and had to know it early enough to give herself time. The box was still dry at the moment she sealed her baby inside. The featherbeds not yet doused with freezing water, the rope not yet ice. When she put the bundle overboard into the twelve-foot cresting waves, she had to know all else was hopeless, or she wouldn't have done it.

A storm blasting from the north would have blown waves away from the lighthouse. So it came from the southwest, and the sea reared up, surged, lunged. Not just huge rollers, each wave incessantly peaked, broke open many times before it reached shore. And not just splashing against the ledges, but exploding against rock peninsulas all around the lighthouse, like out where the ship was already being hammered to toothpicks. Seeing the bonfire and the steady beam from the lighthouse tower, perhaps hearing the placid clang of the fog bell through the shrieking blizzard and screaming passengers, the mother would have known the gale winds would take the featherbed bundle across the inlet to the safety of the lighthouse keeper.

> The span across this channel is enormous, Martha. Even with 50-plus mph winds tossing the mattresses from wave to wave, she would've been submerged by some, thrown clear by others. How could she have survived? What amazing luck it would take for the bundle to skirt the rocky tip of the head where the lighthouse is, where Mary Catherine and the keeper's other children would've been huddled inside at the window watching

their parents scurry from the bonfire to the bellhouse. Or no, wouldn't the children be told to stay away from the windows for fear the storm might suddenly shatter the glass, if this were that once-in-a-lifetime blizzard with icy waves tall enough to engulf the house and tower? But the bundle had to miss these rocks at the tip, then miss the ledges that rise in the middle of the lagoon— not smoothed by eons of caressing waves, these rocks have remained serrated and craggy. As the bundle got nearer, the keeper (how many *greats* before this grand-father?) would've gone into the water. He would've been in over his waist, perhaps over his head, riding the feather-beds, as you suggested, like a boogie board, but not toward a safe, soft, sandy beach. He could've broken a limb, several ribs, certainly risked instant hypothermia (you must remember how cold this water was, even on a mild summer day!) Then with the air punched out of him, panting and coughing up seawater, sprawled and wedged in the rocks like the driftwood that's collected here, he would've still been holding tight to that bundle, his wife helping to pull the mattress ashore. And they would've heard the cries, muffled, coming from inside.

It's incredible how I haven't been able to think of anything else since I got here. My head was so stuffed with other shit the whole trip—you wouldn't believe it if I tried to explain—and now I have been transported, that's the only word I can use. The stillness here is wild, absolutely feral, yet it is serenity, and peace. This is a fixed, sturdy, faithful place, a place seething with strength yet surrounded by uncertainty, violence. I can feel her life here, I can be her, I can describe it for you. How she might've grown, maybe taller than Mary Catherine and the other girls, more broad-shouldered, her hair a different color—darker than these descendants of British earls—and maybe fell in love with one of the assis-tant keepers. He could've been her brother, one of her adopted brothers. A simple story, really. A baby grows to girlhood in this house, on this wind-blown point, and turns to her adoptive brother when the time is right. Or maybe a cousin. We don't know all her cousins, who they were, where they were, they're not on your family tree.

But the time was right. It was right, but I don't know why. Maybe that's how things happened then, not prudish, just no need to talk about it. Two people simply . . . It *is* that simple.

Martha, something happened. I have so much to tell you. But not now. It's still too . . . I don't know, shocking? No. It's not even startling, not that at all, as though I can't be startled by anything. Maybe I'll wake tomorrow and be aghast, I don't know. It's dark now, only the white foam visible when the rollers reach the rocks.

I'll finish this later and tell you then—there's another legend living in this place, a ghost, and maybe the two legends can be put together, the ghost and the ship-wrecked baby. It can make sense. Today everything made sense.

An hour before she had returned to the car and sat in growing darkness writing the message to Martha, Tam had stood on the ocean side of the fog-bell house, in front of a trail of sunlight across the wide inlet. The sun was still above the water but sinking into in a bank of clouds hovering above the peninsula to the west. Each ripple and roll of water had a black shadow, the buoy had lost its red hue. Then she'd released her hair, let it whip and sting against her face, walked back around the bell house, outside the stilts, into the shadow behind it. That's where he was. A man. He had something in one hand, which turned out to be a brown sack from a hardware store, but she didn't assume it was a weapon or anything dangerous nor that his sudden appearance was alarming. She stood still, facing him, her sweater overlapped across her body and her arms holding it closed.

He said, "Are you the ghost?"

"Excuse me?"

"I saw you out here, walking around. I thought you had to be the ghost."

"A ghost?"

She couldn't see his face in the shadows, but his hair was longish and wavy. Not curls but waves, ripples, and the tips flew away from his head in every direction, thick enough to not stand upright in the wind. Suddenly he stepped toward her and put a hand on her arm. He left it there and he squeezed her muscle. "No, you're real." He didn't withdraw his hand. "So have you come out to try to see her?"

"Who?"

"The Lady Ghost. You didn't come out to try to catch her? I've never seen her, but dusk is when she shows herself. She's supposed to be dressed up. Like you. Not exactly like you." He was still holding her arm. They were that close. Now she could see his face, a rugged face but not beat-up, nothing soft but nothing harsh or nasty, a soft gleam coming from his eyes. An expression of wonder beginning to fade, even as his hand stayed on her arm.

"You thought I'm a ghost?"

"No. For a minute, maybe." He smiled, maybe sadly. "I believe that she's here. The way it happens is that she's seen for only a moment then she disappears around a corner. I watched you go all the way around the house. Then you came around this corner and here you are, you haven't disappeared."

"What kind of ghost is she? Who is she?"

"Maybe we should introduce ourselves first?" He squeezed her arm once more then let go. His teeth glinted when he grinned. "After all, this is private property. I'm supposed to shoo you away."

When Tam didn't say anything, he went on, "I'm Nathan Tanner. Nat to my friends. I'm a builder, like everyone else who isn't a full-time lobsterman, and I'm the caretaker of the lighthouse for the folks who own it. They summer here. I came out after work to set some traps." He held up the sack. "Mice, not lobster. Your turn."

"I'm . . . more of a ghost that you thought. My great grandfather and great-great grandfather were keepers here, over fifty years between them. I've come back to . . . Oh, my name is Tam."

"Pleased to meet you." He reached toward her again, stepped even closer, she thought he was going to put his warm hand on her arm or shoulder again, but he didn't. He put the sack down and used his other hand to lift her arm so their hands clasped. Then he didn't let go, and kept his other hand over hers as well. "But it would've been more fun if you were the ghost."

"The ghost. Tell me about her."

He released her hand with one of his—the one that had been grasping hers in a handshake. But still held hers with his other hand, and he turned so they were side-by-side. He dipped and picked up his sack, then they started walking, hand-in-hand. He told her the story. By the time he finished they were already up in the light tower, his breath on her neck, her heart strumming endorphins, like winning the freestyle.

She'd climbed the coil of metal steps that spiraled up inside the tower, two steps behind him, still holding his hand. They'd had to let go as they each climbed through the hole in the floor of the gallery—the little room atop the tower that held the light. Then, like a dance, he'd taken her hand again and guided her so she stood in front of him at the glass. His hands went to her hair, gathering it, combing it with his fingers, smoothing it back. Tam stood facing out to sea, over the bell-house toward the dark careening buoy. Straight down below, the waves were white, engulfing the rocks then retreating. The fog bank rising over the distant peninsula glowed, as though holding the setting sun.

"The keeper thought he saw a shadow move against one of the empty summer cabins. She disappeared around the corner . . ." He continued reciting the story, and his hands slid to her shoulders, then his arms encircled her waist and he edged even closer behind her. In the middle of the story, between sentences, he whispered in a different voice, "Tell me to stop. Just tell me, any time." She said nothing. Thought of nothing except that part of her was part of him, and she didn't know him, so for that moment she didn't know herself—and that was ultimate peace. She never shut her eyes, even as he gathered her skirt up and let his hands slip beneath it to her bare legs. Even when he eased her underwear down by putting his fingers into the elastic band then sliding both his palms over her bare butt, the underwear riding down on his hands. Even when he once again held her around her waist with one arm and penetrated her with one finger, then two. "They never found out who she was." He stopped telling the story and she felt him undoing the zipper on his jeans, so she lifted one leg and stepped out of her underwear that had fallen to her ankles. One of his arms around her waist, one of his hands slid up her back, pressing, pushing gently until she was leaning forward, bent at the waist, her hands on the sill of the tower window. "Tell me no, if you don't want to," he whispered again, rasping a little, but she raised her butt slightly and he slid himself in.

"It's like you *are* her," he said, low and hoarse.

His voice made her shiver, then the shivering didn't stop. She grinded herself against him. Her forehead leaned against the clear glass side of the tower. The red glass was behind them, possibly silhouetting them. With the setting sun breaking out of the fog and shining into the tower, the shape of their copulation could be visible in the red, through binoculars from the east. His rhythm wasn't short and choppy but long, like rollers coming in on a steady wind.

"You're unbelievable," he gasped, before he cried out once, and panted again, "unbelievable."

They stood there until he could no longer stay inside her. He fixed his pants. He pulled up her underwear. He stayed behind her and held onto her, his face beside hers. He said, "Who are you?"

New England Charm

Martha, something happened. I have so much to tell you. But not now. It's still too . . . I don't know, shocking? No. It's not even startling, not that at all, as though I can't be startled by anything. Maybe I'll wake tomorrow and be aghast, I don't know. It's dark now, only the white foam visible when the rollers reach the rocks.

I'll finish this later and tell you then—there's another legend living in this place, a ghost, and maybe the two legends can be put together, the ghost and the ship-wrecked baby. It can make sense. Today everything made sense.

Martha, it's later now. I found a place to stay, for tonight. Tomorrow I'll find something on the island. Anywhere else is too far away. But before I tell you anything else, let me tell you about the ghost. I was told this story a few hours ago, so let me get it down here before I forget. (I don't think I *could* forget.)

This story is about a real woman who became a ghost. It's documented in newspapers, nobody disputes this woman came here and drowned. It was 1931, in December. A well-dressed woman checked into a hotel in Boothbay Harbor, then asked around where she could get an ocean view. Boothbay is a protected harbor, you can't see open ocean from there. So she walked over the bridge onto Southport. She stopped at the general store and asked again where she could get an ocean view, and the shopkeeper mentioned the lighthouse. They say the woman seemed familiar with the lighthouse—she prob-ably nodded and said something like, "Yes, that's what I want," as though she'd forgotten to ask for the light-house but that was what she'd really come for. Or I think maybe she didn't want to ask for the lighthouse by name because she wanted them to think of her as "a stranger," so she asked for open ocean, figuring they'd direct her to what she'd really come to see. So she continued on from the store, walking toward the lighthouse. It was getting dark. The keeper (not our great-grandfather—I'm looking at your family tree, and this happened just one year after Jaruel's son Wolcott had died and a new keeper had replaced him) had walked to the general store, and when he heard from the shopkeeper that a woman had just left there to walk to the lighthouse, he was surprised that he hadn't seen her on the road. She must've hidden from him when she heard him coming. He walked back, looking for her. As he approached the dirt road to the lighthouse, he thought he saw a shadow beside one of the boarded-up summer houses nearby. He called out, but no one answered. He didn't go to investigate, but realized later that he should've. The woman never returned to her hotel. News spread—everyone who went into the general store heard about a well-dressed, soft-spoken woman in her late 40's who'd walked down to the lighthouse but was not seen walking back. Six days later they found her body, just offshore, a little north of the lighthouse, where the tide easily could've brought her. She had an iron strapped to her waist with a belt. They never found out who she was. She had no identification, not even in her hotel room, and the name she'd used to register was probably an alias. They ran ads in the newspapers up and down the East Coast. Detectives worked on the case. But it was never solved. But they say her ghost is still seen, just a flicker of a shadow going around the corner of a building, like the keeper saw that night. And things sometimes happen, like doors slamming and locking, stuff moved around in the lighthouse, that kind of ghost-thing. Lots of theories: that her family had lost all their money in the market crash, that her husband had been killed or killed himself, that she was a bootlegger and had gone out to the shore to signal ships that smuggled alcohol and there met with foul play. But none of these answer why no one came forward to identify her, to see if she was a missing loved-one, and why she would choose to die on Southport.

But think about it, Martha, it hit me like a bolt—or I won't try to describe how it really hit me—but just do the math: 1931. She's in her late 40's. Could a woman in her 50's look like her late 40's? The shipwrecked baby happened in 1875. She'd be 56. Might *she* come back, because of whatever mysterious heartbreak her life had encountered, to die in the place where she had survived? Or could it be her daughter—if she'd gotten pregnant at 15, her daughter would be 41 in 1931. Maybe the shipwrecked baby's daughter came back to end her life (again, for whatever reason) where her mother had survived. Why not? And how creepy to have this story possibly end with a drowning, after all. A drowning, of all things.

But why did no one ever think of this possibility and put the two stories together? Couldn't it be, like I said before, that she grew up to love one of the keeper's sons, or one of his nephews—a cousin? Maybe their natural adolescent lust got her pregnant and. . . whatever happened next was . . . I don't know, her life's big trial?

OK, there's more. I met the lighthouse caretaker, and he showed me around (more on this later). He's pretty interested in all this stuff about the ghost (he's the one who gave me the story). I will talk to him further, for sure.

Gotta go. I'm in a motel in Boothbay where I can send these messages, but I'm checking out and trying to find something on Southport. I'll twist someone's arm to let me stay there. I have to be there.

Paradoxical, she realized, to so emphatically want, or need, to be housed on Southport, and yet also require a means of plugging her laptop to a phone port. But not all of Southport tried to emulate the 19th century. There were numerous lodging establishments, and many bed-and-breakfasts were no longer private homes renting an antique-decorated bedroom and use of a museum-looking bathroom down the hall. The guidebooks enumerated satellite TV, a/c, private baths and phones in the rooms.

When she logged on to send her message, there was an incoming e-mail from Martha that she had downloaded but had not read. She wanted to go to sleep in the same mood she'd carried from Southport, which didn't include anything Martha would say in a message titled *More about Mom!*

She still hadn't read it the next morning and didn't bring her laptop along when, before checking out, she went to wash her underwear and socks across the street at a new-looking laundromat. The car wash sharing the same building said it would open in May. Likewise a freestanding ice cream booth in the parking lot—a trailer permanently rooted with planter pots obscuring the wheels—would open on Memorial Day. When Tam pulled up beside the lone vehicle in the lot, a pick-up parked near the door, a teenage boy and girl came out of the laundromat and got into that truck. The girl was wearing a wool coat, like a Navy pea coat. She clutched the coat tight around her body. The temperature was in the 40's, and the sailor-type coat wasn't unusual for the region. Maybe it was the way she was clutching it, like a blanket, that made Tam remember the coat. The boy helped the girl into her side of the truck, another thing she'd never seen a teenager do. The boy never glanced at Tam, but the girl did—a long look, her face almost plaintive, drained of teenage audacity. Her eyes met Tam's and seemed to cling for a second, as the boy said, "C'mon, let's get going." The high school was just up the road, Tam remembered. Neither the boy or girl had carried a bag of laundry. Later she didn't know if these observations and realizations had only come to her after she'd found what she'd found in the bathroom, and she couldn't remember how much she'd told the police.

Instead of the usual moist smell of clean steam or linty odor of hot fabric, the laundromat reeked, but vaguely. Tam put her underwear in a washer and sat down. The *Boothbay Register* was a big newspaper. Literally wide. Her arms had to spread almost to either side to hold the paper open in front of herself. Articles on water conservation, a YMCA dinner, the purchase of computers for a junior high, and a committee updating the town ordinance, but no *local history* column, which she'd vaguely thought might replicate some of yesterday's sensations.

She put the newspaper down, closed her eyes. There'd been no buzz of seizure-warning since sometime before she'd stepped out of the car at the lighthouse. She didn't remember what else she did in the laundromat during the time before she went into the bathroom. She could still feel him, from yesterday, and she sat there focusing on it, between her legs. They—the sheriffs and paramedic—wanted to know how long it was between the time the kids left and the time she went into the bathroom. She wasn't sure. Her underwear was still in the washer. No, maybe she'd put the clothes into the drier, then stretched, looked at the bulletin board—cars and boats for sale, babysitting services offered—eventually headed for the restroom.

By then her laundry in the washer had masked the vague odor in the main room. But in the restroom, a horrible smell. And a horrible mess. There were only two stalls, both had their doors closed, but the floor of one was covered with blood. Had she thought it diarrhea, she would have recoiled in disgust and immediately backed out the door. But she didn't. Blood is unmistakable. The smell, the texture. Still mostly brick red. Dry and black at the thin edges, with thickened darker lumpy places in the middle. And a garbagy, slimy stink. Some kind of grisly intuition drew her closer to look into the stall.

It wasn't moving, at first—the baby in the toilet. Covered with bluish creamy goo, and the astonishingly neon blue placenta, and more blood. But somehow the head had remained out of the ugly water and bloody mess, and when Tam, using fistfuls of paper towels, pulled it from the bowl and cleared the slime from its face, it sucked a weak bubbly breath.

It was much later than she'd intended by the time she left the motel and headed back to Southport. Maybe they were right to be suspicious after she was so inadequate at determining how long the baby might have been in the toilet. "Surely no more than an hour," she finally said, "probably less." A paramedic had handed her back her wet sweater, smeared with blood. The same one she'd been wearing at the lighthouse yesterday, clutching it around her body the way the girl clutched her pea coat. After fishing the baby from the toilet, it had been obvious that paper towels were insufficient. Besides her underwear in the dryer, she only had the sweater, so she'd bundled the baby then called the police. The paramedic had soft, pre-heated blankets and was able, finally, to make the baby cry, a fragile wail. Of course they asked a lot of other questions, like where did she live, how long had she been in Boothbay, where did she sleep the night before. Her bloody footprints crisscrossed the floor between the bathroom and a row of plastic seats, but didn't go up the aisle between the washing machines. She described the pick-up truck, the girl in the pea coat, the boy whose eye and hair color she didn't know. They cordoned off the restroom and called the state police to send a crime scene investigator.

"It's not mine," Tam said, before anyone asked outright. "You may take a blood test if you need proof."

What they did do was look at her underwear. Not the ones she was wearing, but the clean ones in the drier. None were oversized and none were stained. Besides the bloody sweater, the clothes she was wearing were still clean, and her jeans were not stylishly baggy. One of the sheriffs left and the other asked her not to leave yet, even after the paramedic took the baby to the hospital.

"May I wash this while we're waiting?" she asked, still holding the sweater.

"Not yet, if you don't mind."

The sweater still wasn't washed because she'd decided not to stay any longer after the other sheriff came back. He'd been across the street at the motel where her bed was also unstained and the motel owner remembered her—one of only four or five registered guests last night—as not being pregnant. They took her cell number—she gave a phony—and license of the rental car. They never said thanks.

Tam went back to the motel to get her suitcase and laptop. Other than the bed covers being pulled all the way off the bed and dropped in a pile on the floor, nothing was disturbed. Tam opened the computer.

Tam, here's more stuff about mom i got from G's book (i have something else from G too, see below):

Emily Marr-Burgess's mother, Gilberta Marr, was raised in Hendricks Head lighthouse on Southport, Maine. She actually attended college—a normal school near Portland. Photographs from that time show her on a 5-woman basketball team wearing long dark dresses. Her husband, Leland Irving, came from a well-off Boston family who made their living importing lobsters from Maine. One of the Irving lobster pounds was in Southport. Thus young Leland, spending summers at his family's vacation home in Southport, met Gilberta, home for the summer from her teaching jobs in rural Maine. [An interesting side note: a young-woman schoolteacher almost always was expected to board with a family, living alone was frowned upon. So Gilberta lived with a railroad man and his wife. To get to her schoolhouse, she and the man took a hand-pumped rail car, fall, winter and spring. Gilberta stood on one side, the man on the other, pumping the lever up and down to move the car down the empty tracks.] [See, I'm trying to make this more interesting with these side stories. Hearing about history, or discovering it, especially our personal history, is always fascinating—especially to us!—but putting it into writing, it's so hard to make it come out that good.] Leland would not take over the family importing business. Instead, he went into dentistry and, after marrying Gilberta (who had to quit teaching because teachers were not allowed to be married), he opened his dentistry business outside Boston. Emily Marr Irving was the youngest of the Irving children.

In 1938, with one of his two sons a Lutheran pastor and the other in the army, Leland was getting anxious about his successful dental practice: who would he leave it to after building it from nothing and surviving the depression?

In junior high, Emily wore school dresses with matching bloomers so that after school she could tuck the dress into the bloomers and immediately be ready to play sports or climb trees without first going home. At dusk she went to her father's dental office and went home with him. One day, during the drive home, Leland posed an idea for Emily: since her brothers had gone their own way, perhaps Emily would be interested in going to dental school and someday taking over his practice. But at the time Leland said this, women were not admitted to a majority of dental

schools. Was either of them aware of this? Still, Emily wasn't aston-
ished (at least she doesn't remember being startled). She off-handedly
told her father that she was more interested in sports, particularly
swimming and diving.

[See?? Writing it out, it's all just, this happened and that
happened and that happened then this happened. But
when i think about it, it's like a magnificent scene in a
movie. Like i can just picture mom, the way she would
say "grand" while chewing gum and doing something at
the kitchen counter, whenever we tried to impress her
with something stupid that we thought was so great. i
know *that's* how she looked when grandpa offered her
a pioneer career in dentistry. But i can't write it so it does
that, what it does in my head.]
:)

Like i said, i found this stuff in the book G's working
on—he brought a bunch of pages for mom to look over. i
told him it was some great stuff, or i said something like it
was great to hear about all the things mom did, like life-
guarding, pin-setter at the bowling alley, skiing, diving,
etc. And he said, "Stuff boys do." His voice was very
weird, sarcastic and gloomy. i told him girls and boys can
do the same things. *We* did. He started rambling about
the women search-and-rescue teams at the WTC and
how they couldn't keep up. Keep up with *what*—like
it was a race? Who won? i got kind of pissed. So did he,
and the next day he sent me this e-mail describing what
he'd done at the WTC, look at it:

>FWD: What Soccer-Moms Like You Can't GET.
>They say it was hell, but saying it isn't enough.
>Anything solid was metal, mostly sharp, always hot.
>Any concrete was dust, dust in our eyes, in our mouths,
in our teeth.
>In our hair, in scrapes and cuts, in sweat. Tears were
mud.
>In our lungs. In their lungs. No masks for dogs.
>Their lungs are packed concrete.

>Twelve hour shifts. Dogs in vests hooked to lifelines
>transported by body baskets on wires across the
chasm.
>And fire. Below the crust of debris, it was all fire.
>The way hell is supposed to be, always burning below
your feet.
>And you might fall through into it.
>One man's dog did. Never came out.
>The man waited by the hole. Three days.

Me again: is he cracking up for good this time? Or just
Gary-as-usual? :) He's out of town now, don't know
where, so i'll take a break from being pissed off (and
snooping in his new book).
i know you're in Maine by now, tell me everything!

The low buzz returned to the base of Tam's brain. She left the computer
on but stood and went to the room's only window that looked across the
parking lot to a stand of trees. Patches of thin snow filled hollows in the
shade. Like a photo negative, the shadows were white. The sky was white,
too—overcast. When she put her fingertips against her closed eyes, she
could smell a tint of the bloody restroom. She balled her hands, dropped
her chin, leaned forward with her fists on the windowsill and forehead
against the cold glass, tried to picture his wavy hair pushed back off his
brow, the way his eyes creased as he'd closed her car door behind her
saying, "My ghost drives a rental car."

The day after walking where the shipwrecked baby came ashore,
where fifty-six years later the mysterious woman had thrown herself
back into the ocean to drown—the day after she'd entered the shipwreck
baby's realm and had been generously taken by a man who pursued the
ghost—she'd found a baby.

Tam went back to the computer, hit reply, and Martha's letter was
replaced with a new message window. But she hadn't yet even said everything to Martha about Nat, should she say anything about the baby? Not
that any correlation between the two was anywhere except in her (now)
buzzing brain. She had to get out to Southport again. Perhaps wait for a

news article about the abandoned baby and send that to Martha instead. Whether it mentioned her name as "rescuer" or not.

Because she was still in the motel and plugged to a phone line, she logged on. Martha had answered Tam's message from yesterday.

> Tam, your message is so different from usual! Wow, that place must be really something to have gotten to you like that. You've got this mystery baby's life all figured out and historians have argued about whether she was even real! Just remember: the story says the keeper and his wife had recently lost a child at the time of the ship-wreck, but none of my research shows this. One version said it was their only child, and we *know* that's not true—birth records show 5 (or 6) children born before that shipwreck happened. And none of those children died before the shipwreck. But they probably didn't record stillbirths or babies who died soon after birth in birth records, and that's why the newspaper specified the Marrs had five "living children." A dead baby in the Marr home is still possible. But *my* mystery is still why one child (Mary-Cath) didn't appear in whatever birth records the newspaper historian had access to. Since we're not descendants of Mary-Cath, maybe it doesn't even matter, just fun to be curious! But it *is* important that i know where the usual routes of genealogy research have failed. It would sure help if you could go check. (BTW, that news article was part 1 of 2 so i've asked the Boothbay newspaper to send an archive copy of part 2.)
>
> Now i'm also hung up on another name that appears in some old letters, and i can't find it anywhere in my rough family grid: Vanora Marr. Not that she's a possi-bility for being the shipwrecked baby (she was born before the Civil War) but she did live on Southport. So who is she? (But maybe it doesn't matter, my final product is a genealogical list, not family tree, only one branch is followed, so if she's not on it . . .) But sometimes the best way to investigate loose ends is to go to a graveyard, and since you're there, i can finally cover this part of my

research! i hope a visit to the graveyard will be as special and moving as your visit to the lighthouse obviously was! Let me know!

Dear Martha, I don't know what I'm chasing now. The place that made love to me or the man? A man who seemed to already know me even before he

She only waited a few seconds for the next word to come, but then deleted the whole message.

The same road that went south from Wiscasset off Route 1, through Boothbay and Boothbay Harbor then across the bridge to Southport, also went right past the hospital. That's where the baby was now. Had she given them good enough clues to know where to look for the boy-and-girl parents? Maybe she should leave her name and a real phone number so they could update her if the parents weren't found, or ask more questions. That might make her seem suspicious again. She'd get a blood test, gladly. Maybe they could even tell her if she'd *ever* been pregnant before. Although she'd had dozens of blood tests for annual check-ups over the years, she'd never asked if there was such a test.

Until the road came to West Southport—post office, school, meeting house, lunch cafe and general store, seated around the circle with the flag pole—it was just a pretty rural road through a coastal pine forest ingrown with moderately affluent summer houses, some of which had obviously become year-round residences. In the town circle, though, if you could call it a town, the quiet was not the hush of a prosperous neighborhood (in which case you'd have the steady white-noise of landscaper machinery), but the stillness of off-season dormancy added to the sense of having been abandoned by time—or escaping from time, since it would be this place's choice to be left behind, not a punishment. But *time-forgotten* was also the cliché, travel-guide lingo for quaint small towns. And this one wasn't quaint. It was barely a town. The general store was a square squatting wooden thing with sheds and lean-tos added on, an apartment stuck on top without thought given to "New England architecture." On the other side of a five-space dirt parking area, a wooden garage, just as ungainly as the store building. Not a commercial garage, just a garage. The lunch cafe on the other side of the circle looked more like a temporary building at a construction site, complete with muddy parking lot. The meeting hall looked new but as though built to appear old, a clapboard box with three windows on each side. It had a painted marquee in difficult-to-read script announcing the times of monthly town meetings. The post office was an uninteresting small brick stand-alone building with wheelchair access but no parking lot except on the street circle in front. The school was likewise not built to emulate "New England charm," looking more like a Sunday school addition built beside a suburban church. Speaking of churches, there wasn't one in this circle, but she'd passed one coming in, in this case a traditional New England white-steepled chapel with a generic "Methodist church" sign.

But the town wasn't trying to be what a tourist would come to see. It was what it was and what it had been, continuously, for hundreds of years, despite certain buildings being replaced or enlarged. It hadn't *tried* to stay in the 19th century. The lobster pots stacked beside houses were plastic now, not the curved wooden netted boxes that adorned suburban restaurant walls. The bobbers used to mark location of traps in bays and coves were made of PVC and Styrofoam, sprayed with fluorescent paint. Cars in the muddy parking spaces outside the lunch cafe had American flags fluttering from their antennas. A sign stating "We Will Not Forget" and an outline of the skyline of New York, minus the World Trade Center towers, was displayed in one of the store's windows and in the cafe, facing out. The post office had its flag at half mast for the postal workers who'd died of anthrax. And yet there was this: behind the garage that sat facing the general store, in a patch of lumpy ground no bigger than her motel room, marked off with rusty iron posts supporting a thick rusty chain, gray headstones leaned this way and that. Some were almost worn smooth, many were chipped or cracked. A few had bronze stars on metal stakes pushed into the turf, and plastic American flags on thin wooden sticks planted beside the stars. The dates on the stones were from the early 1800's.

Tam walked through the old graveyard, but none of the stones that were still readable had the name Marr. The breeze was chilly. Snow still huddled in the shade along the edges of the graveyard where it was bordered by trees. She had a quilted coat on today, and jeans and walking shoes. She crossed her arms, leaned forward and watched her feet as she walked out of the graveyard, across the parking spaces and into Barkin's general store.

The store smelled of pizza. At the high counter, a heated display case offered two different kinds of pizza by the slice. There was also, in a refrigerated section of the same counter, some lunch meat and a few deli salads in large cartons. Freestanding at the end of a grocery aisle was a serve-yourself coffee center with tall thermoses of different kinds of coffee, labeled *decaf, Colombian, Mocha Java, French Roast*. The aisles held canned and boxed goods, bread, donuts, cookies. A small table had some produce—oranges, bananas, lettuce, cucumbers. A bank of refrigerators had beer, juice, milk and soda. One aisle had soap and cleaning supplies. The floor and walls were unfinished wood, the ceiling showed the rafters. Near the door, a few photos of the store in various decades were mounted. As Tam studied one beside the cash register, a man came from a back room behind the counter. "Fresh pizza's coming out of the oven," he said. "Hey, Nat, you still here?"

Tam's head whipped around. She didn't see anyone else in the store.

The man said, "Guess not. Hi. You aren't, by any chance, the one who found that baby this morning?"

Again she looked around the store, almost frantically. "What? How did you know?"

"Someone happened to be at the hospital when they brought him in. Stopped by here on his way back. It's like news on TV, a newborn in a toilet. It'll travel fast."

"I thought New Englanders didn't gossip." She thought she heard a foot scuff and turned to look across the aisles again, but saw no one.

"A lost quality. Maybe too many people from somewhere else now."

"Are you from here?"

"I had a summer house here for ten years. Moved here full time two years ago when I bought the store."

"So you're not Mr. Barkin?"

"No, but of course we kept the name. Kept it looking as much the same as possible, too. Original floors and walls. So, you the one found the baby?"

"How'd you know it was me?"

"A tall woman, traveling alone, not from around here. Not many people visit this time of year."

"I'm not a tourist, just here researching . . . family history."

The man nodded without much interest. She knew he'd rather she talk about the baby. But she asked, "That graveyard behind the garage, is that the only one around here?"

"No, there're five or six on the island. If you're looking for the prominent names, try the one just around the corner and down the road."

Again she thought she heard someone in one of the aisles, a shadow that might've slipped from one aisle to the next while her back was turned. She turned and looked, not just a glance. Stood looking down the closest aisle, and listening.

"Want some fresh pizza?"

"No. Just coffee. What time is it?"

"After noon."

"Oh, in that case, yes, I'll take a slice."

The second graveyard wasn't hard to find. When the road forked, and she recognized the route she'd taken to the lighthouse yesterday, she took the other fork, and the graveyard was only half a mile down. It was much bigger than the little one in the town circle, but not big. Maybe the square-footage of two good-sized houses. She sat in the car eating a slice of cheese pizza and drinking decaffeinated coffee, parked on a dirt driveway that pulled off the paved road, made a half circle and re-joined the road. A metal sign called the place Union Cemetery. It was surrounded on three sides with pine forest. Newer monuments were mixed in among old mossy gray granite slabs, stained marble, and badly tarnished bronze. A few larger plots were surrounded with low walls of marble or concrete, with family markers in the center. The ones she could read from the car said Pierce and Orne. She wiped her hands and lips, washed out her mouth with the last swallow of coffee, and got out of the car.

The gentle breeze was startlingly cold. Every time she came out of a building or got out of the car, she was surprised all over again. More surprised by the chill air than that she'd held a slimy newborn just hours ago, or that yesterday she'd bent over and welcomed a strangely familiar stranger, feeling almost like the first time since Denny. And—her shoes crunching last fall's leaves and pine needles and crusty tendrils of ice among the stones—that Denny could come to mind without the heavy pulse in her gut. Surprising, and not surprising. As though normal had always been familiar.

The Marr plot was easy to find, with a replica of a lighthouse as its central monument. In the low marble outline wall around the plot, brass name markers were mounted. Some old and black, their tarnish running into and staining the marble. A few newer. One shiny as though polished— the death date on that one said 2001. She should have brought her copy of Martha's family lineage. Few of the names were familiar, except Wolcott Marr Sr., the second Marr keeper of the lighthouse, 1866-1930, her great-grandfather. His wife Hattie beside him. Another for Wolcott H. Marr, their son. But no Mary Catherine here, and no earlier Marrs. Tam circled the plot, then began zigzagging through other monuments that weren't in an organized family place. There were still more Pierces and Ornes than anything else. In almost the back row, near the shadowy forest that still held snow under the trees, she found a Hiram Marr who'd been lost at sea at age 55, in 1869. His wife's name, Eunice, was below his—she was the one actually buried here. Tam couldn't remember them on Martha's outline, but it was in the car with all her belongings. She started to head back to get it, cutting across graves so she could read the stones. The bodies of the graves weren't outlined or mounded, just the same tufty, winter yellow grass, piled with leaves and pine needles.

She stopped, and when she squatted her head went light for a second and she shut her eyes. She thought, *not now, not now, not now.* And the swimming weakness cleared. In front of her was a double stone. **Jaruel Marr**, it said on one side, and **Catherine, His Wife** on the other. Beside the stone, on Jaruel's side, a bronze veteran star, with the dates 61-65. The thick top edge of the stone, facing up, said **Father** and **Mother**.

She let her knees hit the ground and sat on her heels. Her toes dug into the spongy sod, her hands rested on each thigh. *Here you are*, she thought. Which made her smile. She sat like a statue in front of the stone. Felt the smile go fake and fade. She had no idea where her own father's ashes were buried, or *if* they were buried. Her mother had scattered them somewhere. Off the oil derrick into the Pacific? Tam hadn't asked. Martha probably knew, and Gary. Where had Tam been while her family mourned? With Denny, absorbed in her own stuff, right before he ended it and she woke on the bloody floor . . . *my god, the bloody floor.*

She was breathing through her mouth, staring vacantly at the head-stone. Why had she remembered the bloody floor *now*, and not this morning when she'd stepped through someone else's viscous mess to pick the baby out of the toilet? She closed her eyes again for a long moment, letting her ears pick out the rustle of leaves in the woods, likely a squirrel. A bird trilled, stopped, then trilled again from a new location. She concentrated on the faint scent of moss, of icy snow that's remained untouched on the ground for weeks, or just the smell of pristine cold near the end of winter. When she finally moved, it was to pull slowly her hands in from her thighs and slip them into her jacket pockets. Then she opened her eyes, read the entire stone again.

Father	*Mother*
Jaruel Marr	**Catherine**
	His Wife
Apr. 3, 1829	**Feb. 14, 1829**
March 13, 1906	**Oct. 29, 1920**

What made her eyes slide sideways? Not to the bronze star stuck in the ground on Jaruel's side, but the other way, to an adjacent stone. Only slightly smaller, a single stone, a small garland carved across the top, its creases smoothed.

~~roon~~

J. Thomas
son of
Jaruel & Catherine Marr
DIED
Mar. 30, 1872
at 4 yrs, 2 months, 10 days

As though she could hear the solemn footsteps of the heavily garbed mourners surrounding the grave, on a day that would have been cold like this one, with traces of snow in the shade, and cardinals calling for spring mates from treetops. And she barely jumped when he was suddenly all around her, on every side of her, his chest against her back, his knees on the ground alongside hers, his thighs scissoring hers, his arms parallel to hers, his hands clasped against her ribs, his rough cheek pressed against her face. "My ghost found herself a baby."

The birds went silent. She waited until the boldest one began his call again.

"Yes," she said, "four years old, but that's close enough."

"What?" It seemed like he had her whole ear in his mouth. His breath was warm against her, then it was cold where he'd made her wet.

"Oh," she said, "you mean . . . *that* baby."

"Was there another baby?"

"No. Yes. This one." She didn't want to move from his arms to point to the stone, so she just looked at it. "J. Thomas. A hundred and . . . thirty one years ago. Almost exactly, today."

"Was this what you came looking for?" He opened his mouth against her neck.

"Maybe." She spoke slowly. "The legend says the keeper had recently lost a child when he rescued the shipwrecked baby. But everyone says no, there was no dead child, so the story can't be true. But here he is, J. Thomas." His mouth was still against her neck, moving up behind her ear, and his hands had moved under her coat to her breasts. She said, "Did you hear me?"

"Yes. The rescued baby they named Seaborn."

"You know that story, too . . . and she had a name . . . do you know who she was?"

"That's all, just the legend." He was either trying to whisper, or purposely making a hoarse growl. "A less intriguing one than the Lady Ghost who walks the shore at dusk. And now we know she seduces anyone who's man enough to speak to her. I thought that's why you came here. *She's* buried here."

"Here? Where?"

"Her stone gives her fake name. Louise Meade."

Tam's voice was calm, as though she was going over the assets of an annuity. "I wonder if she's the same person. Seaborn. She came back here, for whatever reason, to end her life." But between sentences, was she humming? "Maybe for unrequited love . . . or lost love . . . isn't that what it always . . ."

His hands worked their way to her skin. Her throat made a low noise when he found her nipple.

"Who was *he*?"

"Who else would she know? There were so many . . . brothers . . . cousins . . . "

"Taboo."

"But would it have been forbidden, since she was adopted?" She meant to laugh but it sounded like a groan. "We sound like a romance novel."

"Isn't that part of the fun?" He released the fastener on her bra, covered her breasts completely with his palms. "The kind of fantasy only a Midwestern housewife could have, being fucked in a lighthouse, fondled in a graveyard."

"How did you know I'm from the Midwest?"

"I didn't," he said. "I don't know anything about you. Let's keep it that way. I don't remember your name, and yet, yesterday, in the lighthouse . . . and now I come across you here like you're waiting for me. I thought I would surprise you more than this."

"I know." She tipped her head back until it rested against his shoulder. "It's like you can't surprise me, and I can't surprise myself."

"Ghosts can't be surprised."

The grave they lay on wasn't Jaruel and Catherine's, and not J. Thomas's. At the far end of the graveyard, at the edge of the woods, is where they ended up. The cemetery was a continual slight grade uphill from the road, with a little dip just before the woods; so, the gravestones rising above them like buildings, the dark woods behind them, they couldn't be seen by passing cars. Her jeans and jacket absorbed dampness from the spongy sod, and his still-clothed body on top kept the chill air from most of her skin.

After he'd been still for a while—holding her head with both hands, his own head face-first down on the wet leaves beside hers, his heartbeat knocking against her—she reached above her head and felt the stone with one hand. Tried to find the carved letters, tried to read them with her fingers. "Is it hers?" she murmured.

"What? Who?"

"Is this *her* grave?"

"The ghost?" Now he really was hoarse. He cleared his throat. "No. But no way I could've stopped to find it first."

He rolled to his back beside her. Exposed to the breeze, she felt her skin prickle, her nipples harden. "I'd like to see it."

"I think I remember where it is. I used to take tourists out here." He was kneeling now. "Wait," he said, when she started to get up.

"Where are my clothes?"

"Wait." He stood and backed up. "You have no idea how you look, lying here, like you rose to the surface, then turned to flesh and blood."

"Do I look like a corpse?"

"*No*, I'm not a lunatic. You look . . . unreal. In another minute I can do it again, and you're not even my type. I've always gone for blond girls with big . . . chests." A puff of stronger breeze made her shiver hard, inside. He stepped over her, stood astride for a moment, looking down. "You're cool, detached," he said, "and it makes me hot. I don't know what it is." He walked away a few steps, picked something up, then came back with her bra and blouse. "I don't want to ruin it, so I'll only say this once—I want you to know I'm not like this. I don't go around fucking every . . ."

91

"Did you follow me here?"

"This is a good place to find a ghost. Now that I know how, I can find you any time I want."

"Or you heard the store keeper tell me where the graveyard is."

He didn't say anything. Was still standing over her with clothes in his hand. Now she was shivering so anyone could see it. Like after a race, at first her accelerated heart, her inflamed muscles made being cold seem impossible. But a swimmer had to wrap up or those same burning muscles would turn to knots.

He walked around her among the grave markers, pacing off a lopsided circle, while she dressed. He didn't look back at her until she was finished, was buttoning her jacket. As though he knew exactly how long it would take her to dress, he turned abruptly and came toward her.

"I can't find it," he said.

"Oh."

They stood for a moment. His hair was too thick to move much in the wind. A few lighter strands were either sunbleached or gray. His eyes no particular color. Hazel, she guessed. Those beautiful, liquid, brown eyes of childhood—like she and Gary and Martha had had—often fade to hazel.

Tam turned and started walking back toward the Marr graves where he'd found her, and as though he was coming upon her there again, he stepped behind her, slipped his arms around her. They were almost the same height, his chin hard against the back of her head.

"J. Thomas," she said. "This was probably their only baby who died as a child."

"Why do you think so?"

"The big stone. And it's right beside where they knew their own plot was. And it's the only one. None of their other children are here. Other children grow up, die somewhere else, they don't get buried with their parents. That's why Mary Catherine isn't here, she must have had someone, a husband, with more claim on her body."

He was silent a moment, then laughed gently and said, "Ghosts can read graveyards—the part not written on the stones."

"I'll read something else too: This big stone, this is how they dealt with it, a child's death. Not therapy or drugs. Put up the big stone, let it manifest all your heaviness, and let it sit and stay out here. But the woman, the ghost lady who came back here to die . . . she couldn't do that, for whatever reason. She carried her sorrow with her. If she were the shipwrecked baby . . . maybe as a girl she would come here to this graveyard, for funerals . . . or she came alone, on her way home from school. Not all these graves were here then, but some were . . . J. Thomas was here. And old Hiram Marr over there, whoever he is, lost at sea before *she* was rescued. But she would see all these other repeated names. The Pierces, the Ornes, the Matthews . . . ancestors, descendants, all related. And she didn't have any. She wanted to be here and belong here. Maybe she thought by marrying, by having children she *would* be part of it all. But maybe she couldn't have children . . . or she lost the baby and then he never married her . . . and that's why she has no descendants. No people who would know her story. And maybe that's why she came back and . . . "

"Why use a fake name, then? Why not the name they gave her, or even one of these other names, so she *would* fit?"

"Maybe . . . by the time she came back, she didn't want to belong to them." She broke from his embrace and turned to face him. "So," she said, smiling, "in the store, you acted like you didn't see me."

"Maybe you were invisible."

"The store man saw me."

"He doesn't have a feel for ghosts." As he had at the lighthouse, he put a hand into her hair, combing it back from where it blew in her face.

His hand tickled her. Tam tossed her head. "Does your feel for ghosts tell you when you'll see me again?" Her hair blew into her mouth as she spoke.

"Maybe . . ." His grin was childlike in his weather-creased face with a day's growth of beard. "I'll find you at the lighthouse again tomorrow . . . at dusk. Your usual time to appear."

A car drove past where her car was parked in the cemetery driveway. He watched it. She noticed his truck wasn't parked behind her car.

"Is there some reason you can't be seen with me?"

"The usual reason."

"Do you have children?"

"God, no! You don't really need to know all this, do you?"

"All what? I don't have children either." She tried to slow down, but words coming out were like hiccoughs she couldn't stop. "I think I never wanted kids, but I don't remember when I decided. People, like my sister, sometimes ask if it's because of my disease. I don't think so, but if it were, it would be a good reason."

"Disease?"

"Don't worry, maybe genetic, but not . . . communicable."

"Okay. But hey, let's keep it like . . . Don't make it real." He took her face in both hands and kissed her. "We've done this twice and I haven't kissed you. How long are you staying here?"

"I'll be here as long as . . . " She sounded like Martha, when she got excited or nervous and was a chatterbox. "Well, when I leave, where will I go? There will be nowhere to go but home—not to the Midwest, I mean to California, and that's . . . not a place I can go right now."

"Answer again. That's not what I asked." He kissed her again. "Go back to *her*. What she came here looking for." He was talking into her mouth, between kissing her. "She's here looking for me, isn't she?" Abruptly, he released her, held his hands up as though in surrender. "God, I've got to go or we'll be doing it again. I meant, are you going to stay here in the graveyard a while? Did you find what you came for?"

"Yes. No." She pulled the same lock of hair out of her mouth. "Wait, how about a person named Vanora Marr? Do you know where her grave is?"

His smile was slow, unamazed. "It's not here."

"You already know that?"

"Vanora Marr Tanner. My great-grandmother."

Did she take a step back? She put one hand behind herself to see how close the Jaruel Marr headstone was, but felt nothing. "What?"

"My great-great grandfather, Nahum, Vanora's father, was the keeper's brother. I guess you and I, we're, sort of, related." He moved toward her, slid his hands down her back, pulled her against himself. "You said the ghost was here because she lost her lover-cousin. I guess I was born to take his place."

"But . . . are you kidding?"

"I managed to surprise you this time."

Martha, do you know what it's like to be the solution to someone's fantasies? You suddenly realize he's thinking about you as he goes about his day, even looking for you, you answer something he's been chasing, calling for, needing, dreaming

She selected all, deleted, then started again.

Martha, Here's the story the graveyard told: Three Marr brothers (out of a family of 9 children) came across the Sheepscot River inlet from Five Islands, early in the 1800's. They were Jaruel, Thomas and Nahum. These are the first Marrs to live on Southport. Later two of their sisters came across and married into the Pierces, the most established family on the island. The three brothers also married, two of them taking Pierce sisters, but Jaruel's wife, Catherine, was (as your family tree says) born in Sweden. In 1869 someone named Hiram Marr was lost at sea. The graveyard (nor your family tree) does not explain who this person is. He was too old (55) to be a son of one of the three brothers—Jaruel, the youngest of the three, would have been 40 at the time Hiram Marr was lost at sea. And he isn't another brother (again, according to your tree). But that mystery ends there, a tragedy in his own time but one that doesn't seem to have given rise to other lifetimes of tragedy. (Sorry for the melodrama, but that's the tone the graveyard gives.) Anyway, I just told you this part because I thought you'd want to know how the Marrs came to Southport, and about Jaruel's two brothers who came and settled there with him, and who had families of their own (including a daughter, the Vanora Marr you asked about), and descendants who still live on the island. (I admit, I didn't get ALL of this from the graveyard.)

The graveyard's more important story does concern the shipwrecked baby, Seaborn (her name), and the Jaruel Marr family. As you've already established, Jaruel became the keeper of Hendricks Head in 1866, after he returned from the war. Your family tree (I'm looking at it right now) says some of his children were born before the war. His oldest, Eugene, would have been 12 years old at the time Jaruel took his post as keeper. But there's something your document doesn't know: In 1872, March to be exact, the Marrs suffered the illness and death of a child. Four-year-old J. Thomas was laid to rest at Union Cemetery in early spring of 1872. Winter's last patches of snow made the shadows white in the surrounding forest, and crystals of ice formed a crust under leaves, crunching under boots and high-topped ladies' shoes, as mourners in their Sunday dresses and suits gathered around the new plot. Maybe thirty people, maybe more, surely Jaruel's brothers and their wives, their children, of course Jaruel and Mother Catherine's other children, including our great-grandfather Wolcott, 5 years old, likely tended by one of his big sisters because of his mother's raw grief. Catherine would have been closest to the open grave, with Jaruel beside her, together dropping the first fistfuls of near-frozen mud onto the small wooden coffin. Maybe she might've knelt, Jaruel behind her, his hands on her shoulders, but remaining stoic under his full beard and stiff Sunday collar. She might've cried into the hole. Not wailing, no histrionics, just quiet, grief-laden sobbing.

It's doubtful the large stone would have been prepared by the time of the funeral, so Catherine and Jaruel (and the other children) would have come back, in a few weeks or a month, maybe when the wild daffodils were nodding under the trees, but not yet in bloom. The big stone was erected in its place beside the plot where Jaruel and Catherine would someday rest. The deep, solemn letters, the little boy's name, his exact age (4 years, 2 months, 10 days), forever making his life eternal, unforgettable. (I hope the irony is just as thick through cyberspace—130 years later, not only was there no record of his life and death so you could include him in your family tree, but we don't even know what his first name was. Perhaps Jaruel? Not wanting to confuse him with his father, they always called him Thomas?) That same year, they had another baby, a son they named Lowell. In fact, Catherine was almost 8-months pregnant at the time of the funeral. Kneeling at graveside would not have been impossible, but throwing herself to the ground would have been.

This would have been the extent of Catherine's outward display of sorrow. The large stone would have been it, would have manifested her anguish. She had other children, soon a new baby to tend. This was her only baby she would lose in childhood. Perhaps she visited the big stone often at first, visiting also the unseen stone in her gut, and perhaps relived over and over how she might've saved her child, carried him from their frozen outpost to a doctor in Bath, some heroic traversing of unpassable roads in unlivable conditions. The reverie calling on her less occasionally at night, a year later, two . . . when her husband rises to trim the wick to make the light burn bright. And it's just a few years later that the March blizzard strikes the coast of Maine and a ship sinks in the narrows of Sheepscot inlet.

The baby that washes ashore in featherbeds was screaming. Not yet speaking, she could've been 2 months or a full year old. Not exactly the rescue of J. Thomas that Mother Catherine had conceived, but yet, at risk to his own life, her husband had saved this baby. And they named her Seaborn.

But Seaborn was not J. Thomas. Perhaps she was olive-skinned and dark-eyed, a dramatic European beauty in the Scotch and Swedish Marr family. Perhaps, with the intent that they would find a family for Seaborn, the Marrs didn't give her their name. What surname could they have chosen for her? The name of the ship that sank? The name of the ship's captain? These are as lost as J. Thomas' first name. Was Seaborn growing healthy and strong on the rocks around the lighthouse, but bruised inside by the unfinished adoption, her flawed reception into the family? Perhaps on her way home from school, she wandered through the graveyard—a graveyard she might've known well because her mother had taken her along when she was too young to leave untended. She passed all the Pierces and Ornes, linked to each other forever, by name, by a birthright that they would lie here, together, in death. And the Marrs were here, too, would be here to join J. Thomas and Hiram. Would she belong here someday? Her name wasn't Marr. But it could become Marr.

Perhaps the young man's parents didn't notice enough to either approve or disapprove. At least until the foundling Seaborn became pregnant at 14 or 15. Would Jaruel send her away to one of those homes, and forbid the boy any contact with her? Or would he demand that his nephew marry the girl? Or perhaps the boy announced his intentions to marry Seaborn and *his* parents recoiled at the idea of someone of unknown ancestry bearing Marr children, so sent the boy to apprentice somewhere, and sent the girl to tend a widower's children. Perhaps they hadn't known she was pregnant at the time. Except *he* knew, and promised he would come get her and marry her, but he never came. Did she lose the baby? Find it the adoptive home she'd never had? Something happened— whatever happened, she was, ultimately, separated from the Marrs—then, in 1931, when she was around 55, Seaborn returned to Southport, and returned to the sea. At last earning her place in Union Cemetery, but without a real name. Just as she had lived without one.

Oh my god, Martha, I just noticed something. Look at your family tree. J. Thomas, 4 years, 2 months, 10 days old, would have been born January 20, 1868—the same day as Mary Catherine Marr. The one without the birth record. They were twins. This validates your curiosity about her— she endured the heartbreak of losing a twin. Maybe *she's* the one we should be thinking about, not Seaborn. If she hadn't died way back in 1899, I'd think maybe it was Mary Catherine who is the lady ghost who came back to drown off the coast by the lighthouse. As a twin, did she expect to die young as well? Did she ever wonder or imagine what infirmity had stricken her twin? The closest girl in age to Seaborn, maybe she was forced to care for her new sister, the baby who came as a replacement for her dead twin. So if that historian didn't find evidence of Mary Catherine being born, where did *you* find her? How did you know she died (and when)? Was there a family bible or something? And why wasn't J. Thomas listed in that same place?

This is long so I'll go now. I'm moving into a B&B on the island.

Tam

Her room in a Southport B&B, actually still closed for the season, was the usual 19th century bed chamber. Antique headboard, table and chest of drawers and rough-plank bookcase with old—likely discarded—books for vacationers to read, mostly *Reader's Digest Condensed Books*. Electricity but no phone, no TV. She could write e-mails there but had to plug into the jack in the parlor to send them. The bathroom access was in the hall, and if there were other guests, she might have to share it. The room had thick creamy walls, blue-flowered wallpaper borders, dark wood trim around doorways and the window and crown molding. The floors were old-fashioned large-plank wood, sanded and varnished, covered with an area rug—dark blue with maroon flowers—that almost reached the four walls. The bed had lacy-edged pillows and a featherbed. She wasn't sure if one slept over or under a featherbed. The shipwrecked baby had been in a featherbed mattress—was this the same thing?

The buxom woman who owned the B&B had, somewhat easily, agreed to open a room in the off-season for Tam, when Tam had said that Nat had advised she stay there.

"When did he say that?" the woman queried.

"Today. We're cousins," she'd added, as instructed. "And you don't have to clean my room or provide breakfast. I can fend for myself."

The house, whose upstairs held the guest rooms, did not have a view of the lighthouse, not even a view of water. It was near the harbor, though—which itself had no view of the lighthouse. The harbor was like another town center, with another dry goods store—this one closed in the off-season—with two non-functioning gas pumps in front. The wharf alongside the store, and another wharf on the other side of the dock, were both piled with plastic lobster traps. The floating dock was between the two permanent wharves, the same floating dock where Gary and Martha had swum in the frigid summer water. This time only three skiffs were tied to the dock, no sailboats tied to pylons in the harbor's deeper water, no tourists with kerchiefs on their hair and sunglasses and red lips upside-down smiling, watching barefoot children shriek at the water's edge. The tide was winter low, and a rowboat, tied to one of the permanent wharf timbers instead of the floating dock, was sitting in mud.

Before going to the B&B, Tam had stood under the Southport Yacht Club sign that spanned the entrance to the dock. The quilted jacket was insufficient in a 40-degree breeze, the sun washed over with a gauze of clouds. The colors of the skiffs were flat. Tam wasn't sure how she felt. Or she felt layered. The chilly atmosphere of the forlorn off-season harbor, the melancholy, equally chilly memories of the last time she'd stood here. The graveyard discovery of one cherished-then-forgotten baby, the only-hours-earlier encounter with another baby, one that was meant to be forgotten. The euphoria of Nat's body up against hers. The absence (since that morning) of an aura-stage buzz. Meaning Denny was no longer with her? And over the top, some kind of brittle, lucid happiness she couldn't fathom, and some kind of longing that made the happiness impossible to hold onto.

She was a guest at the B&B by 3 p.m. She'd used a phone jack in the parlor to send the long e-mail to Martha about the graveyard, written in the car at the graveyard after Nat had gone. The parlor was in the downstairs part of the B&B house, a formal "front room," apart from the kitchen, off to one side of the stairway to the guest rooms upstairs. The buxom woman had explained it was where guests could watch TV and wasn't used by the family.

"Do you have children?" Tam had asked.

"My daughter is 20, off to college and decided to stay when she found a summer job in Portland. She comes home, sometimes, on weekends." She didn't mention a husband, dead or alive. She had ash blond hair, gathered, folded up and held in a clip to the back of her head. Probably Tam's age, or younger. Tam's son or daughter would have been 25, if he or she had really been somewhere in that blood on the floor.

From the parlor window, the woman pointed out for Tam some other historic houses on the street. "Particularly you'd be interested in the Jaruel Marr house in Cozy Harbor," she said. "When Nat's cousins come here, oftentimes that's who they're looking for."

Tam hoped the startled tremor she felt didn't show. "He didn't live at the lighthouse?"

"Yes, but in the winter his wife and children sometimes lived in his house. And of course after he retired, this was where he came to. His son bought it from him and also lived there. He was a light keeper as well, so it was back-and-forth for him too, until he retired. After he died *his* son lived there. And recently one of that son's grandsons came into the house. Nat has done a lot of work on the house. The current resident is another of his cousins. Distant cousin. It's such a big family. What kind of cousin, how far removed, are you?"

"Not very," Tam answered, then asked about another house, which was inconsequential, built in the 1950's as someone's summer house. She stopped listening, and as soon as she could politely do so, she excused herself to go upstairs and take a nap.

In the evening, Tam came quietly downstairs, paused to listen but heard no one in the kitchen. She plugged in her laptop, but turned on the

TV before turning on the computer. Amid game shows and the earliest prime-time junk—reality shows with the world's most obnoxious, audacious, egomaniacal poseurs as "real" people—the last segment of local news was still playing on one Portland channel.

She didn't have to wait long:

Talking head: *Up in Boothbay, this morning, a newborn baby was discovered in a toilet in a laundromat on Route 27. The baby was rushed to St. Andrews Hospital in Boothbay Harbor where doctors have determined the baby boy was small but full term and is in good health. Nurses have dubbed the little tyke Jonah after the Biblical character who survived being swallowed by a whale. Police, meanwhile, are searching for the baby's parents, possibly a teenage couple seen leaving the laundromat about an hour before the baby was found.*

Cut to clip, a suit-wearing police spokesman or district attorney: *"They'll likely face some charges, but for now we just want to find them so we can determine what to do with the child, whose it is, where it belongs. Otherwise he goes into foster care, I understand there's a group home for babies in Augusta, but we haven't dealt with a 1-day-old in years, it's uncertain how to progress from here."*

Cut to clip, the owner of the ice cream booth in the adjacent parking lot: *"Boothbay isn't like that place where those kids had a baby in the restroom at the prom then went back out and danced. We have values here, and I'd like to find this girl and find out who her parents are. It's disgraceful. I could've been the one to find him. I came in today to start cleaning up the shop. I sure wouldn't've let those kids walk away like that."*

Cut to clip, videotape of outside of laundromat, panning to motel. Voice-over: *Authorities said a guest in the motel across the street claimed to have found the baby, possibly even resuscitated him, but has since moved on, leaving no forwarding address. Calls to her cell number have been unanswered. A blood test to rule her out as the baby's mother was not performed.*

Cut to clip, paramedic: *"She had him wrapped in her sweater when we arrived. She had some laundry in one of the machines, so there was no reason to think she was anything other than what she said. But she didn't seem to know why she was in the area or how long she'd be here. She seemed a little confused, but it could've been all the commotion."*

Talking head(s): *Paramedics added that the woman, whose name has not been released by police, probably saved the baby's life by being in the right place at the right time. Someday, Brian, little Jonah may want to thank her. I hope she comes forward.*

And let's hope his mother comes forward too, Janie. In other news, sixth grade students gathered at the Baker farm outside Portland to see what it was like to make sugar in the 1800's.

Tam clicked open her laptop, then groped on the coffee table for a TV remote when the talking news heads switched to commercials and a jangle of hyped-up chatter and music surged into the dimly lit, museum setting, as though a convoy of strobing police cars pulled up outside the shuttered windows of a 19th century Victorian home. Sometimes in the conference room of the brokerage house, the fluorescent lights might be flickering, and colleagues would say "gad, it's going to give me epilepsy." Tam had ignored them, didn't want to admit she knew what they meant.

There was no remote for the TV. Kids with lank hair diving out of helicopters onto alpine peaks, then tipping their heads back and pouring some screamed-out soda name, fluorescent lime green, straight down their throats. Where would jerky kids that age get the money to rent a helicopter? Then little plastic-looking bits of pizza disappearing off a platter as fifteen hands all grab at once and words fly out of the screen like popcorn, then the picture blinking between several smiling, chewing faces, cramming more little plastic pieces of pizza into their maws. Tam lurched off the sofa and around the coffee table. *Next on ET, Jennifer Aniston talks about playing pregnant for a year on Friends and we look back at other TV pregnancies, those that flew and those that flopped. Plus what's happened to Leo DiCaprio, and Hero Dogs! Meet the brave pooches who went down to Ground Zero, sniffing through the debris of horror. Their stories, plus Katie Couric's new love, and Martha Stewart's new book club pits its choice against Oprah's, tonight on ET.*

Tam's fist, her knuckles, hit the off button, her other fist against her temple. *Drama queen*, she thought. She stretched. Parted the thick drapes but could see nothing outside in the dark Maine night, not even a light in the house across the road—probably a boarded-up summer place. Martha would have told her if Gary were going to be on TV. Unless Gary hadn't told anyone. Hadn't Martha said he was acting strangely? So Gary could have appeared on TV, acting strangely, right after the news spot about the confused woman who didn't seem to know why she was here, finding a baby that—they didn't say outright—might be her own.

An hour later, after she watched a documentary on the life of Ulysses Grant, Tam re-read a message she'd gotten a few hours earlier from Martha.

More stuff about mom for my family history. i think i'm getting better at writing it. Tell me if it's more interesting!

Early Feminist

The Irving grandfather [mom's father's father] *had left his lobster importing estate in trust to be used by his grandchildren to go to college—amazingly *all* his grandchildren, not just the boys. So Emily Marr Irving attended a private girls college dedicated to physical education and physical therapy.*

Early Civil Rights Activist [*totally* stolen from G's notes, which he seems to have abandoned at mom's]

Emily's group of friends at college included two Black girls, and in the late '40s at Sargent College, the Black girls—girls who attended the same classes, swam in the same pool, played on the same teams—were housed separately. The group wanted to stay together at the summer sailing camp they were required to attend, so Emily and a friend went to the dean to request permission for the Black girls to bunk in their kiosk. The dean gave a (now) familiar and bogus rationale for the school's policy, that "they" would be much more comfortable if housed separately. No, Emily explained to the dean, they want to be with us. No strikes, no sit-ins or protests were needed. The dean relented, and the college's segregated housing policy was suspended that year.

A World of Women

[i couldn't stop thinking about that nasty comment G made about "stuff boys do."]

During the war, while Emily was still in high school and college, is when she worked as a lifeguard and pin-setter [at a little general store in Southport, with a bowling alley and soda fountain right in the store—have you found it ?]. *There were few men her age who weren't occupied with military training or duty or already overseas. She hitchhiked from Cape Cod to Southport in the summers, and to ski areas in Vermont and New Hampshire over Christmas breaks. Once Emily and a cousin sailed a dory from Hendricks Head across the Sheepscot inlet to Five Islands, a lobster fishing port. They had a beer on the wharf and could see the light at Hendricks come on at dusk, but the light faded as a fog started rolling in, so they left. With no compass and no visibility, the tide pushed them off course and they missed Hendricks Head. Luckily they hit Southport further south, left the boat moored on some rocks, and walked through the fog to their grandmother's house near Cozy Harbor.* [Look, another shipwreck!]

Tam, just got your message. HOW EXCITING! You found something everyone missed! Not only me, but that historian who researched the legend. SHE didn't know there were twins, and one of them dead as a toddler! My understanding of proper genealogy jargon is when you say "ten living children" you mean ten who were *born* alive—everything except stillbirths and those who failed to thrive more than about a day. So i don't know how J. Thomas escaped me. But *both* he and his sister escaped that historian, and she used the same kind of terminology! But with both twins unaccounted-for in whatever records she used, that's significant. (although it's even weirder that *i* found only one. Losing *both* would've made more sense.) i don't remember where i got Mary Cath's birth and death dates. i'll have to go back and check my notes (once i get a name locked in, i pack up the letters or research or what-not that got me there. Probably the bible Mom got from Nana.) Hey, look at my genealogical list—another set of twins further back. But could you go check for me, find whatever archive records would've been available to that historian—are both names missing or did she screw up? (Or did i?)

Your other stories are nice too. Interesting about the three brothers (they're all listed in the list of children one generation further back in my tree). But be careful about speculating. Remember, genealogists don't do that. But even more important, i don't think people in the 1800's think like people nowadays. i mean all the looking back to childhood and making connections to explain how you've failed or why you're alone or unhappy or whatever. i know now we tend to think a person's life is made up of all these important situations, relationships, events, or combinations that each of us feels are crucial, life-changing, significant "big moments" of life. But many (try most) of these things aren't related to each other, they occur at different times and are just completely unrelated to how a person is or what a person is doing ten or twenty years later. i'm not saying people in the 1800's already had this wisdom to get beyond the my-childhood-scarred-me mentality, just that it didn't even occur to them. "Making their way in the world" had a whole different set of obstacles. Just look at those three brothers who came to Southport to start families and build houses and find a way to support themselves. They obviously didn't train for a kind of profession and go look for a job with an employer who paid salary and benefits. It was "i'm old enough to leave home now—so how can i make money and where will i live?" And i think it was the same for women, "who will i marry, where will we live, how will i help him feed and raise the family?" (Oh no, am *i* speculating now?)

OK, now i have to tell you something about Gary. Please keep reading. He turned up, but we haven't seen him yet. Mom got a letter from that horrid dog-person roommate of yours. She wants to know your address. She says she's boxed all your stuff and wants to send it to you. She said she assumes that's why G came to see her. Apparently G went to her house! What's so weird is, mom says his truck is still at his place. If he flew, where's Coach? Mom usually keeps him if G has to travel without him. There's

also a letter from this person to you. Mom hasn't opened it. Send your address quickly so we can send it to you, or should we open it and read it to you?
M

On the coffee table was a stack of slick 3-fold promotion brochures for the B&B, the address and phone number clearly on the front under the photo. It would have been so easy to log back on and send it to Martha.

Invisible

Why is Meryl THAT DOG PERSON *(horrid dog person) and Gary a person with a dog? All-American with a dog. Hero with a dog. Just because he's related? Being related didn't keep that baby's mother from leaving it—leaving him—in the toilet. That other mother from tossing hers overboard (did she have a choice?) I wish someone had left Gary— No, not really.*

Tam was writing letters to Martha behind her eyelids, in bed. There was a breeze outside and the firs made that shushing whisper, sometimes sounding like voices with more edge than a whisper, or maybe someone really was talking in another room, on another floor. Trying to keep their voices down.

Martha, do you know why I stopped having anything to do with Gary?

Tam was almost exactly in the middle, three years younger than Gary, almost three years older than Martha. She shared a room with Martha, so they were alone together almost half of every 24 hours. The three of them, mostly on family vacations, would play together—if you could say swimming or rafting or hiking was *play*. But at times Tam had played with Gary, without Martha. He shared his archery set and lawn darts. When they had time away from swim practice, they threw baseballs or footballs or Frisbees, made forts or prowled the canyon behind their house. Gary had never teamed up with Martha and left Tam out. It was just that sometimes Martha was too young for Gary and Tam, and sometimes Gary was too male for Martha and Tam. But nothing had been the same since Gary had grabbed her leg, then had been the one to pull her from the pool during the grand mal. That was after she'd stopped playing fort or pretending to be explorers with Gary anyway. Still, Gary wasn't finished being Gary.

The high school didn't have much of a swim team. Gary wasn't on it. Competitively, all three of them were too far above inter-school matches with poorly-trained swimmers, the same way a budding musical prodigy wouldn't play in the school band. Gary had special permission to use the school pool to swim laps instead of his regular p.e. classes. Since they went to the club pool after school for team training, his laps during the school day were scheduled as his first period class, a time when few other students had p.e. because no one wanted to get dressed for school only to undress and get sweaty. Gary went to school in his speedo and sweats, carrying school clothes in a bag, arriving early enough so he was in the pool at least a half hour before first period actually started. This same schedule had already been arranged for Tam at the high school before her first seizure, and no one had thought to change it even though she hadn't gone back to the La Costa Swim Club. Nobody, except Gary, seemed to notice that she neither had a p.e. class nor did she swim laps in the morning. She didn't even go to school in a suit and sweats, carrying her school clothes, like Gary did, and surely their mother knew that. When their mother picked them up from school to take Gary to team practice, most of the drive was consumed with his report on his lap times from that morning. Maybe, if they hit a few lights, their mother asked Tam about a biology test or English essay. But no one said boo about the special p.e. arrangement she wasn't using. Except Gary. Every day he either threatened to notify the vice principal that Tam was getting out of p.e. under false pretenses, or told stories of meets where she easily would have won two or three events. He only did this after they left the car where their mother dropped them in front of the school, while they walked to the locker rooms. But after they went into the respective locker rooms—so Gary could leave his school clothes and get a towel—and came out onto the pool deck, Gary said no more. Sometimes he sang from an old children's record they'd had called *Peter the Pusher*, "I sail and I sail on a big ocean ship with a *toot—toot*—out of my way." Peter the Pusher wasn't into drugs, he just wanted people to get out of his way, so he always got a bigger vehicle. At the end of the record Peter learned his lesson and was polite. But now it was Gary's motivation psych-up song for swim meets. After singing, he slid into the water. As instructed by their coach, his first entry was never a dive. He seemed to glare at her as he held the lip of the pool and scissored his legs underwater to loosen-up. Tam read her history book, sitting on the long bench along the pool deck wall. The first week of school, every day Gary heaved himself out of the water after his slow warm-up laps, got a stopwatch out of his gear, and came dripping over to Tam, said nothing, dropped the stopwatch and several dozen splotches of water onto the pages of her book. When the second week began, Tam watched Gary get into the pool from behind the window of the door to the girls' locker room, then read her home-work in the girls' restroom. This lasted another week.

The third week, Gary got out of the car at the curb and stalked off as though he was late. But it was only 7:15, as usual, and first period didn't start until 8. When Tam turned around from saying goodbye to their mother before closing the car door, Gary was already gone, striding across the quad. Tam didn't dally, but she didn't hurry either. So it was strange, when she was inside the locker room and got to the back door that led to the pool area, that she didn't hear anyone in the pool. On first glance, the surface of the water was completely undisturbed, indicating no one was in the water, and no one had gotten out of the water recently. Gary wasn't on the deck fitting his goggles to his eyes, or adjusting the legs of his speedo, or shaking his arms and legs the way they were supposed to before getting into the water. She might have turned away, and avoided the whole fiasco, but a sun-glint caught her eye. It was an outdoor pool, and the sun was low, just starting to send beams over the surrounding cinderblock walls. But it wouldn't glint on a perfectly untouched pool surface. The glint was from a ripple, and the ripple was caused by some-thing floating in the pool. She hadn't seen the something at first because it was over one of the lane markers. Face down, a baby in the water.

She didn't have a seizure, although she should have—the screeching, her own, piercing her brain from inside and out. But at that time her medication dosage was still high enough, though not so high it prevented her from screaming. Just two words, sometimes a third: *help, someone, someone, help, someone come help*. And running: first around the pool once, then back into the locker room where none of the women coaches were in their offices yet. Zigzagging through the dressing area, banging her shins on benches, clanging her hands against metal lockers. Returning to the pool, she finally kneeled on the deck and tried to reach it, but it was too far out. *Someone! help! someone come help!* Then she found a few more words: *Gary, where are you? Gary! Gary, help!*

At what point did her brain quietly ask, *what's a baby doing at the high school pool?* Maybe not until afterwards. When some of the coaches were finally there, both the men and the women, roused from counting tennis rackets and volleyballs in the equipment room or from their morning coffee in the athletic office or lifting weights in the wrestling room. And when other kids started gathering too—the few with first period gym, none of them dressed out yet, most of them laughing. When someone had an arm around her shoulders, when a blurry veil of tears obscured the gleeful faces of the kids, when her own palms over her ears muted their banter and dulled a male coach's bossy exasperation as he ordered them all back to their respective locker rooms—that's when she might've asked herself *what's a baby doing at the high school pool anyway?* After what she'd seen and done in Maine, yesterday in the laundromat restroom, she would not have asked at all, but in the 70's pregnant girls didn't continue going to school, much less have their babies and return to school, much less *bring* babies to school, much less *have* their babies at school.

That's because it wasn't a baby. It was a doll, taken from the home economics room. One of the dummies they used for child care classes, to show girls who got stuck taking Home Ec (because they were too dumb for College Prep, and therefore more likely to get pregnant) how difficult it would be to lug a baby around all day.

And when all the first period gym students were banging locker doors inside the building, when the soggy doll was making a spot on the pool deck, when only one of the female coaches was left out there with Tam—but she had already said "you're OK now" and was stooping to pick up the doll and leave—Gary stepped out of the boys' locker room in his speedo, fixing his goggles to his head. As he started to shake out his arms and legs, he fixed a goggled stare at Tam. And when the locker room door hissed shut behind the female coach, he said, "You wouldn't even get back in the water to save a *baby*? Good thing *you* never went out for lifesaver. Maybe it's a good thing you're a spastic-head and had to quit the team."

In bed after homework, Tam had one of those nights she'd begun to encounter months before, where even a seizure—at least a small one— would have been welcome over the hours of sleepless ruminating she confronted. In between scenarios where she managed to scoop the doll from the pool using a tennis racquet and then just happened to know Gary's locker combination so she could stuff the wet doll inside to drench his sloppy books and papers, Tam thought about team practice and weekend meets. Weighing in once a week, when she and Martha (and Gary) seldom had a problem, and never an overage. They watched some of the other girls, as they got into high school, trying to hide blossoming breasts in tighter suits, closing their eyes in the face of the scale's report that their hips and thighs were growing. The chlorine and warm-water-on-concrete smell of the locker room, the silky undulating calm of the aqua water before anyone had broken the surface, the feel of the bumpy paint on the starting blocks under her bare feet. Meet day, when the little bleachers might hold fifty people, maybe two hundred at bigger meets, at state semis more like a thousand. But after the final kick—lungs aflame, calves knotted, arms of lead—and after her head came out of the water—eyes still streaming chlorine, ears still under- water dead—only her mother's face clear in the blurry crowd, before she even checked the results board to see which lane was the winner. *Lane 4, Tamara Marr-Burgess.* The P.A. system was tinny and fuzzed the words, but the name always came through, a cadence, with Gary's races, Martha's and Tam's often having similar results, but the monotone voice never inferring it had said the name so many times before.

The night after the doll-in-the-pool incident, the idea of being a suffering victor who returns from physical adversity to win again never flickered within her meditated drama. Instead she determined that she would somehow drop the first half of her hyphenated name. It confused too many people anyway. She wouldn't be able to make it official until college, when she processed the necessary paperwork with

Social Security, made sure the university corrected all her records, and changed her driver's license and bank account. But that night in ninth grade, when sleepless melodramatics told Tam the world of swimming was gone, irrevocably gone, she decided she didn't deserve to be a Marr.

Tam hadn't the slightest notion whether her mother would have laid out Gary for stealing the home-ec dummy and planting it in the pool, or just sat on Tam's bed to try to explain, "He's just trying to help, it's the only way he knows how."

Or would her mother have sighed, stroked the bangs off Tam's forehead, and said, "All that training, Tam . . . didn't some instinct come to you?"

Isn't that why she'd never told her mother? So scared for her own pride, she wouldn't even save a baby.

But now, over three decades later, lying awake in a ridiculously high, oversoft antique bed in Maine, she wondered: Didn't it call some other instinct into question?

She remembered how her mother had loved to get them dolls for Christmas. Not dolls to display in a case, dolls to play with. Once, shopping in a toy department, her mother had wistfully remarked that it might be the last Christmas she could get a doll for Martha. Their "big dolls" ate, drank and wet their diapers. The Barbies and knock-off associates dated, stole each other's boyfriends, schemed to get boyfriends back, and, of course, swam in meets, for national titles and Olympic medals. No one, not even their mother, thought it strange that as Tam and Martha got older, the big dolls spent more and more time sitting on their shelves in the closet while the Barbies had the run of the room—sometimes the whole house. No one ever said it looked as though Martha had more maternal instinct than Tam. Who would there have been to say such a thing? Gary waited around until Tam wanted to go prowl in a canyon or throw a baseball. Their mother, when they asked, made clothes for the Barbies: Bermuda shorts and camp shirts, from material she'd used to make Tam and Martha school dresses. How had their mother made sure they had time to play with dolls between swim training sessions? They might have played with the Barbies the summer before Tam started high school, but certainly not after that. The last time she'd visited home, before her retirement, Tam had repacked her old Barbies and accessories. "Maybe an investment," she'd told her mother, "they might be worth something." (That box, with the others, still at Meryl's house.) Martha had long ago given her Barbies to her kids, who promptly wrecked the dolls beyond redemption. Martha didn't feel any urge to protect *dolls*.

How could Tam have known, after Gary's prank, that she might get a second chance to prove she *would* save a baby? A real baby this time. Once there was a maybe-baby she could not have saved, in a puddle of her own blood and urine on the floor. But there was a real, living baby now, in a hospital—they say she's already saved him. But has that baby really been rescued yet? Rescued from what? From being named Jonah? From becoming the butt of some legend about the toilet-baby?

> Dear Martha, I can't remember if I told you my child-ishly convoluted reasons for quitting swimming, something I loved like breathing. Besides understandable fear, it was so mixed up with not wanting to be rescued, but wondering who would save me. Who would get the hero's credit for saving me, who would be the one to tell me I didn't need to be rescued anymore

She selected all, deleted, sat with fingers on the keys, head tipped back, until she realized her mouth was gaping open. She swallowed and started again.

> Martha,
>
> I know you know there have been strained relations between me and G for some time now. I can tell you the reason(s) why, but, like most such situations, the reasons start to look more and more petty as years go by.

But I don't know, maybe this one hasn't become trivial, considering other things that have happened since. You say life has no such connections. How can that be, when Seaborn and Mary Catherine reverberate down through the generations? Anyway, G tried to make up for it once. Arranged for me to meet someone (a man) who did radically affect my life, enough I could've, should've thanked G, but it ended badly and there's no thanks for that disaster, maybe not *all* G's fault. Although I have doubts about that, too.

But until last night I didn't think I'd been thinking too much about past junk. Maybe that's why what happened was able to happen. Still, there's been no plan and I don't really have a plan yet. It's what I've been missing for three years now, a plan. I feel like I want to do more than just find the information you want. I want to reconstruct their lives, Mary Catherine, and also Seaborn, but I don't know the best way to do it. Would it be by adopting a baby of my own and raising it here?

The B&B woman was in the kitchen. Actually Tam waited until she heard the woman in the kitchen, then went downstairs.

"I made coffee," the woman said. She was dressed in jeans and a flannel shirt, her plump body seemed uncomfortably bisected where the shirt was tucked into the jeans. Her hair hung in a ponytail from high on the back of her head.

"I should be the one making *you* coffee." Tam smiled. "Good morning. I was planning to go get breakfast somewhere. I know you're not in the guest business right now. What do you use the off-season for?"

That's when the woman smiled. "Some guests think a Maine winter must be a terrible bore. Others imagine an idyllic seclusion with books and needlepoint by the fire, maybe watercolor or writing poetry." She gave a short, pleasant laugh. "But I do taxes. I have my own office here. Personal income taxes and small businesses."

"And this must be your busiest time. I really don't want to be a bother." Tam accepted a cup of coffee offered by the woman. The kitchen windows were shaded by a front yard full of firs. No grass or flower beds. Between the branches, she could see pieces of a blue sky. "Looks like one of those brilliant, brisk days you're famous for."

"I'll be shut away most of the day." The woman put bran muffins from a toaster oven onto a plate.

"Just tell me where the laundry is. I can take care of my own linens. I'll go get some groceries." Tam split a muffin and buttered it. They were both still standing at the kitchen counter. Other than the flouncy blue window curtains, and the white tile countertop with dark blue borders, almost everything in the kitchen had a lobster on it. Plates, coffee cups, the wall clock, the dishtowel and oven mitts. But the wallpaper border, circling the room just below the ceiling, depicted lighthouses. Cape Elizabeth, Nubble, Pemaquid, Owl's Head.

"By the way, before you go to work, could you tell me Nat's phone number?"

"You don't know how to contact your cousin?" The woman broke off a piece of muffin but didn't put it into her mouth.

"Oh, well . . . He's the one who contacted me, so I never . . ." she laughed. "I don't know how well you know Nat. He likes to be . . . mysterious."

"Yes, he apparently does."

"Pardon?"

"Never mind. He can only be found when he wants to be found."

"When *he* finds *you*, I know." Tam laughed again. The woman didn't. She didn't even smile. She was still holding a broken piece of muffin. When her eyes left Tam's, she looked at the muffin, then nibbled at the morsel as though not sure she would even like it. The shady morning light dimmed. The sun, not visible from the window, must have found one single popcorn cloud.

"It must be such a relief," Tam interrupted the silence, "after taxes are finished, to have—what—six weeks to get ready for the season? And the best part of the year. Winter just ending."

"If not too many clients ask for an extension." The woman broke off another bite, again didn't put it into her mouth. "But Nat helps me," she blurted. "Planting the flower beds out in back, getting the patio furniture out, painting or repairing or . . . anything I need, really. He's . . ."

Tam continued looking into the woman's face even though she'd stopped mid-sentence. When it was clear the remainder of the sentence was not going to come, Tam said, "That's why he recommends your place, he knows it's good."

"He knows *me*." The woman looked up, smiled finally. "He's likely over to Boothbay this morning. He goes about every day to check prices at the lobster pounds and see if anyone's brought anything in. It's too early in the season, but some of the guys have some traps out. He'll stop by on his way back, he usually does, around noon." She was a full head shorter than Tam, so she really did have to look *up*. Tam suddenly felt like a giraffe, looking down.

"Well." Tam put her coffee cup in the sink. "You're troubling yourself for me. I'd like to take you to dinner sometime." Then she retrieved the cup, rinsed it and put it into the dish drainer.

"Sounds fine," the woman said. "Let's all three of us go."

"Three?" Tam felt herself cocking her head. An unfamiliar gesture. She reached for her cup to take a sip of coffee, but remembered she'd already washed it.

"Your *cousin*."

"Oh, Nat. Yes, that'll be fun. He's why I'm here anyway, right? I mean here at your place. We'll help you celebrate . . . a successful tax season."

"We'll celebrate something better than that!" Suddenly the woman was downright chipper. "Well, I'd better get to work. Make yourself at home."

Tam stood a moment more in the kitchen. The overhead light had never been turned on, which let the dappled forest shade outside the window into the room. With the few deciduous trees not yet in leaf, strands of thin liquid light did trickle down to the dead grass, leaves and moss on the ground. She could suddenly understand why baby deer were born with spots. They'd be invisible.

Before leaving the B&B, she brought her laptop back down to the parlor to hook up. She knew Martha would answer last night's message quickly.

> Tam, don't you go cryptic on us too! G is putting stuff on our family website. Weird stuff. (i mean stuff you wouldn't expect so much if you thought he was still doing ok.) Derek says the site's lame and he could jazz it up but i better not let him touch it before i talk to G. and now i don't want Derek seeing what G says before i do! It's how we're hearing from him, we don't know where he is. Except one place he *was*, in Chicago, and we have this letter from your roommate. Tell me your address so i can forward. And stop talking so weird yourself, it's scary! Really, i mean it.

Tam logged off, but packed the laptop in its case to bring with her. She'd be somewhere today, waiting for Nat to find her, where she could have time to think of an answer, and whether or not she wanted to have Meryl's letter forwarded. She could just as easily not open it here as leave it un-opened there, and allow Martha to stop pushing it at her. She slipped one of the B&B business cards into her shirt pocket.

Besides wanting to contact Nat—and she almost believed that would happen at the right moment, the best possible moment, he would make sure of that—she felt driven to do something. But she still knew she didn't have a strategy by the time she got to St. Andrews hospital.

The hospital in Boothbay Harbor was on the side of town closest to the bridge to Southport Island, less than two miles from the B&B. On the way, most of the wharves stacked with lobster traps in the several little bays were quiet, the boats tied up. Only a few sailboats, still sealed over with blue canvass, were anchored in placid water in inlets and lagoons running from the bay behind houses built on wooded, rocky slopes. Some of the houses were obvious summer homes—boarded up, lawn furniture stacked and covered, leaves scattered on decks or porches. But the year-round residences seemed just as closed and quiet, despite cars in the driveway or smoke trailing from chimneys.

The hospital's visitor and emergency parking lot was likewise nearly empty. In the ten or fifteen minutes Tam sat in the car, no one went into or came out of the emergency entrance or the main front door. Choosing which entrance was most inconspicuous was either unnecessary or a crap shoot.

But she was also sitting and waiting to see if what she was doing—whatever it was, not a plan, surely, just an impulse—would incite the buzz of the aura stage. It was definitely there the day of Meryl's frivolous dog show duplicity, although Tam had been as rock-faced as a Moonie while Meryl nervously chattered. And wasn't it the chagrin after detection (not to mention Meryl's unrestrained, even seizure-like breakdown) that had initiated Tam's brain-wave rumblings, not necessarily the deception itself? And wasn't that act of fraud so very harmless, in comparison. In comparison to *what*? To whatever she does today. Like a Q & A conversation with Martha in her head, better than stewing in her own thoughts, which are increasingly difficult to locate and clarify. Could she be just as innocuous and nonchalant as she walked past a receptionist, past nurses and doctors and whatever new parents might be ogling babies in the nursery? Or would a growing clamor in her brain send a soundless signal, and people would sense her intentions, like dogs who perceive oncoming seizures? Whatever intention she may have, and she still wasn't sure. But if she had saved him, she had a right to see him again. That's all. To see if *Jonah* is written in red ink above his bassinet.

But still she sat and waited, because the shame after Meryl's failed ploy was one thing. Her *first* clandestine maneuvering (certainly never as a broker) had ended with a much bigger eruption. Not just gut-wracked sobbing, but eventually everything else on her insides—drool, pee, blood, feces, a baby—gushing to the outside.

Her job with Denny as administrative assistant was one-quarter time clerical, on the university payroll, employee of the State of California. Denny also had a male workstudy student. The workstudy program paid the student, not the university's clerical payroll. So he wouldn't have done any of the bureaucratic paperwork that entangled Tam, but would do the most menial, like pick up wet towels. Meanwhile, requisitioning funds for kickboards, for pull-buoys, for goggles and caps was a labyrinth of account numbers and layers of approval that already took most of the ten hours a week Tam was paid for. But week-by-week she was in the office, or with Denny somewhere else, and was usually at least thinking about the team, for more like thirty to forty hours. Denny had to plan and oversee every team workout, then study and compare each swimmer's daily times, do most of the rub-downs (Tam volunteered to do a few, but he knew she was teasing). Even in off-season, some swimmers continued training, and there was always recruitment. So Tam took over those parts of Denny's job she could, like negotiating with the other university teams for a schedule of exclusive use of the weight room for the swimmers. She arranged for and planned all the logistics for team travel, with a separate budget line in the athletic department. To assist in recruiting, Tam did whatever she could to free up Denny for hours of studying meet results and phone calls just in preparation to woo promising swimmers from everywhere in the country. When these candidates did visit, Tam arranged the dinners and tours and lodging.

One day in Tam's second year working for him—his long bare legs up across his desk, leaning back and holding his own wristwatch to his face, helping Tam test five or six old stopwatches—Denny said, "The workstudy guy has disappeared. Damn I wish you could be paid the money he was supposed to get, instead of them giving us another kid who never shows up so you work more than twice what you're paid for."

In another minute, almost exactly (Tam was holding a stopwatch), they looked up together and their eyes met.

"Are his checks delivered here?" Denny asked.

"I think so."

"You should be paid in more than sexual favors."

"I'm not complaining."

"Maybe we could hire some other workstudy student, one who would agree to . . ."

"Why would anyone agree to donate their workstudy money to me?"

"You're right," he said. "If anything, he'd want to not work and *still* get paid, not get out of work just so he can give us his money."

"Or . . . why not just say the one we have is still coming to work?"

"Will they cash workstudy checks on campus?"

"Without ID?"

"You're right, probably not."

"Did you ask to have my position upgraded to half time?"

"They won't authorize anything more than quarter-time, even when I enumerated what you do here, and it's obviously more than ten hours of stuff. Not counting other *stuff*, of course."

"Oh well . . . I don't mind. It's a good cause. I'm learning something."

"Oh yeah, I forgot to list your erotic enlightenment. Or is that *my* job?"

"They don't pay for on-the-job training?"

"Cheap asses," he said, without smiling. "What if I endorsed the workstudy check over to you *for deposit only*. Wouldn't they deposit it into your account, as long as you aren't taking any cash out right that minute?"

"I suppose as long as this guy doesn't figure out he's still being paid and come looking for his checks."

They'd been keeping their faces entirely blank. As though that would keep them from being, or even seeming, like scoundrels.

But her conscience was clear. It was for the team, Denny's team. (Gary no longer a member.) And the performance of Denny's team meant Denny's job. And Denny's job was *her* job. And more than a job, it was her time with Denny. Not that she would ever ask to be paid for her time with Denny, she would have done it all for nothing. She would have *paid* to do it. But with all the requisitioning and layers of budget lines, sometimes they just needed pencils and clipboards, paperclips, typewriter ribbon, and needed them *now*, so with the extra money, she was able to just go buy these kinds of things herself, from the workstudy money. There were a few changes and tweaks over the next few years, like Tam opened a second personal checking account that was just for the swim team money from work-study paychecks. And, when the ghost workstudy student's checks stopped coming, Denny located a new workstudy student and persuaded him—without telling Tam how—to deposit his check into his account then write a personal check for the same amount to Tam, which she then put into her swim-team account. She rarely used that money for herself.

But that first day when they'd inadvertently flirted with the plan (and never voiced a final affirmation that it was what they would do), Tam had stood, her eye-contact never breaking from Denny's, crossed the small room and sat on his desk, beside his shins, facing him. But didn't touch him until he raised his leg, nestled it across her thighs, hooked it around her body and used his swimmer's muscles to ease her sideways until she was directly in front of him, between his chair and the desk, his legs clasping her. She put her hands on his knees. Slid them slowly up his thighs.

He'd already helped her to be bold, like this, ready to make moves to arouse him. But her own arousal peaked, so to speak, with the first thrill of adrenaline. That was enough, she'd decided. It was delicious, in fact, the rush of heat, the bright spot in her gut, the stimulation of knowing you're stimulating. Any more than that—if she were to let herself go into the *paroxysm of passion* she'd read about in new novels that extolled a woman's ability for sensuality—she might find herself too close to losing control.

But it wasn't sensual passion that occasioned the third grand-mal. Passion of another sort. Two years into the ghost payroll ploy—supplying them with not only clipboards, but Gatorade and scented oil for rubdowns (which she and Denny borrowed then didn't return to the swimmers, after they thought it was too weird)—already warped by her own over-dose of hormones, the house of cards fell, *Denny* blew it over. But it was more like cinder-block walls crushing her. Was Denny really untouched by the demolition? Was his alarm that she could be expelled justified, or was there some other conspicuous jeopardy, one only he could feel? Or was it just that old hackneyed fear of *forever* that made him abandon her and their baby before it had eyes or legs. And then her body abandoned it. Whether or not she can blame him for that . . . another abandoned baby had found her.

The off-season stillness was not going to be beneficial. In quiet hospitals, nurses and doctors, orderlies and aides, therapists and phlebotomists could work without haste, could move vigilantly among beds—or rows of newborns in bassinets—and would notice if they were being watched. But busy hospitals, crowded with newly arrived and distressed patients, were the epitome of havoc. People flying here and there. Sometimes more *here* than *there*, and *there* could be completely abandoned while everyone was *here*.

That's what Tam was thinking while she watched two cars of people pull into the parking lot at the same time and park side-by-side. Six adults, four in one car and two in another, plus two children under ten, got out of the cars, met and moved toward the hospital in a cluster. One of the women was holding a baby and two other women were on either side of her, with arms around her, as the whole swarm hurried toward the emergency entrance.

Tam immediately got out and followed them. The emergency waiting room had one short window-enclosed counter with one receptionist. In front of that, two chairs with a magazine-strewn coffeetable. The throng of extended family assailed the counter, completely obliterating the receptionist from view. The unseen baby was crying. The two children were pushing the magazines around on the table, looking for the things waiting rooms always supplied to entertain them. One adult woman turned around twice as Tam passed, but she was only looking back at the children, telling them to sit down and be quiet. Tam went through the double doors and continued on down the corridor, past the tiny E.R. (nothing like TV), following signs toward obstetrics.

It wasn't a big hospital, but they hid the babies somewhere. You wouldn't think they'd want families of new mothers roving everywhere, towing children who would stare at the mostly old, bewildered faces of infirm people in chairs or on gurneys left parked in the hall awaiting a treatment or x-ray. But likely they also didn't want the new babies to hear the screaming from delivery rooms (could everyone on the obstetrics floor hear the screaming?). She went along every corridor, each floor's rectangular circuit of hallway, searching for that big glass window where people gathered to press their noses, engrossed in watching babies sleeping or drooling or screaming their heads off. Seaborn probably screamed, but no one would have known. By the time she got to the top floor, Tam thought she heard something. A faraway wail.

Where the elevator opened, the main hallway that would have continued around the corner to the right had been partitioned off, so the 3rd floor was the only one that could not be walked in a complete circuit. Instead, to the right of the elevator, the corridor turned left, but soon dead-ended at the wall, creating an alcove where a few sofas and chairs and been arranged with a window overlooking the harbor. It was not an outlook over the tourist-recreation section of Boothbay Harbor. A spit of land, housing many of the hotels, restaurants and shops, blocked that part of the bay from this view. But a twin port—subdued, less guide-book-scenic and more workman—lay behind the tourist chic of Boothbay Harbor. That was the waterfront view in the hospital's windows. An old shipyard boat landing housed a rusty tugboat and a few other smaller vessels. There were no lobster traps stacked on that pier. Just below the hospital, which was on a slightly elevated bluff, private lobster wharves were attached to near-shack dwellings on the shore across from the tugboat wharf. The road from Boothbay to Southport lay along the edge of this part of the bay. Yesterday Tam had seen a fox run from mud flats on the water, across the road, through a private summer home's garden, and into the woods. Now, like yesterday, the tide was low, and the moldering shapes of two wrecked ships that had been rotting there for eighty years were dark, oval islands in the bay. There were no masts, no deck rails, no decks. Just vague outlines of boats.

Tam had moved from the elevator, straight across the hall, diagonally, to the window in the corner alcove. There had been no one in the elevator with her. But there was one person sitting in the alcove. Anyone exiting the elevator and bustling off to the left—in the only direction there were any hospital rooms—might see Tam at the window but wouldn't see where the other person was sitting on one of the sofas against the interior wall, unless they walked from the elevator straight into the alcove to view the shipwreck shapes in the bay, and then, sensing another person there, turned around, as Tam had done. It was the girl from the laundromat.

"You . . ." the girl said, her voice frail, and she was starting, awkwardly, to stand.

"No, stay there," Tam said. She turned halfway back toward the window. "Don't make it look like you're talking to me."

"Who are you? What are you *do*ing here?"

"Same thing as you?"

"I'm . . . But you're . . . You're the one . . . But why did you come here—?"

"You shouldn't have worn that coat," Tam said. "It's the coat they know you wear." She was staring at an oil painting on the wall opposite where the girl sat—a seascape, of course, with a price and business card affixed to the frame.

"I'm already busted. They already know. I'm supposed to be at home."

The seascape was not a stormy one. White-sailed schooners in a dazzling harbor of wharves, hotels, cafes, colorful dots of people strolling the waterfront. It could have been Monte Carlo, it could've been Boothbay. "What are they going to do to you?"

"I don't know."

"What about him?"

"Him?"

"The father."

"Father? Oh— He's . . . He's at school." The girl might've been sobbing, or about to.

"So what was the crime," Tam muttered, more to herself. "Abandoning a baby? And only a mother can do that? Just because it wasn't hurt, it wasn't killed, and those were the only things they could've pinned on the father, *he's* scott free?"

"His parents sent him to a school in Massachusetts," the girl choked.

"Are you OK?"

"It almost hurts more . . . afterwards. Could hardly walk. That's how I got busted. My parents brought me here last night, for a check up. But I didn't see him . . . the baby. They don't know I'm here now. Someone named him Jonah."

"Wretched name. You don't have to keep it."

"But I . . . I won't be . . ."

"Won't be what, his mother? I don't see how you can get out of that."

"I don't want to get out of it!" The girl finally began full-fledged weeping, but silently, bent over double onto her own lap. "God, I stink," she blubbered. "It's such a mess . . . afterwards."

"Wait here," Tam murmured. She got up and left the corner alcove without glancing at the girl. The hall was empty. She walked down to the other end, passing the big nursery window without stopping, only shifting her eyes sideways and seeing there was one person, gowned and masked, moving among no more than a dozen bassinets. After the nursery there was a false hall, a passageway with a door, probably an entry into the nursery. The only things in the passageway leading to the closed door were a covered trash receptacle and a canvas hamper, the green of a nurse's scrub gown trailing out. Tam got to the other end of the main corridor. There was a nurse's station with one nurse seated behind a high counter and behind a computer screen, barely visible. A sign on the corner of the wall said *Post-Partum*. Tam turned the corner and kept walking. The doors to the rooms were halfway closed. TV's could be heard in some of the rooms. Someone was singing softly. Tam turned around and walked back. The nurse was still buried behind the high desk and flickering computer screen. As Tam passed the nursery window again, looking sideways without turning her head, the gowned person was leaving the nursery out a back door. Tam stopped in front of the nursery window, just far enough past the passageway with the hamper that she wouldn't have been able to see into it even if she was looking.

She stood still, listening. She heard a door and a wheeled cart, she heard the rustle of cloth as whoever it was who'd just left the nursery removed their green robe and stuffed it into the hamper. She heard the snap of latex gloves being peeled off. She hurried into the stairwell beside the elevator and listened until the elevator came, opened, closed, and left again.

When she got back to the girl, Tam had already sorted through some plans, discarded some. Her car keys, her key to the B&B and the B&B business card already in one hand, she sounded like a veteran conspirator, decisive, resolved, "Take my car, go to this place, go to my room, first one at the top of the stairs, and wait for me there."

"What?"

"Just do it. If you want your baby. And leave your coat here."

The girl was already standing. Already taking the keys and card from Tam's hand. She put them onto the sofa while she slipped her arms from the peacoat. She kept looking at Tam, her mouth partly open. When she was all the way out of her coat, she whispered, "I won't have any clothes. And I need these huge pads . . ."

"We'll get everything you need," Tam murmured back. "We'll have someone to help us." She picked up the coat and left, not even watching to see that the girl got onto the elevator. But when she turned into the passageway with the hamper, she glanced back and the girl was gone, the corridor empty.

It was still before noon. If the B&B woman was right, and if she hadn't already missed him, Nat would be coming back to Southport soon, and would have to go over the short bridge, roughly two hundred yards down the road from the hospital. Tam had counted her footsteps, estimated at about a yard each, rounded it off to two hundred. And in the two-hundred steps, not a single car had passed her. If they'd discovered the missing baby yet at the hospital, they hadn't sent anyone to search the road, Highway 27, from Boothbay to Southport.

With the walk, and carrying the small bundle—cradled in a sling made from a sheet and tied around her shoulder, hidden under the peacoat—Tam was warm, but she couldn't take the coat off. Her arms were in the sleeves, her hands free. Through the coat, she could press her elbows close to her body and support the baby hanging in the sheet, but if a car passed, she could stand normally, her arms free and hands showing, so no one would assume she was holding a baby.

At the bridge, there was a wider sandy shoulder. She'd noticed, the few times she'd crossed, that a car was commonly parked here. Different cars each time: someone fishing in the gut, someone's domestic, maybe a salesman. Once she'd seen a man here getting out of a car with a satchel. It didn't seem an unusual place for a person to leave their car or wait for a ride. She sat on the low wooden rail on the roadside leading up to the bridge, let her lap catch the baby as she lowered her body to sit. The motion of walking, rhythmic soft bumping against her body, hadn't upset him. He'd been asleep when she picked him up from his bed. He hadn't woken when she'd used cuticle scissors to remove his hospital bracelet and slipped him into the sheet sling, nor during her exit from the hospital, down the elevator alone and out the front door. As easy as if she were invisible. The cars that had carried the family with the sick child were still in the lot, but her rental car was gone.

When the baby started to stir and make fretting noises, Tam got up again and walked slowly to the bridge and back, a ten-foot span. She didn't sing or use her arms to pat the baby. Two cars went by in about twenty minutes. A man came out of one of the cottages near the bridge. He walked on his wharf, behind the heaps of lobster traps, tossed a ciga-rette into the water then got onto a boat tied to the dock. Like most lobster boats, it had a tiny half-shelter big enough for a person to stand in if steering the boat during inclement weather. It looked like one man could handle the boat, certainly wouldn't need more than two. The man was out of sight on the boat. He was probably making the rhythmic tinking sound, clear but faraway, that Tam could hear through a breeze moving the firs on Southport. Then the gravel crunched and Nat's truck was pulling off the road.

She didn't even see his face. They were both moving, as though his arrival was choreographed. Nat was getting out of the truck the same time Tam was hurrying to get to the passenger side and get in. He bolted around the front fenders and caught up to her, grabbing her arm, but she didn't turn to face him. His presence was breathless, fiery, forceful. "No, get back in, let's go," she hissed, trying to get the door open. It was locked. The baby was whimpering a little, wedged between Tam's body and the passenger door. Nat's hands were on her shoulders, then sliding down the back of the peacoat. She thought he might sink down and try to crawl up inside the coat with her. His hands seemed to not know what to do, tugging a little at the coat, the sleeves, then flying back up to her head. He held her head hard with a palm over each of her ears, his forehead against the back of her skull, his breath savage against her neck. He hadn't spoken yet, but when he finally did, his voice was raw, as though he'd been screaming. "Just when I thought . . . you could never . . . find another way . . . to drive me utterly off the edge . . ."

"Nat, we have to get out of here."

"I can't believe . . . the ghost . . . walking to Southport . . . without a car . . . alone in the wind . . . my god, yes, get in the truck, get *in* . . . "

His urgent closeness was suddenly gone, then he was back in the truck, leaning over to unlock her door. He was holding onto her arm, pulling her into the truck by the same arm she was now using to try to support the baby. "Okay, I'm in, just go, get out of here," she said, panting, or tried to say it, but he hadn't moved himself back to his side of the truck. He was still holding her arm, his other hand gripping her jaw, his mouth against hers. The baby's fussing broke into a weak cry.

"What's that?" Nat pulled back.

"Let's go. Please, go and I'll explain."

He didn't go. He was pulling on her coat, so Tam stopped resisting. She lifted an edge of the coat for him to see the sling. The baby wasn't visible. "It's the baby from the toilet. I took him. So we have to go. Let's *go.*"

His hand was on the sheet, on the crying baby's head. "You . . . snatched the baby?"

"I . . . decided to do it. I did it. I knew you'd be . . . I waited for you here . . ." Suddenly nothing she could say made a lot of sense. But he didn't seem to notice. His hand touched the baby's body through the sheet. The crying grew louder, but he didn't seem to notice that either. Instead he kissed her again.

"Oh my god, woman . . . if you only knew how hot I got seeing you on the roadside, a perfect image of the ghost, I almost drove off the bridge. Like a ton of rocks, I swear, I couldn't breathe, I was on fire. I was going to fuck you right there for all the world to see, because I knew we'd be invisible, you're a goddamn *ghost* . . . but now you even have a baby, you *stole* a baby—you were goddamn waiting for me with a stolen baby— Where are we supposed to go?"

"The lighthouse. Go there."

"Are you . . ."

"Yes, crazy, probably." She used both arms now to hold the baby, tried to jiggle or rock him to ease his crying.

"But of course, why *not* the lighthouse." He put the truck into gear and pulled back onto the road. Tam didn't watch out the windshield. She uncovered the baby's face and put the tip of her little finger into his mouth. He quieted for a moment.

"Drop me off, then go back to where I was staying. The mother is there."

"The mother?"

"*His* mother. She can feed him. I hope."

"You've got the renegade mother stashed away, *too*?"

"It all just happened. I don't know what I would have done if she wasn't there."

"Does Sara know about this?"

"Who's Sara?"

"My . . . your landlady."

Tam looked at him. The side of his sculpted face, his wavy hair pushed straight back as though facing a stiff wind. She also noticed the bulge in his lap. Maybe because he put his hand there and adjusted himself. "What were you going to say? *My* what? Do you live there too, and didn't tell me? Does she keep a guest house in back?"

"No, I have my own place. We're sort of . . . involved . . . I guess."

"Sort of, you guess?"

"Well, there's no ring or . . . I can certainly keep putting off any further . . . development." He grinned, closing up all the white creases around his eyes. "Until my ghost is ready to stop haunting me."

"This isn't funny."

"It's fairly horrible." His hand slipped to the back of her neck and he leaned over to kiss her again.

"The road!" she yelped.

"I know every curve by heart. But yours I need more practice . . ." He let go of the wheel and his hand—which had seemed so confused by the coat before—was inside her shirt and on her breast in a second.

"Nat!"

He chuckled, returned that hand to the steering wheel, the hand on her neck pulling her sideways, down almost into his lap, muffling the sound of the baby crying, just as they rolled past the flagpole circle with the general store and post office. "Stay down, now," he said.

She relaxed, lying on her side with the baby nestled on the seat against her chest and stomach. He quieted too. He slept again. And just before they got to the lighthouse, just as Nat turned off the paved road and onto the bumpy path leading onto Hendricks Head, Tam lifted her hand from the baby and elicited a dark moan from Nat when she found him through the front of his jeans.

After making sure the baby was safely in the middle of the big bed in the lighthouse's master suite—with Nat behind her dragging on the peacoat, searing open her clothes as she settled the baby—they'd disintegrated to the floor. A wooden floor with only small throw rugs, so they'd slithered ten feet in the process of ravenous coupling, until Tam's shoulder jammed against a wall. Then the baby slept, exhausted in his hunger, while Nat went to get the mother.

Waiting for Nat to return, Tam wandered the keeper's house. The master bedroom where the baby slept between four tall bedposts was downstairs. Nat had said it was the only addition made to the house when these owners bought the lighthouse ten years ago. It had changed the outward shape of the formerly square wooden-frame farmhouse, a small extended wing with continuation of the sloping red roof, but unless Tam compared it with older pictures of the lighthouse—of which there were many framed on the interior walls—she couldn't really distinguish that the new part was different, added on. Couldn't distinguish visually, that is. They'd tried to match the wooden floors, and all the interior walls had been repaired, replastered and painted. There were no seams. The decorating ran thematically true throughout. But it wasn't original, and once she knew, it would be difficult to overlook.

Nat had told her that the owners had also removed an interior wall or two, making the main living area downstairs into one large room—combining bright kitchen and airy seating area—instead of the several tiny rooms that would have allowed the keeper's family to conserve heat in the winter, huddling together in the kitchen while the parlor, with a view of the ocean, stayed brittle as ice. Now as one big room, it was furnished with a white tile kitchen, the electric stove an island with wide shores of countertop. The dishwasher had a pine-paneled front, so it was less conspicuously the wrong century, and a compact washer-dryer was stacked inside a tall pine cabinet. There were light English pine spindle-legged tables and glass-fronted curio cabinets in the seating area. And the nautical motif everywhere. On a plaster-covered ceiling support beam—remnant of the wall that had once closed the kitchen off from the parlor—oars of various shapes for various types of craft were mounted. A tall brass oil lantern sat on a table pedestal in a corner. Antique blue plates, a tattered piece of flag from some storm-tossed ship, snow shoes, a life saver's ring were all displayed on walls, along with dozens of paintings or photographs of the lighthouse. More than one frame held postcards of Hendricks Head through the decades, from the kind of hand-painted matte postcard of the early 20th century, to versions from the 60's and 70's where a cartoon of a lobster was added on top of the glossy photo scene. There were maritime tools on every wall, several globes on end tables, and a large brass telescope aimed out the light-pouring windows toward the Atlantic.

At the bottom of the staircase, a closet-sized room with a porthole window. A museum office with tiny desk and backless stool for a chair, old navigation devices on a shelf, labeled: sextant, echo sounder, liquid compass. On the table surface, a cracked leather-bound log book, binoculars, a Morse code telegraph beside a fax machine and laptop computer. A framed poster showed the differences between a whale boat, brigantine, cutter, schooner, and brig. Another a chart of the maritime buoyage system.

Upstairs two more bedrooms and a bathroom. White lace bedspreads, the same English pine furniture, maritime posters, photos and apparatus on the walls. One bedroom was L-shaped, a full-sized bed in the main part of the room, a single in a little alcove with its own private window toward the sea. Perfect for sisters who may not mind sharing a room, but the older one would need her own space, a little privacy, even in 18-whatever with four, five, or six siblings in the house.

No. No one would sleep alone in the 19th century. Except the baby who might have a narrow rocking crib made of wood placed on the mother's side of the parental bed. A bed that nightly knew many comings and goings, as the father rose to trim the wick on the lighthouse lantern, and the mother awakened to the baby's cries.

On the way downstairs, Tam paused in the doorway of the office. With the ocean on three sides of the lighthouse, nearly every window in the house looked out toward water. Only the front door faced down the neck of land, down the road. The porthole window in the keeper's office kept watch over the Sheepscot River inlet, where the Lady Ghost body had been discovered several days after she disappeared. Tam sat at the little desk and opened the laptop.

> Tam, you've been dropping hints about something that's happened there, and it seems i haven't taken the bait, like i'm not interested. i've been waiting for you to tell me, didn't want to push.
>
> But what's this about adopting a baby? Agencies will only consider you if you have a stable home, and usually

only if you're part of a couple. It takes years. Unless, i suppose, you opt for an older child. this would be exciting, but i hope you'll come home to do it.

Haven't heard from G. Not pushing there either. But mom's worried. Have you seen the website? You didn't say what you thought. How about the boy and dog running away in the distance? Telling us something? i check it every day to see what's changed, it's how he's contacting us I think.

i sent the letter from your dog friend to general delivery at Southport, express mail, should be there tomorrow. Go pick it up there. -m

Tam picked up the binoculars and sent her eyes out the porthole window. Across the wide, choppy inlet, the opposite peninsula was hazy, blurry, the green of the firs dull and smeared. Almost the same color as the dank grey of the rocks whose sharp edges, crags and pitfalls were smoothed and shadowy. The coarse water was worse than angry. The gray-green indifference too cold to even grant the rocks a layer of green slime. Near the opposite headland, a white boat nodded up and down. A man leaned over to grab for a pink fluorescent lobster trap float.

She listened for the baby. Listened for Nat's truck on the sandstone road. Heard the changeless breath of wind and water, moving in, moving out, and the distant complaint of gulls, which could also be a man's shout, faraway, out on the water, near the rocks around the lighthouse. From how much further away than that could a human voice be heard?

www.marr-burgess-family.com

Welcome to
The Marr-Burgess Family Website

your hosts:

Gary Marr-Burgess *(author, triathlete, sports therapist, adventurer, martyr)*

Martha Marr-Burgess Richter *(historian, chronicler and keeper of the family tree)*

Tamara Burgess *(mystery woman who would emigrate from California)*

Emily Marr-Burgess *(athlete, cook, counselor, coach, artist, free spirit)*

 Sample Gary's books

 Gary's Latest Triathlon Results

 Gary & Coach **iN HELL**

 Mom's Watercolors

 Read Portions of Martha's Family History

 What Tam's Been Up To

 Message **FROM HELL**

 Message from Martha

 Message from Mom

 Message from Tam **(wherever you are)**

 Where Gary's Going

Each Necessary Task

Tam's first thought had been: this is better. At least the swimming pool image was gone. Even though the replacement picture hardly depicted the family, such as it was, *now*. Ever dramatic Martha and her suppositions into Gary communicating some brand of unspeakable distress through the website. An obvious ploy, the new words added in red, another way to boast about his exploits in NYC. Then Nat's truck had crunched up the road, idled, sighed, and doors had slammed.

When she'd finally returned to the website, after dark—the teenager and her baby tucked into the white lace bed in the upstairs dormer, Nat in the master suite breathing rough and rhythmic like surf, the shutters wide open, the picture window framing restless water blacker than the sky—she went beyond the website's front page. Outside the porthole window, visible from here and not from the bedroom, the beacon from the light tower bled a little light onto the rocks and water.

Looking at a computer screen in a dark room meant the subliminal flicker was even more palpable. Doing e-mail, she tried to keep her eyes on the keyboard, not the screen. When a computer had been her partner in a livelihood, she'd used screen filters and had a professional in ergonomics set the lighting in her office to defuse the danger of strobe-induced seizure. A flat laptop screen was always better, but still, she shielded her eyes with one hand, as though looking far into a bright horizon.

She didn't click the icon for Gary's books or triathlon results. Then she noticed he'd changed the icon for what had been search & rescue. A jet flying at a peculiar angle. How excessive can you get, Gary? Only a few other icons had been changed, the bizarre face or stick-man-thing for his personal message, the sailboat was a new item hinting he was setting off on one of those male-midlife-crisis adventures. The icon for "message from Tam" was also changed, although there wasn't and never had been any message from her, and now a picture insinuating she was off alone on some tropical island with a computer. His snide guess at where she'd gone showed *his* biases, not hers.

She went back to the jet, which, if anything, was *ascending*, not crashing.

Waiting for the page to download on the slow lighthouse dial-up, she looked out the porthole. Mary Catherine, sitting here, might have her speller open on the secretary desk, would look up from the rows of words at a schooner or brigantine (she'd know the difference without a poster) making its way up Sheepscot River to harbor in Wiscasset. If it were night, like this, the beam from the light tower might shimmer on the wet rocks but wouldn't illuminate the murky form of the ship, the ghostly sails sliding by in the darkness. She'd be spelling words quietly aloud, listening for the new baby's cry from upstairs, thinking of the people on the schooner eagerly awaiting a new port, and how secure they felt seeing the lighthouse lantern glowing, and how perhaps they paused for a moment to reflect on the meaningful life of a lightkeeping family.

Gary had acquired photos, maybe he shot them himself, dark and grainy—the computer screen might even be abrasive if she touched it—people in elephant-nose masks, or with their hair fuzzy with ash, strung together with ropes, maneuvering through wreckage of unrecognizable pieces. He'd added portions of phrases in red letters.

Steel beams were slick with ash and dust
if you fell,
**   it would be into a pile of steel swords**

Then she noticed a sound icon and used it. A hologram voice spoke from the computer's speaker. Familiar, despite being crudely reproduced, the voice chanted or recited—most of the words Gary had printed among, around, even over some of the photos. But she could tell it wasn't Gary's voice, despite not having heard him for at least five years. . . the last time she was home? When she retired? She didn't even remember if she saw him then. She guarded her eyes with both hands, cupped around her brow and temples.

pulverized concrete, pulverized glass
every worker had to take decom showers
                    after every 12-hour shift
            With cars still burning in the garages below
a cloud of noxious fumes rose

It was Bill Kurtis. Gary had taken Bill Kurtis, narrating one of his documentaries about Ground Zero, and put the voice on his website.

The cloud a mixture of burning fuel
asbestos and carbon monoxide gas
                    Haz Mat experts monitored
                        the atmosphere hourly

The Kurtis voice ended. The remaining words unnarrated, accompanied by some kind of chafing bagpipe music, too rickety to make out a melody.

Going down into it, like cave explorers,
except this cave with no floor, no bottom,
                            bottomless
                snarl of hot metal and spiny steel,
No floor, no ceiling, no walls,
just festering smoldering holes,
                    darker than any darkness
            mark the trail with spray paint to find our way back.
Pretzeled rebar and steel
and malicious barbed objects and insidious dust.
                Fucking dust! Eat it for breakfast, lunch,
                    the cream in our coffee.
If the hole had been full of water instead,
I might've gotten in there
                        and found something.

It was Amazing Grace, of course, the buzzing, thrombosis-raising bagpipes. The back arrow to *home* cut the noise off. Tam glanced out the window to see if a cutter (schooner?) was still making its way through the Sheepscot's tidal current toward Wiscasset.

The sailboat icon, sure enough, was a proposed trip-around-the-world. Predictable that this would someday be his course, and not very original.

> Hey folks, We'll be putting our things into storage and setting sail soon. But first we've got to clear out and simplify our lives. Here's what's available, if anyone's interested:

> > 3 packages malomars (generic brand)
> > brand new toilet brush
> > box of rubber bands
> > last year's issues of *Smithsonian* (12)
> > 2001 San Diego County phone book
> > framed picture of you-know-who on the starting block
> > (. . . BANG!)

> > Charting our route: Guam, and the place where what's-her-name's plane went down and was never found (we could S&R there . . . I guess that's just S, right? No R there anymore either), Hawaii of course, Japan, and something between Hawaii and Japan. Thailand's somewhere out there. And Vietnam. We'll S&R Vietnam, right Coach? (Anyone to R there? Where is there anyone left to *R*?)

She returned to the home page and sat with her eyes closed, deciding between the page that used to be Message from Gary (she'd never read it before, why start now?) and the page that used to have her dog show photos (she hadn't posted them, it was either Martha or their mother). That page was now marked with the flying fish icon, and she was assuming the dog show photos were gone. She was right.

> She was slick and slippery as a bass
> cutting through water without a splash
> vicious in her lane, a barracuda
> unflappable under pressure as a Buddha

But something weird happened one day
The fish grew wings and flew away
Did she evolve to some higher life?
Or was she running away from some horrible strife?

Come back flying guppy
You can splash with my puppy
The water is safer
Than reading the paper

How long had the poem (if you could call it that) been glowing on the screen while Tam again gazed out the porthole window? She was hearing more than seeing: the conjoined swirl of uneasy air and water. A ship, a cutter or brig, swept upriver on the wind, would sound the same. From inside, from across the channel, you couldn't hear the flap of sail, creak of rope or groan of waterlogged wood. Mary Catherine might never have been on a ship. So close to water, but always rooted on this rocky shoal, she would look up from weeding the garden or hanging the wash, or just stand outside the house, her dress and apron billowing like useless sails behind her, and see the ships every day, going and coming from Wiscasset or Boothbay Harbor. She might hold baby Seaborn. . . no, Mary Catherine was only 7 when Seaborn arrived. So she would hold Seaborn's hand—a girl seven years younger, who would grow up to help Mary Catherine with the laundry, cooking and sweeping—and she would tell Seaborn about the ship she'd arrived on, the storm that broke it to icy splinters on the rocks out there near the Cuckolds (or was that Sequin Island), and the harsh frothy water that had washed Seaborn to the light-house.

The creak she heard was not a ship. It was Nat's socked feet padding through the kitchen. Tam logged off and closed the light keeper's laptop. Then Nat was in the doorway. He squatted beside the stool where Tam sat, nearly pulled her to the floor in a clumsy embrace, his head in her lap. "Ghost in the dark," he muttered thickly.

"Are you sleepwalking? Nat? Are you awake?"

"Yes. I wish I weren't. I hafta go. Can't stay all night."

"We can't take her and the baby back to Sara's place. Where will—"

"No, you stay. No one'll come here. I'm the only one . . ." He burrowed his face into her lap. "Tomorrow . . ." He raised his head and pressed his cheek against her stomach.

"What about tomorrow?"

"I'm going to start dropping my first traps of the season. Want to come out, troll the mouth of the river around Dogfish Head, see the lighthouse from the viewpoint of a ship?"

"That would be . . . wait . . . on a boat? No."

"Afraid of getting sick? Ghosts don't puke, do they?"

"I don't know. I haven't been on a boat for a long time."

"Since you arrived as a baby tied between two featherbeds." He looked up slightly, his face between her breasts.

"No. Since . . . I'm epileptic and almost drowned once. My brother had to—"

"Nothing real. Make up another reason."

"Oh . . . okay. She survived a shipwreck and washed ashore, then grew up vowing never to set foot in a boat or ship." Tam put her hands in his unruly hair. "Or . . . no, how about if we . . . try it with someone else. Someone who had lost her twin brother, and he'd been replaced with the shipwrecked baby." She ran her fingers along his scalp, raking through his thick hair. "So I could never look at a boat the same again . . . even though my father . . . my papa . . . guides ships to safety with his lighthouse."

"Do that some more," he groaned. "Do it forever."

"But you have to leave."

"Yes, I can't be waking up here."

"Is there someplace you always have to wake up?"

"Not always. But . . . It's never here."

"Who would know?"

"My truck . . . parked out there . . . anyone can see . . . everyone knows it's me."

In the short afternoon before dark on the third full day at the lighthouse, Tam sat in the fog-bell room and opened the oversize envelope Nat had picked up at the post office. Martha hadn't just forwarded Meryl's still-sealed letter (Martha proving how good and un-nosy she is), but a note from their mother as well. That note unsealed, so Martha would know its contents. But she'd wait for Tam to bring it up, prattle about some asinine kids' project she'd involved herself in, then as soon as Tam mentioned it, Martha would be serious and anxious, show the true color of her immersion in the Gary drama.

After seeing Gary's name in her mother's handwriting, Tam put that note aside and opened Meryl's letter.

Tam,

Cancel my subscription, I can't take any more of your *issues*. You did nothing but pout and brood and sulk about yourself. Why couldn't you find one shred of pleasure and satisfaction in teamwork and partnership? If not with me then at least with a dog. A lot of weird loners discover how to relate to and trust someone by training a dog. Even your deranged *brother* might know this—but no thanks, I don't want anything more to do with him *either*. Thank you very much for siccing him on me. I'll gladly ship your junk to you COD, just give me an address, I'll be happy to be rid of the last of you *and* your crazy family. I thought as long as your things were here, you might, just *might* try to talk to me, to come to some understanding, even come back. But *no*, you had to send your *big brother*. And what a piece of *work*. He just shows up on my front porch. And looks like he hasn't changed his clothes in weeks. I thought you had a stalker or something. He does seem to know about dogs, though. He knows what terriers are bred for. But he was really pissed off that I didn't bring my dogs to Ground Zero to search for survivors! What a *jerk*. I really think he's demented, and on this one thing, I'll grant that you had good reason to have issues with your family. But now I get this lunatic on my doorstep out-of-the-blue telling me how selfish I am for having show dogs. Like anyone *asked* him! At first I thought you'd told him what to say, but it was *more* than you'd ever say, and then he started in on Ground Zero and this combating evil shit, and I remembered you said something about him being some kind of big-deal there. He called it egocentric for us to do foo-foo showing instead of using the dogs for the betterment of mankind. Where'd you *get* this guy? After he calls me names, he offers to help me teach them to go into little crevices and find survivors or body parts! He said they could've searched places even the professional search teams couldn't access. I'd have liked to let them access the back of his leg. But since he scared the shit out of me, showing up all dirty like that, I only had the door open a crack and got it shut and locked and chained as fast as I could after I said I'd send your stuff to you so *leave me the fuck alone!*

Meryl

p.s. I need an address of where you are.

Where she was. There was no address for the fog-bell chamber on Hendricks Head. She clicked her nails on the closed cover of her computer. Nat had brought it, with her suitcase, from the B&B. He'd had to get them when Sara wasn't home. He'd left some money and a note Tam had written, thanking Sara for opening her establishment a few months early. He'd removed the rental car.

Tam folded Meryl's letter. She should have opened the other folder Nat had given her, but instead unfolded her mother's note.

Tam, hope you are well. Martha has told you we are worried about Gary. Maybe he just needed to get away, but it doesn't look like he's on vacation, from what we can tell. Martha told you about the website. I know you think you can't do anything, but maybe you should come home. We think he's looking for you. If you were here, he could find you here, we could help him, if he ~~needs~~ wants help.

Love you. Mom

Standing on twelve-foot stilts bolted right into the bedrock, on the outer-most tip of land of Hendricks Head, the fog-bell structure was connected to the house only by an uphill wooden ramp that began at the doorway to the screen room. From the light tower, one could look over the fog-bell house, out to sea, or look down onto the scaffolding that had once held the bell on the structure's roof. But from inside the fog-bell chamber, the view was only of the sea. No windows toward the lighthouse. There was no electricity. Tam read by 3 o'clock window light. It would soon begin to dim. The room, already chilly, would grow colder.

The fog-bell chamber was furnished as an austere bedroom, maybe the most authentic space at the lighthouse compound—one plain wooden single bed with handmade quilt, one plain wooden table, braided rag rug on the wooden floor, a row of hooks on the wall for clothing—except no bedroom would have been here. Would great-great-grand-father Jaruel have thought to remodel the bell house as a bedroom for one of his daughters, as she grew older, as she began to need the privacy and modesty of a young woman? But he himself would have had to come here regularly, to set the mechanized chain-contraption that would keep the bell tolling through half-a-day of roiling mist, dense enough to obscure a view of either the light tower or fog bell from the main house. Perhaps he could train Mary Catherine to work the apparatus and sound the fog bell. Could she sleep, then, through a thickened night with the bell tolling right above her?

Would it be like a lonely lover's call, enough to lull her to slumber, with the knowledge that all who heard it were safe? Or was it the 19th century version of a fluorescent light, aural tumult instead of visual tremor? Her mother's note, still open on her lap, her limp hand still holding it, did seem to flicker. She closed her eyes on it, and on the hum in her head. With her eyes closed, she folded the note. Perhaps the chiming bell could have brought both: dull headache, the buzz, white-out confusion even in the dark—all spelling the lamented memory of a lover. Denny. Who was Mary Catherine's Denny? Her own dead brother? Someone else?

A dizzying meditation like she thought she'd never have here. *Here*, where a phone never rang, the fax machine in the keeper's berth never spit printed sheets into its tray, the television never tuned to news of machine guns versus rock-throwers or little girls abducted from their beds. Here, where when the baby stirred at night, his mother held him before his first cry. Her milk had come readily, robustly, and she laughed at the wet stains on the big T-shirts she wore. (Nat had brought an armload of his own undershirts. Acquiring girls' clothes might have aroused some-one's notice.) Even the girl didn't seem to wish for the noise of a radio or stereo. She sang to her baby, Christmas carols it sounded like, perhaps the only soft melodies she knew.

The one time the television had been tuned to a news broadcast, it was local, from Portland. It was their first full day at the lighthouse, early evening, Tam and the girl with the baby on the big bed in the master suite. The local newscaster read the story without cutting to a taped interview or field reporter sent to Boothbay for more info. Just a still photograph of the outside of St. Andrews hospital, and 4 lines:

> *A newborn baby is missing from St. Andrews Hospital in Boothbay Harbor. Nurses discovered the baby missing yesterday and notified police. The baby boy, named Jonah by nurses in the hospital, had been born the day before in a public restroom in Boothbay and found in a toilet by a tourist. Authorities suspect the baby's mother, an unnamed minor from Boothbay, took him from the hospital.*

Tam got off the bed and turned the television off.

"Well, *I'm* nailed," the girl had said.

"We don't need to watch news anymore."

"How d'you think we're going to get out of this? Stay here forever?"

"That won't be likely."

"*You* can leave anytime, they don't know who . . . like, what's your name, anyway?"

Her back to the girl, Tam slowly closed the pine cabinet doors, obscuring the blank face of the television. "How do you like the name they gave your baby?"

"Gross."

So they'd re-named the baby Jared and the girl called him Jerry. He wore only diapers and a blanket, a blanket big enough to completely envelop him with enough left over to drape over his face when the girl carried him outside for some brisk, sweet air, usually at dusk after the early lobster men would be back in port. Not out onto the slick rocks where the waves splashed. But not on the road side of the house either, where someone might see her. She napped heavily in the afternoon with the baby beside her, bathed and changed him, helped cook a meal three times a day, holding the baby while she ate. The past two days Nat had been there for lunch, and again for dinner. There was a dishwasher, but Tam filled the sink with soapy water and did each dish, languidly, by hand. Nat asked her why.

"It's quieter," Tam had said. "And slower."

Of course, when he'd asked, he was right behind her, pressing her up against the sink, his hands feeling for her fingers in the warm water, his body an outline of hers. "I like the way you think," he'd said.

"I want to know more about how it was back then."

"Back when?"

"You know, 1875, 1880, around there."

"Has she gone to bed yet?" His wet hands out of the water, he began lifting her skirt. She was wearing her traveling jumper again. Not to travel, but because it seemed right to move from room to room with loose material brushing against her thighs.

"I don't know." She didn't stop him. He paused, just let himself press against her underwear, his hands damp on her stomach. "But I'd like to know what they would eat and where they got it. What homemade soap is like. Washing the sheets and cloth diapers by hand. Hanging them to dry, would they smell of the ocean? Those kinds of things."

"I love this dress." His fingers peeked into the elastic of her underwear then retreated. His hips pulsed against her. "You wear it to drive me crazy, don't you?"

"I wish I had something more like she would wear."

"Let's say you do. Let's say it is."

"Then I would have a whole lot more on underneath." She lifted a dripping pan into the drainer as he pressed her harder into the sinkshelf. She had to hold onto the counter for a moment and push back to keep her feet from leaving the floor.

"I'd get so hot undoing everything," he said, "in the short time we have here before someone comes in."

"And there are so many children. I have . . . some younger siblings. Mother's putting the littler ones to bed. And the keeper, or father—papa—will be back from the tower soon."

He slipped a whole hand between her legs, still outside her underwear. His face, his breath hot and wet against her ear, whispering, "What's your name?"

"Mary Catherine"

"Who's that? Not Seaborn?"

"No, her older sister. She was . . . *I* was seven when Seaborn . . . arrived."

"How old . . . are you . . . now?" He spoke with the same rhythm as his pelvis.

"Now I'm . . . maybe sixteen."

"Who would I be?"

"My cousin."

One of his hands disappeared. She could feel him maneuvering the fly of his jeans. "Yeah, there was no one else. Everyone was related. Maybe I'm your father's sister's son, loaned to the lighthouse in the winter when there's no work for a lobsterman." He put his penis inside the leg of her underwear, pressing it against the cheek of her butt. "But this might be as far as I could go . . . in the house . . . with people around . . . with all your clothes to get through . . . and I might come . . . just from this."

When he'd stepped away, he'd grabbed a dishtowel to catch the wet running down her leg before he dropped her skirt.

A day later—today—when he'd brought her mail from the post office, he'd also handed her a tattered manila folder. "My mother gave me this when I moved up here." They were in the bright, modern kitchen, just before noon. He took a mug from a rack and poured cold coffee from the carafe.

"You aren't from here?"

"Portland. I bought my house from another distant relative. You've fallen into a quagmire of kin." He sipped. Licked his lips. "*It's our ghost who had no family.*"

"But Mary Catherine did." Even standing up at the counter, Tam's legs felt constricted. She was wearing her jeans today. She had to wash the dress yesterday. It still hung from a line she'd stretched between the light tower and the yard's picket fence, still damp from having flapped there in a morning mist.

"So who is this Mary Catherine? You're not the mystery woman anymore?" He was sitting on a barstool, on the other side of the white-and-blue tile counter, smiling at her over a white glazed mug with an anchor printed on the side.

"Mary Catherine was probably a ghost, too," Tam said, surprising herself. What did she mean? Maybe that nobody noticed her, not after adopting Seaborn, the saved child who replaced Mary Catherine's dead twin. But maybe Mary Catherine was still a ghost, a second phantom prowling the lighthouse. Where did she die? And how or why?

"She's one of Jaruel Marr's, the lightkeeper's children," Tam had finally added, aware of Nat's benign, near glassy smile in a ticking silence.

"I'm going to need a roadmap to know who you are." The baby had cried upstairs. "My cue to leave. One of these days I'll drive you over to my place after dark, show you what I'm doing to the old house." He'd tapped the frayed folder.

Tam put her mother's note back inside the big envelope with Meryl's letter. The humming had quieted while she'd sat still with her eyes closed. She heard only the whoosh of ocean outside below the fog-bell chamber. She opened Nat's folder.

> *Nat, this was written by my Aunt Lottie around 1920. Now that you have the house, I thought you should have this. —Mom*

Life on Southport

My mother was close to her Aunt Mary Jane Marr Pierce. She spent so much time as a child at the Pierce house, and told us often of those fondly remembered times, more or less 1855 to 1869 when she married. I've preserved her memories as best I could here.

The Warren and Mary Jane Pierce house was at a quarter mile distant from their nearest neighbor, Warren's older brother Samuel and his wife. Mary Jane must have taken comfort in their lights on winter nights when the weather kept women with young families housebound for days. Her house stood at the southern end of the harbor with a clear view of the pinkies and small schooners at anchor and the vessels coming into Pierce's wharf to sell their catch. Two young maples stood sentinel in front of the house. Warren said they would give protection against the fierce north and west winds, but Mary Jane probably wouldn't see that they helped, since the front door had to be nailed shut each winter. It was always a happy day in spring when it could be opened again. West of the house, a fishhouse and wharf extended into the gut that separated the property from Joe's Island. This gut flowed with the tides from the end of the harbor down the length of Joe's Island and out to sea. To the south stood a barn that housed a cow and sometimes a pig. A henhouse and yard stood nearby the back door.

The garden plot, surprisingly deep for an island that was all granite ledge, allowed them to raise all the vegetables they needed. There were apple and pear trees, too (Last time I saw it, one lone pear tree still lived in the front yard. It was the most pampered tree on Southport.). There was no reason for Mary Jane to grow flax, since dress lengths came in on every vessel from Boston and Port-land.

The kitchen was half the house. It had a large cooking fireplace with ovens. Though Mary Jane had an iron stove as well, she always seemed to prefer her fireplace. As a little girl, I remember her sitting in the doorway of the ell, smoking a pipe. It must have been quite a thing in her day. I also remember the big fireplace and my mother told of the meals Mary Jane cooked there. She would have had strings of braided onions and bunches of herbs and dried flowers hanging from the beams.

The other half of the first floor was also one big room. This would have been the parlor and not used for anything but weddings and funerals. But in this case, since there were no other bedrooms except two little ones in the attic, it was a bedroom for Warren and Mary Jane and whatever babies were there. After Warren's death in 1851, the room was a dormitory for the younger children and their mother. My mother was but a year old when Warren died and she became close with Mary Jane when her own mother sent her there often to help out. This was not a healthy family. Warren died at the age of 38. Abbie and Izetta, mother's cousins, died in their early 20's in childbirth or the results of it. Another cousin, James (the eldest son, named after my grandfather, Mary Jane's brother) died at 33. Glory might have lived longer but she was drowned. One other son, Nahum, I don't recall what became of him. That left only Mary Jane and one daughter, Lydia, at any such times that I can remember. They were both very dark, thin-faced women, small in stature with shoulders bent from care.

After his father died, James became the man of the family. My mother remembers him knitting potheads for lobster traps. He lobstered, clammed and fished, went deer hunting and perhaps shot fur-bearing animals as well. There were raccoons, skunks, foxes, and mink that turned white in the winter and were sold under the name of ermine. Mary Jane and the girls, besides cooking, washing and cleaning, had to knit caps, mufflers and mittens, sweaters and stockings, and the fisherman's big mitts which were boiled to make them dense and waterproof. They had to braid rugs, piece quilts, and do all the sewing for the family. My mother would often spend a week with the family, sewing and mending. This helped my mother's family, since for that week she would be fed from Many Jane's food stores. There was always a bucket of lobsters, cooked, cooled and ready to eat, in the sink. When any of the younger children came in, saying they were hungry, Mary Jane would say "Get a lobster and eat it outside." They would much rather have had bread and molasses.

My mother met my father when she was fifteen but they were not married until she was nineteen. My father was stationed by the Lighthouse Service in Portland, but the trip was easy. He made regular visits, on the lighthouse boat, to check on Hendricks Head. Mother was also often there to visit those cousins. In her childhood the lighthouse was a small dwelling with a tower on the roof, but some years after they were married, my father was ordered by the lighthouse service to build a much more extensive compound. The new dwelling house was spacious, for the times. The bell tower, built even later, was further down on the rocks and was connected with a walkway. The light tower was a hollow brick building. My mother said she was afraid of it, yet remembers climbing the brass-railed, iron staircase with her cousin Eugene, Keeper Jaruel Marr's son, cringing at every ringing footstep. Of course Eugene was going up as unofficial assistant to his father, to trim the wick or check the oil or wind the large clockworks. He and all his brothers stayed with lighthouse work, but it was Wolcott who took over at Hendricks. Wolcott was many years younger than my mother, born only a few years before she was married. Other babies were born at the lighthouse just before she married. The year she was 18, when she wasn't sewing her trousseau or helping and visiting her Aunt Mary Jane, mother was often at the lighthouse to help her aunt Catherine care for the children. One of the younger ones was named Mary, whom Jaruel and Catherine might've named for Jaruel's sister, my mother's beloved Aunt Mary Jane. Although my aunt, this girl Mary could've been like an older sister to me, as I had none, only brothers, but she was a shy one. I have few memories of her, as the Lighthouse Service required father and mother to travel from Southport. After I married, I only visited Southport in the summers, since mother and father lived there again after he retired, but I haven't been back since we moved mother here with us after father died.

by Lottie Marr Gordon

Tam sat for only a moment longer, letting her eyes slide up the thrum of names. Jane, Mary, Catherine, Jane, Jaruel. Then she took her computer and left the bell house. Out on the walkway, her hair blew sideways like a flag. She left her shoes in the screen porch and padded through the dim kitchen, past the coffee pot's red beacon on the dark sinkshelf, and into the keeper's office just below the stairway.

Martha, I won't claim to have remained chaste since Denny. But can say I was untouched since him. Til now. This man, we play a game, but he's so real, with me, beside me. In me. Nothing I say can explain it. Not his creased smile, his outdoors-in-the-wind hair, his sculpted arms, his no-color eyes—but the way he looks at me, his hunger a profound caress, his profound touch a lifeline

She selected all, let it stay for a moment—white words on black background, then deleted and started over,

Dear Martha, I think I just found your double in our lineage. Another scribe of family history. Someone named Lottie Marr-something (why did all these Marr women keep their maiden name as a middle name?) But do you think we all have kindred doubles? At first I thought mine would be Seaborn, the adopted stranger, but it isn't her.

We're all fine here. At least we know what we're doing each day in the short term. The Marrs' lives were likely the same. Finish each necessary task. But never dream of what could have been, or what might be. Actually could be a serene existence. Is it too late for anyone in the 21st century to live it?

Tam

When she came out of the keeper's office, she saw the girl in a rocking chair in the living room, facing the ocean-side windows and nursing the baby. The girl's name was Jill. Tam stood behind her, trying to imagine seeing an old lady in a rocking chair smoking a pipe. Her name would not be Jill. But Jared, the baby's name, was a good compromise.

Outside the window Tam's dress billowed like a corduroy banner. Every time she went to take it off the line, it still felt damp.

Jill shifted, looked over her shoulder at Tam. So Tam came around the rocking chair and sat on the sofa. When she wasn't nursing the baby, the girl wore a bra with cloth diapers stuffed into the cups to catch leaking milk. While nursing, she removed her t-shirt and lowered one bra strap, then usually draped the baby and her upper body with a sheet. Today she was not covered. Tam could see a starfish tattoo on the girl's chest, just above the bald back of the baby's head. He made grunting noises. Jill looked up and smiled. "He's my little piggy." In one fist, the baby held Jill's finger. "Do you have kids?" Jill asked.

"No." Tam peeled an afghan from the back of the couch and wrapped her shoulders. "Aren't you cold?"

"I swear, this makes me *hot*." The girl giggled. "Not hot like *hot*, but, like, you know. Like it could be *summer*?" She bent to kiss the top of the baby's head. "Did you ever want kids?"

On her lap, Tam hooked her fingers through the afghan's mesh. "I knew it was a bad idea. What do you usually do in the summer?"

"Last summer my dad let me run twenty traps. So, like, I could check ten every day."

"Lobster?"

"Yeah, duh!"

"So it was your summer job."

"Yeah. I, like, sold them mostly to, like, neighbors having parties or whatever. I, like, undercut the pound's prices a little."

The kitchen door gasped. Nat's bootstep creaked the old hardwood. Tam leapt and flung the afghan over the girl's chest, including the baby.

"I hafta switch sides in a minute," the girl said.

Tam looked up to Nat squinting a grin at her from the kitchen where he'd already poured himself a cup of coffee, this time kept warm for him. "I have news, girls."

Jill didn't look up from watching herself shift the baby to her other breast under the afghan.

"They think she took the baby on her own," he said, "so there's no way in hell they're going to think to look here. They don't really know where to look. But they're asking store clerks to be on guard for anyone stocking up on baby items, or if diapers and whatnot are being lifted."

Tam retreated back to the sofa. "If they think she did it alone, who do they think is going to go shoplifting for her?"

"Maybe a ghost?"

The girl snorted a quiet laugh.

Nat came into the living area. "No, don't worry, you were truly invisible, the perfect crime. But they don't know if she doesn't have some friend somewhere helping out. I'm sure they're grilling all her pals from school."

"They won't know anything," the girl murmured, singing it like a verse to the baby.

"But our hideout's about to be invaded." Nat looked out the window, perhaps at Tam's dress still whirling on an eddy of breeze caused when the house and light tower bent the linear wind. "Some friends of the owners are visiting the area, and he wants them to have a tour. So day after tomorrow, when they're here, I'll want you girls stowed away in the fog-bell room. I'll tell them I've been painting it so we can't go in there. Also we'll have to tidy up a bit, remove obvious evidence."

"No problem," the girl sighed, standing. She whispered, "Asleep," and moved slowly toward the stairs, still shrouded in the afghan.

Nat didn't stir until the girl's footstep moved across the upstairs bedroom floor. He advanced toward the window, as though to peer through the brass telescope. But then swung around behind the sofa, his coffee cup deposited onto the end table, bent swiftly, his hands on either side of Tam's head. "It'll be dark soon," he rasped in her ear. "Can the ghost appear at my house tonight?"

"How'm I supposed to get there?"

"She'll hide out in my truck. Startle me. Nearly scare me off the road where it swings dangerously close to the water."

"What happened to my cousin awaiting times he'll find me alone during my housework?"

"That's good too—four people in three different centuries can fuck simultaneously." One hand still on the back of Tam's neck, he swung a boot over the back of the sofa, the rest of his body followed.

155

"Nat . . . Sara . . . where does she think I am?"

"I told her you got what you came to find." Kneeling beside her, then one leg climbing over hers, he pulled her shirt from the waistband of her jeans, pushed her bra up at the same time. "I said your goodbye." His hands on her breasts, like holding two soap bubbles.

"And paid her, I hope?" Tam closed her eyes. His mouth, even his day-old beard like a whisper against her skin. "We were supposed to have dinner," she murmured. "The three of us."

"*That* wasn't going to happen." A nipple in his mouth.

His boots were sandy, not muddy. The next morning, before Jill had come down for breakfast, Tam had to look for a vacuum to get the sand from the sofa cushions. What would Mary Catherine have done if her cousin clumsily got sand or mud on the furniture in the parlor?

Later that afternoon, Tam asked Jill if she could hold the baby for a while. "You may need a break," Tam suggested.

"Why? I can't, like, *go* anywhere!" the girl snickered, but she settled the baby into Tam's arm.

Tam had gathered her dress from the line at midday, when it felt dry, before it could become damp again in an evening fog. She wore a long-sleeved white blouse under the jumper, and her hiking boots. A shawl made from the afghan knotted around her shoulders. Then she took the baby into the fog-bell chamber where she was keeping her own computer and satchel of papers. With the sleeping baby on the crook of one arm, Tam spread Martha's genealogical list on the wooden table.

John Marr of Kittery, Maine, and his descendants:

John Marr m. Catherine Surplus, b March 9, 1703
    John Marr, Jr. (Aug 3, 1720)   Elsie Marr (Sept 22, 1729)
    James Marr (Oct 3, 1722)   Surplus Marr (Sept 15, 1731)
    <u>William Marr (Aug 4, 1725)</u>   Dennis Marr (July 10, 1735)
    Jane Marr (Aug 30, 1728)

William Marr m. Ruth Spinney, b. April 18, 1742
    <u>John Marr</u> (Aug 3, 1755)   Olive Marr (Aug 3, 1755)

John Marr m. Mary Cornish (birthdate unknown, died at over 100 yrs old). *John Marr served under General Putnam in the Revolutionary War*
    John Marr (Sept 8, 1780)   Richard Marr (March 6, 1792)
    <u>Thomas Marr</u> (April 1, 1784)   Alexander Marr (May 11, 1794)
    Dennis Marr (May 3, 1786)   William Marr (Jan 1, 1801)
    James Marr (Feb 16, 1789)

Thomas Marr m. Lydia Trafton, b. March 9, 1786
    Izetta Marr (Aug 28, 1812)   Jothan Trafton Marr (Jan 13, 1827)
    Lydia Marr (Jan 23, 1815)   <u>Jaruel Marr</u> (April 3, 1829)
    Thomas Marr (June 5, 1817)   Lemuel Marr (March 20, 1832)
    Mary Jane Marr (Sept 20, 1820) Marinda Ann Marr (May 26, 1835)
    Nahum Baldwin Marr (Nov 18, 1822 - d. Sept 27, 1823)
    Nahum Baldwin Marr (second of this name, Aug 4, 1824)

Jaruel Marr m. Catherine Westman (Sweden, c 1830)
    Eugene Clarence Marr (May 10, 1854)
    Cedelia Ann Marr (November 20, 1856)
    Mabel Verona Marr (September 23, 1860)
    <u>Wolcott Garrett Marr</u> (December 15, 1866)
    Mary Catherine Marr (January 20, 1868, died March 24, 1899)
    Lowell Herbert Marr (May 11, 1872)

Wolcott Garrett Marr m. Hattie Hatch (Portland, 1869)
    <u>Mabel Giberta Marr</u> (June 16, 1891)
    Garrett Eugene Marr (June 7, 1893)
    Thomas Perry Marr (February 19, 1897)
    Wolcott Hamlin Marr (December 3, 1898)
    Gracie May Marr (1899, d. in infancy)
    Charles Simeon Marr (August 3, 1900, d. in infancy)
    Herbert Loring Marr (May 6, 1902)
    Clara Etta Marr (April 14, 1904)
    Catherine Marr (January 15, 1906)
    Arthur Ficket Marr (June 6, 1910)

Gilberta Marr m. Leland Irving, b. *November 15, 1889, d. 1963*
(Gilberta dropped her given name of Mabel, kept Gilberta and used Marr as her
middle name. She also gave Marr as middle name to all her children.)
    Simeon Marr Irving *(November 9, 1922)*
    Garrett Marr Irving *(June 22, 1924)*
    Lee Marr Irving *(Sept. 12, 1929)*
    Emily Marr Irving (February 19, 1931)

Emily Marr Irving m. Daniel Burgess, b. *July. 9 1926, d. February 28, 1978*
(Became Emily Marr Burgess. In honor of Emily's lineage, Daniel and Emily were among the
pioneers of the hyphenated family name, a practice long used in Latin American countries where
Daniel had worked as a petroleum engineer prior to being married).
    Garrett Marr-Burgess *(May 3, 1953)*
    Tamara Marr-Burgess *(June 26, 1956)*
        (later dropped Marr and became Tamara Burgess)
    Martha Marr-Burgess *(January 7, 1959)*
        (m. Michael Richter and became Martha Marr Richter)

John, John, William, William, John, Thomas, Thomas—no wonder they got poetic and decided to mix it up with Nahum, Jaruel, Wolcott, and Lowell. Some of the other names were obviously old surnames from other family branches, thrown in as middle names but sometimes as first names, like the aptly dubbed Surplus Marr (certainly enough was enough, although his mother only had to have seven. But perhaps Martha hadn't been able to locate offspring who didn't survive in the 1700's.).

The baby was heavy. He slept like dead weight. The crook of her elbow was damp and developing an awkward ache. Her spine felt pulled out of whack toward that side. A twinge shot up her neck.

Not a family tree, but a genealogical list (as Martha had pointed out more than a few times.) But now she realized it meant this document would show no continuation of the descendants of Nahum Marr, who was Jaruel's brother and Nat's great-great grandfather. She couldn't see her name juxtaposed to wherever Nat's name would be, how far apart, how many branches and limbs away in the tree was he? How did all these people in sparsely populated 18th and 19th century Maine find someone unrelated to marry? Maybe because everyone had litters instead of families. What was with William and Ruth? *Oh*—there's the other set of twins. But like with Jaruel and Catherine's twins, the mother wasn't a Marr—so twins aren't a hereditary Marr trait, just luck, or accident. Still, how did this Ruth get out of having more? Some of these women were still grunting out kids into their late 40's.

One-handed, Tam put her computer on the table on top of the papers. A droplet of thick white sputum had collected at the corner of the baby's mouth. His lips pursed and worked a little, his body stretched then relaxed into deadweight again.

dear martha, i don't have your last message in front of me so don't know if there was anything to answer. i have no free hand to hit the shift key so am forced to use this annoying email custom. but i still refuse to make the sideways smileface.

yes i saw the website. what can i say. do i even know g well enough anymore to know if he's cracked or that's just how he is or what he's become over the past 20 years? maybe that's too bad, that i don't even know my brother well enough to know if he's off the deep end. it's not an easy thing to rectify since drifting apart didn't 'just happen to us,' was caused by his same grotesque idea of interpersonal communication, so maybe what he's displaying now is more of the same, now that i think about it. he was just younger then and his weirdness not as developed.

imagine what it would be like to not know your brother for reasons outside your control. if he were taken away, or dead. i don't think of g as dead so the estrangement has never seemed tragic. i think seaborn's story involves estrangement of the more distressing kind, and i think it was probably unfortunate for others besides seaborn. if she did come back and drown herself in the 1930's. what more logical explanation for the nameless, family-less, pastless woman wandering down the old beach road to the lighthouse, resolved to throw herself into the sea? who else but seaborn? but why here? she had to have lived several decades somewhere else after leaving here.

so if she came back here to die, it was because her life's melancholy was here. but how could it be melancholy to be rescued from death and taken in by a large, dutiful, family, and one with lineage? a family still mourning the loss of a child.

did the marrs want seaborn? mother catherine already had another baby since j.thomas, another boy. likely her wound had healed enough that seaborn was not needed as a surrogate. besides, catherine was a besieged light-keeper's wife with a garden and animals to tend, meals to prepare with the roots she dug from the thin-soiled ground and the meat she hacked from carcasses she'd dressed. then clothes to mend and sew and knit and wash. floors and dishes, dirty faces and hands to scrub. her trips to the cemetery had grown fewer these past three years. suddenly an inauspicious late-season storm brings a new baby to tend as well? a baby not her own. was keeping seaborn even her idea? thankfully she had her older daughters, cedelia, mabel, and mary catherine. but cedelia was born before the war, before her father became light keeper, was 19 years old in 1875. wouldn't she be married and out of the house, likely having babies of her own? mabel, 4 years younger, soon to follow. so it was mary catherine, 7 years old. they'd all lost a brother but she'd lost a twin. still she was the one called upon to tend seaborn. to hold her, wash the rags they used for diapers, and feed her. how would they have done that, were there bottles with rubber nipples? had rubber been discovered? would she have to soak a rag in milk and guide seaborn to suck it? would she put tiny teaspoons of boiled cooled milk in seaborn's mouth? would they know to boil the milk? her brother had been an ebullient companion, equal opponent in racing and hiding games, equal cohort in sneaking tastes of molasses from the jug, equal shareholder of mother's attention when there was an adventure to recite or defeat to cry over, equal source of warmth in the child trundle bed they would have shared. In fact, might she not have been there with him when the tremors of death first rumbled inside him?

instead, a girl herself, she's given this helpless baby. removing mary catherine even from the world of her younger brother, lowell, closer to her age than seaborn, but she wasn't free to play with him, to roam the woods or rocky shore or explore the spooky echoey light tower. no time to join him when he fished or hunted or was given his own lobster pots to tend. he played alone or with cousins and second cousins. the island was full of marrs. why wouldn't mary catherine be resentful? so she didn't cleave to seaborn as a sister.

seaborn would have known. it doesn't make mary catherine bad. even as girls too young to comprehend adult remorse, they both built lives on sorrow, on loss. separate lives. i understand them both. but mary catherine is the one i see through now.

can you tell me how mary catherine died? did she ever marry?

also, what is a second cousin, and what is a first cousin once-removed?

oh i think you thought i might adopt a baby of my own? not now.

t.

It took two trips from the fog-bell structure to bring the baby back to his mother and her computer to the keeper's office so she could send her e-mail. (She tried computer under one arm, baby cradled in the other, but upon standing, her heart beat suddenly quicker, harder, and her head went light. She imagined herself stumbling, convulsing, dropping him.)

Jill was sleeping upstairs. When Tam put the baby down in the curl of her body, Jill closed around him like an anemone. The room smelled faintly, not unpleasantly, of sweat and milk. They planned to air it out that evening and again in the morning before the owner's friends arrived for their tour.

Tam filled a mug with the coffee she kept warm for Nat. She would have to make a new pot as soon as she sent her message to Martha. He still stopped for coffee twice a day at Barkin's store, saying they'd wonder where he was keeping himself if he didn't.

After the e-mail was dispatched, Tam noticed she'd also sent a message yesterday after reading the memoir Nat had given her, but had never checked for an answer from Martha. How many days had she been here? Three or thirty? The condensed daylight hours and extended hush of windblown night made every day a drawn-out morning or forever evening. Instead of returning to her webmail, she stopped at the family website. She'd never been very good using the track-pad to move a cursor instead of a mouse. Hand-eye coordination might be in the jittery part of her brain. It took three tries to hover the cursor onto Gary's

 Message **FRoM HELL**

you think i went to find Tam—
i went there to see Bill Kurtis—
the only one who understands
but he needs to say—
they're all over the place
tripping us choking our dogs
and no one notices them but me
and when i point they're gone

close my eyes— stumble over legs, feet, ears in piles
like leaves against a fence—
searching through moonless starless dark where hands
dangling down brush my face—
dew soaking my feet is blood—
every concrete hunk i step across catches my boot and
is a head i'm tripping over, falling face forward into the
agonized grimace—
Here, i scream, here and there and there— i point and
point, but there's nothing there.
he can't even smell them— his nose tough, crusty,
turned to parched rawhide—
he gags, coughs, can't smell—
bait my hook with fingers, cast out into the dusty sea,

reel in elbows, a knee—
sharks butt against the bottom of my board— they bob
to the surface, it's a shoulder, a ribcage—
swim through it, gary, swim to shore—
mark and fetch it, coach—
will he bring me a shredded half a face?
he's gone too. have to go look for him. go look
go look go look go look go look

Tam when you disappear I know what you're doing
i never told you, you wouldn't let me—
i was saving you from a world of heartache
but don't let this happen to us too
your not in the picture anymore
this much i can fix, this much i can save
save us, gary, save us
save this family we're becoming unbagged body parts

Her toes, then calves, then the muscles in her butt contracted. Not involuntarily. She squeezed her fists and flexed her biceps. But especially her gluteals. Flood the heart with venial blood that was languishing in extremities, have the lungs engorge it with oxygen, then back to the heart to be propelled to the swooning, precarious brain. Tingling, her fingers deftly put the cursor on another icon.

 ## Message from Mom

> Gary, please call. Your garage isn't big enough to store a boat. Where have you stored provisions and equipment for a sailing trip? Where's Coach? Did you take him to Chicago with you? When you see Tam, please bring her home for us. She needs you, Gary. We're counting on you.
> Love you. Mom

Tam left the website, went back to her e-mail and sent a postscript to Martha,

p.s. don't tell g i'm in maine.

The words seemed to quiver on the screen for a moment before disappearing, on their way to Martha, leaving Tam's heartbeat shuddering, too heavy.

By fall of her sophomore year, Tam and Denny had rearranged the swim team office so it could accommodate a mattress hidden behind a row of file cabinets. One of the first times they used it—still autumn, still warm outside and thrumming with air-conditioning inside—Denny had said, "I had lunch with your brother today. Mr. Sportswriter. I think he's happy. Or at least not circling-the-drain anymore over not making it to the Olympics."

"He can't even spell. You didn't tell him I'm here, I hope."

"Girl, I don't tell anyone you're here." He'd kissed her cheek, then behind her ear.

"Did he ask anything . . . about me?"

"Like if you'd joined the team?"

"Like that."

"Kind of."

"Don't tell me any more." She'd rolled to her stomach, her head resting on her crossed arms, face turned away from Denny.

"Anything the matter?" His hand passed up her back, under her shirt.

"How could anything be the matter while you're doing that?"

"Okay." His fingers traced a little more heavily around each bump of her spine. "But you know, this thing about swimming. Not swimming. I still don't get it."

"I hope you don't lose too much sleep over trying to get it."

"I just mean . . . wasn't it hard to give it up, to just quit?" Both hands now, he kneaded the skin and muscle over her shoulder blades.

"Harder than losing a . . . pet, I suppose. No, it wasn't like a pet. Harder than losing a leg. Like losing your favorite leg, your *best* leg."

"Not much world-class swimming without legs."

She rolled to her side, still facing away from him, and pushed her back and butt against him. "I like what I'm doing instead."

"What do you mean?"

Her hand on his thigh, "I have *your* legs instead. So . . . I think I'm over it now. Especially if I don't talk about it."

"Okay."

But lying there with Denny, his hand drawing lines up the two legs she did still have, she'd realized she'd spent less and less time picturing where she would be now, if she were still swimming; and that the times spent sleepless in bed—remembering the glass-shattering explosion of her body hitting the surface, the sweet burn in her lungs, the slick-solid feel of the pool's lip when she was the first to hit—were fewer. But she'd also been making excuses for not attending his team's early meets. Of course she'd never gone to any of Gary's college meets, and she'd also not ever gone back to attending any of Martha's meets. She hadn't been to one since she'd quit the team. But she'd been around the pool other times, usually timing Denny's laps, sometimes watching him teach a general-ed swim class that was part of his contract.

After she'd been with Denny for another year, he once suggested she change her major to phys-ed, then he could groom her to be assistant coach and maybe someday she could take over the women's team. She thought about that idea more than she'd realized at the time.

She left with Nat after dark, after supper. She'd wanted to make a slow-cooked beef stew, but the smell might have lingered too long. The owner's friends would be there around noon tomorrow. So she opened two big cans of chowder and made biscuits—from a refrigerator roll. No flour was kept in the pantry over the winter, Nat had said, because it was too difficult to hinder mice. Nat slurped loudly, looking over his spoon at Tam. Jill put a drop of milky chowder broth between the baby's lips. The teakettle screamed. Tam and the baby startled, then Tam got up to make tea while the baby cried.

"He don't like sudden noises, do he?" Jill cooed to the baby. "It woosily be so quiet here."

"Since babies aren't born knowing baby-talk from regular talk," Nat said, "why do people think they need to use baby-talk?"

"I guess it, like, lets everyone else know that *you* know you're, like, talking to someone who, like, doesn't understand?"

"What?" Nat laughed.

"Careful," Tam said, bringing the teapot to the table. "Maybe he does understand."

"Yeah," Nat said, "in some deep innate part of his brain, he'll know he spent his first weeks at a lighthouse. Maybe he'll be drawn to return here someday, not even sure why . . . or a hundred years from now, after he's dead."

"*Nat,*" Tam reproached.

But Jill was absorbed with trying to calm the baby's escalating wail. She touched another droplet of broth to his tongue and his face contorted further. "He be off to beddy-bye to get his num-num," she sighed, getting up.

When Jill was out of the room, Nat said, "At least she doesn't say *like* when making goo-goo talk at the kid."

"Just be glad she's doing such a good job."

Nat had pushed his chair from the table, grasped Tam's arm and tugged, more like invited her from her chair to his lap. She was still wearing the afghan around her shoulders like a shawl. He put a hand on each of her thighs, then clasped her hips, then one hand back on her arm. "You're all muscle and sinew."

"Life here is hard work. Even for women. No time to get soft."

"You hide your soft places. In layers of wool and buttons and snaps, and behind your stoic Mainer front."

"Who can I trust to strip it away—since I was 5 years old I've known the weight of loss, of no longer being heedless, of caring for others before myself."

"But now you're a big girl who knows what adds a ray of joy to her bleak world."

"Yes. He comes into my parents' house and repays their hospitality by taking their daughter's chastity."

"He can sneak her to *his* house—the biggest offering he has to propose."

"But he's not proposing."

"He can't. She's his cousin."

"Maybe once-removed."

"Nothing will remove that he can't."

The drive to Nat's house was all of ten minutes, but she lay on the bench seat, seeing only black branches of firs passing quickly overhead, between slices of black starless sky. His jeans and rubber boots smelled briny. The tires crunched and threw pebbles on the lighthouse's dirt road, then ran fat and tacky on the asphalt. The one stop was at the circle where the general store, post office and cafe would be dark now, at 7 p.m., feeling more like the hours after midnight. Then the truck turned and Nat's right hand left the wheel to rest on Tam's hip until he needed that hand to open his garage door. A dim light was on as he lowered the door behind the truck.

"It didn't have a garage," she said before sitting up. "I read your history thing."

"They tore down the barn in the 20's and built the garage. I installed a new door."

When Tam sat up, she saw her rental car parked beside Nat's truck.

The garage was behind the house. He took her hand and led her through the dark, through dead grass swishing at the hem of her skirt, over mushy leaves decaying into mud beneath her boots, around the side of the house to the front. Two big deciduous trees were dimly skeletal against the sky. She could hear water slapping pylons, a faint creak of rope, a remote buoy bell. Lights in other houses on the east side were visible, but the water was not. It was just there, somewhere in front of them. It was the harbor and was far more secure and subdued than the piece of open Atlantic intimidating the front of the lighthouse. Some darker hulking structures further ahead, also on the harbor, were the backs of the buildings on the wharf, the seasonal drygoods store and soda fountain where her mother had set the candlepins for bowlers on stormy summer afternoons.

"I wonder if we ever came this far down," she murmured.

"Excuse me?"

"The summer we visited here, I was going into ninth grade."

"You're not Mary-whoever anymore? You were here before, for real?" He squeezed her hand. "I used to come up in the summers, too."

"So we were here together—another time, for real. It was 1969."

"I would've been 18 and out all day checking traps. I got to work for one of the bigger lobstering fleets. I bought this house about twenty years ago and have worked for myself ever since, carpentry, care-taking summer places, my own traps, this and that."

"So you didn't live here then?"

"Not in 1969. Would I have noticed you?"

She dropped his hand. "You would have seen . . . I would've been . . ." She clasped the blanket tighter around herself. "You might've seen my brother. He rowed a boat all over the place. My sister was the one who loved the graveyard . . . then. And my mother . . . they all swam in the harbor. I would have been the one just standing there. Wishing I were somewhere else." She took a few steps into the front yard. "That's why I feel I know Mary Catherine."

"Not the shipwrecked orphan?"

"I'm not an orphan. I tried to pretend when I first . . . was diagnosed. Like Mary Catherine, I lost something that was part of me."

"What did Mary Catherine lose?" He stepped up behind her, surrounded her with his arms.

"That was her *twin* in the graveyard, J. Thomas . . . remember? Back when you found me there. How long ago was that?"

He seemed to be humming or moaning in her ear, before he said, "And how do we know it wasn't this Mary Catherine, the mystery woman, who came back in 1931?"

"I thought of that, but she died in . . . somewhere around the turn of the century."

"How?"

"I don't know." Tam stepped forward, and Nat moved beside her, one arm around her shoulders. "There are those songs about widows looking out to sea for years after their fishermen husbands were lost in storms." She stopped, her skirt catching on a bent tree stump. "But my branch of our family were the ones on shore, lighting the beacon, building the fire, launching the rescue boats, doing the saving, if anyone could be saved." She raised the afghan, displacing his arm from her shoulders, then settled the afghan over her head, wrapped the ends around her neck. "For them . . . us . . . calamity didn't come from the ocean."

He took her shoulders and turned her to face him. "Then why won't you come out in my boat?"

The tree stump snagged her skirt again. She tugged it loose. "You didn't ask what I lost."

"Got sidetracked by your seductive story. I assume you meant you lost someone."

"Yes, I did. But if you'd asked, I was going to tell you what I lost after I had my first seizure. The thing that made me special. The thing that was going to be my life. But I did, also, lose a . . . someone . . . maybe two someones . . . sort of . . . ."

They looked at each other, full in the eye, without moving, for longer than they had in any of the days she'd been there. Then he shook his head. "No, don't start. Let's not include real life. Don't ruin it." He smiled, laughed a puff of breath into her face. "I'm so turned-on right now. I reread that thing before I gave it to you, about my house, and thought of bringing you here, then could hardly stand it, I wanted it so bad."

Tam smiled, too. Her legs went weak. "Have you made many changes, or are you too sentimental about the past?"

"I'll show you."

"Where's the pampered pear tree?"

"There's the stump." He tapped it with one boot.

The first floor of Nat's house had been, like the lighthouse, opened up into one big room, kitchen on one side, sitting area on the other. His staircase leading to the bedrooms was in the middle of the back wall. Also like the lighthouse, the windows facing front were likely in the same place and were the same size the windows had always been, although now modern double-paned weather-tight windows with screens. But the windows to the west, on the side of the sitting area, were almost wall-to-wall, with no coverings. Unlike the lighthouse, the decor was wood paneling, knotty pine—walls, cabinets, window shutters, floors, furniture, a gentle gleaming swirl of woodgrain. The upholstery was dark green, the counter tops sage. In the daytime, light would brighten all the wood inside to the color of sunshine. At night, the window wall was black but the wood still gave back a darker version of the brilliance it must have enjoyed earlier.

In the middle of the glass wall, a slider, and outside the slider a wooden deck overlooking the tidal gut that ran along the house from the harbor. Nat was leading her through the room, holding her arm. The slider opened at his effortless push, like an automatic hospital door, and she stepped out. She smelled the briny gut, heard sighing fir trees, bubbling water, tink of a harbor buoy—no it was a windchime hanging from an open trellis overhead. She saw the steam rising from a hot tub built into the deck.

"Nat . . ." She turned to him.

He was unbuttoning his shirt. She raised her hand to stop him, but he caught her wrist, backed her up against the glass wall. "I just finished it. Be the first one in with me. Then I can say no one's been here before, because it'll just be a ghost, a memory of something that never happened."

"Nat, I don't want—"

"Please." He unknotted the afghan, her fists holding his wrists.

"Not here."

"I know, I'll break my window if I bang you up against it." He couldn't get the straps of her jumper down, couldn't unbutton the blouse underneath it. He lifted the skirt and found long underwear.

"No, I mean . . . not in the tub. I . . . please, no."

"Damn, woman, is this how they dressed? How did their men . . ."

Tam broke away, rolled sideways and went back into the house. She knew he would follow so she didn't look back and didn't hesitate, lifted her skirt and climbed the stairs, her boots resonant on the wood steps, his joining in cadence behind her. "As a girl, at the lighthouse, she would never have done it in a bed," Tam said. "But if Mary Catherine eventually married . . . even if he was her cousin, once removed or second cousin . . . they worked all day, then climbed the stairs to bed together. She carried a candle, the only light, and when they got to the bed chamber, he took her arm, drew the candle close and blew it out before they'd undressed. That's how she knew what he would do that night."

Tam entered the first bedroom she found and felt for the light switch. The room was only illuminated for a second before he reached past her and turned the light off.

The baby was peevish while they cleaned and aired out the lighthouse. Jill sour. Wanting to do a reckless job and go take a nap before the visitors arrived.

"You can sleep in the fog-bell house while they're here," Tam coaxed.

"Damn straight I will." She slapped at a windowsill with a featherduster. "Little punk barely let me close my eyes last night."

The kitchen had to look cold and untouched, no smell of coffee lingering, no sensation of oatmeal eaten there that morning. Tam sprayed disinfectant to clean the counters. Jill flipped a broom, grumbled "*yuk*" when she had to push a few damp cereal crumbs and raisins into the dust pan. The upstairs windows were left open all morning. The afghan replaced on the back of the sofa. Tam wore jeans and stowed her jumper with her luggage in the fog-bell structure. The baby's things stuffed in a bedroom closet.

It was a brighter afternoon than the day before. Jill lay on the single bed, the baby tucked in one arm beside her. Tam sat at the table in the fog-bell chamber. No one could stroll anywhere on Hendricks Head and be able to look into the chamber's windows, so Tam could gaze out. No boats were passing in Sheepscot River. Neon lobster trap markers and the red anchored buoy bobbed and tipped on dazzling whitecapped rollers. Even Sequin Light was distinctly a tiny white rectangle out on its rock island.

The baby fretted. Jill groaned but didn't move. Then muttered, "I'm so tired my teeth hurt."

The door to the lighthouse screen porch squealed, footsteps tapped on the walkway, voices buzzed, and Nat's voice answered, louder, "We can't see the fog-bell house today, I've had a painter working there and he took the key. I'll have to make sure he leaves it when he comes back to finish. The fog bell used to hang aloft—up there—but now the alarm is automated. Some years osprey have come to nest in the old bell scaffold."

A woman's voice, piping, laughing, and Nat's answer, "The Coast Guard knows when the fog is bad enough, they can sound the horn. All computerized. It sounds every Tuesday at 11, like how they do tests of air raid sirens. And sometimes the ghost makes it go."

Another laugh.

"No joke. She's seen here often. One time the door to the light tower slammed shut behind me—you'll feel how heavy that door is, we'll go on up there—but when it shut, somehow the latch swung back over the loop. I had to climb out that little window. Yeah, she came here and drowned in '31, before the light was decommissioned. So the first few years she would ring the bell. No wind, no fog, but the bell would suddenly toll, just once." The footsteps pattered again, his voice moved up the walk. "When it was automated and recommissioned in the 50's, there was no technology to remotely sound an electronic fog bell, except the ghost. *She* could. Sometimes she did."

Metallic clanks were Nat fumbling with the lock on the light tower door. "Put that rock there so she can't slam the door on us again." Tam could even hear, or thought she did, the muffled booms of feet stamping up the winding metal staircase.

The baby's whimpers shifted into the "hunh, hunh, hunh" before he would suck a load of air and let loose a real wail.

"No no no *no*, little boy, you've already sucked Mommy dry, *please* let me sleep."

By the time the feet boomed back down the light tower steps and the heavy door scraped shut, the baby was all-out crying.

"Quiet him," Tam whispered.

"I'm trying, can't you *see*?" Jill was finally sitting up, trying to jiggle the baby into surrender. "This is just so *whack*, hiding here in a stupid freezing-cold box on legs."

"What's wrong with you?" Tam hissed, but she didn't reach for the baby to try to do better at quieting him.

"*You* try this, it's not easy, I'm so tired I can't sleep. My body aches like, I don't know, I been *raped*."

"Stop being so melodramatic."

Outside Nat's voice rose, as though a volume knob had been turned. "Hear something? Yeah, like the wind is whispering when there's no breeze at all, a voice calling or crying, sure . . . any of those. She's always here. Sometimes she's silent or not in evidence for weeks or months. And the lighthouse is empty most of the year, how do we know she doesn't take human form and live inside . . ." The screen door squalled again, snapped shut, then the inner door to the lighthouse kitchen closed, and there was no more sound until the guests' car doors thudded, engine whooshed, and tires crunched the gravel road.

World of Women

Did it seem like Martha's answer took more days than usual? Or was Tam going to her e-mail less frequently? Or was the elapse of time normal, just drawn out by a 19th century pace?

Tam, your question about Mary Cath—you're not trying to think she was epileptic, are you? A woman her age, one would primarily assume childbirth. If not that, then TB or diarrhea (no kidding) or the flu.

About cousins—1st cousins have the same grandparents, their parents are siblings. 2nd cousins have the same great-grandparents, their grandparents are siblings. Cousins, whether 1st or 2nd or beyond, are in the same generation. Once-removed means removed from generation—mom's 1st cousin would be our 1st cousin once removed.

But remember, Tam, You were supposed to be checking Mary-Cath's birth records for me, to find out if her record is missing from wherever the other Marr birth records were archived. Now we know MC had a twin, possibly the pre-shipwreck dead Marr child referred to in the legend—so am guessing also no birth record for him. Why? Born at home, yes, but there are records for the others. If no birth records, also no death records? You're there, you can look for these things. Although right now they don't seem as important as when you decided to go look. A genealogist's focus has to only be on who survived—lived long enough to produce the next generation.

About G—sorry, I think mom may have already told him you're in Maine, in his private e-mail. But who knows if he's checking it.

-m

Instead of going with her own computer into the fog-bell house, where she usually composed messages before coming back to the phone line to send them, Tam stayed in the keeper's office and answered right away.

I'm not a genealogist. Won't be checking any archives. That would kill Mary Catherine.

She's struggling with her feelings about Seaborn. And with strange, quiet inner rage—suppressed, clamped tight, uncomprehended—at her younger brother. Maybe at two of her brothers, the younger and the one just ahead of her. The younger for his helping to heal their mother's heart. And because he was born with no knowledge of J. Thomas, her double, her sibling-partner. Lowell is blissful, ignorant, the beloved youngest. Mary Catherine seethes because Lowell's whole life was given to him. Her sisters and other brothers were too much older to grieve much about J. Thomas. Their lives given back to them. Especially Wolcott, only two years her senior. He could've—perhaps should've—been her confederate, but was already learning his trade as a lighthouse keeper. The loss of J. Thomas hadn't swayed that course. So no one can, or no one will share Mary Catherine's chronic lesion. No one knows how it feels to be given charge of Seaborn, who survived when she shouldn't have, delivered by Mary Catherine's parents from the frigid brine. Does Mary Catherine also resent her mother for letting J. Thomas die, perhaps in the dark of night, of a mysterious, violent apoplexy, but magaging to rescue Seaborn, then nurturing, loving Lowell? Did it seem to Mary Catherine that her mother set her aside when she set aside her grief over her twin and looked only at the developing futures of her living children? And so, perhaps illogically, she resents Seaborn.

So what would birth records tell me about anything? The who-cares of a date over one hundred years ago. Death records—no thanks, if it's going to be childbirth.

No mention of said child. It's too much to pile on Mary Catherine now, 16 or 17 and in love with her cousin.
oh never mind

She deleted everything and instead wrote:

Martha, Tell Mom thanks-a-lot. Is G going to show up at my door?

Which door would he come to? None were really hers. Nat had been taking her to his house for an hour or two these past few days. It was easier than trying to be discreet in the lighthouse. Jill staying up, sullenly watching late-night variety shows on the TV in the master suite. Anyway, Mary Catherine couldn't have partaken in trysts at home. Even if her father made the fog-bell structure into a bedroom, he would have given it to Mary Catherine's older brother Wolcott, already serving as assistant keeper—*he'd* be the one rising to sound the bell through a soupy mist. Then once married, whether to her cousin or not, Mary Catherine would no longer belong to the lighthouse, would live in a husband's hand-hewn dwelling. Unless the man she married could become the keeper. If someone produced a full family tree instead of Martha's genealogical list; if someone followed the descendants of Jaruel's brothers and sisters, would they find Mary Catherine cataloged there as a spouse?

So-and-So Marr (or Tanner?) m. Mary Catherine Marr (b. 1868, d. 1899)

Would there be a list of children? Five or seven? Or did the first one, coming too late in life, kill her?

Maybe before any covenant had been spoken between them, Mary Catherine's cousin had come of age to be on his own, had gone to work in the interior as a logger or to apprentice with an apothecary or, most typically, as a seaman. Mary Catherine would have stayed on at the lighthouse for several more years, seeming unmarriageable as she waited for the cousin no one knew she still clung to, until a local widower, perhaps with small children left motherless by typhoid or the flu, came to speak to her father. A man who worked the shipyard in Bath or lived upriver on the Sheepscot beyond the tidal influence, sent his apple crop to Portland on the steamers that came into Wiscasset. In the dark with him at night, lying still while he floundered with her flannel nightgown, she would be thinking of her cousin, wondering where he was, at sea on a merchant ship or trawling for cod off the coast of Canada, the ardent hands she'd known growing gnarled, freezing to ropes or rigging if it were February or March. Hearing the muffled knock on the door downstairs, while her husband huffed and heaved above her, of course her heart would keen for a second, supposing it's her cousin—he'd gone looking for her at the lighthouse and they told him where she'd been relocated. Then, cold and sticky, alone in the bed after her husband went downstairs to assist the neighbor who'd come to say his mare was in foal and needed assistance, Mary Catherine would remember a time she *had* used her brother Wolcott's room in the fog-bell tower to meet her cousin, and similarly someone had banged on the door—of course it would be Wolcott, come back to his room. The giggles and secretive rustlings would have made her brother turn, red-faced, and steal away.

Tam had never thought of anyone else when she was with Denny, so the knock on the door couldn't have been someone she wanted to be with instead of him. And it was Gary.

Tam hadn't slept in the fog-bell chamber because there was no heat, no light, no clock. But she'd been staying there later and later, waiting for Jill to drag herself back upstairs, feed the baby a final time and collapse in her unmade, clammy bed. This time, when Tam returned from Nat's house, she couldn't tell who was weeping softly in exhaustion, the baby or Jill. She'd checked the baby that afternoon while Jill napped on the sofa. He had good color and seemed plump enough, if a little gamy and crusty around the eyes and scalp. The baths Jill had performed morning and night had dropped off to every other day.

But Tam was too tired to wait for Jill and the baby to quiet down and go to sleep. She took the afghan from where Jill had left it balled on the sofa and retreated to the fog-bell house. She fumbled in the dark to remove her clothes, down to the thermal underwear she wore under her cotton jumper. On the internet that morning, she'd researched 19th century clothing. In the hour or less Mary Catherine might have had with her cousin, wherever they stole away, he would have to get through not only a wool or muslin skirt, apron, bodice and shirtwaist, but also maybe bloomers, a petticoat, a chemise that went to her knees, and long coarse-knit stockings. The long underwear was the best Tam could muster in duplication. Nat said he was going to get her some clothes, at least a long coat and pumps, so the next time guests came—he expected some in a another few days—she could dress as the Lady Ghost in vintage styles from the '30s and appear on the shore while they were up in the light tower.

That night in the fog-bell tower she dreamed of Denny. One of those dreams where she still works for him, has worked for him all these years, but no one has noticed that she hasn't been carrying out her functions because there are others working for him, many others, too many other people always around so she and Denny never have a chance to resolve what happened between them so many years ago and can only plug each other with sulky glances through the hustling crowd. Until the end of the dream . . . when he would finally be close enough, put a hand on the back of her neck, or wrap both arms around her from behind, his cheek against hers, some kind of pact gestating in the air between them, but nothing uttered aloud, and almost as soon as he was with her, he was gone, the whole scene evaporating as she woke sluggishly. The familiar intimacy of him still against her body, her brain struggling with how to make up for 25 years of detachment, of doing nothing—both in the office and with their connection, not even knowing what their connection is, unable to come up with a single word to define it. Then realizing she doesn't have to because there's nothing to define. Except the already decades-old estrangement.

As always, by the time she was unavoidably, undeniably awake, she was feverish from the effort to come back to herself, or the effort to *not* come back. Certainly, a form of the aura stage. She might stay in a stupid haze for hours, or all day.

And as though expecting a knock on the door, every creak or tick of the old house—ceaselessly adjusting to the wind or indecisive temperature—sent her eyes out the window to see if it was Gary skulking about.

It hadn't been difficult to surmise what Gary knew or guessed, the time his knuckles rapped on the coach's door when she was in there, with Denny, on the mattress wedged behind a row of file cabinets that made a false wall dividing the office. Tam hadn't ever gone to Denny's apartment at the beach. The office, a few motels, once or twice in the weightroom at night—that way it was easier for Tam to assert she'd been at school, in the library until it closed at 11. She still lived at home in college.

Three years before, the summer Denny had helped her slide away from virginity, Gary had finally moved out when he'd gotten his first sportswriting job, but he still came back with laundry most weekends. Tam would do her own laundry, with Martha's, early Saturday morning, so there'd be no possibility she'd end up folding Gary's undershirts and socks come Sunday. She'd moved into Gary's room, washed it—floor, walls, ceiling—with disinfectant. She'd wanted to switch Gary's mattress for her own, but couldn't do it alone. Her mother said "I don't think that's necessary." So she washed her own mattress cover in a double dose of bleach, flipped Gary's mattress and covered it. She put anything he'd left behind into boxes and threw them (not gently) into the basement. When Gary was in college, their father had hired a contractor to put a separate entrance onto the house, a door with its own concrete slab of stoop that ushered straight into Gary's room. The lock used the same key as the main front door, but still, Gary was afforded the right to come and go as he pleased, to get home late without waking them all with his heavy footstep through the kitchen. He'd been given their father's old Volkswagen when he was 18, and when he was 23, took it with him when he moved out. Tam had bought her own used Japanese compact with the money she saved from her job with Denny—her real paycheck, not the ghost work-study student's check that she used mostly for team expenses. But when she'd moved into Gary's room, their father had considered sealing the private entrance. "I'll get a locksmith next week to change the deadbolt." He'd already served four bowls of clam chowder from the tureen—the red Manhattan-style chowder that he preferred. Any Friday he was home, they had his clam chowder. The thick milky New England chowder was her mother's choice, which they had more frequently, but only when their father was out on the derrick.

"We need to know that you're home, safe," her father had said, after his first spoonful of soup. "You shouldn't be traipsing around."

"Why was it okay for *Gary*—?"

"Gary's a boy."

"So what? Does that mean—"

"It means a lot of things I think you know."

"You think a boy can't get into trouble?"

"Not the way a girl can."

"You're such a hypocrite, you were all for Title IX, but when it comes to *trusting* me—"

"Just simmer down, young lady."

For fear she'd have a seizure? She left the dinner table and tromped to her room—her old room. All her things were already in the new room. She sat erect, her back to the door, on her old bed, on the bedspread that matched Martha's. She didn't cry. She'd already learned the toe-curling, fist-squeezing, butt-tightening exercise for sending blood from her extremities back to her heart where it could quicker get up to her brain. And she presumed anger was dangerous. Frustration and anger combined even more so. Although she didn't yet know the extent.

The dishes and spoons continued to clink in the dining room. Voices murmured. Footsteps thumped into the kitchen and back. Tam finished her circulation exercises and was warm. She stared at the curtains her mother had made—patterned with fall leaves in every burning color—and thought about getting up to open a window, and wondered whether or not she would ever come and go that way, like kids did on television shows or the movies, meeting disreputable friends. But she wasn't a kid, and Denny wasn't a hippie or dropout or in a motorcycle gang—he wasn't someone who would throw rocks at the glass or tap the pane with a stick, although the phone was also not an option. Neither of them had to say anything to know that. A few times, in the decades after it was over, Tam had wondered about the built-in secrecy she and Denny had maintained. Was there such a thing as sexual harassment in those days? How far ahead of the times was Denny to worry about propriety in the workplace? Or was there an actual rule prohibiting faculty from intimate relations with students? That's possible too. Something neither of them had to articulate aloud, they both just knew. So she wasn't sitting on her tightly made former bed infuriated that Denny wasn't ever going to ring the doorbell and escort her to and from his car, but that her father would reduce her to using a window.

Tam didn't flinch when the door opened and Martha slid softly from the doorway to her own bed. "Did you forget where your new room is?"

"I guess I don't have a room in this house."

"You could come back in here with me."

"I'd rather move out of the house completely."

Martha's mattress squeaked a little. She started brushing her hair with the brush she kept on her bookcase headboard. Her hair was still long. Their mother trimmed the ends a few times a year. The brush in Martha's hair didn't sound like cracking fire or grass roots being ripped from the earth or tires on wet pavement. It was as almost soundless as a sound could be, and still be felt somewhere else, like Denny's finger on her leg.

Martha stopped brushing. "Remember when you and Gary used to have a secret club and didn't let me join?"

"No."

"Well, you did. Mom told me not to worry. That someday it would be like you and me were in a club, and Gary would be the outsider."

"That much came true."

"Yeah, it's good he moved out. He'll be easier to take in smaller doses." Martha's hairbrush clattered back onto her headboard. "Anyway, that was a good excuse to get away from the clam chowder I know you love so much."

"It was no excuse. It's not fair."

"Well, if you'd stayed you would have heard mom stick up for you. Dad's gonna leave the door."

And she'd never thanked either of them. The number of times in three years that she'd used the separate entry after nine o'clock was pathetically low anyway. But the Friday night three years later, in 1978, when Gary had come looking for her, she would have probably come home too late to use the front door, if he hadn't been so persistent with his interruption.

Tam and Denny had been just lying quietly on the mattress, one condom already spent an hour ago. A little before seven the phone had rung. Denny might have been asleep. He moaned, then neither moved, Tam counting the rings . . . seven, eight, nine. Several moments after the phone stopped, Denny murmured, "Who would call the office this late on a Friday?"

"Maybe it's our workstudy kid, wondering where his money is."

"He knows where his money is."

"No, the first workstudy guy who stopped coming. Maybe he finally came back."

"Why would he come back?"

"To get those first few checks we got before we had to invent a new guy."

"The new guy's real, too."

"Okay, maybe it's him."

"Not if he knows what's good for him."

Their whispered voices sounded little different than the sound of their movements against the old, thin sheets Tam had brought from home to cover the musty mattress. He began stroking her again. He touched her all over with his hands, his cheeks, the insides of his arms, his calves, his thighs. "You swim on me," she'd said once, so to tease her he'd caricatured various strokes, called it the 4x4 relay: *breast stroke* when his hands and mouth were absorbed there, *butterfly* when his hips and shoulders undulated, *freestyle* when he turned her over on her knees ("or is it the dog paddle?" he chuckled), and *backstroke* when he flopped to his back and invited her to straddle him.

They were probably up to butterfly or freestyle when the knock battered the door. They froze in the new silence. Then the pounding started again.

"Someone's obviously looking for you," Tam whispered.

"Maybe it's a custodian hammering something."

"Think so?"

"No. It's an asshole at the door." He heaved himself from the mattress, pulled on his shorts and golf shirt and went barefoot to the other side of the file cabinets. Tam curled in the sheet as though hiding, although she would be unseen even if the knocker came into the office, unless he craned to see over the file cabinets for some reason. But no one came in. Instead Denny went out. Tam heard the door shut behind him. He couldn't be pretending to be leaving the office and heading to the parking lot, not without shoes or socks, without his car keys and satchel. Voices resonated, low and slow, like faraway thunder, but not an argument or altercation, just two male voices in an empty hallway without any other workaday sounds to obscure them or make them as insignificant as they should be. Then the door opened and she heard Denny say "Okay, will do," before he was back inside, the door shut behind him, and a few seconds later was squeezing past the last file cabinet and sliding onto the mattress. He got back under the sheet with Tam, held her like a stuffed bear, but he didn't remove his clothes.

"Who was it?"

"You don't want to know."

"Why? What did he say?"

"It was your brother."

"To visit you?"

"No. He didn't say much. He wanted to know if I knew where you are."

"Did you tell him?"

"Yeah, I said we were in here fucking like bunnies."

"Really?"

"Sure. Didn't you want him to be first to know?"

"You didn't really tell him, did you?"

"No. I said maybe you were at the library."

"Did he leave?"

"Yeah, but we should be quiet for a while, in case he comes back and listens at the door."

So they were silent. The building after hours had that plugged-ear feeling of mute throbbing. But they were able to be silent together, without an awkward need to fill their shared space with the distraction of chitchat. So it wasn't surprising to Tam that Denny asked no questions. He'd never even said, "Tell me what happened between you and your brother." If he had, the answer, if she answered, would have seemed so frivolous. If it was even one thing, or a list, or something she could specify. It was just *Gary*. And that was no explanation. Except to her, and maybe Martha.

The phone rang again.

After the second ring, Denny had said, "This can't be good." He got up to answer. All he said was "Yeah" when he picked up the receiver, then "Okay," several times, but never said goodbye.

"My brother again?" Tam came from behind the file cabinets, the sheet around her shoulders, trailing behind her.

"Yeah." He'd held her, put a hand on the back of her head like cradling a newborn's flimsy neck. "You have to go. Your father . . . Gary said your father died."

Tam jerked back from the embrace. "What *exactly* did he say?"

"Tell Tam our father died and she should get her ass home." His wrists were on her shoulders, his hands on her neck, fingers in her hair.

Her palms were flat against his chest as though she was struggling to get away. "It's a trick. It's Gary . . ."

"You'd better go and find out. What if it isn't?"

"What if it *is*?"

"If it's a trick and you go, that's better than if it isn't and you don't go."

She'd gone home, and it wasn't a trick. Which made it almost a trick, if she could have accused Gary of killing their father so that he could track her down with Denny in his office.

But all that nearly forgotten upon sight of her mother's pale, drawn face. No red lipstick, no upside-down smile. And Martha's puffy, slimy face in their mother's lap. The rest of Martha sprawled on the sofa beside where their mother sat. Tam, kneeling in front of the sofa, stared at her mother's hands smoothing Martha's hair over and over. Martha's eyes were closed, face contorted, more tears oozing out from between her lashes, while their mother's shaky, weak voice recited the facts. Their father had suffered a fatal heart attack out on the derrick that morning.

They'd called for a helicopter and flown him to a hospital in Long Beach, but it was too late.

"He was under a lot of pressure lately," her mother continued. "He felt badly for not being here more, but he hoped you would be proud of him for what . . . what he was doing . . . going through."

"What was it?" Tam whispered, still staring at Martha's closed eyes. Martha was no longer convulsing with silent weeping.

"Something the oil company was doing that they shouldn't . . . weren't supposed to do . . . he reported to the EPA. They couldn't really out-and-out fire him, but they stopped giving him any assignments. Other people were there doing his work. But he had to keep going out to the derrick on schedule, or they'd use that as an excuse to fire him. He had to be there . . . three weeks at a time . . . no one speaking to him, no work to do. A whistle-blower . . . they tried to intimidate him. Other ways. He had to just ignore. . . all of it. It was hard for him. He wanted to tell you all, when it was finally over . . . how he was doing the right thing."

"Did they . . . " Tam swallowed, tried to prevent her breathing from growing more labored. "Maybe they . . . killed him . . . and made it . . . look like . . . natural."

"No, Tam." Her mother reached for her face, but Tam rose to her feet. Actually she was helped to her feet. Gary was gripping her arm. She jerked herself free, tried to ignore him.

"Go get yourself something to eat," he said.

"I'm not hungry."

"Then go get Mom some tea."

"It's not necessary," their mother said, but Gary was holding Tam's arm again, pulling her toward the kitchen.

"Fuck *off*, Gary," she hissed.

Gary turned the water on and started filling the kettle. Tam turned to leave, to return to her mother and Martha, but Gary said, "That's a grand thing to say to Mom. Where were *you?*"

"None of your business. I was at . . . having dinner." She stopped in the doorway but didn't turn around. "Denny knew where I was having dinner and came to tell me."

"*Denny*? You mean Coach Clarkson?" The water stopped. "That was pretty quick—he got to where you were supposedly having dinner pretty damn quick." The kettle clanked onto the stove.

"Because he's my employer . . . he always knows where I am . . . because in case I have a seizure, they have to call him."

"That's crap. Go take a shower." Water on the bottom of the teakettle hissed as the burner heated up. "How long d'ya think he'll keep it going with you if people started to know?"

"Eat shit."

More guests were coming to the lighthouse. Nat had brought a long rain-coat, a straw hat and scuffed brown pumps from the Salvation Army. "The ghost will just appear on the rocks and walk away," he said. "Then I'll get rid of them and come find you." He looked around the kitchen and sitting area. "But clean up again. I can smell baby. Open every window this afternoon. What's wrong with the little mother lately?"

"I don't know. Post-partum depression? Or teen angst."

"Bad combination. Someone might get murdered. Have you thought what you're going to do about her? I mean, another month is about all we can have here."

"I haven't thought that far ahead."

"Well . . . good, don't try to figure it out now. First things first."

"The guests."

"The ghost." He leered but didn't touch her. "I won't be by tonight. Tomorrow morning, around ten? Stay in the fog-bell house. When you hear us go into the light tower, come down. Walk at the water line, going around toward the north. It'll be low tide."

At one, after she'd cleaned the kitchen, Tam had to go wake Jill. She made sure the baby was covered, then opened all the windows in the fetid dormer and pulled the covers away from Jill's frowzy body.

"Go away, my teeth hurt," Jill groaned, grabbing for a sheet down by her feet.

"No, we have to clean and air the house."

"*Again?*"

"It's sort of like washing your hair. Once in a lifetime is never enough."

"Bite me."

The baby woke and cried, not very loud.

"Is he okay, is he getting enough to eat?" Tam asked, gathering the sheets in her arms. "Are *you* eating enough?"

"He gets everything I've got. C'mere, little man, shut up, okay?" Jill still didn't get up, but pulled the baby close and kissed his head.

Tam pushed the sheets into one of the pillowcases. She couldn't do a wash until after the guests were gone, or they might detect the humid, soapy smell. Everything had to be cold and stale. She found clean sheets in a drawer in the master suite.

"It's getting too cold in here for him," Tam said. "Take him . . . I don't know, I've got all the windows open everywhere."

"Why do they have to be allowed up here anyway?" Jill finally sat up, holding the baby. She was, as usual, only wearing underwear and one of Nat's undershirts. Now her hair was probably real bedhead and not some kind of bedraggled-chic style. "He has to eat, could I have some privacy?"

"Since when have you been modest?"

"I guess I don't have a room in this house, do I?"

"None of us do, honey." Tam wondered when before she'd ever said *honey*. Chilly, brackish air puffed through the windows. "Keep him warm."

"I *know*." Jill took the baby into the bathroom and shut the door.

Tam finished the cleaning herself, then carried the pillow cases stuffed with dirty sheets up to the fog-bell house. Another trip for the garbage sack of dirty diapers Nat would have to haul away at night. She wanted to go for a walk, or sit by one of the open windows, but someone might see her. Lobster boats were slightly more numerous every day, which meant *one* might be in the Sheepscot inlet, but one was enough. Mary Catherine, on a rare afternoon with nothing to do, might take Seaborn for a walk the mile or two up the beach road to visit her brother's plot in the graveyard—of course she wouldn't have to hide if she left the house, and could have gone for a walk anywhere during daylight. But if Mary Catherine had an idle afternoon, and the bad luck for it to happen on a day when her cousin was out placing his early spring traps, she would stay at the lighthouse, would wander from window to window and up to the tower looking for his dory in any of the coves around the head-land. Not seeing him, she might flip through the last reader she'd finished before leaving 8th grade, or bake a special loaf of cinnamon bread for her cousin (with no worries of the scent lingering in the air). She might work on a pair of mittens she was making for him, or the multi-colored scarf she was knitting for his birthday, or she might write a letter to one of her married sisters.

March 28, 1885. Dear Mabel, The sun came out today, but still blowing cold off the water. Mother and Father are into the harbor to see about the Pierces' heifer they've got up for sale (and no doubt checking to see if anyone's brought a catch into the pound). They'll likely be stopping at the cemetery on the way home. Perhaps foreseeing my melancholy, Mother took the little girl with her today. The girl doesn't seem as happy here as she should. After all, didn't Father and Mother give her a place to grow up? She's ten now and finally has daily chores, as she should. Today I've hung the winter bedding to air. Too early, you'll say, but you know I could never wait for spring. Always anxious to get past the last of March and on into April. March never had anything good to offer, as you'll recall. Wolcott's taken on the full job of assistant keeper now, but we hear he may be off soon to Two Lights or Cuckolds, to his own post. Hattie likely can hardly stand the waiting as it would mean a wedding date. Lowell shows no signs of deciding on one thing over another. Hunting, fishing, lobstering, trapping, playing with balls, they are all the same to him. Mother says the baby gets to play the longest. Cousin Nahum (Aunt Mary Jane's younger boy) is here often to help. I know the fishing fleet has a strong call to many a young man, yet it is our hope that he'll want to learn the post of assistant keeper when Wolcott moves to his new station, and Father may make over the fog-bell house for the new assistant keeper's quarters. His smile seems to brighten my gray days this time of year.

Tam went down to the keeper's office with her laptop, thinking she had time to write a longer message to Martha. But first she had to get Martha's latest reply, one that had been waiting a few days.

T-
i put some of my history thing about mom on the website,
a revision of what i sent to you before.
(i'm hoping g will see it and be pleased i'm finally using

the site, or maybe mad i stole his research for his book about mom. either way, maybe he'll come home or at least call). here's the url, you can go directly:
www.marr-burgess-family.net/fam-hist
hey what about those archives? what've you been doing? you ok? maybe g's there with you now?
-m

 Read Portions of Martha's Family History

A World of Women

During the war, while Emily Marr was still in high school, there were few young men who weren't occupied with military training or duty or already overseas. One summer when she was in high school (around 1945), Emily and an older cousin went to stay for a month with her Grammie Marr in Maine. [This was Lighthouse Keeper Wolcott Marr Sr.'s wife. Mom's summer visits to Southport were long after he was dead.] Emily was told secretly by her Grammie Marr that her cousin had been sent to Maine for the summer to get her away from a boy she'd gotten "too involved" with. Emily was given the covert duty of staying with her older cousin and watching over her to make sure she didn't try to "get mixed up with" boys on the island that summer, as well. They swam and sailed and went to dances at the Pavilion near the bridge to Boothbay. On rainy days they bowled duck pins at the general store in Cozy Harbor, where there was also a soda fountain and the local kids would be there. One time Emily and her cousin sailed a dory from Hendricks Head across the Sheepscot inlet to Five Islands, a tiny lobster fishing port. They had a beer (Mom was only 15 or 16 years old!) on the wharf and could see the light at Hendricks come on at dusk, but the light faded as a fog started rolling in, so they left. With no compass and no visibility, the tide pushed them off course and they missed Hendricks Head. Luckily they hit Southport further south, left the boat moored on some rocks, and walked through the fog back to their grandmother's house near Cozy Harbor.

Early Feminist

Walter Irving, Emily's paternal grandfather, had left his lobster importing estate in trust to be used by his grandchildren to go to college—amazingly *all* his grandchildren, not just the boys. So Emily Marr Irving attended a private girls' college dedicated to physical education and physical therapy. Summers, Emily worked as a lifeguard at swimming pools in Boston or Cape Cod, and, during her visits to Maine, as pin-setter in the same general store in Cozy Harbor. Emily would sometimes hitchhike from Cape Cod to Southport, (and, over Christmas breaks, to ski areas in Vermont and New Hampshire). The college also required a summer session so the students could complete their outdoor field and water sports requirements. Emily and her classmates had to learn to maneuver several different water craft, including rowboat, canoe, single scull, double scull, coxed four- and eight-woman sculls, and a sailboat with jib and mainsail. Besides swimming all the strokes and the lifeguard techniques (which she already knew) Emily learned four kinds of dives: swan—frontward and back, and single pike, frontwards and back.

Early Civil Rights Activist

Emily's group of friends at college included two Black girls, and in the late '40s at Sargent College, the Black girls—girls who attended the same classes, swam in the same pool, played on the same teams—were housed separately. The group wanted to stay together at the summer sailing camp, so Emily and a friend went to the dean to request permission for the Black girls to bunk in their kiosk. The dean gave a (now) familiar and bogus rationale for the school's policy, that "they" would be much more comfortable if housed separately. No, Emily explained to the dean, they want to be with us. No strikes, no sit-ins or protests were needed. The dean relented, and the college's segregated housing policy was suspended that year.

Martha,

Just like you've been researching Mom's life your own way (and how dubious is G's interpretation?), I've explored Mary Catherine my own way (No archives.). She was alone in that family. Just looking at the birthdates—the two sisters 8 and 11 years older than her, married and on their own by the time Mary-C was out of little girlhood. Wolcott was a mere 2 years older, but boys grew up quicker then, he had his life's work already stretched before him, and we all know a girl was relegated to the home. By the time she was 13 or 14, her time to venture into the woods or row a dory among the islands in the harbor was over. And Wolcott, 15 or 16, is already going about a man's life—a life of purpose, aspiration and vigor, where he'll guide and rescue people at peril—what use did he have for a younger sister, perhaps a sickly one? No one noticed her habit of keeping vigil by the window at night, when it was foggy and the in-coming ships would need the salvation of the light. Any thought he has for a girl of a year or two younger would be the one he plans to marry. Or if his sister's life crossed his mind at all, it might be to thwart attentions she receives from boys her age. (Can you imagine a certain brother doing something like this? I can.) As far as Mary Catherine's younger siblings, there's only the baby brother Lowell, 4 years younger. He's still a 10-year-old dragging mud into the house when Mary Catherine's 14—the one who sweeps and scrubs. Still carrying his arithmetic and reader to the schoolhouse, still being sung to in bed. Mother hasn't had to tear her attention away and give it to any new little one. Except there's Seaborn, 7 years younger than Mary-C. Maybe father had said, "God brought us this baby to make up for taking J. Thomas," but secretly Mother knew Lowell was her bequest for giving up J. Thomas to God. An impish little boy like J. Thomas had been, into everything, bringing pranks and giggles back into the lighthouse, and mother did smile, and began to more frequently laugh. The two somber girls, Mary Catherine and Seaborn, are left, one to care for the other without choosing to. Perhaps no one wonders why Seaborn has little laughter in her, and likewise why Mary Catherine couldn't set aside her babyhood grief over losing her twin. They're merely adopting the doleful countenance of an adult wife, like their widowed Aunt Mary Jane Marr Pierce, who Mary Catherine had spent much time with, helping to sew and mend. The girl cousins at the Pierce home likewise already wore the morose expression of widows. But, more importantly, and perhaps inspiring Mary Catherine to more frequent visits, there were boy Pierce cousins as well. An older boy who'd taken over as patriarch when his father died—became the man who ran the lobster traps and snared the fur for trade, a man whose supper is placed before him the moment he comes in and sits himself at the table, whose clothes are taken from him and hung to dry, whose boiled wool mittens are inspected and mended before he can put them on again. But the younger teenaged boy at Aunt Mary Jane's house, Nahum, wasn't expected to become a man so soon. Like Lowell, the Marr's youngest, Nahum's boyhood was preserved, yet still, he would have chafed at his brother's place of deference among the girls, while he's merely the one asked to fetch water, to fetch firewood, to seal the windows with scraps of wool. But Nahum's cousin Mary Catherine Marr, near his own age, maybe born the same year, would have quietly come to take his mittens, help him shuck his boots, even peel the wet wool socks from his feet. Little does she know, while father and mother are in Cozy Harbor this day, or some other day, they'll meet a man, a widower from Sheepscot who's come to the island to visit his brother, a shopkeeper or minister, someone father and mother know and have reason to visit. The widower is interested in finding a second wife.

T

Tam stayed online, glancing first at her crestfallen stock portfolio, then began to research wedlock in the 19th century. Her searches—"marriage in the 1800's," "marriage and engagement in the 19th century," "history of courtship and engagement"—kept producing lists of canned essays for sale to high school and college students, mostly about *Pride and Prejudice*. Nothing to help better interpret Mary Catherine's family. "Arranged marriage in the 1800's," and "attitudes toward spinsterhood in the 1800's" brought little except more school essays for sale. But one attempt on the search (she didn't remember which key words) produced a long rejoinder on a genealogy newsgroup discussion about the history of first cousin marriages and laws that prohibited them.

> After about 1850 an intolerance toward first cousin marriage arose in American. Prior to 1850 first cousin marriage was not uncommon, but the occurrence of first cousin marriage in the United States began to diminish in the second half of the century and many states began making laws against it. Marriage among cousins became equivalent with vulgar and uncivilized behavior.

Over an hour had passed. The incoming-mail tone interrupted. Martha had already answered.

> tam, i don't know where to start. i'll get to your strange letter in a minute. first about gary. mom got a weird message from him. i can't remember every word. something about _the water babies_, (that story mom used to read to us. i brought that copy I found to show mom and i think he took it). he said his naughtiness would come out in prickles all over his skin, he would be marked, so no one could hug or touch him. that word i do remember, naughtiness, because it's not a gary word. then he said it's his inadequacy, his failing, his ineptitude. words like that. so mom and i went over to his house. finally talked her into using her key. no smoking gun but what a mess. needless to say, no boat being prepared for a cruise. looked like a robber ransacked the place, except things like tall piles of pennies and dimes and nickels lined up on the kitchen counter. the phone machine had something like 23 messages, capacity filled. mom didn't want to listen but i said we had to. again nothing to directly explain what's going on. people wondering where he was. but

several, some of the earliest ones, from a vet. saying they needed to discuss some possible treatments. later asking if he was coming back for his dog. did your roommate happen to mention if he had coach with him?

now tam, about you. what's going on? I know you're not in a library researching life in the 1800's. so where'd you get this stuff about boiling wool mittens and that old-fashioned accent you're slipping into? and you can't possibly know how anyone felt about anything. maybe i'd better fill you in on a few facts: the lighthouse was replaced and completely rebuilt in 1875. that's the same year as the storm with the shipwrecked baby. the family moved into the *new* lighthouse in sept of that year. so the family would have been living in the marr house in cozy harbor during the storm. of course jaruel would have still been keeping the light, camping out in the unfinished new quarters, so the rescue *could've* still happened. but i just got that 2nd article by that historian in boothbay. she had some other reasons to prove the legend wasn't true. she found this novel published in 1900 that contained a shipwreck story on southport island—a baby floating ashore between mattresses, rescued by the light keeper, the whole same thing. so she says the legend is really a passed-around retelling of the novel's plot, retold and retold until people began to believe it was a true story they were telling.

but tam, regardless of how or why the legend got started, how much truth there is, please try to realize, there's no evidence the family ever adopted any child! even if there was a storm, a shipwreck, a rescued baby— i said IF—the marrs had six children already! why would they keep her? she could've easily been adopted by someone else on the island or jaurel marr took her to a doctor who might've known of some other couple who'd recently lost a child. i know you want to relate to this shipwrecked child adopted into the family, but, please, this thing with g is enough for us to handle right now. we need you to keep a steady head. come home. or no, wait there and see if g finds you. then come home.
-m

Martha,
Why couldn't it be the other way around—the novelist
heard the legend then used it to write his book? And it's
turned out that Mary Catherine is the one I understand.
Perhaps through her, I'll see Seaborn. (Can you tell me
anything about second marriages in the 1800's. under
what circumstances were such marriages ever arranged
by parents?) Must run. T

She didn't know where she had to run. Still an hour before she would
heat canned food for supper, then the slow evening still stretched in front of
her, with no visit from Nat that night, no drive to his house near the harbor,
no climb up the shadowy staircase to dark bedrooms on the second floor.
Anytime she looked, she could see the two forms ascending the stairs, hard
heels hitting the raw wood, her step lighter, his heavy, not in unison, not in
rhythm. At the top, one of the bedroom doors is open, framing a window
illuminated by the moon, and the woman stops, silhouetted in the doorway.
Undoes her hair, flings her head so the heavy reddish wave sways from one
side to the other, her arms up to push thick locks out of her face. The man
moves toward her, but she shuts the door. One hand on the knob, he raises
the other, but doesn't knock. Palm flat on the door. He says, "Good night
then." His voice gruff, embarrassed . . . angry? Mary Catherine knows
she'll have to submit to the widower soon. Not a widower any longer—her
husband. Her cousin hadn't answered her frantic letters, begging him to
come back to forestall this marriage. It's been a year, maybe two or three,
since Mary Catherine has been left with only one staid brownish photograph of her cousin in his new seaman's garb, and his laughing imprint in
her memory. His buoyant face and crooked smile are Denny's. And Mary
Catherine, silhouetted in the moonlight, looks more like Meryl.

She went back online, but in a few minutes the baby began crying
and didn't stop, and was loud enough that she knew Jill had him downstairs. So Tam saved the search results for "The Water Babies" and left
the lightkeeper's office. Jill was on the sofa, her feet on the cushion and
knees drawn toward her chest. The baby was propped on her thighs, so
the two would have been facing each other, except the baby's eyes were

squeezed shut as he cried, and Jill's head was thrown over the back of the sofa, eyes staring toward the ceiling.

"Is he okay?" Tam asked.

"Ask him." Without looking at the baby, Jill put a hand softly on the baby's head. "I think he's hungry."

"Should you drink some milk or eat some yogurt?"

"We don't have any."

Tam got a glass of water and brought it to Jill. "Here, at least stay hydrated." Tam sat on the arm of the sofa while Jill drained the glass, then slid off the arm and sat beside her. Their shoulders touched. The baby, still crying, was also going to sleep. "Seems more like a poor imitation of crying, now."

"That's the sign of a bad actor, can't even make you believe what he's *really* feeling."

"Are you making me believe what you're really feeling?"

Jill rolled her head sidewise to look at Tam. She didn't even seem startled at how close they were sitting.

"This reminds me," Tam said, breaking her gaze from Jill's puffy, listless face and focusing instead on the baby. "I remember when I was 8 or 9, my sister and I were settling on either side of our mother on the sofa where she used to read to us. She had two sides, so there was room for both of us to see the pictures, but my mother sort of pushed me away and said 'you're getting too heavy to lean on me like that.'"

"Nice."

"Did your mother read to you?"

"I don't remember."

"It's a lot closer memory for you than for me." The baby was asleep, and Jill's eyes were closed. Her hair was matted to her head, pushed forward on one side, standing straight out sideways on the other. "I still remember some of the books she read to us. She read to us even after we could read them ourselves. Sometimes our older brother yielded his superiority and sat in the room to listen. *The Wizard of Oz*. The real book, not the movie. *The Yearling. Black Beauty.* And our favorite was *The Water Babies.* Maybe because we were all on a swim team." The baby made a shaky sigh and Jill echoed it, smiling slightly. Tam continued, "It was about a poor orphan who escapes harsh child labor in 19th century England, is turned into a water-dwelling nymph with gills, living in the beautiful land of underwater where all the water babies have as many sweets and hugs as they want, and do nothing all day but play, no brutal masters to serve."

Sailors probably didn't read much, if at all, but easily a captain or first mate could have picked up the book in England, while serving on a cross-Atlantic vessel. Then, coming home on one of the smaller ships that brought goods from Portland and Boston, making stops in Wiscasset and Boothbay, the book made its way to Maine. Maybe old Hiram Marr who died at sea—when his duffel was unpacked, there was a copy of *The Water Babies*, brought for his son or daughter or favorite niece. Then passed around among the family, possibly Mary Catherine found it in a trunk that stored her cousin's dead father's clothes, when she went there to find a shirt to make over for him. (Why would this dead uncle have saved a book? Perhaps a long-forgotten Christmas surprise for one of the daughters, those dreary girls who would view a fanciful moral tale as useless rubbish.) So the book ends up in the lighthouse. In Mary Catherine's room that she shares with Seaborn. And at night before sleep, she reads to Seaborn, the tale of Tom the chimney sweep who learns how to be good, and how to be clean, by living underwater as a nymph, enduring punishments like the prickles all over his skin for stealing the sweets he would have gotten anyway, if he'd just waited and stayed good. This was one of Mary Catherine's defects of character, that she would read such a story to Seaborn, who could have lived the last of her short life underwater if she hadn't been washed ashore in the mattress. But perhaps Mary Catherine didn't slyly take the book out and call to Seaborn to come hear the story with any plan that it would astonish Seaborn into tears. When the little girl gulped back her terrified memory of being pitched into the turbulent ocean—an image of something she couldn't actually remember, but perhaps was often told of, by Mary Catherine—Mary Catherine would have stopped reading. Would have understood.

Would have also remembered her cousin, Nahum, and how she'd let herself imagine serving with him to light the way for lost or imperiled mariners. Instead, at that moment, he was conceivably on the salt-washed bow of some vessel too small for the squall it had encountered off the coast, and there hadn't been any letter from him. The photograph she keeps was one he'd sent to his mother. (That black-clad woman thinks she tucked the photo into her leather trunk.) Now as Seaborn looked at Mary Catherine gravely, with eyes too-large and too-dark to belong to this family—and as Mary Catherine began to conceive her cousin's playful hazel eyes lost inside a storm-ravished seaman's slicker hood— Mary Catherine's head went light, and her sight was washed in white spots, a shudder stiffened her body for just a second, the book fell from her hands. The next thing she discerns is Seaborn's voice calling to her from far away, softly, as though not wanting anyone else to hear her call, holding Mary Catherine's hands and pressing them to her own face. Mary Catherine raised her head and the last spots swam away, her jaw began to ache and her fingertips to tingle. Seaborn, still clutching her hands, watched her come back. Perhaps, in that moment they became sisters.

Jill was asleep, her breathing slow and deep. Her head had rolled to one side, away from Tam. Her astonishingly white ear with five small hoops seemed naked, revealed. Tam eased herself off the sofa, then brought the afghan in from where it had been airing outside and covered Jill's lap, including the baby, also asleep, drool oozing down his neck.

> Martha,
> I sent that last message by accident before I finished it. I was saying that I don't strive to unite myself with Seaborn, except that through understanding Mary Catherine, I can get close to how Seaborn might've lived, what she thought and felt, and what might've happened to her. I understand that it could have been Mary Catherine's one big weakness that she didn't, for a long time, let Seaborn feel wanted and welcomed. She was the one person who probably *could* have helped Seaborn feel included, needed. And then she finally did, in her own way. When at some point, through understanding Seaborn's experience—being one whose rescue meant the loss of ever knowing who she was, who she'd been meant to

be—Mary Catherine realized she always had possessed an aspiration to share in the noble work of the keeper of the light, realized it when it was no longer possible.

Your reference to The Water Babies (or G's reference) reminded me, so I looked it up. The author died in 1875. Maybe while a storm far across the Atlantic from his home in England bruised the coast of Maine, and a real waterbaby was being tossed from the sea. (Play Twilight Zone music here.) Do your children like it? I mean, has it lost whatever zing it held for us, with a new generation more enthralled by child warlocks and galactic combat?

T

After eating mushroom soup (which did claim to have some cream) Jill was able to feed the baby, and they both immediately went upstairs to bed.

The next morning at 9:30, Tam changed into her jumper, with nylons she suspected Nat had pilfered from Sara's bureau. She wore a sweatshirt under the jumper because the raincoat wasn't very thick. But the coat covered everything anyway, and came down to her calves. So, along with the straw hat and pumps, her silhouette could pass for 1930s vogue.

She changed in the fog-bell house, Jill and the baby curled together on the bed. Jill's eyes were closed, or they could have been slits, observing a dim, blurred image of Tam attiring herself in the absurd outfit. But, even if she were watching, Jill didn't ask any questions. Tam sat at the little desk, no mirror in front of her, no laptop beneath her fingers, just the bare wooden table. Just the sound of water washing the slippery rocks around the head, the dull bell on the red channel buoy, the velvety whisper of breath from the bed behind her. Finally tires on gravel. Thumps of car doors.

"There's your cue," Jill murmured.

"Pardon?"

"Is it *ever* worth it?"

"Excuse me?" Tam was standing. The light from the window didn't quite reach the narrow bed. But she could see Jill was sitting up now, leaning against the wall.

"You know, doing, like . . . *whatever* will get a guy turned on."

"Courtship is mutual, isn't it?"

"Courtship?" Jill snorted softly. "Yeah, what-*ev*. Mutual. Then look what happens." The baby was anchored in Jill's arms. "Does it always stay mutual?"

"That's an old story, honey. You think you're the first one?"

"Do *you*?"

"I'm hardly likely to get pregnant."

"That's not all. I mean. . . Like, it's more than that. Look at us, we're like. . . like we're not anywhere. I mean like no one cares where we are."

"Someday you may wish that were true."

"Whatever."

Voices began to seep from the house's back porch. Tam put her hand on the doorknob. "Can you stay up here until I come back?"

"Whatever."

"Get under the blanket if it gets cold." The boom of the light tower door signaled Tam had to go. She hurried down the ramp from the fog-bell house, then turned sharply away from the lighthouse and tower, down toward the rocks under the fog house where the timbers were anchored. By the time Nat and the guests were at the top of the tower, scanning the horizon, Sequin Island and the Georgetown Peninsula, Tam was picking her way carefully, dreamily, along the rocks near the water's edge. One hand on her hat, eyes alternately out to sea or downcast toward her feet, wrapping the raincoat around her body as spray doused her hem and stockings. She couldn't hear Nat's feigned gasp, nor his breathless exclamation to his guests, his hoarse, hushed re-telling of the Lady Ghost of Hendricks Head who had her own veiled reason to come back here to drown, but not to sleep in perpetuity underwater, instead to roam the shoreline forever in search of something. Something she may have never had in the first place. But, for her enigmatic reasons, thought might have been here. Might be here still.

Tam followed the curve of the Head. Nat's plan was that when she was on the rocks on the other side of the house, he would bring the guests down the light tower. Tam would go into the house through the French

201

door in the master suite, then immediately go upstairs to the bathroom on the second floor. The guests might want to go out on the rocks, and, naturally, the Lady Ghost would be gone. They wouldn't stay out there long, probably clad in the wrong footwear, but if they started to linger, Nat knew where to find a lobster trap marker that had broken free and washed to shore, a perfect authentic souvenir for them to bring home and hang in their rec room, so the discovery would incite a return to the car. If either guest had to use the restroom, Nat would show them back into the house to the master suite, where they wouldn't notice the wet, drying outline of Tam's footsteps on the floor boards.

Tam waited in the upstairs bathroom. She didn't remove her damp, slightly salty clothes, except the nylons which felt like sausage casings. The Lady Ghost would have worn stockings held up with a garter belt. The combination was still not a complete undergarment, far less preclusive than clothing fifty years earlier, or in fifty years to come (what better chastity belt than panty hose?). Most of Mary Catherine's apparel would have contributed toward repressing her (or someone else's) impulses. What else was a corset for? Chemise, shirtwaist, layers of petticoats, woolen stockings, the body-armor union suit—the same clothes she and her cousin had feverishly unwrapped in the scant time they could evade supervision, might prove a deterrent for the widower, at least for a while. She went to the window, parted the gauzy curtains only slightly. When she heard the car grinding away down the dirt road, and before it was out of sight, Nat was behind her, hooking one arm around her. The curtain a veil across her face as she turned toward him, her hand once again holding the hat.

Fog Warning

tam, seems like a ticking bomb, waiting for g's next shoe to drop. nothing new, except he added to the website, not sure how long ago. you should check it out—he's talking to you.

i've been tinkering with the f-tree. (sorry, genealogical list, not a tree). look at this. marr, jaruel's father. i added that his wife died in june. 1835. look at her last child. born may 1835. i know so many names, it's hard when you're not looking. here it is:

Thomas Marr m. Lydia Trafton (b. March 9, 1786 & d. June 1835)
  Izetta Marr (Aug 28, 1812)
  Lydia Marr (Jan 23, 1815)
  Thomas Marr (June 5, 1817)
  Mary Jane Marr (Sept 20, 1820)
  Nahum Baldwin Marr (Nov 18, 1822 - d. Sept 27, 1823)
  Nahum Baldwin Marr (second of this name, Aug 4, 1824)
  Jothan Trafton Marr (Jan 13, 1827)
  Jaruel Marr (April 3, 1829)
  Lemuel Marr (March 20, 1832)
  Marinda Ann Marr (May 26, 1835)

note: Lydia Tafton was 26 when she had her 1st child and 49 when she died a month after having her last child.

Thomas Marr had five more children with his second wife Nancy Taylor
  Mark Llewellyn Marr (1840)
  William Taylor Marr (1844)
  Nancy K. Marr (1847)
  Georgianna A. Marr (1850)
  Ansel F. Marr (1855)

so check out his 2nd family. he's over 70 when the last child is born. don't have a birthdate for this 2nd wife. how much younger was she? he's over 50 when they married. this thos marr didn't know when to put it away.

no i never did read water babies to my kids. Derek is almost 12, he reads adult books.

if mom doesn't hear anything directly from g in another day, she's going to call back some of those messages on his machine.

-m

Fog had dropped down from last night's gray sky. Not only were Sequin Island in the Atlantic and the Georgetown Peninsula across Sheepscot Bay completely lost from sight, even the houses across the small inlet to the east had disappeared. The lighthouse and surrounding rocks down to the placid sea were cut adrift like a trance. Except the automatic and synthetic warning signal from the fog-bell house that resounded every sixty seconds. From the keeper's office, Tam spotted a speaker attached under the eave on the fog house.

She had logged on to check her portfolio. It was faltering, still not completely collapsing. She'd thought she should, like Martha, do a little tinkering with it. The phone-connection icon flashed, then the screen informed her the connection had been broken. The same instant the phone rang, and the fog horn let out its scheduled peal.

"Why the hell don't you answer the phone?" Nat, obviously in his truck, slightly out of breath. His cellphone staticy, as though his voice was coming over a Morse code machine.

"I just did."

"I let it ring about fifty times."

"I was on-line. They must have call-waiting on the phone line and it eventually cuts off the computer hook-up."

"I don't care if they have a phone hooked directly to the moon. Get dressed and go outside."

"What?"

"Am I breaking-up? Get dressed . . . same clothes. I'll find you . . . outside."

"Are you bringing more guests? How many people usually visit this time of year?"

"What's the matter with you?" Then his voice softened. "Look at the fog, woman. It's the stuff for ghosts to appear and disappear into. Get out there. The ghost might find what she's come back for." When he stopped talking, the open sound of the phone was like air continuing to breathe against her ear.

"How far out are you?"

"Half hour."

When she heard his truck come, too fast, down the dirt road, Tam was on the tip of the head, on the edge of the rocks behind the house. Nothing on the other side of the house seemed to exist—the house itself swimming in mist, beyond that, the rest of the head, the sweep of rocky shore toward the small crescent beach, the boat dock and boat house, all swallowed in impervious white. On her other side, the sea touching the lowest rocks was dimly evident, the slosh of almost motionless water into the crevices. Above, the top of the light tower as well as the fog house, from which still came the dispassionate warning, were gone. A more poignant reply came from the fog warning on Sequin Island.

At the last moment, before leaving the house, she'd lifted the baby from where Jill had huddled with him on the sofa after nursing. Tam held him now, asleep, wrapped in a full-sized blanket. On top of that, another blanket across her shoulders and over her head like a hood. She held the two ends closed with one hand, the other arm cradling the baby's weight. The pumps had been slippery the last time she walked here, so she hadn't changed from her rubber-soled tennis shoes. The placid mist was chilly, even wintry, but also brackish. The blankets began to feel damp, heavier. She licked salt mist from her lips like froth.

His footstep silent, she heard Nat's breath first, and then he was all around her.

"I saw you, I watched for a while . . ." He panted, his head resting on the outside of the blanket hood, against hers. A little behind her, mostly beside her, his hands moved down the front of the blanket, found her arm holding the baby. "What do you have?"

As though his coarse breathing was now hers, the dense air became more difficult to inhale. "Maybe . . . she had . . . lost a baby." She turned her head toward him, but found the blanket hood covering her face. "So when she comes back to walk the coast. . . maybe sometimes she has the baby, and sometimes she . . . doesn't."

"She couldn't be the mother of the shipwrecked baby."

While the fog warning sounded, Tam tried to use her shoulder to sweep the blanket away from her face. "Not that baby. Maybe . . . there's another." The baby squirmed a little, and muttered. "Or . . . she . . . the ghost could be the shipwrecked baby. Or could have known her."

He slid a hand inside the blanket, around the back of her neck, so her hair, her hot face were set free in the mist.

Tam drank the air, then heard her voice, softly hoarse, and she listened to herself as though listening to someone else: "So the baby she's holding could be herself. . . or she mothered her own lost baby. . . Her legacy. She comes back, hoping . . ."

"Someone will find her."

"Or to find someone." A gentle lap of water spit a few drops of foam against her leg. "Is the tide . . . ?"

"Let's go."

Nat stopped her on the porch. The fog warning, almost directly over-head, wailed, and the baby cried. "Hey," Nat shouted. As though assuming Tam might disappear, he pulled her with him when he went to the door to the lighthouse and used his shoe to push it open. "Hey, come get the kid! Come here!"

"What the hell—?" Jill came to the door wearing only her usual big undershirt and dirty white socks.

"Take him."

"He's okay," Tam said, turning so Jill could take the baby from her arm.

Nat was already pulling Tam toward the ramp to the fog tower when Jill answered, something about a sex toy, but most of her words were lost in another blast from the fog warning.

For Mary Catherine it would not have been a mechanical blast but the bell tolling above where she lay in the narrow bed. She'd come with her cousin, Nahum—her father had sent him to set the chain mechanism that kept the fog bell chiming for several hours. The official assistant keeper, her brother Wolcott, was away that morning. Perhaps the fog had prevented him from returning from up the river at the lobster pound. These were the times Nahum filled in, and Mary Catherine had learned how to assist him. Mary Catherine and Nahum would have overladen the little wooden bed, with both their bodies and all their clothes—her skirt and petticoat and bloomers and stockings and high-topped shoes; his trousers and woolen socks and boots. The bell would have been hard pressed to drown their giggles.

Tam didn't let Nat take off his boots. Nor his jeans, nor did she remove her sneakers or long underwear from under her skirt.

"Please tell me there're no panties under this," he rasped as he ripped the fly of the longjohns. "Fucking a ghost should be easier than this."

Mary Catherine might have kept a threaded needle in the hem of her apron at all times, to have it handy, and indeed found it practical when she must repair her clothing before returning to her chores.

"It'll never be easy for her. But this kind of strife she doesn't mind."

"Why?"

"It's what *she* wants. *She* chose it."

The fog warning sounded again, and they did not resume conversation, for ten, eleven, twelve, thirteen or more warning blasts.

"Hope this fog holds—I've a big bundle of diapers in the truck bed, anyone could see." He was half-sitting, half-lying on the narrow bed, hands behind his head, leaning against the wall. Tam likewise reclining, seated between his knees, resting against his chest.

"If anyone comes, the girl will let us know." She slowly gathered the sheet and wadded it between her legs. She would have to wash it, and her long underwear, this afternoon.

"How?" he muttered. "She's probably in another teen-angst stupor."

"She's doing okay, under the circumstances."

"The circumstances being that someone *else* took a risk to get her baby for her."

"There are a lot of risks happening out here." She closed her eyes, waiting for the fog warning. Hadn't it been several minutes? The rise and fall of his chest felt like a rocking boat, unsteady, like she might tip and slide to one side or the other.

"Such as . . . ? You mean us?" He wrapped his arms around her. "So, how does that go? You can pick your bedmates but you can't choose your relatives. Or both?"

With his arms holding her, the sensation of falling one way or the other was gone. "Oh, that reminds me, I figured out . . . you're my fourth cousin. It has to do with how many generations ago our relatives were first cousins. Four generations."

"Then we're not incest."

Tam opened her eyes. "Cousins weren't allowed to marry, even back then. Mary Catherine was in for another huge heartbreak."

"Who's this again? The one you think became the ghost?"

"No, the first Marr lightkeeper's daughter, the second Marr keeper's sister. She was the one who lost her twin brother. Her first heartbreak. Maybe she would someday replace him with a baby." She traced the shape of Nat's hand, where it lay on her stomach. "But maybe it'll be a girl baby, and she'll name her Jane Thelma."

"Thelma Jane sounds better."

"But it has to be like her brother, J. Thomas. And Jane, for her cousin Nahum's mother Mary Jane." There was more light coming through the fog house windows, still diffused, not a candid sun. The fog was lifting. "Meanwhile, though, Mary Catherine is the one who cared for Seaborn, growing up. They finally formed a bond. She called her CeeCee, or maybe Sissy. They could have used that name back then without meaning weakhearted. Sissy would have alerted them—Mary Catherine and Nahum—when someone was coming to the fog-bell house. But maybe, with the bell still tolling, they didn't hear Sissy's warning. Or maybe Sissy couldn't see the dory coming through the fog, and it was too late for a warning."

"Who would be coming?"

"The assistant keeper. Mary Catherine's brother."

"That makes sense." He lifted one arm to rub his eye or scratch his head. His other arm tightened on Tam, as though to maintain her stability. "You know, lighthouse keeping wasn't all a man with a nautical uniform and a pipe, looking out to sea with a periscope, guiding ships to rescue." His other arm returned to help hold her. "The reason the light-house keeper had to have an assistant was so one person would always be there to keep the light lit while the other tended his crop, his livestock and his lobster traps—his *real* livelihood. And they had wives in order to have someone to keep the vegetable garden and the chickens, make and mend the clothes."

"And have children, and have more children."

"And they had children so they could have a bigger hay crop, more lobster traps, and a steady stream of lighthouse assistants."

"With their brothers as the keepers, the daughters couldn't always be-come lighthouse *wives*, if that's what they wanted. But now, even if Mary Catherine's brother took a post as keeper somewhere else, her father will withdraw his offer of assistant keeper to her cousin." She used her little finger to move strands of hair from where they were tickling her eyelashes. "After her brother tells their father what he found in the fog-bell house."

"A cousin with his hand in the jewelry box."

Dim clangs from the buoy in Sheepscot channel meant the sea was in motion again, the wind had come up.

"How're they gonna keep from getting pregnant, anyway?"

"Same way we do?"

"They didn't have condoms, or— you're using birth control, aren't you?"

"It's too late for that."

"*What?*" His body jolted beneath her. His hands jerked away from hers, his fingers gripped her shoulders, pushing her upright.

"I'm too old to get pregnant," she smiled, feeling floppy as a rag doll. "At least I thought I was until I saw my sister's family tree."

"Jesus, woman." He pulled his leg from her other side, so he was sitting on the edge of the bed, and Tam, leaning forward to sit up on her own, was slightly behind him.

"I wonder if that's what the men said then, when the wives told them they were pregnant again."

Nat stood, tucking in his shirt, his back to her. When he turned, his gaunt face was overcast for a static moment before igniting into a grin. "Just make sure it stays a ghost baby."

How did she tell Denny? *Did* she ever tell Denny?

There were no drugstore pregnancy tests in 1978. Only calendars. And the lab at the university student health services. She bypassed the latter, suspecting results would come with counseling sessions: one-sided mock-friendly consultations. Three weeks late was getting close to missing two periods. And still no forecast aura of cramping. When would the nausea start? Maybe she was going to wait until she awoke with queasiness before telling Denny. But also possible she'd decided to tell him that day. She'd always assumed she did. But what if she didn't?

He was swimming. It was not unusual for him to be doing laps before 8 in the morning. The team would be in the training room by 9, then a team meeting followed by the usual work-out—laps, time trials, starting drills. Tam didn't expect to be with Denny in the office until later in the afternoon, and she had classes herself, so after staying at the pool to transcribe times for him, she would pass the clipboard back to Denny and leave before 9, with no more than a sidewise glance from him—a glance that still glinted with his conspiratorial smile, for a second. So arriving early was another way to occupy the realm that existed only when they were alone. The pool, when they were there in private, was part of that realm now, not just the province of her past—a world of clean-chemical scented humidity and powerful movement through water she could have, should have belonged to. But it was okay now, to be on the deck while someone else swam, if they were alone, and if the swimmer was Denny.

Skylights threw plenty of sun into the pool area, and the disturbed surface of the water bounced lasers of radiance around the walls. A visual agitation, but a familiar one—Tam did little more than shield her eyes, and felt no instability. She sat on the first row of bleachers, beside his towel and sweatshirt, where his tennis shoes, tongues cut out, were askew on the deck. If Denny didn't notice her during a freestyle flipturn, then he surely would when he switched to backstroke. But he didn't stop and completed 400 yards of every stroke, not at a race pace.

When he finished, he stayed in the water. He braced his upper arms on the lip of pool in his lane, elbows bent, chin on his hands. Then, underwater, his body curled, flexed. He brought his feet up against the wall and pushed off, gently. Floated away on his back. She always waited in the bleachers, but that day Tam stood and approached the edge of the pool. She stopped about a foot from the lip. The nearest she'd been to the brilliant aqua in eight years. Why today? Maybe because the closer chlorine smell might bring on her first wave of nausea? Perhaps that's why she stayed there. Hoping? But Denny was coming back, floating face down until his fingers found the deck. Once again resting his arms there, chin on his palms, yet kept his feet braced on the wall, ready to push off, goggles still over his eyes. By now, usually, he'd be toweled off, throwing sweats on over his still-damp suit and skin, getting his clipboards and notebooks from her and heading toward the weight room.

"What're you doing?" Tam asked.

"Thinking."

Tam lowered her body, squatting, not quite kneeling so she wouldn't get her pants wet. She reached to touch his arm where white hair held crystal drops of water.

Denny raised his head. "Not here. The guys might—"

"Sorry," Tam said.

"Unless you're going to get in with me!" His hand darted to catch her wrist, but she was quick enough to stand and jump back in one motion. "Damn, you're like a cat."

Tam laughed, thought Denny would heave himself out of the water then. But he didn't. Her heart started to race, and she said, "Maybe you're right, we should be thinking together."

"Meaning . . . ?"

"Meaning . . . What if I was . . . ?"

"Was what?"

211

"What if I decided . . . today I won't jump back? Let you pull me in?"

"What if you dove in yourself?"

"What if you held me like I was a baby who couldn't swim?"

"What if we took our suits off and fucked like seals?"

"I don't even have a suit anymore."

"Perfect." But his goggled face didn't show the usual buoyant verve. Is that why she didn't say more?

She stood, one foot, maybe two from the edge. She took a step back. "What were you thinking about?"

He finally raised his goggles to the top of his newly shorn head. "We might have some trouble, kid."

"Gary?" Her stomach flared, but not the anticipated morning sickness. They hadn't mentioned Gary in the month since her father died.

"What? Why—?"

"I don't know, never mind." She forced another smile, hand on her fluttering stomach.

"Know that phys. ed. swimming class you're getting credit for without ever showing up?" He finally did pull himself out of the pool. Water streamed off him like he'd been oiled.

Tam turned to get his towel from the bleacher bench. "Don't tell me you're going to make me swim a meet in order to get credit." Her voice bright. She breathed deeply. Everything was steady again. "Remember, I do your grade sheets."

"No, it's not you . . ." He dried his face, then left the towel around his shoulders. "But our workstudy kid is doing the same thing."

"Why?"

"It's how he . . . It's what he gets in exchange for the money from his paycheck."

"Oh." Tam took another step back and sat on the bleacher. "I wondered why he would do it. You never told me how you got him to."

"Yeah, well . . . I think he told someone."

"About giving us his paycheck?" Tam picked up Denny's sweatshirt, held it on her lap while he dried his legs.

"Not quite. About taking a ghost p.e. class. I had another guy come ask me how he could arrange to do the same thing."

"Oh, *yeah*—you know what? I think someone came to ask about that once when you weren't there."

"*What?* You're kidding." He took the sweatshirt from her and pulled it over his head. When his head came through the neck hole, he said, "When?"

"I don't remember. Maybe . . . two weeks ago? I've been a little . . . pre-occupied with . . . something else."

"Yeah, I know." He sat beside her, looked quickly over his shoulder as he put a hand over hers. Her stomach burned again, but sonorous this time, not dangerous. "What'd he say?" Denny asked.

"I didn't know what he was talking about. He said something like it wasn't fair that some people got out of their p.e. requirement by making deals with coaches. I thought he meant *me*. I thought he was talking about. . . us."

Denny stood, looked again toward the door to the locker room, took a step back. "What'd you say?"

"That I didn't know what he was talking about."

"Why didn't you tell me?"

"I don't know," her eyes fell. "I didn't know you'd made this deal with the workstudy guy. I'm sorry. I had other things on my mind. As soon as I knew that it didn't mean Gary had . . . "

"Gary had *what?*"

"You never know what Gary'll do. I don't trust him, and now he knows about us."

"Yeah, and now someone probably knows something worse than what Gary knows." He knotted his towel around his waist. "Or at least just as bad. God, and it's all *connected.*"

"What are you afraid might happen?"

"*Besides* someone finding out we're using a workstudy paycheck for team expenses?"

"But how is it connected—that Gary knows about us and that the workstudy guy is getting p.e. credit without—"

"So are *you*, Tam. Won't it look like ghost p.e. credit in exchange for some nooky in the coach's office?"

"Nooky? Is that how . . . ?"

"Sweetheart, no." He sat again, the towel wrapping his legs like a tight skirt. "But look how it *looks*. What if someone saw us a minute ago, me standing here with my speedo in your face?"

"But we . . . what does it have to do with the workstudy guy?"

"Maybe it doesn't . . . but the workstudy money trail, it leads to *you*. And you're getting ghost p.e. credit, besides being my, what, employee? That leads back to me. And us having . . . you know . . . on top of all that? It's . . ."

"Not a very good role model?" She took the edge of his towel between thumb and finger.

"For *one* thing." But he grinned. "And you want to send me into weight training with a hard-on? How's that for a role model?"

"You'll be great."

"We'll see about that. For now, get your hand out of my towel, young lady." He scooted away from her so he could reach under the bench for his shoes. "Let's talk later, okay? I didn't want to scare you. You'll be in the office, right?"

But she was asleep on the mattress when Denny finally got to the office sometime between 6 and 7. The mattress wasn't visible until he came around the end of the false wall of file cabinets, but he would have known she was still there when he came through the door, despite the lights being out, the typewriter covered, the coffee pot cold, because the back of her chair was wearing not only her pantsuit blazer but her blouse as well. Her pants folded, on the seat. Her bookbag on the floor, propped against the desk. If he'd turned the lights on at first, upon entering, she might have known, might have woken. But it was still dark when he came around the file cabinets and sat on the floor beside her, leaning against the backs of the files.

"What time is it?" she murmured. She could barely see his outline but thought she could almost see his eyes. It was nearly darkroom dark, in a room with no windows, so it could have been any time.

"I don't know. Won't they be expecting you at home?"

"It isn't always a problem. The one who tries to control me doesn't live there." She moved back a little to make room on the mattress. "God, that reminds me, I was having a dream that you wanted to name our kid Gary."

"Gary Marr Clarkson. I guess he'd be a swimmer."

"My last name is Burgess."

"Oh, right."

"What happened this afternoon?"

"Team meeting ran late. Then had to do a few of those one-on-one pep-talks." His head tipped back against the file cabinets. She couldn't see if he closed his eyes. "And I stayed and did more laps."

"What are you getting in shape for?" She smiled and stretched her legs, still under the sheet.

"Just thinking."

"Again, or still?"

"I think best in water."

"So you haven't been thinking clearly whenever you're with me?"

"That must be it." He pushed himself forward and crawled onto the mattress. Tam lifted the sheet, and he edged over beside her. "So, like you said, I haven't been a very good role model. For you."

"That was my mom's job, and my dad. My dad—did I tell you how he stood up to his bosses after he ratted on his evil oil company? And look where I ended up."

"Stealing workstudy money and sleeping with the boss." He had one leg over her, one hand cradling her head, his mouth against her ear. "But this isn't where you're ending up."

"I'm not complaining."

"I know. But I'm going to tell the workstudy guy to stop sending the checks. I'll tell workstudy he's terminated. He's already got his side of the deal. You should close the account, but we'll hang onto the money, for now, in case . . . if we somehow have to pay something back." His hand moved to her shoulder, sliding her bra strap down.

"There's not enough to pay back two years' worth."

"I know. Maybe it won't come to that. If we quit now. You would be expelled if anyone found out, so now's the time to stop, since you've applied for graduation."

"Luckily I can keep working here after I graduate, I'm regular university staff, not workstudy. And maybe after everything . . . after I'm settled

I can come back and do that second major in phys ed. Learn the ropes of coaching." She turned to face him, so she could reach around and unhook her bra. But Denny's hand returned to her face, his thumb tracing the shape of her mouth before he kissed her.

"We don't have to decide that yet." His voice barely above a whisper.

The baby was fussy, his nose running. Tam felt for a fever, but there didn't seem to be one. "Keep him warm," she told Jill.

"You shouldn't'a had him outside," Jill moaned. She was, as usual, on the sofa in a wadded nest of throw-blankets and pillows.

"Probably not, but he wouldn't already have a cold just a few hours later." The stale smell of soiled linens and sour humid skin—or maybe just the smell of baby—hung like invisible fog in the house. Tam removed a discarded dirty diaper from the coffee table. "Did you get the new diapers out of Nat's truck and throw the bag of garbage in?"

"What'd'ya think, I'm a moron? Or that I like to keep bags of dirty diapers around all the time?"

"I think you're acting fairly ungrateful."

"You want me to be grateful?" Jill shifted the whimpering baby to her other arm. "Grateful that I haven't got a lousy CD to play? Big whoop, like wow, I get to stay up and see what band might be on Letterman every night, in case it's *not* like some old geezer from the 60's."

"What do you want? To go home and leave your baby all over again and pretend like nothing ever happened?"

"What I *want* is for *some*thing to happen. *Nothing's* happening. Nobody comes to visit *me* and take me on walks for hot sex."

"That's none of your business."

"Like *I* was ever any of *your* business?"

The baby sneezed and blew a bubble out of one nostril. Jill suddenly laughed and dabbed at the baby's nose with toilet paper. Tam smiled too. "Bubble boy!" Jill switched to her sing-song voice. "Little Jerry says, don't be mad, mommy."

Tam pushed aside a wadded comforter and sat on the sofa.

Jill was sitting sideways, her feet stretched out—now the bottoms of her bare feet against Tam's thigh. She wiggled her toes and said, "I don't mean to be so awful, but you know, it's getting close to spring, and, like, prom is . . . it'll be time for prom, and . . . "

"You've got your prom date," Tam said, nodding down at the baby. He was falling asleep, but his breathing sounded like sucking the last bit of liquid from a glass through a straw.

"I know. But, like, not going will feel so skank."

"In the long term, it won't matter at all. You'll never think about it, whether you did or didn't. It won't change anything, and you won't—"

"*Okay*, I get it, so like, when I'm old I won't care. But what about *now* when I *do* care?"

"Life is full of disappointment." Tam stared at Jill's toes, each with a tiny island of old nail polish.

"What-*ever*. I take it that means *you* never went?"

"For one horrible moment I thought I might have to when my mother assumed I would be deprived unless my brother took me."

"Oh, yuk, I know kids who went with a cousin, but not their *brother*, who everybody would *know* wasn't really a date."

"Yes, a cousin might've changed my mind." Tam tucked the comforter over her own lap and Jill's feet. "But I didn't really want to go. I was afraid I'd— that something awful would happen."

"What, get left while your brother went and sucked face with one of your friends?"

"Hardly." Tam laughed a puff of air. "That would have been a relief, except not if it were really a *friend*." She reached across Jill's legs and gently stopped her from picking at the crust forming around the baby's nostrils. "But I didn't have many friends. I was a loner—by choice, not by cruelty."

"I guess I can picture that. But what were you afraid of about prom?"

"That I might have a seizure. I'm epileptic."

"Oh." Jill added the last handful of mashed toilet paper to the three rock-sized wads already on the coffee table. "So that's why your mom and brother were . . . protective?"

"No. Not my mom. Well, maybe she was. Just not the way I wanted. She should've protected my resolve, not let me stay scared."

"Maybe she was scared, too."

"I don't think so," Tam laughed again, again just air. "She still had my brother and sister to carry on normal lives. So she didn't even stop to think that the reason I didn't want to go to dances *wasn't* that I didn't have a date." The last of that morning's fog dissolved and the day's first ray of sun put a spotlight on the brass telescope near the window. Tam smiled, but felt too lazy to get up and move a chair into the splotch of sun.

"What'd your brother say when your mom thought he should take you to prom?"

"I don't remember. I'd already stopped listening to him years before. Probably, 'why would I ever go anywhere with a spastic-brain like her?'"

"Wow, I'm glad I don't have a brother." Jill startled when the baby hiccupped. She pulled her feet away from Tam's leg. "Is he still, like, mean?"

"He's still a know-it-all blow-hard mama's-boy. I guess. I haven't had much to do with him for years. My sister tells me he's sort of disappeared. That he might be having some sort of break-down. I'm sure they assume traumatic stress from being a big hero rescuer at Ground Zero last year." Tam gathered her hair to the top of her head for a moment, her eyes on the radiant telescope. "And she says he's been leaving messages for me on our family website."

"Wow, what's he saying?"

"I don't know. I haven't looked."

"Really? God, I'd be, like, looking every *hour*."

Gary's website communiqué was not in "message from Gary (from hell)" but on her own, always blank, message-from-Tam page, the icon now changed to an incoming mailbox.

Message *to* Tam

You chose to feel alone, an outsider. The more you wallowed (what you thought was silent stoicism) the more they focused everything on you. It was poor Tam, poor afflicted Tam. You got what you wanted I guess. Who do you really think was left alone, to sink or swim (as they say) on his own, to succeed, to excel, to conquer. But I fooled you. I got a disease of my own. An inflamed brain of my own. Two inflamed brains from the same bad seed. And something else—what I did, I did for your own good. I think you've secretly blamed me for that for too many years. It was no different than pulling someone from under the rubble. You had to be extracted. I'd do it again. I love you.

Tam read the message three times then went to her stock portfolio. Did Gary think post traumatic stress disorder was a brain disease? Did anyone with post traumatic stress *know* they have post traumatic stress? Didn't they just think they were reacting appropriately in a troublesome world? And the thing he *thinks* she blames him for, he couldn't be referring to pulling her from out of the pool, from out of her swimming career.

She barely glanced at the stock portfolio when it came up. Instead she decided she should do more research for Martha, so she could at least say she had. Her first search was for Hendricks Head. After basic lighthouse index sites, two of the items on the search results said "Lady Ghost of Hendricks Head" and "The Beautiful Stranger."

The Beautiful Stranger
She had registered at a Boothbay hotel as Louise G. Meade and had brought with her what appeared to be a

trousseau (but no husband). Then set off
on a walk to rugged Hendricks Head—
and never returned.

During the last week of November, 1931, a beautiful young
woman registered at the Hotel Fullerton in Boothbay, Maine.
Louise Meade had come to Maine with a brand new traveling
bag and new clothes, yet the outfit she was seen wearing was
all black. She insisted on paying her hotel bill right away, as she
was going on a long walk and wanted to be sure the bill was paid
in the event she got lost. She never returned. The next morning
a maid discovered her bag had never been opened. A search
began. Police were told that a girl answering the same description
had asked for information concerning the best spot on the coast
to view "rugged rocks with a heavy surf." She was directed to
the area around Hendricks Head Light. Early on the morning
of December 3, a woman's terrified screams were heard in the
woods along the road in West Southport. Six days later the body
of the woman who had registered at the hotel as Louise Meade
was found below a rocky ledge on the shore near Hendricks
Head, an area frequented by rum runners. Believing at first that
the girl had committed suicide, officials were surprised to discover
a waterproof pouch beneath her blouse carrying a cryptogram.
Strapped around her waist was an electric iron, and in her pocket
a small calendar with only a small checkmark on the date two
weeks prior to when her body was found. An officer in the Signal
Corps First Area deemed the cyptrogram to be a rum runner's
code. Apparently a large cargo of illegal liquor had been taken
ashore less than a mile away a short time before the discovery
of the body. Two claims of lost daughters came from men named
Meade, but in both cases the physical description didn't match the
mysterious dead woman.

Parade Magazine, May 21, 1972

Lady Ghost of Hendricks Head
Rose O'Connor
(as printed in 1956 in the Lewiston Journal)

These years she is seen mostly at twilight and so she has
become known as the Lady of the Dusk. Sometimes she is seen
in the very bright moonlight and there are those who swear they
have seen her when the fog comes rolling in, picking her steps

lightly and easily over the rocky coast, a creature more shadow than substance as befits a ghost. The last time she was ever seen alive was at the chill twilight of a December afternoon in 1931. She had asked for directions to an open sweep of ocean, "to get one last good look," because "she was going West."

Was It She?

The lighthouse keeper THOUGHT he saw her that December afternoon. It was almost dark, just those last minutes of afterglow before darkness settles down. He was on the lookout for her because he had heard about her, up at Charlie Barkin's store. The wondering had started even then as to why such a well spoken woman with that vague label "lady" stamped all over her should be walking unescorted on a rugged coast that soon would be drowned in darkness. It was almost dark and he was almost home. He knew every inch of the area around him. Through the winter-stripped trees he could see the summer cottages looming up darkly a short distance from the road. He knew all the people who owned those cottages, could tell them from any distance.

And then he saw something flicker just for a second, off near one of the cottages, it was like a shadow, slipping around a corner of a house. He stopped, listened, called, but there was no answer. Night was coming down fast. He called again. Two or three times. Now the twilight was so thick, the outlines of the cottages were melting into the shadows.

If he saw her, he was the last one ever to see her alive. He always was certain that he had seen her and he forever regretted he had not stamped through the heavy underbrush to get to the cottage on the shore. Whenever she is seen now, it is usually at the precise moment when the twilight is melting into blackness and she is seen just an instant, so quickly that no one ever is sure she is there or if it is just a trick of the twilight.

Many Stories

Stories have sprung up about her in the last quarter century. There is the story that her family fortune may have been wiped out in the stock market. But why did no one ever come forward, if she had been from a family of position or wealth? Some say because she was dressed all in black she must have suffered a recent death and could not face life any longer. But again, wouldn't someone have missed her, wouldn't someone have realized she was the woman trying to be identified through the ads in the papers?

Why did she come to Southport? She seemed to know the territory, be familiar with the landmarks. She did nothing, during the few hours she was there, to arouse suspicion other than walk off down a lonely road in the late afternoon of a December day. And 25 years ago, Southporters knew most of the summer residents. They usually came back year after year. There wasn't the transient travel of today. Yet nobody ever came forward who knew her. The name Louise Meade meant nothing to anyone, yet it is an acknowledged fact that when people assume false names they take one that either has the same initials as their own name or sounds very similar.

Illegal Liquor

A story persists that she was mixed up with liquor smuggling, that she had gone down to the coast that late afternoon in 1931 to signal a liquor boat. That was the Prohibition era and the broken coastline of Maine in those years has a history that has never been written. Those are the ones who say she died because she knew too much or because she double-crossed someone.

"Nonsense!" says Mrs. Charlie Barkin of West Southport who was born a Brewer and has generations of coastal Maine behind her. "She wasn't that sort. I talked with her. She was a nice woman. A refined woman. A lady!"

The stories too, have made her a beauty. "She wasn't," says Mrs. Barkin. "In her 40's I'd say, maybe late 40's. Not a beauty, no, but nice looking."

"Nice looking" by Maine standards often turns out to mean beautiful by people given to more lavish turn of expression.

Came By Bus

The story of Louise G. Meade begins on the afternoon bus to Boothbay Harbor on Tuesday, Dec. 1, 1931. The day was windy, with ominous clouds blowing across the sky, but there was sunshine, off and on. Maine was clinging to late autumn. Nevertheless it was not the kind of day nor the time of year to lure visitors to the Maine coast. Persons on that bus, that afternoon almost 25 years ago, were all "natives," getting back home before the short afternoon ended. Still, there was nothing about her to attract attention on the bus trip to Boothbay Harbor. A woman all in black, sitting quietly, apparently quite certain of every planned detail of her journey.

She checked in at the Fullerton Hotel, now no longer operated in The Harbor. Anything unusual about a woman checking in at a hotel in a resort town in December? Not at all. She could be on a business trip, or looking over summer property as many cottagers do before the Maine winter "sets in." Her quiet manner, her composure, her quiet dress gave no reason for any hotel clerk to look at her questioningly.

Later, checking back, they found that she stayed at the hotel but a very short time. She unlocked the suitcase she had brought with her. There was never anything in that case to identify her. Labels had been removed, each and every one, with care. The only label ever found was that of Lord and Taylor's on the dress and coat she had on when she washed up on shore. Somehow, those labels had been overlooked.

It was learned, too, that she had asked several persons where she could get a very good view of open ocean. Those she had talked with in town told her to go down to the wharves because there was as good a view as could be found of the famous harbor of Boothbay. But that did not interest her.

Seemed to Know Territory

She started on the road to Southport. Now, the road curls around the harbor, and although Hendricks Head is as the crow flies, "just over there" from Boothbay Harbor, it is a hike to undertake on foot, especially on the short afternoon of a windy December day. She knew about Hendricks Head, that is for certain, because when she met Mrs. Barkin, the name was not unfamiliar to her.

Mrs. Barkin was on her shift at the West Southport Post Office inside the store. The afternoon was drawing to a close and it was getting windier and cloudier so Mrs. Barkin went over to shut up her hens for the night. Could be that by morning, snow would be falling. She had just stepped back up to the porch of the store, when she saw the lady in black. The woman was walking along the road, almost in front of the store.

"She was medium height," recalls Mrs. Barkin whose memory is sharp as a tack, "and she was dressed in deep black. I remember thinking I had never seen her before and in those days I knew most everyone who came to Southport, winter or summer."

The woman stopped when she saw Mrs. Barkin. "I'm on my way to the ocean," she said. "Which way shall I go?"

"Why, over there's the harbor," said Mrs. Barkin, nodding across the highway.

"Yes," the woman looked over her shoulder at the road to Cozy Harbor, "but I want a sweep of the open ocean."

"You're near Hendricks Head," Mrs. Barkin said hesitantly.

Hendricks Head? Yes, that was what the woman was looking for. How would she get there? Mrs. Barkin gave her the directions. "It might be dark before you get back," she warned. "And it's lonesome."

The woman thanked her and left. Mrs. Barkin watched for just a second, then hurried back to the warmth of the post office. This was no afternoon to visit the open coast of windy Hendricks Head where the surf smashes in even on quiet summer days.

As the wind heightened and the clouds thickened Mrs. Barkin thought of the woman walking along the road to the Light. She discussed it with her husband. They weren't disturbed, but it seemed a little strange.

"You didn't know her?" said Charlie.

"No," said his wife, "I never saw her before." Mrs. Barkin was keeping an eye on the highway to watch for the woman's return.

Then Mr. Knight, keeper of the Hendricks Head Light, arrived at the post-office-store. The minute he came in Mrs. Barkin asked him if he had met the woman on the road.

"I didn't meet anyone."

"But you couldn't have missed her. She couldn't get down past your road this fast."

"I didn't see a soul," insisted Keeper Knight. He listened to the story. A worried look came over his face. "I'll keep an eye out for her on the way back home," said Keeper Knight. "Kind of funny, isn't it?"

Retraced Her Journey

Later of course, when they retraced her footsteps easily followed in the sandy soil, they found that Mr. Knight had walked right by her. She must have heard him coming, long before he came into sight on that quiet road. He was hurrying along, not giving a thought to meeting anyone, and she had dodged into the woods on the north side of the road near the top of Beach Hill. She had stood there, quietly, watching him walk by and when his footsteps had died away up the road, she had stepped out of the woods and continued her journey.

The lights of Keeper Knight's own home were in view when a movement, way in at the shore, near one of the cottages, caught his eye. He barely saw it, but he could swear it was a person, a woman moving swiftly, maybe running. He shouted. He shouted a couple of times. It was almost too dark now to see anything clearly.

He was home in a matter of minutes and he told his wife about the woman and about the movement he thought he saw. It was really dark now. His wife had not seen anyone on the road.

"Curious"

By the next morning everyone in Southport was a little worried. The woman in black had not returned. "We became curious," is the way Charlie Barkin puts it, so Willis Brewer, a Southport fisherman, went looking for her. He had no trouble picking up her tracks. He found where she had stepped off the woods up at Beach Hill. And then he followed her path to the beach where, they have always since believed, she probably watched the water.

The sound of Mr. Knight's returning footsteps must have disturbed her. At least that is how Charlie Barkin has figured it out and he is no Sunday-detective. Charlie has come up with some pretty good solutions to many coastal mysteries, has unraveled many tangled clues that have tripped up some of the smart city boys.

"I figure," he says, "when she heard Mr. Knight returning, you know how sounds travel near the water, she took the road over by the Conner cottage. She must have seen the lights in the Light House residence, because she retraced her steps about 100 feet, then went west down on the little beach west of Conley's cottage."

Maybe she watched Mr. Knight walk home, barely making out his figure in the growing darkness. Certainly she heard him call, because he shouted several times. There has never been any doubt in the minds of those who tried to solve the case that the movement Keeper Knight saw was Louise Meade. Evidently she had thought the dusk was deep enough to hide her and, too late, realized he would see her so she had slipped around the side of the house and that was when he saw her.

The general theory is that she drowned herself. She is listed in the medical records as suicide. Charlie Barkin goes along with the latter, but not with the first.

Charlie Barkin's Solution

"My theory, and mind you, this is just my own theory, is that she sat on the beach and took poison. No autopsy was performed so there was no proof. But here's how I figure it. When she was found it was in a spot a few feet south of this beach. She had a leather belt fastened around her wrists and then the belt was run though the handles of an electric flatiron and through the handles of her handbag. One hand was hooked on her belt. The other hand, the thumb, was inside the catch of her bag which was partially opened. Now I've seen plenty of drownings, some accidental, some not. And I've yet to see a person who cast himself into the water, regardless of how great was his desire to die, but what at the last moment, when it was too late, that will to live made him reach out, trying to grab back life. This woman's hands had not moved. That's why I always will believe it was poison."

The Search

Charlie Barkin, who among all his other duties for years has been one of the guiding lights of the Southport Volunteer Fire Department, goes on with his story: "After six or seven days I asked some of the firemen to help search, so on Sunday, Dec. 6th I took one or two men and scanned the shore, starting at the lighthouse. Stanley Forest with other firemen started at Conley's cottage, working toward our group. Stanley arrived at the ledge south of North Beach at about the time I arrived on the north ledge. Stanley was gazing into the water and all of a sudden said: 'There she is!' The undertow was washing the body up near the surface, then letting it back into the depression about six feet under at that time of tide."

They tried to identify her. The labels on her clothes, the only identifying mark ever found, were Lord and Taylor, the fashionable New York City store. But those labels never helped at all. Detectives came down from New York City, and her description was broadcast to every police department. People were interviewed, Missing Persons Bureau was checked and rechecked. Newspapers carried the story. Nobody ever came forward to say they ever had even heard of this well dressed, well spoken, well behaved gentlewoman.

Finally on January 8, 1932, the Town of Southport buried her. They buried her in the old cemetery on the road to Hendricks Head. Names on the monuments in that cemetery are names noted in Maine history, sea captains, early settlers, Southporters. There is no Potter's Field in this town. There is no need for one. So they took the woman known as Louise Meade to "their" cemetery and gave her a decent burial.

Not Forgotten

Already many of the younger generation do not even know where the lady in black is buried. Charlie Barkin can take you right to the spot. It is under a giant tree, a little off to one side because this is a cemetery of families and the only place for a single grave is "off-to-one-side."

Of late years she is seen usually only at deep dusk, down around Hendricks Head. Not always in the same place. Some people say they have seen her in the bright moonlight, that dazzling white moonlight that bounces off the sea. And a lot of people claim the fog brings her back. They say they have seen her when those thick peasoup fogs roll in and the fog horns start talking up and down the coast. Most people see her in the last few minutes of twilight, when the first stars are beginning to brighten and everything looks a little blurred, a little strange. That is when she comes back most often, picking her way over the rocks, moving along toward the water, so intent on what she is doing, that she seems not to care if she is glimpsed for a second as she goes on her journey.

A Note to the Reader
This story was written for the Lewiston Journal, magazine
section, on July 14, 1956. This appeared 25 years after the event
happened. I had heard the story many times from my grandfather
Charles Barkin. I wanted to preserve it for my children, so it was
copied from a faded newspaper. The grave is located in Union
Cemetery, in West Southport.
    Robert D. Forest

Martha, I've found two online articles about the ghost—the
other lighthouse legend. But I still think this legend and
the Seaborn legend combine into one story. Go look at these
two versions of the ghost (search ghost+Hendricks+Head),
one says a young woman—a girl. The other says in her
40's, even late 40's (and could 50's pass as 40's?). I guess this
Louise Meade couldn't be Mary Catherine (dead in 1899),
but she could be Seaborn, or she could be Mary Catherine's
daughter. I'm thinking Seaborn had no daughter of her
own, but perhaps if Mary Catherine had a daughter, it was
Seaborn who raised her. Seaborn's own daughter would
have only known her mother's story, with no reason to care
about Mary Catherine's life. But if Seaborn raised Mary
Catherine's daughter, they would both remain nameless
strangers to the world, and Seaborn would tell the girl
Mary Catherine's story. It was *that* story which would
drive the girl back to the place where her mother had lived
and loved. And yes, Seaborn could've told the girl both
stories—how she herself was rescued as a baby at that spot
(and, in being rescued, she lost whatever name, and life,
she would have known), and how Mary Catherine had lost
her lover and her dreamed-of life in the same place (lost
him to the sea, but in a different way)—so the girl would
have come back to that site to die. There are other distinct
differences in the stories. . . the scream, the cryptogram,
the false claims for lost daughters. . . Rum runner? Maybe
she was both. Seaborn had no way to support herself and
raise a child. Maybe Seaborn had already met her own
fate in the prohibition underworld, so the motherless girl
or woman was exacerbatedly distraught. Traumatic things
can build up until . . .
I suppose this only makes you think of G.

http://www.digitalhistory.uh.edu/historyonline/childbirth.cfm

Dying to Have a Baby - The History of Childbirth

by S. Mintz

During the seventeenth and eighteenth centuries, between 1 percent and 1.5 percent of all births ended in the mother's death as a result of exhaustion, dehydration, infection, hemorrhage, or convulsions. Since the typical mother gave birth to between five and eight children, her lifetime chances of dying in childbirth ran as high as 1 in 8.

Death in childbirth was sufficiently common that many colonial women regarded pregnancy with dread. In their letters, women often referred to childbirth as "the Dreaded apparition," "the greatest of earthly miserys," or "that evil hour I look forward to with dread."

Given the high risk of birth complications and infant death, it is not surprising to learn that pregnancy was surrounded by superstitions. It was widely believed that if a mother looked upon a "horrible spectre" or was startled by a loud noise her child would be disfigured. There was also fear that if the mother looked at the moon, her child might become a lunatic or sleepwalker. A mother's ungratified longings, it was thought, could cause an abortion or leave a mark imprinted on her child's body. At the same time, however, women were expected to continue to perform work until the onset of labor, since hard work supposedly made for an easier labor. Pregnant women regularly spun thread, wove clothing on looms, performed heavy lifting and carrying, milked cows, and slaughtered and salted down meat.

Most women were assisted in childbirth not by a doctor but by a midwife. Most midwives were older women who relied on practical experience in delivering children. During labor, midwives administered no painkillers, except for alcohol. Women were merely advised to "arm themselves with patience" and prayer and to try, during labor, to restrain "those dreadful groans and cries which do so much to discourage their friends and relations that are near them."

During the second half of the eighteenth century, customs of childbirth began to change. One important change was the introduction in 1847 of two drugs - ether and chloroform - to relieve pain in childbirth. By the 1920s, the use of anesthesia in childbirth was almost universal. In 1900, over 90 percent of all births occurred in the mother's home. But by 1940, over half took place in hospitals and by 1950, the figure had reached 90 percent.

The substitution of doctors for midwives and of hospital delivery for home delivery did little in themselves to reduce mortality rates. It was not until around 1935, when antibiotics and transfusions were introduced, that a sharp reduction in the maternal mortality rate occurred. In 1900, maternal mortality was about 65 times higher than it is today, and not much lower than it had been in the mid-nineteenth century.

http://www.digitalhistory.uh.edu/historyonline/uscourt.cfm

History of Private Lives
Courtship in Early America

In seventeenth and early eighteenth century New England, courtship was not simply a personal, private matter. The law gave parents "the care and power for the disposing of their Children in Marriage" and it was expected that they would take an active role overseeing their child's choice of a spouse.

By the middle of the eighteenth century, parental influence over the choice of a spouse had sharply declined. One indication of a decline in parental control was a sudden upsurge in the mid-eighteenth century in the number of brides who were pregnant when they got married. In the seventeenth century, the percentage of women who bore a first child less than eight-and-a half months after marriage was below ten percent. By the middle of the eighteenth century, the figure had shot up to over forty percent.

As parental influence over courtship declined, a new romantic ideal of love arose. By the late eighteenth century, love letters, particularly those written by men, had grown more expansive and less formal. Courtship letters changed by the nineteenth century from brief notes to longer, more effusive expositions of feelings and emotions. Yet even in deeply impassioned letters, the kind of love that early nineteenth century Americans sought was not transient passion, but was motivated by mutuality of tastes, companionship, trust, and shared interests.

Yet ironically at the same time that courting couples were often so open in their expression of their affection, young women, in particular, more openly disclosed their fears of marriage. "There can be no medium in the wedded state," noted one Massachusetts woman. "It must either be happy or miserable." While men were likely to stress the pleasures marriage would bring, women, in their correspondence, expressed fears about marriage. It was a "sad, sour, sober beverage" bringing "some joys but many crosses." Women often associated marriage with the loss of their liberty—often linking marriage with loss of self—and forebodings about the dangers of childbearing—often omitting children from their fantasies of an ideal marriage.

To move from "girlhood" to housewifery had become a rite of passage so difficult that many young women experienced a "marriage trauma" before taking or failing to take the step. Many women wrote that they "trembled" as their wedding day approached, that their "spirits were much depressed," and their minds were "loaded with doubts and fears."

In colonial New England, marriage was regarded as a social obligation and an economic necessity, and virtually all adults married. But by the early nineteenth century, the number of unmarried women increased to 11 percent. Between 1780 and 1820, young women between the ages of 14 and 27 enjoyed unprecedented opportunities to attend school and to earn a cash income outside of their parents' home. Marriage was regarded by young women in a new way—as a closing off of freedoms enjoyed in girlhood.

http://www.nightbeacon.com/lighthouseinformation/articles/
Women_Lighthouse_Keepers.html

Breaking the Barrier:
Women Lighthouse Keepers of the U. S. Lighthouse Board / Service

One of the first non-clerical U.S. government jobs that were open to women were positions as lighthouse keepers, although others did serve in staff positions at the various district and headquarter offices. Typically those appointed as keepers were actually the spouse of the assistant or head keeper; they assumed these professional duties to assist their spouse or took over when their husbands became ill and/or died. Nevertheless, many of these intrepid widows, and women appointed in their own right, served their country for many years with distinction in a time when employment for women was extremely limited. They were true trailblazers.

See Also
Abbie Burgess
Ida Lewis
Fannie Salter

p.s. Martha,

I'm doing some research and getting somewhere now. I suppose you know there was a coincidentally-named woman lighthouse keeper (assistant to her husband, of course) named Abbie Burgess. It seems she was only famous for *being* an assistant keeper, and for one time keeping the lights burning during a month-long storm when she was alone. That's OK, but there was another one named Ida Lewis who actually saved as many as 25 drowning people *herself* and President Ulysses Grant came to visit her.

Also, on the Coast Guard's website of statistics for Hendricks Head, it says the fog bell house was built in 1890. Mary Catherine would have been 22. And 9 years before her death. Yes, this still works. That's where she met her cousin. Perhaps for the last time. Her brother Wolcott came upon them there. Perhaps Seaborn away at school, Mary Catherine long finished after 8th grade, still at home, awaiting the time she and her cousin could announce their plans to be a lightkeeping, lifesaving family. But plans and decisions cut short when Wolcott discovered them together there. But I need to know: when did Wolcott get his first assignment as assistant keeper somewhere else, and when then did he take over at Hendricks?

Tam rose from the desk to look out the porthole window at the fog bell house. In 1890, when it was built, Mary Catherine wasn't 16 or 17 but 22. For a woman who died at 31, the span between 16 and 22 was almost a lifetime. The difference between herself at 16 and at 22 is the distinction between a girl who did nothing more in high school but go to her classes and do her homework, and a young woman who'd lived and had conceived loss. Her father, then Denny—the whole world that was Denny—and whatever was in the mess she left on the floor of his office. Did anyone ever suspect it was a crime scene? Did Denny, as he mopped or scrubbed, wonder if she'd tried to commit suicide? By then the blob or morsel of essence that could have been something else, a part of him, would have been just a thicker, tackier, gelatinous piece of crud stuck harder to the floor than the thinner spread of blood and urine. Residue of a life Tam had lived. He might have scraped it up with a plastic knife from a morning bagel, or maybe used the wingtips from an old winged-victory trophy.

Mary Catherine's life between 16 and 22 was devoted to her illicit consortium with her cousin, Nahum. The first years Mary Catherine shared with him, they'd met in boathouses in winter, in toolsheds, in henhouses or barns, even in the woods on a cushion of needles. She'd left school after 8th grade, so spent the days when he couldn't steal away to see her occupied with her only recognized vocation, in the home, pretending it was for him—as though the house she cleaned, stew she boiled, scarves she knitted and trousers she mended were his. Her parents, Jaruel and Catherine, might have thought she was bashful, retiring. The other children grown and growing, thriving, her parents might have finally had time to worry about her, perhaps bearing in mind her melancholy might have to do with her twin lost so many years ago, and therefore they said nothing. In 1890, was a girl of 22 with no apparent suitors becoming an old maid? Perhaps, once, her mother discovered Mary Catherine slumped on the floor, a fallen broom and dust pan beside her; Seaborn, 15 years old (and recently had also left schooling behind), sitting beside her adoptive sister, Mary Catherine's head in her lap. Mary Catherine's body seemed to quake, as though silently weeping. Seaborn—Sissy—with one of Mary Catherine's hands in her own, palm-up, rubbed Mary Catherine's wrist and looked at her mother in the bedroom doorway. No words exchanged. Her mother might have assumed Mary Catherine had swooned in some kind of distress or sorrow she couldn't bear. Outside the house, the taps of hammers and rasp of saws and crack of lumber as the fog bell house was being built. Nahum might have been hired on as part of the crew building the fog tower.

A moment after she'd become still, Mary Catherine would open her eyes and smile up into Seaborn's face. The bliss of just knowing her cousin was here on Hendricks Head today meant neither her usual nor her secret routine would be dull or hollow.

Tam's e-mail alert sounded. Perhaps an answer already from Martha?

You thought I wanted you for a lover? I wanted us to be like sisters. Now that I know your creepy family, I'm glad, no thanks! First your deranged brother coming here, waving some book in my face, supposed to prove why you shouldn't be training dogs. Training dogs, my ass. You never did jackshit with my dogs, just stood there at the end of the lead. If they showed well, it's because *I* trained them. So tell your pushy mother I don't know where her babyboy is and I didn't touch her darling daughter and your precious shit is all packed up waiting for you to send enough money for me to ship it and, thankfully, get it out of my sight forever.

Tam deleted the message, and the same moment Jill said "Hi," from the doorway. Tam jumped from the chair.

"I wasn't, like, looking over your shoulder. I didn't read it." Jill's voice not apologetic or soothing. Her increasingly usual petulance.

"I know. I'd just turned it off and you startled me. How's the baby?"

"He's sleeping. Finally. I hope he, like, knows to breathe through his mouth cause his nose's stuffed."

"We can prop him a little more upright."

"Okay. Hey . . . " One of her white-socked feet atop the other, knees turned in toward each other, the girl didn't move out of the doorway even though Tam was standing there, obviously ready to leave the office. "I, um . . . guess I should tell you. I used this computer they keep here and went on line to, um . . . I e-mailed my mom."

Tam just stood there for a moment.

"I mean, I . . . I didn't tell her where I am. I didn't say anything about *you*."

"How did you e-mail her?"

"I have my own Hotmail account and I just went online. I've checked my e-mail a few times the past few days. My mom has been e-mailing, like, every hour almost. Not really, but . . . *lots*." The girl put one socked foot over the other, dipped her chin and picked at an already ragged cuticle. "I was checking to see if Branden had sent anything. But he didn't."

"The father."

"Yeah, him. The supposed father. Probably, like, rowing crew for his new preppy school . . . 'scuse me, *academy*."

The little room seemed dim, Jill almost colorless. Some of the morning's haze was already returning, or else it was later in the afternoon than she thought. Especially since she thought she heard tires on the gravel outside.

"That can't be—"

"Why not, it's almost four." Jill finally turned and left the doorway.

"I mean, he was just here."

"Maybe he's horny again."

"That's enough of that," Tam said.

"Oooo, if you add a *young lady* to the end, you'll sound just like my mom."

"The same mom you were so anxious to e-mail and maybe get all of us arrested when they trace it."

Jill turned and rolled her eyes. "They can't trace Hotmail. It, like, goes through a central computer somewhere else."

"You'd better not—"

They snapped to silence when Nat came into the kitchen. "'Evening, Ladies."

Tam stood rooted until Jill padded away and up the stairs.

"Did I interrupt something?"

"Not really." Tam went toward him and didn't stop until her body was up against his, her head on his shoulder.

"What's the matter?"

"Sit down with me, okay?"

With his arm around her, they started together toward the sofa in the sitting area, but Tam stopped. "Wait, let's go back to the fog bell house."

"What's up?" Nat's voice followed her.

Tam was already going through the screen porch and out to the board walkway to the bell house.

Nat's footsteps hurried after her. "Did *you* see him too?"

When Tam whirled to face him, her hair whipped across her face. She clawed at it, but Nat held her shoulders, then his fingers drew her hair aside and pushed it back. The wind had an icy edge. Waves hitting the rocks sounded brittle. He stared into her face, his eyes squinting. "Every time we're together, I wonder how many more times . . ."

"I do too." She moved closer, wrapping herself with her own arms, looking for protection from the wind. "But—who? Who did you ask if I've seen?"

"Folks have sighted some guy poking around. Just sort of driving here and there." As he spoke, he began moving up the ramp toward the fog house again, gathering Tam in one arm beside himself. "Sometimes he gets out of his car and walks around. Could be anyone, looking for summer property, someone's real estate agent. I wondered for a second about him being a detective."

"Oh." Tam sat on the bare mattress and started taking off her shoes. She'd stripped the bed after they'd been there that morning, but hadn't brought the clean sheets back yet.

"Now you don't seem too worried."

"It's . . ." She kicked her shoes away then pushed herself further back on the bed, but didn't unfasten any other buttons, snaps or zippers. "I don't think it's a detective." She sat looking at him until he joined her on the bed, both of them sitting with their backs against the wall, feet on the mattress and knees propped up.

Nat didn't take his boots off. Then he leaned sideways, hooked an arm around her waist and lay down with her in front of him. "It's cold without the blankets," he mumbled. "This one might not be a masterpiece."

"No, I just thought you'd like to come out and hear more about her—Mary Catherine."

"Have you figured out how she's connected to the ghost?"

"No. Maybe, but listen. Remember the first time in the lighthouse, you told me to say no if I wanted you to stop? Well, I *didn't* say no, but I didn't say yes either."

"Are you saying I—"

"No. But for Mary Catherine, that's how it was after she— after her parents arranged for her to marry a widower."

Tam flinched when Nat worked his hands under her flannel shirt and t-shirt. "Just to keep my fingers warm. Go on."

"One day her parents had gone into Cozy Harbor and they ran into a man. Maybe he was buying lobsters. Or he was a friend of the man who ran the lobster pound. Maybe Jaruel was bringing his catch to the pound and his wife, Catherine, had come with him that particular day, so they could stop at the cemetery on the way home."

"These names are running together."

"It's Jaruel Marr's wife. Your great-great grandfather's sister-in-law."

"Too many people related in too many different ways."

"Well, they met this man and found out he's a widower. And they also know they have this dilemma—Mary Catherine, their daughter. She's not married. She's 22. Maybe 23 by now. It's been several months since Jaruel has already taken care of the other problem—her cousin Nahum."

"Oh, I remember, the cousin they caught . . ." He edged his hand down under the waistband of her jeans.

"Yes. Wolcott had caught them together in the new fog bell house. Her father took care of that by going to Nahum's older brother—their father was dead—and together the two men convinced Nahum he'd better sign on with a merchant ship. It was time for him to set out in the world, make his own way. The excuses they gave. But the three of them knew it was only because of Mary Catherine, because a scandalous liaison between cousins had to be terminated. Nahum took his medicine like a man and left home to be a seaman. By dead of night, maybe that same night Jaruel had come to see his older brother, Nahum's bags were packed and his brother took him to the docks in Boothbay. If there wasn't a ship moored there that was hiring on, they would spend the night and push on to Wiscasset or Bath the following morning. So Nahum was gone. And perhaps it had been more than months, maybe a few years now. Perhaps his family heard from him occasionally, but if he'd written to Mary Catherine, her father would have discovered the letter in the mail he picked up at the general store, and it never would have made it to Mary Catherine's hand. When she never replied to his letters, Nahum stopped writing, believing her heart had been weak after all, she had forgotten him, replaced him with another."

"You've got this all figured out." His hand worked farther into her jeans.

"But she wanted to be a lightkeeper, stay in a lightkeeping family. With her cousin, together, they'd learned to polish the brass, trim the wicks, keep the oil warm."

"You can keep my oil warm."

"But now what other choice does Mary Catherine have but to marry the widower who will have her. Maybe her mother suggested to her that the taint of losing her maidenhood to a cousin would be known and that no one else would ever want her. Her parents worked in concert. Eventually, after an informal ceremony by the county clerk, that night in his bed in his house up past the tidal waters of the Sheepscot River, Mary Catherine knows that saying no is not an option. Still, she doesn't say yes. She simply must submit. When he . . . ."

Nat's hand, resting outside Tam's underwear, slipped between her legs.

"She simply must forget her cousin's sweet hands, his mouth, the way he touched her, because this man, he only pushes at her, ruts like one of his animals, so instead of thinking of Nahum's warm body, his crooked smile, his gentle fingers, his ebullient but soft conspiratorial laugh, she only lets herself think of her brother—the one who caused all this. Wolcott. The one who told her father what he'd found in the fog bell house."

"She thinks about her brother during sex?"

"To hate him, like she hates what's happening."

"Kinky. You want to pretend to hate it?"

"No, not weird at all, when a brother ruins your life. What kind of claim of *protection* could he make? Protecting you from being happy? From having someone who wants you, who brings other choices and possibilities to make your life whole again, someone who loves what you can do, accepts what you won't do, and still wants . . . ."

His voice simmering behind her ear, "What won't she do?"

"I couldn't . . . *wouldn't* swim anymore. How did he think Denny had anything to do with *that*? With Denny I had something else, maybe something better, something that would last, I was going to—"

"What are you talking about?" His words joined faint chimes of the channel buoy.

Seabirds screamed before she answered. "My brother, I think he—"

"Your brother? A real brother. You're talking about *your* brother?" Nat jerked his hand out of her jeans.

"I think it's my brother . . ."

"I don't want to hear this crap." His body no longer curled around hers. "I meant it, no real lives. You don't want to hear mine."

"What, that you're not just 'involved,' you're married?" Either he was pulling even further away or she was curling into a smaller ball. Or both.

"Engaged." As he spoke, the bed jolted beneath her. He stood on the mattress and stepped over Tam, then thumped to the floor. "Yeah, we're supposed to do it this summer. Does that make it better for you? To picture me figuring a way to explain to her why I'm going all the way to Bath so often— sure can't admit it's so no one who knows me will see me buying diapers, and that I'm driving all over looking for a different dumpster to pitch the shitty ones. But does that make you hot? To imagine me lying to her about how fucking busy and tired I am so I can't fuck her as often—"

"No I don't like that at all." Tam's eyes were closed. She heard a soft whisper or rustle. Also the buoy, gulls screeching, ceaseless swoosh of water against the rocks below them. She waited. For it to start. The aura. For the resonance of Hendricks Head to recede. For all sound to disappear except: the mute vibration. The silent floating rays of light. Loss of peripheral vision. Or loss of all but peripheral vision. All with her eyelids still closed. Like they said in Illinois, during her first turbulent thunderstorm, a tornado is closest to touching down when abruptly, during the gale, everything stops at once. No wind. No rain. Black quiet.

The violent howl might start with a hum. But instead of a first hint of the thin warning buzz, Nat said, "Hey." Tam opened her eyes. He had one foot on the chair and was tying his boot, his chin was dipped but his eyes looking up, as though over reading glasses. "Is it too late for me to take it back?" His boot back on the floor, sand gently rasping underfoot against the boards. The other boot was already tied. He said, "Hey," again, and

Tam dragged her eyes from his boots to his face. "I'll make it up to you." He smiled. "We're not finished with the story, are we?"

She stayed and slept, not meaning to. It was 7 by the time Tam went back through the screen porch into the kitchen. "Did you eat anything?" Said more to test how her voice would sound than in anticipation the empty room would answer. She looked for a dirty saucepan or empty soup can or microwave dinner package. There was a cereal bowl and spoon in the sink. The television was on, muttering in the master bedroom. Tam left the kitchen without eating.

Her computer had been left on in the keeper's office. Her e-mail software still open, but hidden by the screensaver's blue sky, puffy clouds, and bi-wing airplane puffing back and forth. As she sat and touched the cursor pad, the screen showed the in-coming message alert that had been waiting there who knows how long.

Tam, so much since yesterday. mom and i found out coach is dead. we went to the vet who'd left messages on g's machine. he had an acute lung ailment. probably caused by work in the wtc. we're pretty sure g's going to come looking for you. don't look for logic in why he would do this. tam, whatever problems you have with him, remember he's not well. mom found all his meds still here. new prescription, none used.

i have to tell you, mom is worried enough with all this, so i did tell her you and i have been in email contact all this time. she was relieved but a little hurt. you know. so i want to give her your address, that ok?

so you say you're doing some kind of research. i guess you mean on the internet since you said you won't go to the actual archives. you might have found the answers to your questions there, but in case you haven't: our great-grandfather wolcott marr joined the lighthouse service in 1890, assistant keeper at portland's cape elizabeth (nana

born there), then the cuckolds fog signal station, then
came home with his wife and children to be keeper at
hendricks in 1895.

tam you could e-mail mom. wetpaint@icom.net

It works. The Hendricks Head fog-bell structure built in 1890. Wolcott
leaves home in 1890. Before embarking on his lighthouse career at Cape
Elizabeth, Wolcott's last familial duty is to inform their father that the
new fog-bell house has been used for a licentious meeting between Mary
Catherine and their cousin Nahum Pierce, to urge his parents to get the
young man into a profession that conveys him away from Southport and
to seek a reputable union for Mary Catherine elsewhere.

But there were probably years before the widower offered his dead
wife's vacant post. Years that Mary Catherine remained at home, with
Seaborn as she grew out of girlhood. After the first two or three days of
silence from her beau, Mary Catherine learned of Nahum's defection into
the merchant navy as casual family news, her father's voice between loud
sips of his bean soup at supper, "Mary Jane's boy Nahum took himself to be
a seaman, finally settled on a calling." Mary Catherine's hand reaching
for, finding Seaborn's under the table. Years ahead to spend at this silent
clutching. Sometimes it was Seaborn—Sissy—doing the clasping, whenever Mary Catherine foundered while hanging the wash, while beating
a rug or milking a cow. Sissy might think of these as Mary Catherine's
swoons. Her spells. She knows how to hold her sister's body until it
softens.

By the time Mary Catherine was bedded by the widower, at 26 or 27,
Wolcott would be back, keeper at Hendricks Head, his children playing on
the tide-washed rocks, in the forests, at the crescent-shaped beach of
the cove beside the Head—and attending the same school on Southport where Mary Catherine had sat across the aisle from Nahum during
winter months. Wolcott's daughters sleeping in the dormer Mary Catherine had shared with Sissy. Someday, before the new century was ten
years old, Wolcott's eldest daughter would leave Southport to attend normal school near Portland, then work as a schoolteacher in inland, rural

Maine. But there was no choice like that for Mary Catherine between 1890 and 1895 when her brother returned and the house on Hendricks Head—where Mary Catherine had hoped to live, tend and keep the comfort-giving light burning with her cousin Nahum—was given by the Lighthouse Service to Wolcott and his family. Their parents Jaruel and Catherine would retire. The light in the tower would remain an oil flame and kerosene lamps would continue to glow in the parlor for years after the new dim electric bulbs flickered inside Jaruel Marr's retirement house three miles away in Cozy Harbor.

Sissy would be expected to make her own way in the world. There'd been no offers of marriage to the orphan, so she followed Mary Catherine as close as she could, took a post in a tavern in Wiscasset where the seamen came ashore for ale. There she occasionally heard of Nahum Pierce, his promotions in rank, what new ships he'd signed on with, the foreign coasts he'd seen or touched, the wife he took in Portsmouth. On Sunday, she visited Mary Catherine at the widower's little farm at the end of the tidal waters on the Sheepscot River, sitting with Mary Catherine in the dark, smoke-scented kitchen—never the parlor, that was for formal company—as Mary Catherine grew larger under her skirt. When the widower went out for firewood, Sissy might whisper, "He's been to Spain." Or, "His second child born last year." Or, "They say his ship comes often into Bath." Or she thought better of it and kept these things to herself, protecting Mary Catherine from further despair.

But before that time, in the five years left at Hendricks Head before her father would retire, before her brother would return to become the second Keeper Marr, Mary Catherine and Sissy tacitly shared their estrangement from life, each austere melancholy day. Hurrying to finish their chores so they could walk to the cemetery where Mary Catherine has shown Sissy her twin brother's marker. In the summer they might sit there to do their embroidery or darning, no longer wanting to gaze out to sea between stitches. There have been no letters to answer. Sissy with a cold stone in her own stomach, doesn't have to express anything to Mary Catherine; it's understood that Sissy languishes because her adoptive brother Lowell has never returned her tender gazes.

Maybe one time their solemn days were disturbed, when Sissy reported to Mary Catherine that a man had been spotted, lurking around the island, nearest to the harbor, and on the road toward Hendricks Head. Wearing a sailor's peacoat and a nautical cap. Sissy hadn't seen his face. She was on her way home from delivering eggs to the Barkins who lived above the general store. *It could be him*, Sissy would contend. *He doesn't want anyone to see him looking for you.*

Even though her heart staggers, Mary Catherine suspects it could also be Wolcott, stealing back from Cuckolds just to check to make sure she's still living properly at home, isn't receiving any visitors. The scant family talk at the supper table says Nahum is far out at sea, so she could really have no hope it was him.

If not her lover, then certainly her brother. Who else could it be?

Crying Along with Him

Just as clearly as she knew that Gary was in Southport, she knew this: whenever his course collides with hers, hers is the life that changes lanes.

And of course Gary would know where to find her. He wouldn't aimlessly drive the circuit road around the island, or hike the trails, or sit at the Cozy Harbor dock waiting for lobster boats to come tie up. He knew she was at the lighthouse, and her comprehension of that was more than a sensation. In the morning she discovered things had been moved around in the front room. The brass telescope turned inward as though to probe ceilings and corners of the kitchen and sitting room. A broom reclining on the sofa. Then the following morning the computer was left turned on, the dial-up connected, the website waiting under her screen saver with Gary's body parts dream glowing. A copy of *The Water Babies* next to the coffeepot, already filled with fresh coffee before its 7 a.m. timer kicked in. Tam began locking the doors at night. Nat had a key, but he'd stayed away for the past thirty-six hours. The baby was sick, coughing, sputtering mucus.

Tam spent the edgy, quiet afternoon hours on line in the keeper's office.

www.sdakotastate.edu/athletics/staff/clarkson

Dennis Clarkson

Assistant Athletic Director

South Dakota State University
Bob Golbreth Athletics Building
Brookings, SD 57007

Phone: 605 922-2200

Fax: 605 922-2001

Office Hours: By Appointment
Email: coach.clarkson@sdakotas.edu
Education: BA, physical education, Fullerton State University

Background:

As a prep and college swimmer, Dennis Clarkson specialized in the 200 and 400 meter butterfly and breaststrokes. He was a member of an All-American 200 medley relay at Medesto Central High School. He went on to swim at Fullerton State, was a Pacific Coast Conference finalist in the 200 and 400 breaststroke from 1965-1969, and received the 1969 "Workhorse Award."

Prior to his tenure at South Dakota State, Clarkson spent the previous two years as an assistant men's and women's swimming coach at University of Nevada Las Vegas. Before that he was men's swim coach at San Diego University for 8 years. While at San Diego and UNLV, Clarkson coached various swimmers who qualified for the NCAA Championships and National Championships, including athletes with Olympic Trial Time Standards. In 1985, Clarkson became the men's and women's swim coach at South Dakota State University. In 1994, he accepted a post as assistant athletic director, continuing as men's swim coach until 1997. Coach Clarkson's prep-star son Ben is preparing to become a member of South Dakota State's swim team in the 2003 season.

Twinges of vertigo, the threshold of agitation, a restless jitter in her limbs she can sense but not see. But Tam holds it off, the same resolve Mary Catherine must have built—after she realized just how consequential it had been for Wolcott to discover her with Nahum in the bell tower—to not ever again let her brother have that kind of influence.

Did Mary Catherine giggle when her brother knocked on the bell house door? Or maybe Wolcott didn't knock. Why would he knock? It wasn't a private residence, a bedroom. It held the mechanics for the fog bell, and maybe one little cot for whatever man might have to stay there twelve to twenty-four hours to keep the mechanism going. When Wolcott came in that day, with the fog bell tolling above, Mary Catherine might not have even heard him, until Nahum, her cousin, slowed above her, turned, and she could see past Nahum's shoulder, over the mound of her petticoat and skirt bunched above her raised knees . . .

she could see Wolcott in the doorway, behind him nothing but the mist that was blotting the Head from the rest of the island. Instead of giggling, Mary Catherine might have felt the aura, the white-out foreboding, the invisible flashing or light-headed signal for one of her spells. Would she, just for a second, have wished for Seaborn to be there?—her cousin didn't know it happened, and only Sissy sensed what to do if Mary Catherine swooned. If she had, it might have averted Wolcott's attention from what he'd witnessed when he first opened the door. If Mary Catherine had had her grand mal *then*, and if she'd died from it that day, her lover would have mourned her forever, and her brother would not be accredited as her rescuer.

Had Tam felt the aura when Gary knocked on the swim team office door? No, her brain had been too lit with other hormones that day, and she'd missed the portentousness of where that knock would lead. Not just to news of her father's death. Past that, after that, to the day Denny would say, "Reality's come knocking," days or a week after she'd tried to tell him about her condition. "I can't risk this," he'd said.

She'd thought he'd guessed or figured out she was pregnant and meant it was the reputed baby he couldn't risk. The realization that he probably didn't mean that at all, that instead it had to do with Gary, washed over her in bigger and bigger waves, twenty-five years later on Hendricks Head, Maine.

It did not end where the ending began. McDonald's was just off campus, but not a place an athlete usually liked to eat, especially a vegetarian. Tam and Denny ordinarily went to a Greek cafe, mostly carry-out but with a few small tables scattered with old issues of *The Reader*, often opened to the personal ads, and Tam would read them aloud—*SWM, 9", seeks fun-loving SWF for walks and snuggles. Try-it-u'll-like-it*—over salad with feta cheese and olives, and their favorite, spanokopita, since they had decided to become vegetarians the previous year.

"Every few years I get this craving for French fries that won't quit," Denny had said. Was his grin forced, or could she have noticed it then?

"They're fried in lard, aren't they?"

"That's what makes them so attractive, the taboo, the lure of animal fat."

But he hadn't stopped with fries; he'd ordered a Big Mac with cheese. Tam tried to stay true and at least avoided the beef; she got a fish sandwich, but she knew the block of pasteurized fish flakes was cooked on the same grill as the burgers. She held it with a thumb and one finger—Denny said her hand looked like a crab's claw holding a sandwich—and peered at it, waiting to see if she would feel as queasy as she knew she ought.

"Greek food is greasy, too," Denny said. "That filo dough has to be fried."

"I know." She put her fish sandwich down on the tray. "I wish Kung Food would open a place nearer to school."

Denny took a huge bite of hamburger. "Is tofu really as sexy as everyone's making it out to be?"

"How about almond butter and honey on whole wheat? That's pretty sensuous."

"Sounds like sticky paste on cardboard."

McDonalds was teeming at noon on a school day. Tam and Denny had one small table, not a booth, more an island on a pillar, with two stools on pillars bolted to the floor on either side. Other toadstool tables and chairs lined up beside and around them, all brisk with students, either alone and trying to balance an open textbook along with a tray on the tiny table, or in pairs and threes. The restaurant, awash with mumbling din, peaked periodically with a spike of laughter, or a shout to someone recognized across the room.

"You don't like your fish thing?" Denny asked.

"I don't think I feel well," Tam had said, even though she couldn't locate any curl of nausea.

Denny looked around as he chewed, then took another bite. With his mouth full, he said, "Um . . . I think . . . well. . . reality's come knocking. Don't you think?"

"Meaning?" She pushed a finger into the top bun of the fish sandwich. "Health food's all a sham? Or . . . " She looked up suddenly. One of Denny's cheeks bulged out as he chewed. His elbows on the tiny table, his hands holding the remaining portion of his burger steady in front of his face, his eyes focused there, on the food, not on her. She asked, "Did someone find out about the workstudy money?"

"No. But maybe we should hide the trail even more."

"We already stopped it."

"I know, but . . ." He'd been working on that mouthful a long time. "I have to . . ." He swallowed but continued chewing without taking another bite. "I can't . . ." He swallowed again, put the hamburger down and picked up his soda, held the cup and drank from the straw, his eyes closed, until the last of the liquid rattled. He hadn't even touched the French fries that had supposedly provoked this whole lunch.

"I just can't risk this," he'd said.

"*This*—? What's that supposed to mean?"

With the straw, he poked at the ice still in his cup. Looked down at what he was doing as though he were fixing a watch. "That . . . I think we should go our separate ways. I think now's the best time."

"Now? You mean now that I'm—"

"Look, I almost got you expelled. What kind of person is that for you to be with?"

"It's a person I . . ." She couldn't be the first to say *love*. "I wasn't about to be expelled. Not even close. No one even *knew*. You're using it as an excuse—" She abruptly crumpled her untouched sandwich inside its wrapper.

"No, Tam. Look, it was fun, a *lot* of fun, but . . . think about it. I used you. I got loads of extra clerical hours, some extra money, let you take most of the risk. I'm a big bum. You're graduating, your degree's in, what, finance?" Suddenly a succession of words coming out of him, and now he was looking at her. "You'll get a much better job at a bank or something, you don't need to be saddled with a floundering swim coach at a school considering doing away with swimming so they can give more of the bucks to football."

"Is that what this is about? You don't have to support us. I was thinking about grad school in phys-ed or phys-therapy. I could help you, be your assistant for real."

"Tam, don't. I shouldn't have let you think that way. Maybe you shouldn't have been with me in the first place. If anyone had known or found out . . ."

"I can't believe this."

"I know how bad it seems. But you'll forget this, Tam, in no time. By this time next month, you'll be able to look forward and see yourself a year from now, two years from now—"

"And twenty years from now, it'll almost be 2000, so damn what?"

"Tam, come on. I thought we both knew . . ."

By then she was crying. Actually gulping hiccups to forestall crying, but tears and snot obliterating not only her vision but any semblance of composure. She pushed greasy napkins into her eye sockets, smelled ketchup, felt a clammy shred of lettuce on her cheek and angrily snatched it away with her other hand.

"I'm sorry, but I do have to think about my career, such as it is, going nowhere fast. If—or when—I have to get another position, I can't afford any kind of . . . thing on my reputation."

"It's not a *thing*."

Maybe he didn't even understand her, through the blubbering. By then, his strategy, if that's what it had been, of doing it in public so there wouldn't be a scene, had broken down. After sweeping the trash and food from their table onto a tray and leaving Tam alone, head down, crying, to throw it all away, Denny, strangely enough—or not so strange, considering what he had been saying—draped her sweater over her head and led her from the McDonalds like a prisoner who doesn't want to be recorded on TV cameras. He kept his arm around her, and she submitted, let herself be guided through campus, seeing only her own feet, sunny sidewalks, and grass when Denny took shortcuts. She recognized the wooden steps to the old gym's auxiliary building where the swim team office was located. She recognized the cool smell of their dark office, the tiny aisle leading around the file cabinets, and she let her knees buckle there, curled into a fetal position on their mattress, no thought to her dignity, she wept, then quieted when Denny lay beside her. Neither of them said anything for an hour or more.

Then Denny whispered he had a meeting with the assistant athletic director, would she be okay alone for an hour?

Tam nodded. He didn't kiss her when he left. He rustled softly in the outer office for a moment, but didn't turn on any lights. When he left, he closed the office door with a soft click.

Tam thought she kept her eyes closed for the entire hour Denny was away, but she didn't sleep. A clock somewhere in the office was ticking. She'd never noticed it before. The air system came on and off. Students in the hall of the old building went past the door with brassy laughter and boisterous voices, swelling then receding as they passed the door. Her brain chanted in rhythm with the phantom clock, *He won't leave me, he won't leave me.*

When Denny returned, gently, as though to a sick room, there was nothing more to say, but they said it all again anyway.

"I don't know why you're doing this."

"I just can't risk it."

"You say you've been a bum, but you're really being one now."

"Tam, I'm not like a tenured professor. I could get fired."

"For what? You're a good coach."

"A good coach who boffs his student help."

"Why do you say it like that?"

"No matter how much fun we both were having, it *looks* like me taking advantage."

"I thought we cared about each other."

"We did. We *do*. That's why we have to do what's best for each other now."

"This isn't best for *me*."

"It seems bad now, but look at the big picture, someday—"

"That's crap. That's such crap. You're being wretched. You're horrible. I can't believe you could do this."

It went on and on. She would cry. He would stroke her like a dying animal. She would calm a little. They would be quiet for a while. Then they started over. Her face was a puffy, slimy horror. Her blouse and skirt wrinkled, damp with sweat. She could smell the rank distress seeping from her pores. The aura had never been a smell. In fact, three years with Denny, four years off her meds, sometimes she'd almost forgotten about it, frequently forgot to be on guard for signs of loss of stability. Even climaxless sex had become more a habit than conscious holding back out of fear the culmination would trigger a seizure. So the stench of terror exuding from her body that afternoon didn't warn her. Didn't warn her enough.

It's an echo of the terror she recoils from now, as though she can smell a tint of it again, and her gut throbs now with the nausea she never felt then, even seconds before she was writhing on the swim office floor, gushing bodily fluids from every orifice. Because she suddenly understands what he was saying.

What were the rules, written or unwritten, in 1978? Could Denny have been fired for an affair with an undergraduate? There was no such thing, yet, as sexual harassment—was there? And how would Gary know there might be a pregnancy. He wouldn't. All the cues and signals flying past her fuzzy brain, even just two days ago with Gary's enigmatic message on the website—but not until Mary Catherine's doom is sealed by her brother Wolcott could Tam picture Gary, steely faced, uttering into a telephone, "You break it off or I'll tell someone it's going on," and Denny losing his year-round poolside tan on the other end, his sweet guileless face falling, his honest heart plunging, grasping his dilemma.

http://www.fredonia.edu/aaoffice/index2.htm

History of Sexual Harassment

The following is an abbreviated history of sexual harassment decisions:

•**1964 Civil Rights Act**—broadened the employment discrimination section, Title VII, to cover sex discrimination

•1972 Education Act Amendments—prohibiting sex discrimination at schools and universities that receive any federal funding

•1976—*Williams v. Saxbe* - conditions of employment applied differently to men and
women were forbidden under Title VII as sex discrimination

•1977—First charge of sexual harassment of students brought under Title IX of the 1972 Education Act Amendments

•1980—*EEOC Guidelines on Discrimination Because of Sex* were formalized and became official

•1982, 1983—Two federal circuit courts of appeal identified two basic varieties of sexual harassment: (1) Quid pro quo ("this for that") and (2) hostile environment

•1986—U.S. Supreme Court ruled sexual harassment on the job is illegal discrimination
even if the victim suffers no economic loss

•1991—*Robinson vs. Jacksonville Shipyards*—nude pinups in the workplace can constitute sexual harassment

•1991—*Ellison v. Brady* established the "reasonable woman" standard

Dear Denny,
Look at that, the first sexual harassment charge brought just the year before! Were you aware of it? Of course, you had to be, it was threaded into title 9, the savior of women's swimming. And by 1991 they'd decided, finally, that women were reasonable. Perhaps decided by then we could pick our own lovers without our brothers' approval.

She hadn't even typed in an e-mail address. Even so, she sent it, and when it didn't go, sent it again, and after a third time, deleted it.

Message *to* Tam

You chose to want to feel alone, an outsider. The more you wallowed (what you thought was silent sto-icism) the more they focused everything on you. It was poor Tam, poor afflicted Tam. You got what you wanted I guess. Who do you really think was left alone, to sink or swim (as they say) on his own, to succeed, to excel, to conquer. But I fooled you. I got a disease of my own. An inflamed brain of my own. Two inflamed brains from the same bad seed. And something else—what I did, I did for your own good. I think you've secretly blamed me for too many years for that. It was no different than pulling someone from under the rubble. You had to be extracted. I'd do it again. I love you.

Dear Martha,
Did you ever know what G meant in this message? I do now. Love me? He hasn't ever met the meaning of the word.
T

Upstairs, the baby cried, a frail keen, like an animal caught in a trap too long. Perhaps she also heard Jill's voice, tenderly, wearily trying to sing the baby to sleep—or crying along with him.

When she sent the message, her software announced incoming mail.

Tam, it's mom.
I know you think you have to look for something there. You're not going to find it. When Gary finds you, please bring him home.
Love you, please come home.
Mom

Tam, what's really going on there? G must've found you by now. he's sick but not stupid. what's been going on all this time?
-m

Martha, you may as well ask me, why do you let yourself be used in this man's stories? I don't know if it's his story or mine, maybe that's because it doesn't matter whose story it is. I'm always the luminary.
You can tell mom.

Again she deleted the first version and started another.

Martha, am trying to figure out how to answer this, why it's so important to continue doing what I'm doing, (even though seeing G is becoming imminent, and will likely ruin everything). Maybe this will explain: Are you one of those who hides in air-conditioning all summer? In Illinois when it gets about 90 and the humidity is thick and pungent, you assume it's right to stay inside in the thin, cool conditioned air. But if you're forced to go out into reality, your skin dry and chilly, you're instantly drawn into the fever, its arm around you like a friend, a steeping bath and the scented bath oil is your own acrid essence. And you instinctively absorb that this is also right. Once you're out there, you know it's right. Perhaps it's the slick sheen on your body, that you get from no other contact. The caress of warm breath, quickened only by your arrival. Other people might still think of it with apprehension, too oppressive to give yourself to. I know there are people who would consider him as low class, unable to discipline his animal urges, a betrayer, a debaser, a self-absorbed user. Perhaps you would wonder why I think about his touch with appetite, why I would want his humid body to induce that oily coat of sweat on me. These who wonder would be the same people who would never go out in the summer. And I had been one of those people, staying inside in the safety of air conditioning.

Deleted.

Dear Martha,
A hundred years before sexual harassment policies were being conceived . . . Mary Catherine was in love with her cousin Nahum, their secret incandescence neither a hostile environment (until her brother decided it was one) nor quid pro quo. It was not love but marriage that was quid pro quo. A hundred years before the courts decided a woman could be reasonable, Mary Catherine was given in marriage to a widower. This for that. He'll make her a respectable (reasonable) woman, she'll give him her body. Or she'll let him take her body, but never give it. Her resistance was stoic indifference. A hostile environment? For him or her?

Frigidity can be right in one bed, but that doesn't mean resistance is always right. Mary Catherine knew, as I know, how a man's desire can make her alive with her own. And the power a woman has to make a man want her, to give him a secret life he'll think about during toil or travail.

Before she found her cousin, Mary Catherine's life was just bereavement over what she'd lost. She was a little girl, no one could accuse her of wallowing, seeking the attention of pity. Losing a twin, they say, is like losing part of yourself (perhaps like losing a child?) . . . or like losing a part of who you were. You see why I understand her?

But her cousin—he brought joy back to her. And the purpose. The sense that her place, her calling was at the lighthouse. She stopped tarrying in the graveyard. She'd brought Sissy there previously, when she was still Seaborn, when she was still a little girl's burden. Mary Catherine had brought her to the graveyard, perhaps so Seaborn would comprehend whom she would never replace. Perhaps Mary Catherine had unkindly said, "If you'd drowned in that mattress, you'd probably be here beside him, but without a big stone like his, maybe with no marker at all, since you weren't part of the family." Seaborn, a pigtail in her mouth, stared solemnly at the headstone, understanding.

In the 1880's, Mary Catherine and Sissy didn't habitually return to the graveyard together, not until after Mary Catherine's cousin Nahum went away to be a merchant seaman. By then the thin ice of cruelty had melted from Mary Catherine's connection with her adopted sister. By then it was only Sissy who had known of Mary Catherine's euphoric secret, and only Sissy who sat by—a tranquil, steadfast restorative—when Mary Catherine swooned. But Mary Catherine was too consumed with her own bliss to know that Sissy stole off to sit in the graveyard, alone, sat in the place where she could never belong during times when Mary Catherine needed their bedroom to be with Nahum. It wasn't until afterwards, when they once again sat there together, that Mary Catherine learned of Sissy's long unspoken feelings for Lowell.

How had this happened? Little spoiled Lowell. Was he Sissy's Nahum? The youngest son. The youngest was allowed to stay a boy, to play and dream, the world of grown-man responsibility not his. What was attractive in that, in a man who wouldn't grow up, who dabbled in many vocations, who might never marry, or maybe would try to make the gesture later in life, only to keep daring and dreaming just months before the date approached?

It's the dreaming, isn't it? I didn't dream for so many years. Denny now only dreams about his own, real child. Just like Mom—after that whole world of women opened every door for her, she ended up with only aspirations for her son. But a dreaming man, who puts you in his reverie . . . who embodies doors thrown open, not slammed in your face, that's all Mary Catherine and Sissy wanted.

Mary Catherine wasn't lucky enough to ever find another who could restore and arouse life in her like her cousin had. The widower's want of her was pig-want. He didn't see her as the center of a whole story. She was the means to an end. Which became her end.

Deleted

Martha, yes G is here, haunting the lighthouse, I suspect I'll see him soon, all-too soon. The baby is sick and the girl, his mother, depressed. I haven't

seen Nat for almost two days and am burning for his touch

Deleted.

Tam slept with the door to the master bedroom locked. She knew the sound of Nat's truck on the sand drive would wake her and she could be at the door to release it before he was through the kitchen. The baby's cries were distant, like dreams, like the serenity nature-sounds tapes she used to always have with her. It was only the sound of the fax machine in the keeper's office that woke her, repeatedly, through the night.

Barely past dawn she stood, dressed like Jill in one of Nat's undershirts, looking at the sheets she'd taken from the fax machine's tray.

The first one:

```
. . . . . −. −  /  − . −−  /  . . /  . −−  / . .
. . . . . −. . /  . −− /  . −. . . −. . . −
. . .    −−−. . . .     . . .    −−−. . .      . . .
−−−. . . .
```

The other three:

```
. . .    −−−. . . .     . . .    −−−. . .      . . .    −− −
. .     . . .    −−−. . .
```

Behind her the coffee machine hissed into action at 7 a.m. The baby had been crying for ten or fifteen minutes, now ebbing and fading until his voice once again melded with his mother's monotone croon. Tam folded the papers, weighted them with a coffee cup, then turned her back, stood holding another empty cup in both hands, waiting for the coffee maker to finish. From upstairs, either a recurring moan or the girl was still singing. Floorboards creaked. Wind whomped against the big window facing the sea. Except the coffee tinkling into the filling decanter, they were the same sounds Mary Catherine might have listened through, those days when she didn't know if her cousin would come or not. Or after he was gone to be a seaman, she still listened for the familiar sounds of his arrival that she knew she would never hear again. During the last days the family lived in the lighthouse in 1895, awaiting Wolcott's return to take over the keeper's duties upon their father's retirement, Mary Catherine listened to the sounds of waiting, but anticipation long gone, and she wondered how Nahum would ever find her after she goes to marry the widower in Sheepscot near the head tide, farther from the sea than she had ever lived. The murmur upstairs is Sissy, melancholy as she packed a small valise. No wedding trousseau or hope chest, just her two or three skirts and blouses, woolen stockings, bloomers and petticoats. She also wouldn't be moving with the family to the house in Cozy Harbor. 20 years old, she knows she should have departed long ago, when she left school at 15, but had stayed to remain near Mary Catherine, and

Lowell. And, on such a day, in 1895, listening and waiting, Mary Catherine would only hear the triumphant return of Wolcott and his family.

"Hey." Jill wasn't visible, still at the top of the stairs. "I think your man's here."

"What? I didn't hear— Which one?"

Jill made a snorting sound. "How many d'you *have*?"

"I didn't hear his truck, I thought you meant—"

"He's, like, in a boat. I think it's him. He's all dressed like the Gorton fisherman."

"The what?"

"That fisherman guy in ads for frozen fishsticks."

Tam realized she had one hand pressed over her strobing heart. She put her fingers on the outside of the coffee machine, as though to see if it was warm. "How's the baby, is he eating?"

"Yeah, eating, and breathing. Poor miserable thing. We're going back to bed now, so you two can, like, please keep it down."

Tam removed the coffee decanter and put her cup into the flow of coffee streaming from the machine. When her cup was full, she put the decanter back. She still didn't hear Nat's boots approaching the porch. There weren't any trees on the head to visually tell her the volume of wind outside, but the house creaked a little, and something outside rattled. The open ocean off the tip of the head was shredded by surly whitecaps. When she opened the front door, she could hear water smashing against rocks, and the wet-river sound of wind through dead grasses and dormant coastal brush. It was only just dawn. The seabirds had just begun calling. A cloud ceiling hovered, but not low enough to be fog. Tam had her jeans on, but no sweater or jacket over the undershirt. Coffee still in her hand, she only meant to stand on the porch a second, to see what Jill was talking about, but she saw him, not in the choppy Sheepscot inlet, but in the cove on the other side—the little bay that was cradled by Hendricks Head yet this morning was uneasy with white-tipped rollers. He was in a sailing dinghy, smaller than a one-man lobster boat, but bigger than the skiffs the lobstermen used to get from wharves out to their vessels anchored in a lagoon or harbor. It had a flat back, two oars and a single mast, swaying back and forth like a pendulum, but there was no sail attached.

She slipped her bare feet into tennis shoes she'd left on the porch, crossed the gravel drive and began to make her way to the rocks as Nat used the oars to maneuver the dinghy close to shore. He was wearing a yellow rain slicker and hat with a long tail that protected his neck. He stood before the dinghy crunched against the slabs, threw a small anchor up into the rocks beyond where the waves splashed. He had thick leather gloves that went past his wrists to his forearms, oilcloth pants that matched the slicker, tucked into knee-high boots. Although anchored to the rocky shore, the dinghy still roiled in water five or six feet out. Nat stood looking at her, holding the mast with one gloved hand. His body skilled enough, lithe enough to move with the dinghy, so his stance was sturdy, his gaze steady. She watched his supple knees and hips absorb the upwelling and subsiding. Water dropped from the brim of the hat.

Tam hugged the coffee cup to her chest, one arm atop the other, shivering, Nat's undershirt billowing around her. "Are you . . . ?" But her voice was blown away.

"I came for you," he shouted.

"Where's your truck?"

"I realized, she's been wandering the coast, looking out to sea, waiting. So she isn't looking for anyone to come for her by *land*."

"What—? The ghost—?"

"*You*." His knees leaned and shifted to keep his body erect. "And if it *was* rum-runners you were signaling, they'd come dressed as fishermen."

"Nat, I can't . . ."

"You look cold, woman. Come aboard and I'll warm you."

"I have to tell you something!" Tam shouted louder.

"I know you do. Come here then." He leaned forward and grabbed the anchor rope. Although completely hidden by the slicker, she could see his body work with agile power, pulling the bobbing dinghy closer without losing balance. Then he put one boot out on the rocks, still holding the mast, held a gloved hand out toward her.

"Nat! It's my brother who's been—"

"Your brother the lightkeeper?"

"My brother the jerk. My famous hero brother who writes—"

"Forget it for now."

"I can't, he's really—"

"Not *now*."

"But he's—"

"*No*, dammit." He jumped from the dinghy, bent to pull it father onto the rocks.

"What's the matter?"

"We have to get back to *this*."

"I'm not going out on a boat."

He stared for a moment, then dropped the dinghy's rope. "No, you're not. Not now." He came toward her, rising as he climbed the rocks toward where she stood. "I can't recreate— Not after . . . not now. It has to just *happen*. It's always just *happened* for us. Why are you stopping it now?" He ripped the yellow slicker hat from his head.

Tam resisted an urge to touch the lock of hair falling forward onto his brow. "I'm sorry, I didn't know—"

He turned and headed toward the house, the big boots squeaking in the sand.

Tam followed. When she got to the front porch, the boots were already empty on the steps, the gloves tossed onto a bench, and he was stripping himself of the slicker and oilcloth pants. Underneath he was wearing longjohns and a sweatshirt with some kind of faded sports insignia.

"I'm sorry," she repeated. "We can—"

"We *can't*. I was trying to get something going, but you're not letting it happen. Your damn brother can't exist . . . and not your father or mother, your boss or your best friend." He flung the pants on the porch floor on top of the slicker.

"I notice you didn't mention husband."

"You're not wearing any ring."

"I took it off."

"Liar." He jerked the door open and pushed past her into the house.

"Oh, now you want the truth?"

"No, forget it. Just— forget it." He took the coffee cup she'd set on top of the fax sheets, filled it, and raised it to his lips, looking at her over the rim. Maybe even glaring. His eyes hot and hard, but also asking a question.

"What, Nat?"

"Nothing." His gaze dropped. He lowered the mug without ever taking any coffee into his mouth. He picked up the papers. Tam wasn't sure what he was looking at. The kitchen lights weren't on, a late-winter dawn still just breaking. He held the fax sheets in one hand, coffee cup in the other, his jaw working. Then he said, "Someone's contacting you in Morse code."

"I know. What does it say?"

"I knew this stuff once. I almost went into the Coast Guard. I'd have to brush up. But I can see the SOS at the bottom. God, weird. Like *she's* using our technology to make contact with you."

"Not a she. It's my brother, he's here, somewhere, and I'm—"

"No, goddamn it, *no*. This crap about your family is ruining it." He crumpled the papers and threw them. The coffee followed, not thrown but the mug put down so hard coffee splashed across the counter top. He stood with both hands flat on the counter, arms stiff, shoulders tight and head hanging. Then his fingers curled, his hands closed into fists. His voice splintered, "It's going to end, isn't it."

"No, it doesn't have to. I . . . ." She approached him slowly, as though cautiously, but she was still a body's length away. "I need you, Nat. Stuff is starting to get so complicated."

"But—" He raised his head, shoulders shaking. He turned toward her, his face distorted, eyes squinting almost shut. "Nothing has ever been so . . . raw and intense, and now . . . How is this going to end?" He wiped his nose and one cheek with his palm, but his face continued collapsing.

Tam froze. "Now you're ruining it for me."

"What?"

"You're the one who's always—"

"Playing, right? Never dedicated enough to make a go of one thing. So I said I'd marry her, and I will, but— it's this summer. It's *this* goddamn summer, and today's, *what*? What *is* today? Is it April already? Already goddamn *April*?" He turned, his knees buckled, his body slid to the floor, his back still upright against the cabinets but head in his hands, his breath heaving.

Tam thought she heard the stairs creak, a footstep pad back into the bedroom upstairs. She listened for a moment, trying to put herself into the soft retreating footsteps. In all the times she'd resolutely eluded a demonstrative storm, ever since Denny, she'd still never felt so inert. Her feet mired in glue, her hands benumbed deadweight. By the time she moved through the suddenly boggy air in the kitchen and was kneeling in front of Nat, his harsh breath was steady, his body wasn't heaving. He lifted his head, and as though on cue, he was the one to move, to lift his arms and cup her face in his hands. After a moment he pulled her closer and kissed her. His face was damp, his lips salty.

He said, "Can't we save it a little longer?"

Tam touched his chin with her tongue. "You're briny. Did you know the ocean's saline is almost the same as the human body's?" After he kissed her again, she continued, "They called her Seaborn, born of the ocean, the womb that brought her . . ."

"And then she returned to it to drown."

"Maybe. I don't know yet. If it was Seaborn, or maybe Mary Catherine's daughter."

He stared into her face, as though searching for something. But now his eyes, although tired, were calm. "I'm not trying to force you, but I thought you like to be with someone who makes you do what you want to do, what you're pretending to be afraid of."

"What brought you to that conclusion?"

"What you said, in the bell house the other day. She doesn't say no but she doesn't say yes." He squinted, winced, and said, "God, I sound like a defense attorney at a rape trial."

"Or Mary Catherine on her wedding night."

261

Another flinch, and his smile was sour. "You had to remind me again?"

"Wedding nights aren't what they used to be, are they?"

"Shut up." He slid his hands into her hair and took gentle fistfuls.

Tam shut her eyes. "Not yours. Mary Catherine's. Not only to endure the vulgar rutting of her new husband—he smells of manure, not of clean salty fishing boats. But to bear it while also knowing her sister Sissy has packed a valise and arranged a ride to Wiscasset—probably half a day's trip in a wagon stacked with salted, dried cod—and that she'll take a lowly position as a barmaid. By the 1920's, that's how she'll get mixed up with rum-runners."

"Wait," he pulled her head closer until his forehead touched hers, "you know Maine had prohibition before everyone else? I don't remember when it started. Way back."

"Oh. I'll check on that. But a little wine couldn't change how Mary Catherine's grim wedding night in 1895 is like a dire ceremony over losing everything: her cousin lover away to sea without a word, five years gone; and now her family leaving the lighthouse—her home, and the safe passage she'd envisioned continuing to provide there—and turning it over to her betrayer brother."

While she spoke, Nat's hands had relaxed and he slipped his fingers through her hair, gathering it, releasing it, combing it again. "When summer comes and these people want to use their lighthouse, I can stash you somewhere else. But—"

"I know. We have to clean up this thing with this girl and her baby."

"Yeah, true. But I was going to say, a man and a ghost . . ." his voice dropped to a hoarse whisper, "people can see him, but not her. If I— if we did it with people around, nearby, what would they see? Can you . . . ?"

It was only getting close to 8:30 but felt like a whole day had been spent, by the time Nat put on the oilcloth pants and some old work boots he kept in the base of the light tower, then headed up the road on foot toward Barkin's store for his morning coffee ritual there. There had been some frail whimpers from the baby at one point, no singing from the girl, then everything upstairs had quieted again.

Tam, no i don't know what g meant by 'extracting' you. maybe from your extreme fear of swimming? you can ask him when you see him. start some communication. it'll be good for both of you. i think he did go off the deep end, as you say, (more literally he's off his meds) when his dog died. i forget, sometimes, to cut him some slack when he acts crude or reckless, like when he reamed me out over not getting what he went through at the wtc. g-as-usual i said. yes, i suppose for him it is usual. his condition is so much worse than yours, and yet look what he's accomplished. mom and i hoped you'd understand this about g and not hold him to a standard he can't meet. but i'm just as guilty, i realize now. he wants so badly to be what you think he failed at being—the courageous person he tries to show to the real world, but sometimes it's just too hard for him and he crashes, usually just to his family, but now it's probably a complete break down of every facade he ever built.
-m

From the keeper's office, Tam could glance into the dark kitchen where she'd crouched with Nat. It seemed morning was having difficulty lighting the sky, still unable to prevail, and the explanation came as rain on the roof. A steady thrum, suspending seabird calls, deadening the toll of the buoy. The coffeepot sighed, reminding her it was still on, still an inch of coffee in the decanter and grinds in the filter needing to be cleaned. She'd sponged the coffee from the counter after Nat left. Otherwise the kitchen was clean. Linens could be washed, but she had to wait for Jill to rise again. As long as the baby slept, that was good—he seemed to wear himself out crying as long as he was awake. Of course, she supposed it was not good if he stopped crying altogether.

What would Mary Catherine do, after washing the breakfast dishes in her new husband's cottage? There was always knitting and mending. Probably a lot of it, saved up over the years he'd lived without a woman.

Dirt crusted in corners. Sheets lank and dingy. She simply sat at the table she'd just cleared and cleaned, drained of verve by the daunting onus stretching out permanently in front of her. Not knowing whether she can be everything her new husband expects, and what will she do, without Sissy, about the foreboding traces of the aura. Her mind numb and flashing at the same time, her hand gropes for something to read. Just as she'd read to Sissy when Sissy was little, Sissy had begun to read to Mary Catherine of late, sometimes as Mary Catherine rested after a swoon, other times as she embroidered pillowcases she'd never want to use now in this dismal coal-mine of a dwelling. What might Mary Catherine have to read now, likely only her new husband's family Bible—not the Marr Bible, that stayed with Wolcott—or the only book she'd been able to bring from home, *The Water Babies.*

Tam had moved it from the kitchen to the sitting area, and she didn't feel inclined to move from where she was. The computer was already on, already logged in.

http://www.digitalhistory.uh.edu/historyonline/housework.cfm

History of Private Lives

Housework in Late 19th Century America

by S Mintz

Prior to the twentieth century, cooking was performed on a coal or wood burning stove. Unlike an electric or a gas range, which can be turned on with the flick of a single switch, cast iron and steel stoves were exceptionally difficult to use. Ashes from an old fire had to be removed. Then, paper and kindling had to be set inside the stove, dampers and flues had to be carefully adjusted, and a fire lit. Since there were no thermostats to regulate the stove's temperature, a woman had to keep an eye on the contraption all day long. Any time the fire slackened, she had to adjust a flue or add more fuel.

Throughout the day, the stove had to be continually fed with new supplies of coal or wood - an average of fifty pounds a day.

At least twice a day, the ash box had to be emptied, a task which required a woman to gather ashes and cinders in a grate and then dump them into a pan below. Altogether, a housewife spent four hours every day sifting ashes, adjusting dampers, lighting fires, carrying coal or wood, and rubbing the stove with thick black wax to keep it from rusting.

It was not enough for a housewife to know how to use a cast iron stove. She also had to know how to prepare unprocessed foods for consumption. Prior to the 1890s, there were few factory prepared foods. Shoppers bought poultry that was still alive and then had to kill and pluck the birds. Green coffee had to be roasted and ground. Loaves of sugar had to pounded, flour sifted, nuts shelled, and raisins seeded.

Cleaning was an even more arduous task. The soot and smoke from coal and wood burning stoves blackened walls and dirtied drapes and carpets. Gas and kerosene lamps left smelly deposits of black soot on furniture and curtains. Each day, the lamp's glass chimneys had to be wiped and wicks trimmed or replaced. Floors had to scrubbed, rugs beaten, and windows washed.

According to calculations made in 1886, a typical housewife had to carry water from a pump or a well or a spring eight to ten times each day. Washing, boiling and rinsing a single load of laundry used about 50 gallons of water. Over the course of a year she walked 148 miles toting water and carried over 36 tons of water. Women also had to remove dirty dishwater, kitchen slops, and, worst of all, the contents of chamberpots from their house by hand.

Laundry was the household chore that housewives detested most. On Sunday evenings, she soaked clothing in tubs of warm water. When she woke up the next morning, she had to scrub the laundry on a rough washboard and rub it with soap made from lye, which severely irritated her hands. Next, she placed the laundry in big vats of boiling water and stirred the clothes about with a long pole to prevent the clothes from developing yellow spots. Then she lifted the clothes out of the vats with a washstick, rinsed the clothes twice, once in plain water and once with bluing, wrung the clothes out and hung them out to dry. At this point, clothes would be pressed with heavy flatirons and collars would be stiffened with starch.

The last years of the nineteenth century witnessed a revolution in the nature of housework. Beginning in the 1880s, with the invention of the carpet sweeper, a host of new "labor-saving" appliances were introduced.

http://www.mainehistory.info/history.html

A Brief History of Maine

Extract from Maine Almanac (1980)

by Jim Brunelle

1851—"The Maine Law"

The temperance movement had its origins in Maine, and to one degree or another dominated the political life of this state for more than a century.

The world's first Total Abstinence Society was founded in Portland in 1815. A state organization of temperance societies was formed in 1834, and within a dozen years had developed enough political clout to force the enactment of a state law prohibiting the sale of alcoholic spirits except for "medicinal and mechanical" purposes.

Under the fiery leadership of Portland's Neal Dow—known internationally as the "Father of Prohibition"—Maine approved a total ban on the manufacture and sale of liquor in 1851. Five years earlier a similar, but weaker act had been passed, but authorities were unable to enforce it. The new act was stronger, though those who sought to obtain or sell alcohol still found the ways and means to skirt the law or avoid detection.

This so-called "Maine Law" remained in effect, in one form or another, until the repeal of National Prohibition in 1934.

After being online so long, the ringing of the fax machine bewildered her for a moment. But when a sheet of paper started feeding through the printer, Tam got up and left the lightkeeper's office.

Mary Catherine's transactions with her family might wait in the future while she endured weeks or months of repetitious silent days of household chores. Then when she did go with her husband to see her parents in Cozy Harbor every other or every third month, her mother's recitation of news would slip from sibling to sibling, births and illnesses, harvests and cows freshening, sows having litters and foxes raiding henhouses, children passing from 2nd reader to 3rd. Mary Catherine would nod, murmur "Oh really?" or "That's nice." She would return to her husband's bleak residence just as weary, just as broken. It was a different sojourn that fostered Mary Catherine, that kept her lugging water and cleaning soot, scrubbing shirts and darning socks, kept her emptying rank bedpans from under her loathsome marriage-bed. It was the Sunday evening when Sissy found a ride from Wiscasset up the road beside the Sheepscot to the head tide. Sissy saw sailors every day, and a medley of sailors meant abundant accounts from other ports. And sporadically one of these anecdotes brought news of Nahum. In return, Mary Catherine didn't shy from telling Sissy all she knew of Lowell. That he was still unmarried— not surprising, as he still spent one day repairing a wooden dory, the next tinkering with a steam engine tractor, and after that would put to sea for a catch of stripers.

After Tam had sat for a while by the picture window where rain still blurred the view of the Atlantic, and Sequin Island was invisible through the subdued storm, she went back and retrieved the sheet from the fax tray.

> Last time I was at a hospital (probably years ago) I talked to the EEG tech, asked him what kinds of people have to do this, only nuts like me? He said people come to the lab to get tested for multiple sclerosis, dizziness, headaches, numbness in their limbs, blackouts and seizures. Here's the part for you: Even epilepsy patients go there to get temporal lobe surgery to eradicate their seizures, or they have long-term monitoring to find out where exactly the seizures are starting in the brain so they can excise those parts. And he told me that most of the serious epileptics in long-term monitoring have depression or anxiety, too, and often have "subjective" seizures when there are no clinical signs or EEG waves to prove it. So some seizures are real and some are psychologically driven—i.e. FAKES. There are so many patients who come in and say they have blackouts

when their EEGs are normal. Some are very obviously acting, or else believe it so thoroughly that they bring the convulsion on themselves. One of the docs told me that any of us, given the right conditions, could have a seizure. From lack of 02 to the brain, or after having been poisoned in some way, or from a brain infection, etc. Think about it, I've never had a seizure, but does that make me NORMAL?
G

Something Here

The last thing she thought she'd be looking up on the internet was post traumatic stress syndrome, which now, she discovered, they're calling a *disorder*, not a syndrome. Insurance usually pays for treatment of *disorders*, less often for *syndromes*. So that's why Gary thinks it's a brain disease? And why Martha is so tenderly fretting about it?

Dreams, inability to love anyone (but himself), reclusiveness, marital problems (as if any woman could stand to live with him even in the most blithe of his moods)? Inability to concentrate (on his insipid instruction pamphlets for buffoonish guys who play softball then drink a six-pack on weekends)? Insomnia and irritability? Isn't that Gary-as-usual, Gary-as-always-was? And don't these add up to almost anyone who's experienced anything?

Mary Catherine has had her beau taken from her, waylaid by dark of night. Her parents have given away her refuge, her home, her future life to the brother who instigated the departure of her lover. They've forced her to go live in narrow quarters with a stranger, to wash his clothes, clean his house and cook his food all day, so while she may be alone for hours, the vague consolation of her former solitary days, her austere walks to the cemetery, her nighttime vigil at the window over Sheepscot inlet while Sissy slept in the trundle bed behind her are all also, like her cousin-lover, like the rest of her life, gone. Then, in the mire of mounting loss, she must lie and succumb while her body is rudely penetrated by someone—something—as vulgar to her as her cousin was delicious. The sweat that slithers between his skin slapping hers, his rank breath in her face—it is only endured through listlessness, leaving her body and sending herself up the chimney like smoke to fly the sky where she might, in her mind's eye, see Nahum hauling a net of cod, coiling heavy rope, at watch on the stern, a sorrowful meditation hardening the creases growing around his eyes and the knots of muscle rising under his skin. He speaks little and retires to his quarters alone, never writes letters home and won't read those he receives. His officers complain that his hands aren't as sure on the nets and ropes as they might be; that he's too much the dreamer, the loner who won't accompany his mates to a tavern nor smile at the pretty bar maids. They say that notwithstanding the strength in his body, his lack of verve and enterprise won't even raise him from second mate to first, despite how he does habitually volunteer for the night watch, and stands as though tied on the bow, staring into the darkness of black nothing stretching in front of him.

Mary Catherine likewise stares into the blackness of her room, after the husk of her husband's body is snoring beside her. And if at night she twitches, her arms stiffen, her head throws itself back against the headboard with a thump, her urine gushing uncontrolled won't soil her nightclothes any more than they already are. When she wakens, her heartbeat the flutter of a dying bird, her tongue raw or bloody, she'll rise in the darkness to wash her bloomers, her nightgown, even peel the sheets from around his benumbed hulk, and by morning the evidence of her tumult will be gone.

When Sissy comes to sit with Mary Catherine, on some Sunday mornings before the speakeasies open—when Mary Catherine is alone because she declines joining the women's auxiliary at her husband's church, declines even attending services—Sissy has decided to censor the news she hears from the sailors and seamen as she serves their illegal ale in the windowless back room of the tavern. Sissy worries of Mary Catherine's delicate health, seeming to grow even more frail, worries that some news of Nahum might cause Mary Catherine to swoon worse than she ever has, to never stop the rigid twitching and thrashing until her fragile body can thrash no more and is still forever. So when Sissy has heard of Nahum's marriage in Baltimore, or maybe it was to a belle in a port town on the Gulf, she prattles to Mary Catherine cheerfully, instead, about how modern the world will be—with machines to do the wash and stoves that heat evenly without dirty coal or wood—in the new century around the corner.

"A new century means little to me," Mary Catherine answers, her voice lethargic. Her hands on her lap, although holding socks and a darning needle, are lifeless.

Dear Martha,

So what did they give G for PTSD, Prozac, the yuppie-med? G hasn't met a real med. And I've been off mine for 20 years. Going off didn't make me more likely to bolt off somewhere or stalk anyone. If you haven't seized in a year or two, they want to wean you off the meds. I begged my doc to let me stay on, but finally couldn't get them filled any longer. So they leave you on your own, every day feeling for, checking, controlling the propensity you might implode. And how about Mary Catherine, there were no meds for PTSD or PPD . . . not even any words for these things . . . are they even really DISEASES? No, those D's are just emotional depressions. There was nothing to call Mary Catherine's torment . . . except probably hysterics. The old use of that word, you know, the same root as hysterectomy, when they tried to extract the distress by delivering the female organs. Her real disease was carried deeper, in her DNA or genes. So the loss of her child, and her own early death, would presumably thwart any future return of the aberrance later in the family tree. Future generations will remember her brother, Wolcott, highlight him in their genealogy, brag about having descended from a lighthouse keeper. Nobody will start their ancestral list from Mary Catherine's name. Look at her death date, 1899. I read that the death rate soared in the first months of 1900 because so many elderly, sickly people got whatever boost of adrenalin, of anticipation and hope, wanting to live to see the new century. So thousands who would have died in August, September, October through December . . . they rallied, saw the new century come in, then succumbed. Not Mary Catherine. How could she feel she even had a future in the new century?

Did I ever tell you why I broke contact with G, as much as I could? He ruined my life.

T

By May of her senior year, a week or two before graduation, Tam had been off her meds for almost four years, and had long since stopped inching through each day as though treading gingerly on the edges of a pond with a crust of ice near shore but a deep open hole in the middle. Of course Denny had been the primary reason, not that he knew it, but their pact, bond, secret world—whatever he would call it—had helped her forego or forget always being mindful, guarded, cautious. Until she thought the deep open hole might not be there anymore. But it was. Or was back as soon as he was gone. As though for those three years, Denny had held her hand while she padded, then walked, then began to skate around the outside edges of the ice. Faster and brisker, more graceful, more bold, maybe even turning and skimming backwards. But when she lost his hand, where else would she go but be flung into the middle and straight down the hole?

Because she'd been crying for more than an hour since Denny left the office, when it first started, she thought it was still just the wobbly fatigue of feral sobbing. For a second she may have registered how dangerous this was, this kind of unrestrained discharge of sorrow, persisting despite abject exhaustion. All before her cognizance was gone, too. But there may have been five seconds, as she was drawn into the curl of a wave of lightheaded void, when her perception moved from weeping to *oh no, I can't, not now,* and then to nothing.

What happened in between, and how long it actually was, she could only guess subsequently, when she woke—not really woke but more came to, or came back—in the sticky, twisted, putrid aftermath. Where had she been beforehand? She hadn't stayed sobbing on the mattress behind the file cabinets. If she had, the whole mess could have been dragged out the door and disposed of, neatly. But she'd been at his desk. Couldn't stay on the mattress that smelled of him, and of them together. So she'd walked, wailing, around the office, and ended sitting at his desk. That's why she found herself under his desk, or half under, her body cranked around and between the legs of the chair, her face glued with blood and drool to a short leg of the old wooden desk, the back of her skull in the cleft between the bottom drawer and the coarse industrial carpet. And as though someone had placed her mouth to protect her tongue, her teeth were clamped on the desk's leg. It hadn't completely saved her tongue, though. Her old scars were bleeding.

Her first awareness was only where her head was. The rest of her body not yet retrieved. Then she located her hands, at the ends of contorted arms. One arm straight but twisted almost 360 degrees, most of that arm plunged into the metal trashcan, lying on its side, her hand buried in the rubbish, as though searching for something she'd discarded but now needed to recover. Her other arm was ratcheted under her back, her bunched fist was the knot she was beginning to feel against her spine.

She'd started trying to move before she discovered the extent of her body's purge. She pulled her arms in like bird wings, then pushed her palms against the carpet to slide out from under the desk. Her head hung like a puppet with a broken string. When she tried to get up or crawl away from the desk, her knees ripped away from a gluey wetness. She rolled her hips to a sitting position. Her skirt, dark and damp, was scrunched against her thighs, her skin stained with streaks of dried blood, and between her legs a viscous black puddle. During the seizure, her thrashing legs had spread the mess, and her hands must have been in it too, because smears and streaks painted the side of the desk, the seat of the chair, and the carpet in a body-length radius. Hands on the rug on either side of her hips, she pushed herself back away from it, her feet dragging through until she found the muscles to lift her shoes over the thicker clumps. It took every determined kernel of force she'd ever used to burn through the last 50 yards of a freestyle race, just to pull her feet under her weight and then push on her legs to stand, holding onto the back of the chair, her arms joining in the strain to right her body. Her eyes never left the stain, the disaster left under the desk. Although her guts felt heavy, leaden, pulling on her to let her body return to the floor, she also knew there was a vacuum inside her now, whatever had been in there, whether it was a baby or just most of herself, was gone.

Tam left her laptop in the lightkeeper's office and slipped out through the screen porch to go lie down in the fog-bell house. The rain had stopped, but, although there was no fog, the cloud ceiling still hung low, narrowing the view of Sheepscot inlet to a long horizontal. Grayish water chopping along a grayish rock coast under a bleak gray sky. It was barely noon when she straightened the simple covers and lay on the bed. It was almost one-thirty when she sat up. She may have slept in between. She still felt fatigued. Achy and fluish.

Is it April already? Already goddamn *April?*

Nat was right, if it had to end—and obviously it did—there still had to be a way to not let it just grind into the ground. Mary Catherine didn't have that option, but Tam could. Nat at least had tried, and now it was her turn—to conceive of some way both to end it, and still leave it in the sublime.

When Tam came back down the ramp from the fog-bell house and entered the lighthouse, the baby was crying upstairs. His voice was feeble and sometimes he just seemed to be sputtering, but then the longer rhythmic squalls began again. Tam sat heavily on the sofa, as though the trip from the fog tower had been exhausting. For a moment she looked at the copy of *The Water Babies* on the end table. The cover's illustration showed Tom, the chimney-sweep-turned-water-nymph, with a lacy collar of gills around his neck, eating something from the gnarled hand of a big-nosed witch wearing opaque-lensed spectacles. Then Tam noticed a marker, a stickynote as an index tab, barely showing. She picked up the book and found the place the stickynote marked, near the end of the book, a sentence highlighted in neon green marker:

'You may take him home with you now on Sundays, ~~Ellie~~ Tam.
He has won his spurs in the great battle, and become fit
to go with you and be a man; because he has done the
thing he did not like.'

How Gary could Gary get? She didn't throw the book down, but placed it slowly, just as it had been, as though expecting Gary to come check to see if she'd read his message, and didn't want to be found out. Then remembered Gary had left the book by the coffeepot, not here. She'd already moved it, if in fact he'd come back to check. But the house had been locked the past two nights.

The baby still cried. There was no sound of Jill walking back and forth with him, no thrum of Jill's voice humming. Tam again pulled herself up and climbed the stairs, but his crying seemed to get no louder when she got to the second story bedroom. The reason was easy to determine: the baby's voice came from the closet. That's where she found him, bundled in a blanket and nestled in a basket of dirty clothes. His face was red, his eyes squeezed shut, one fist pummeled ineptly near his ear. Tam stood for a moment, holding him. He'd stopped crying when she picked him up, but soon began again. Other than being crusty around his nose and eyes, he didn't seem in imminent distress. His diaper wasn't dirty. He might have been heavier than the last time she'd held him. She wasn't even surprised that Jill would leave the baby (again) and try to go back to her usual life. The peacoat, hanging in the closet since they'd come to stay here, was gone.

Tam took the baby downstairs, to the master bathroom to wash his face. While the water was running, warming, she thought she heard a shout outside. She saw no one from the window that looked out to the cove. But then noticed Nat's dinghy was gone from the rocks. Not for a moment did she suspect that Nat had crept back and taken his boat without coming inside to see her again. Yet her heart thumped harder than it had at the prospect of Jill abandoning the baby.

The baby in one arm, she hurried to the big window in the seating area, but the overcast, ground-level view held nothing but agitated white-peaked water. She went out the glass doors, the baby's weary voice rising to near screams while she rushed to the light tower, then squeezed him awkwardly in one arm while she fumbled with the heavy door. She didn't take the time to prop the door open with a rock—let the ghost slam the door behind her if she wanted. Tam ducked inside and began booming up the metal coil of steps. She had to crawl through the hole to the galley on knees and one hand, the baby hiccupping, tucked against her ribs with her other arm.

Because of the red shading on the east half of the lantern pane, most of the cove where Nat had come in the boat was not visible from the tower. But, in the familiar scene she hadn't viewed since the first day she'd been up here with Nat pressed behind her, she saw his dinghy, just coming around into view from the cove into the open water off the head. Two people on board. One in a dark peacoat. The other in the yellow slicker and hat Nat had left on the porch when he'd walked away up the road just as the light rain began that morning, in boots, oilcloth pants and thermal undershirt.

The person in the peacoat, obviously Jill, was crouching near the stern. The man in the yellow slicker was rowing. He was heading around the front of the lighthouse, but going into deeper water, probably to ensure he cleared the rocks that extended into the water from the head. The dinghy bucked over each crested roller. Then suddenly, straight out in front of the lighthouse, the man stopped rowing and stood up, holding the mast, his feet spread, and his body began swaying—the dinghy rolled harder.

Tam had to lay the baby on the galley floor while she lowered herself through the hole and found the first step. Then snatched him up again, turned precariously before plunging down the coil. The ghost had not slammed the door shut hard enough to lock it, but the door was shut. Tam pushed it open with one shoulder and burst out, running, through the screen room and back into the house where she deposited the baby in the center of the bed, rushed back out but caught herself with both arms on the doorway, turned back and pushed a pillow on either side of the baby.

Back in the sitting room, the boat was now visible from the picture windows, but Tam didn't stop to watch what the guy standing up would do next. She went out the glass doors, through the small grassy yard and swinging picket gate and out to the rocks.

Now she could hear him singing. "I sail and I sail on a big ocean ship with a *toot . . . toot . . .* out of my *way.*" She could even hear Jill's giggle. Now she was sure.

She couldn't dive until she was past the half submerged rocks, until the water was at least to her knees, slippery rugged shale still beneath her tennis shoes. At first her jeans just felt heavy, sucking at her calves, the rubber of her soles sliding between rocks, until one foot slipped down suddenly and she was wet to one thigh, so she pushed off and lunged forward. Then the icy explosion of her body's entry made it seem she would never breathe out again.

But she did breathe, every third or fourth stroke. Each sharp intake stabbed her laboring heart. Yet the strokes came readily, steadily, her muscles and tendons fell into an understood course and cadence. Head down, each wave crested over her, so her arms could continue reaching and plunging, her sodden shoes continued kicking, her ears filled with the numbed roar of water, blotting any voices from the boat. Her uncapped hair plastered to her face made vision more difficult during her measured gasps of air, but she squinted up each time and adjusted her trajectory, keeping the dinghy in her sight. The incoming tide sucked against her headway, but it also drew the wayward dinghy toward land, so at last the boat loomed just in front. Tam's last few strokes were more erect, her head up, her feet scissoring underwater, and her hand groped for the gunwale like it was the lip of a pool, only higher, like a nightmare of a race where you've won but can't ever reach the concrete edge that's suddenly too high, bobbing frantically, swashed out of reach over and over.

Then she had it. The boat tipped toward her as her other hand also took hold. She heard Jill's screech as the gunwale tipped down close to the chopping water, but Tam didn't stop trying to thrust one leg into the boat.

Waving in her vision, a yellow arm, a hand extended. He was standing, no longer holding onto the mast, so Tam grabbed Gary's arm with both hands and kicked off with her legs against the dinghy's hull. She went under, into the frigid galaxy of sparkling ebullience beneath the grey choppy surface. When she popped back and broke through, Gary was no longer on the dinghy. Tam again thrust her body out of the water and this time did hook a leg over the gunwale, then flopped down into the boat.

"God *damn*, you're a crazy-woman," Jill shrieked, laughing.

Tam, up now, fumbling for the oars, bellowed back, "You left your goddamn baby alone to go off with—"

"Your brother."

"*You don't know him!*" Seated, Tam leaned into the oars, still shouting at Jill crouching in the stern. "He could've been some crazy lunatic, and you left your baby to go off with him!"

"Wait," Jill shouted. "Aren't you going to wait for him?"

"He can swim. Didn't he tell you that?"

Even the strenuous effort of rowing the dinghy didn't keep Tam's teeth from clacking. Her arms, shoulders, whole ribcage shivered cruelly. She rowed with her chin craned over one shoulder, watching to see that she was directing the bow toward the head. There was little peripheral vision left over to look for Gary, but she heard him, his voice repeating a mantra as he paddled, probably a tranquil breaststroke, somewhere parallel to the dinghy.

"What's the big deal," Jill sulked. "He said he came to get you. Why can't someone come to get *me*? Jerry was safe, unless he, like cried himself to death. Like, you think I shouldn't be allowed to *do* anything?"

"Don't you think," Tam panted, "your life would be . . . totally different now . . . if you hadn't . . . put your baby in a toilet?"

"I *know*." The girl started to cry.

"You might still . . . be in school . . . he'd have the things a baby . . . usually has . . . toys . . . a crib . . . playpen . . . whatever . . ."

"I've thought the exact thing, but—"

"But you're hiding . . . in a lighthouse . . . with a baby . . . that was stolen from . . . a hospital. Do you think . . . you can just . . . *do* anything . . . you *want*?"

"But I knew you were still there to, like, watch him, and, like, what would *you* do?—this good-looking guy comes in telling me he's there to rescue me."

"From *what*?"

Over the harsh sound of her own voice, struggling to push words from her heaving ribcage, over the swash of the oars in the waves, the waves against the boat, the girl sobbing, Tam could still hear Gary's hoarse voice, farther away, behind the boat, not a harangue, not a song, but a chant. "Tam, you swam. Tam, you swam. Tam, you—"

The prow hit rocks. Tam stood and hopped from the dinghy, keeping one hand on the gunwhale, sloshed through the knee-deep water furling and foaming over the slippery rocks, keeping the prow up and dragging the boat higher onto the head until it was fully locked on shore and Jill could disembark onto the flatter, drier shale. Jill was clutching the peacoat to herself the same way she had when Tam had first seen her leaving the laundromat. Her chin tucked in the collar, eyes lowered as though watching her feet pick their way through the tufts of grass.

"He'll probably need to be fed," Tam said. The girl nodded.

The cadence of the sea hitting the rocks and Gary's voice continued behind them.

"We'll try to figure out how to get you out of this, get you home so someone can help you look after him properly."

". . . you swam . . . Tam . . . you swam . . . Tam . . . you . . . swam . . . Tam . . . "

Jill stopped and looked back. "He's kind of, like . . . whacked out."

"Just ignore—"

"Tam . . . you . . . swam . . . you . . . swam . . . you . . . *Tam* . . . *Taaaam swaaaam* . . .*"* Gary's breathless incantation had mutated. His voice alien and wild, inflamed, a delirious wail, unrecognizable, and yet, obviously, he was weeping.

Tam's hand was on the collar of Jill's coat. She tugged as though to stop the girl from continuing toward the house, then jerked harder and the girl unclenched her arms, letting the coat slide from her body before she hugged herself again. "Get on up to the house, hurry," Tam said, then turned back toward Gary with the coat. He was still in water to his shins, his eyes squeezed shut. Tam slung the coat around his shoulders, held onto his waist, took his arm, and guided him out of the ocean.

Tam, I'm frankly disappointed in you. You must've blinded yourself so thoroughly to what goes on in our family, is it possible you still don't know that G is bipolar? Has been since his mid-20's when it typically becomes evident. I think at the time he told mom not to tell anyone—but how could we not know something was going on when suddenly he was in the hospital but didn't seem "sick." Where were you? I would've thought you'd know by now. Yes, he's supposed to take meds, and he won't ever wean off. When he stops taking, he flies or crashes, or both. Yes, over the years I've heard you make cutting comments about him, or just as cuttingly ignore news about him. And I admit I can get impatient with him, too. When he's on his meds, he's supposed to be normal, and if his personality is sometimes too strong, that's just Gary. But I do always suspect his judgment when he makes new plans, decides new ventures—is he manic? is he working off unrealistic kinds of energy, causing him to, I don't know. . . not act like he's in the real world? After the WTC he was changed. You mention PTSD. Of course this, too. And if he handles it badly, worse than others, can't you try to understand why? He couldn't save anyone, not even himself.

-M

Martha,
"By now" I do know.
-T

Gary was sleeping in the master bedroom. Jill had fed and bathed the baby and was sleeping with him upstairs. Tam, in the keeper's office, with the peacoat now thrown over her own shoulders. She could nap in the extra bed in the dormer, or in the fog-bell tower, but either way, she might not hear if Gary tried to leave, or if Nat arrived. She'd called his cellphone from hers, and—just pressing the nine digit—she left a message in Morse code, dot-dot-dot-dash-dash-dash-dot-dot-dot, three times. For the other call she planned to make, she would use the light-house land line.

Tam put her head down on the desk and closed her eyes. There wasn't much chance he would get up soon anyway. She knew the kind of sleep she presumed Gary was sleeping—the dead rest of complete bed-rock exhaustion.

After she'd dragged herself from the floor of Denny's office, some-where between 9 and 11 p.m., she'd sat on his chair, feeling for the throb of heartbeat in every part of herself, her comprehension moving from fingertips to arms to shoulders, down her spine, down her guts to the hollow tumor-place, huge and empty. She counted the ticking clock, lost her place, started again, eventually realized she was only counting one-two one-two one-two. She forced herself to stand, to recognize her legs, knees, ankles and feet. It might have been three minutes or a half hour since she'd come to consciousness. She remembered a towel that had been on the coat tree for months—Denny had come back to the of-fice one day still wet from the pool, without changing in the locker room. Another time that he'd swum his thinking-laps too long. But now it was here to wrap around her bloody clothes, and, although it was late and the campus abandoned, to hide the photograph that she took from the wall—Denny in a frozen butterfly.

But she didn't drive herself to the hospital. She went home. Used the private entrance to her bedroom that her father had wanted to seal. Balled the stained clothes, with the towel, under the bed. The framed photograph face down on her nightstand, pulled her nightshirt over her head, and curled in her bed on one side, asleep, without stirring, for over twelve hours.

When she woke, she lay without moving for a moment before real-izing that her mother was sitting behind her, on her mattress, but her mother didn't touch her until Tam rolled to her back. Her mother's face—drawn, strained—clouded even more.

"What's this on your face, Tam?"

Her mother's hand there, not trying to wipe it away, but brushing lightly over Tam's skin.

"Blood." Tam felt her voice coagulate on the word. Her swollen tongue muddying her voice. "And dirt."

"Were you in an accident?"

"No. I . . . it must've been a seizure."

"Oh no. Where? Why didn't they take you to the hospital?"

"There was no one."

"Did you hurt yourself anywhere?" Her mother's hand holding her face, cupping her chin. "Your tongue?"

"Sore. I'm okay. Just tired."

"How did you get home, were you able to drive? I'm sorry I wasn't here for you."

"I didn't want to wake anyone."

"Martha was here. I was with Gary." Her mother's fingers slid up to Tam's brow. Tam felt she was just a head on a pillow; forced herself to become aware that her arms were crossed over her chest, clutching the sheet that covered her from the shoulders down. She loosened one arm and let it slip from under the sheet, and her mother took hold of her hand. "It almost makes sense, Tam, you seizing again now. I know we've had a hard time, these past few months, with your father— I've wanted to tell you more, but . . . waiting for the right time. And now . . . With Gary . . . Gary's been . . . " Still holding one of Tam's hands, her mother's other hand didn't stop stroking a lock of Tam's hair over and over to the side of her face, as though training a wayward cowlick. Her mother's eyes concentrated there too, on Tam's fore- head, as if unable to look Tam in the eyes until she could make her upside-down smile, which wasn't the same without the red lipstick, but was finally there.

"You just rest, honey. You're graduating and have a big exciting future to think about, choices and new opportunity. Don't worry about going back on meds for a while, that won't change anything."

"I don't care what I do," Tam murmured.

"Sure you do. You'll be going into the world, meeting new people—"

"I don't want to meet anyone."

"Oh Tam, you'll feel differently in a day or two, we all will. You'll be okay, Gary will be okay. We're all going to see things differently, better, look forward—"

Tam pulled her hand from her mother's and rolled away, her face against the pillow. Again, her voice thickened, curdled. "I wish I hadn't quit swimming."

Her mother now standing beside the bed, one hand on Tam's shoulder. "What's that, honey?"

Her mother waited, as though knowing the silence was not obstinacy but effort.

"I don't want to look forward."

"You think so now. But you will. Go back to sleep. I'll bring you some soup in a while, before I go back. . . before I have to go." Her mother was straightening the sheet, folding the blanket down so it only covered up to Tam's waist. "Martha will be home from school soon—it's already almost two—if you need anything later."

Martha had never come into the room, not that Tam remembers. Certainly not the way Sissy had stayed the course by Mary Catherine's side during and after every swoon, every longer spell. Except after Mary Catherine was married and Sissy gone to work in Wiscasset. In those years Mary Catherine was alone after every occurrence, without the luxury of being able to sleep through the ground-zero of physical depletion. And without her mother to sit on the side of the bed, fondle her hair, feel her forehead and cheeks for fever, and hold her hand, Mary Catherine rose every morning and stoked the fire, cooked the hotcakes or biscuits, made the strong black coffee. Whether she'd woken with her bloomers and sheet wet with sweat and urine, or whether she'd risen with a surge of nausea and vomited into the dirty bedpan before taking it to be emptied outside. It started after three years being in the widower's house, in his bed. Weak, weary beyond words, Mary Catherine thought back to the last time she'd had to wash rags for her monthly time, and realized her misery had found a way to go lower.

Mary Catherine had long ago relinquished the disposition to turn to her mother for comfort or solace. Probably as far back as the loss of her twin, when Mary Catherine's child-grief couldn't be detected, absorbed or soothed by her mother's adult sorrow. Sorrow her mother bore, as

Mary Catherine did now, silently, through the daily tasks of housekeeping, cooking, sewing, preserving, garden-tending, and providing libidinous gratification for her husband. And when her mother's concealed misery was assuaged by a replacement boy-child in Lowell—followed by the dramatic rescue of Seaborn, and then the daily, weekly, yearly passages and fortunes of her other children—Mary Catherine's proclivity not to seek out her mother for consolation was sealed. Original melancholy over the loss of her twin eventually softened through time, helped by the devoted passion of her cousin and looking toward their shared guardianship of the lighthouse. She never coupled the distress over the loss of Nahum with the prior loss of her twin, but now, with her bulging belly on her frail frame growing heavier by the day, she thought of her mother, pregnant at J. Thomas's graveside, and wondered if this was her own replacement child—replacement of J. Thomas *and* of Nahum, who might, even now, be on a doomed voyage, and wouldn't, after all, ever return to find her. But no, it couldn't be that. If J. Thomas or Nahum were to reappear, it would not be in the form of another man's seed, a man who forced her in the dark to spread her legs.

During Mary Catherine's pregnancy, marked by growing disconsolation, it's also possible Sissy would have tried a different tack to bring Mary Catherine about, like the abruptness of smelling salts, and would have revealed to Mary Catherine that her cousin was married, that his children were already growing, attending school, crawling across a firelit floor to their father's knee or standing with him on a windy bluff learning to identify the shapes of schooners, cutters and brigantines.

Either way, Mary Catherine lay in bed at night and thought about Southport—about the lighthouse, solitary and stalwart on its windy, rocky, salt-sprayed neck of land; and about the graveyard, the serene afternoons spent there, the sweet breeze through the pines and mulchy softness of the needles and leaves beside the mossy graves. Before her time comes—before the agony of labor shreds her; when her fragile body might not survive the prolonged loss of blood and sweat, the lack of nourishment; when loss of oxygen triggers a massive apoplexy—she'll return to the island, to the graveyard and then on to the lighthouse, one more time.

So if Mary Catherine were to go to Southport now, pregnant, living 30 miles away, and go without her husband's knowledge, how would she get there?

From the lighthouse, it's less than a mile to the graveyard. It's three miles to Boothbay Harbor where there's a hospital, but how can she force Gary to walk beside her or follow her there? Instead, she can walk to the general store, then another quarter mile south to Nat's house near Cozy Harbor, and her rental car in his garage. When Nat answered her call to his cell, she told him she needed her car to go into Boothbay Harbor.

He said, "Let me pick you up."

"No. Too many cars coming and going. I'll walk over, after dark. Then I'll bring the car back to your garage, before light."

"What are you doing?"

"You don't want to know."

"Is it illegal?"

"Funny thing to ask, now."

"You sound strange."

"It is strange to be on the graveyard shift, so to speak, the night shift for family business."

"When ghosts are out."

"Tomorrow, around noon, in the graveyard. Okay?"

"Noon. Okay."

"It might rain. Again."

The clouds had hung heavy all afternoon and into evening. When dark came there were no stars, the air was damp, and no breeze picked up. The air, the obscure clouds, the heavy fir branches hung somewhere out of sight above her as Tam walked the beach road toward Barkin's Store. She wore the Salvation Army raincoat, the straw hat, her jumper. On her feet, tennis shoes, and she carried the shabby pumps.

She hadn't been there more than four times, and had barely peeked at the route, mostly had been reclined on the seat, when Nat had driven her to his house at night. But she found the way easily, past the cluster of harbor buildings, the drug-store-bowling-alley that would remain closed until June, the blank outside wall and 50's era unconnected gas pumps, lit by only one yellow bulb under the eaves. Past the back of the harbor buildings, the water on her right—which she couldn't see but could smell—was not the harbor but the gut that likewise rose and fell with the tide beside Nat's deck.

Nat was outside the garage, just standing in the dark. He didn't move as her rubber soles quietly crunched the sand on his driveway, nor as she drew near enough that he would have seen her through the darkness, but when she was close enough to him, he reached out to pull her against himself.

His hands on her shoulder blades, his face against her hair, neither spoke until he finally said, "Now you're the briny one."

"Yes. I went for a swim today."

"Oh." He backed away and held her at arm's length. "Then you must be . . . Wait, you're not taking anything with you."

"That's because I'll be back, before light, like I said."

She was. By 2 a.m. the car was again in Nat's garage. Nat was, again, standing there, but this time inside the garage, in bare feet. He didn't turn the light on even when the door was completely shut behind the car.

"I heard you on the driveway," he said, his voice muted, as though someone else was near enough to overhear. "I couldn't sleep."

"I hope you can now."

"Will you stay here?"

"No, I've left that silly girl alone long enough. Tomorrow . . ."

"In the graveyard."

Perhaps Mary Catherine knows she won't live to see the new century. The smaller, warning spells have been more frequent—her sight goes flashing white as she bends over a washtub, as she rises after lighting the fire. She hangs onto the back of a chair until it passes. Sometimes while on the way to the table, his supper in a plate in one hand. "What's the matter?" he demands, so she releases the back of the rocker and shuffles slowly around the table to serve him his stew and mashed turnips. She knows that after it happens, she'll be buried in her new husband's family plot, somewhere inland, beyond the head tide, not on Southport, not in the salt air within walking distance of the craggy coast and the lighthouse. Nahum isn't there either. But J. Thomas is. So she has to go one last time, to the cemetery around the corner from Barkin's store. Now that she finally realizes what must have happened to J. Thomas, what kind of paroxysm took him suddenly in the night. The same failing that has led to her swoons and is now looming even more forebodingly.

She didn't sleep at the lighthouse again. By the time Tam was standing shrouded in the woods on the edge of the cemetery, still wearing her jumper but this time with Nat's yellow slicker covering her because the air had turned to a liquid drizzle, she had already gotten and read her mother's e-mail letter. The message now stored on her computer, her computer folded and zipped into its case, sitting atop her suitcase farther back in the woods.

> Dear Tam,
> I don't know how it happened, that there were things I should have told you, tried to tell you, and never found the right moment. Time passed and we all went on with life, and you found success in Chicago, and it seemed time had taken care of everything. I had no idea that over the years, in passing or some kind of conversation, the issue of Gary's illness wouldn't have come up, and that you still didn't know. You were still in college, involved with your own life, we all presumed you had a steady boyfriend who kept you away from home so much. After your father's death, I welcomed this kind of comfort and distraction for you, someone who meant the future, to make you forget losing your dad that way, so suddenly. I had always meant to tell you, someday, that his death was not due to a heart attack, but a grand mal seizure. They told me afterwards. One of those things he carried around all his life, probably showing symptoms, even having petite seizures that nobody knew about. But you were in such a vulnerable time concerning your own condition, how could I tell you the same thing had caused your father's sudden terrible death? Especially after you had another bad seizure right before you graduated. That time is so clear in my memory

because it's the same time Gary had his break-down. I tried to tell you but you were weak and groggy. Gary had been found by the police living in one of the lifeguard stands at the beach. He had a crate of books, a sleeping bag, some waterbottles, a radio, a typewriter, a few other things. When they tried to deliver him home, they found his apartment stripped bare. I never did find out what he'd done with all the furniture and his clothes. He hadn't been to his job at the newspaper for over a week. But they told me his last assignments had been almost gibberish, reports on high school athletics full of embellishment, tall tales written like potboilers. The police thought he was high, but after we checked him into a hospital it didn't take long to get the diagnosis. They said he could handle it with medication, that he would live a normal, productive life if he could be responsible about his meds, and he was. For how long now, he always was.

Back during that time when Gary was in the hospital, for three or four days, one thing he told me was that he thought it was his fault that you quit swimming. He didn't tell me why he thought so. He said you would know. It might be one of those things he only imagined and you don't have any idea either. I don't want you to think this worry was a cause of his breakdown, then or now—it's physiological, not emotional. But I told him what I hope you've always understood, that we were right not to push you, if you didn't want to swim again. You had to be ready on your own, not just do it because someone else asked it of you, even though it broke our hearts—even Gary always knew you were the best swimmer, you were the one who might've made it.

It always seemed to me that your father's death shattered our family. I've thought about this because it seemed so unlikely, because your father had to be away from home so much of the time, that his death could have initiated such a chain of events, Gary's breakdown, you moving away and seldom wanting to come home. Compared to many of my friends, I'm lucky to have three children who have done so well. I do sometimes wonder, though, what I could have done differently to make your adulthood even better.

Martha and I will be here to help and support Gary when he returns. I know you'll help get him home. If you can't come with him, we'll understand. But your family is still here, Tam.

Love, Mom

Nat came on foot to the cemetery, through the trees on the opposite side from where Tam stood. He'd likely walked from his house, then cut through the woods behind Barkin's store. Maybe he'd even gone into the store for coffee first, let himself be seen to throw off any suspicion that he wanted to avoid being seen. For Tam, even walking from the lighthouse with her suitcase—and staying off the road, in the edges of the woods so she wouldn't be noticed—wasn't as difficult as the trip Mary Catherine now forges, starting with the note she leaves her husband saying that she's gone to visit her mother who is suddenly ill, then a laborious walk into Headtide, a jolting wagon ride with a farmer to Sheepscot, another ride in a minister's buggy from Sheepscot to Wiscasset. There, in the legal front part of the tavern, she endures the stares from the seamen— she is so overwhelmingly pregnant—as she motions for Sissy to meet her outside. She wants Sissy to come with her the rest of the way, but Sissy can't leave her post; it's near suppertime, and after the tavern serves fish soup and biscuits, the men will move to the hidden room and drink heavier. Sissy begs Mary Catherine to wait, to go lie and rest on the bed in her room at the boarding house next door. But unable to delay Mary Catherine's mission, Sissy sends the boy who sweeps the tavern floors to borrow a buckboard and horse. She wants the boy to take Mary Catherine onto Southport, but Mary Catherine says no, she'll drive the buckboard herself, she'll return the horse by midnight. Sissy will be waiting. It is another three hours into Boothbay and an hour after that to Southport. It is dark and chilly, and there's no way Mary Catherine will be back to Wiscasset by midnight.

Nat was draped in a camouflage rain poncho, picking his way through the headstones, looking down, then he stopped at the one where he'd found her, only a few weeks ago. Jaruel and Catherine Marr, mother and father. Tam stepped out of the woods. Her feet made little sound on the moss and sodden pine needles. But a spray of rain, or wind-blown water shaken from the trees, spattered against the yellow slicker, and Nat turned. His face was gaunt and tired, but creased into a smile.

She found his hand in the folds of the poncho. "Thanks for leaving your raincoat for me."

He squeezed her fingers, but didn't answer.

"We can get out of the rain, go under the trees."

"Wait." He pushed the poncho hood off his head. His hair was already wet. "We still never found her grave. Louise Meade."

Tam looked down at J. Thomas's stone, darker from the rain, the words harder to read. "If we were here in 1898 or '99, that grave wouldn't be here."

"Then whose would we be looking for?"

"Mary Catherine's parents' stones wouldn't be here yet either."

"So it's this one. The dead brother . . ."

"It's a place Mary Catherine visits."

"She's here to see her brother?"

"Yes. And no. The mystery, now, of what had snuffed his life has become suddenly lucid for her, and should have been for years. But her twin is forever a boy. If he'd become a man he might've been a friend of Nahum's, their cousin. Perhaps one of them would have become the keeper at Hendricks Head, the other assigned to be assistant, with Mary Catherine as second assistant, sharing the work in thirds. So Nahum wouldn't have gone to sea. But none of that happened, her twin's toddler body rests here, and Nahum's not buried here. Still, there's something here, more than just her twin, that lures her."

Nat released Tam's hand and took hold of the two sides of her hood to pull her close. "That's good."

"So it was only Mary Catherine's imagination that could bring Nahum here in the flesh, this day, to find her, one last time."

His arms around her, he turned so his back and the wide poncho faced the road. "To anyone looking, there's only one person in the graveyard."

It's Mary Catherine. Standing in her dark cloak and hood. A passerby wouldn't discern she's pregnant. But no one passes. And eventually she kneels, then sits. Something pulling downward, the sensation like a low moan coming from her body. Mary Catherine is silent, though. Supposing that it's his back she leans against, not a gravestone. His hands feathering through her hair, not the moist breeze. His lips on her throat, not a spring drizzle.

Tam and Nat stood, his hands cupping her head, his face against her face, against her neck, his feet planted on either side of hers. Perhaps only her hands grasping his waist held her upright. No car had passed yet on the road. No birds twittered in the trees. The whoosh of wind in the tops of the trees was the sound made by his breath against her skin. She shivered.

"Come on." His quiet voice no intrusion, could be felt, almost held. "You're right. Up under the trees."

The poncho and slicker made a tarp big enough for two people. They sat and faced the graveyard, Nat behind Tam. She leaned against him. The drizzle seemed to be absorbed by the branches of the firs above them. The cemetery was gloomy without being shrouded. Dark but clear and distinct. "It's like the air is water," she said.

"A hundred percent humidity."

"Then it should feel like swimming. I wonder what they called it then?"

"The damp chill of a Maine spring."

"Consumption weather."

It's one reason why Sissy worries when Mary Catherine doesn't return by 10. Or would be the reason for someone else to worry, anyone who doesn't know of Mary Catherine's spells. The widower comes into the tavern at 10:30, looking to see if Sissy accompanied Mary Catherine to visit their sick mother. Sissy says no, then . . . *yes*, she had, but she'd returned to work her shift. But, she adds, if the widower will lend her his horse, she'll go and fetch Mary Catherine back right now. He's not on horseback, he says, brought the wagon to return Mary Catherine home. She shouldn't be out in her condition, he says, and without her husband. But if her time has come, you shouldn't be there, Sissy insists, she'll need me.

Mary Catherine nestles in the mulch and moss, her cloak both under her and covering her. Drops of water patter in the forest, close beside her and farther away, as mist condenses in the firs and drips from the tips of needles. Any of the soft sounds could be his footstep. And the next sensation would be his hands, his arms, lifting, carrying her. Away from the pains which have begun to anchor her here to the ground.

Nat held Tam tighter and pulled her with him as he lay on his side. "I don't know if I'll be able to . . . do anything"

"That's okay. This is perfect."

"It's wet, cold and miserable."

"And perfect."

"If this is so perfect, why am I—?"

"It's okay to be sad. You won't always be."

Had anyone ever said any such simple thing to Mary Catherine, when she was 5 and her twin died, when she was 22 and Nahum left for the sea without so much as a goodbye message? If so, it wasn't at the former moment, when her stoic but grief-stricken mother wouldn't have understood a child's lesion; but the latter, when Seaborn would know what to say. And Tam had repeated it to her brother, somewhere past midnight, when she'd finally seen him clean and in a bed in the hospital, after doctors had decided he should at least spend a few nights, while she arranged to get him home, so they could confer with his doctor in California and re-establish his medication protocol.

It had been surprisingly easy to get Gary to go with her to the hospital. Probably because she told him that he could take her home, that she needed him to take her home, but that she needed him to be rested and fed and healthy. And back on his meds. He was the one to say that.

"Do you have to take something every day, to keep you normal?" he'd asked during one of the long periods of time waiting in the ER for test results or for a room to be ready.

"Not anymore," she'd said. "Not for a long time. Maybe never again."

Gary had been washed by the ocean, but had scrapes on his face— above his days-old beard—and bruises on his legs from the rocks off Hendricks Head. His hair had dried saltwater-stiff and matted. His muscles twitched. His hand shook signing his name. His clothes, which she'd washed then dried at the lighthouse before bringing him to the hospital, were again in a pile on the floor.

Tam had picked up his pants and folded them, put them on a chair. Staring at a news anchor on the TV screen mutely delivering silent information, Gary had said, "Every time I won a race, mom wondered how many you would have won."

"How do you know?"

"I think she did."

"You were wrong."

"Then maybe I wondered it," he'd said.

"Mom only wondered why I didn't have your guts."

Gary had turned away. "So what were you doing in the lighthouse with a girl and a baby?"

"Rescuing a doll I should've fished out of the pool a long time ago. Now I have to figure out a way to rescue him again, get him and his mother out of that lighthouse, without anyone knowing I'm the rescuer. Any suggestions?"

"Yeah, let someone else be the hero."

"I wish you'd thought of that before you pulled me out of the pool."

"You wanted to drown?"

"I wanted to win."

"Then you shouldn't've quit."

"I thought I found something else, but you rescued me from that— from him too."

His eyes, now looking back at her, seemed smeared with confusion.

Later, when he was settled in a room, medication started, his eyelids half closed, his movements no longer twitchy, he'd mumbled, "Nobody wanted me to say it was horrible, too horrible, just so horrible . . ."

"You don't need permission to be sad about it," she'd said. "Or scared, or horrified. But I wonder if . . . Is it only man-made violence that's horrifying?" Gary was asleep. Tam went on, now mute like the television, *You might imagine that your ancestors on a tranquil seaport island, shaping their lives from the ocean and the land around them, couldn't, or wouldn't experience any of the scary kinds of things we're aware of now. You might presume that, unlike our restlessness, their serenity would just move like the seasons, like the tide, more then less, brighter then dimmer, but always imbued with calm knowledge of who they are, and the fundamental security of their hand-built house, their fire, their barn, the food that would come without fail from the ocean, the work expected of each, and the children that would come year-by-year, most surviving, some not. And some mothers would not either. But the traumas of the times: whether it's witnessing ships go to pieces before their eyes—drowning and freezing hundreds of bodies that would never wash ashore, husbands, sons, lovers, cousins, brothers, some of them were men, or boys, who never wanted to go to sea—or bleeding out the remains of a past and a future . . . should they just accept these as predictable parts of their domain? Or was their horror equal to jet crashes and military destruction? Can the loss of a lover, the compelled agreement to give oneself to another as wife, the loss of who you were and who you could've become, be the same as what soldiers and rescuers undergo?*

"They knew some hard sorrow," Tam said. "And that's how we know them."

"Who?" Nat's quiet voice still wasn't a whisper.

"People then. We don't think back to the happy times they might've had with a roasted goose and holiday pudding. That's for Christmas carols. When we want to know them, we dig for their misery."

"Then right now you know me pretty damn well."

"It's how you know anyone."

"What are we going to do now?" Nat's body, behind her, curled slightly. His head pressed against the back of hers. Both of them still wrapped in the poncho. "I'm sorry, I can't . . ."

"No." Mary Catherine's last time here, it wasn't her dead twin or her lost lover who came to her. It was Seaborn. "Listen."

Drizzle dripped into the mulch. A church bell somewhere. No, it was a harbor buoy wind-chime at the store up the road. A woodpecker hammered a tree. But no swash of the cold foam against the rocks.

"What are we listening for?"

"I'm waiting. I think I'll hear them go past to pick up the girl and her baby."

"Who will?"

"Whoever comes for her. Probably her mother."

"How did they find out?"

"I, *like*, called her mom and, *like*, told her she could go get her daughter."

"But they'll find out it was you . . ."

"I used the lighthouse phone. I tried to sound like one of her friends. I think I'm still invisible. They won't know who took the baby and stayed with the girl there."

"She won't tell?"

"I don't think so. I don't think she knows my last name." She paused. "That's always been a little confusing."

"Fingerprints?"

"Who's going to bother? I didn't call the police, I called her mother. I said Jill had only been at the lighthouse for a few days. She'll find the girl and the baby, everyone already assumes the girl took her own baby, why bother to look for anything else? If they ask the lighthouse caretaker, what's *he* going to say? And remember, guests visited the lighthouse just a few days ago and they didn't see anything."

"Does the girl know this is going to happen?"

"She halfway wants it to. If she tries to tell a story, it'll be too—"

"Yeah, too fantastic for them to believe—a nameless woman with no past showed up to steal her baby for her and hide them both in a lighthouse."

"But this woman has a past. And she has to go back." Staring out at the soggy cemetery, she couldn't recognize or pick J. Thomas's headstone out of the uneven columns of granite slabs.

"To her past?"

"To her family."

"Will you come to visit again?"

"It wouldn't be the same. We'd be different and disappointed."

Under the poncho, he slid his hand up her body to her face, then just left his palm on her cheek. "How are we going to do this?"

"I don't know. But this feels right. No more than this."

"I guess so. It does."

"Except," Tam brushed away the poncho covering their heads, "you can't hear the ocean from here."

"I suppose not. You'll hear it in California."

"Mary Catherine can't go with me."

But Mary Catherine wants to get closer to the ocean. It's time to return to the lighthouse. There's nowhere else to go. The pain, screaming from inside her body— She knows it's coming. The baby. The seizure. She never realizes the patter, getting closer, the pounding— it's hoofbeats, not her own heart. And Seaborn also knows, the lighthouse is the closest place. It's the only place Seaborn would bring Mary Catherine that night.

 ## Message from Tam

There was no proper ending to make a goodbye out of. Nor, I suppose, a proper goodbye to make an ending out of. I am sorry about that. How seldom life is a satisfying story. I think you won't be as unhappy as you fear. I think our memories will be good. And I think you won't continue to look for the Lady Ghost of Hendricks Head.Because you now know her, she may cease to come, at twilight, to the lighthouse. And so here is the rest of that story:

Mary Catherine, when she lost her lover, and lost the life she'd hoped for in a lightkeeping family—what could she do? Appeal to the government to give her a lightkeeping post of her own? Women had already been successful light keepers, but had any of them received an appointment without first having a man—a husband, father or brother—who had the post and designated her his assistant before he died and left the job to her? And would Mary Catherine even want the life without Nahum to share it with her? Even if she thought being a lightkeeper would assuage her, by the time Wolcott returned to become keeper of Hendricks Head, Mary Catherine's illness was real, not imagined. No one could accuse her of quitting because there was nothing to quit. She could have run away, as Seaborn had, instead of entering into the unwanted marriage. But duty and tradition had bound her. Or perhaps she wanted to always be somewhere where Nahum could find her. Staying in the region, by marriage, was the only way.

And so, eventually, Mary Catherine did become pregnant by the widower from Headtide. Before the baby came and he owned half of it, she wanted to return to Southport Island, to the places that embodied the aspirations she'd dared hold, and had comforted her after her dreams were gone. First to the cemetery where her twin was quickly becoming forgotten (so much so that, a hundred years later, some historian would proclaim that the Jaruel Marr family had *not* lost a child and therefore the legend of Keeper Marr rescuing and adopting Seaborn could not be true). Perhaps Mary Catherine's own mother had stopped visiting the gravesite, the plot put down closest to the one that would be her own. After all, there were grandchildren tumbling about at the lighthouse, and doubtless many more from the other Marr siblings, which meant there were others in the cemetery as well, this one and other untold graveyards, on Southport or wherever the lives of Mary Catherine's brothers and sisters had taken them. We only know of Wolcott's progeny, including two of his own offspring, Charles Simeon and Gracie May, who died in infancy. But at the head of Wolcott's list, healthy and stalwart, my grandmother Mabel Gilberta, who would have been 8 years old when Seaborn brought her aunt Mary Catherine, already far into a difficult parturition, to the lighthouse, late one night in 1899.

To the house Mary Catherine had hoped to share with her cousin Nahum—to be partner in his toil, a friend in his long desolate winters, a wife to his body. To the rescue-station lighthouse now kept by Mary Catherine's brother, the same brother who'd sought to protect her by eliminating the possibility she would ever die bearing her cousin Nahum's child while he, in wretched grief, knelt outside the door of her girlhood bedroom. For that much she might have thanked Wolcott, if the connecting of such thoughts were possible to her now. If she opened her gluey eyes a sliver, as the lighthouse door cracked open, she would have seen his face, just for a second, before he gave way and Seaborn barged through with her armload of calamity. His face, gaunt, clouded, growing furrows of worry she'd never seen before—were she capable she might have realized there are parts of his life that she knows nothing about.

Up to the second floor, to the dormer with the trundlebed, that is the room to which Seaborn carried Mary Catherine. The ground-floor master suite was not a part of the lighthouse then. In fact, the dormer had not yet been re-configured into the L-shape. The extra space was still a closet or storage room, or separate small room for a younger sibling. Whose room would this be in 1899—Gilberta's? By this date she had three brothers, the youngest only just turned one. The bigger bedroom would be needed for them, all sharing one bed, with the small extra room round the corner for their elder sister. In fact, this was the year Gilberta had lost another baby sister, Gracie May. The house might have already been dreary with death, or perhaps Wolcott's wife Hattie was still pregnant with the doomed baby and the surprise arrival of a semi-conscious Mary Catherine after ten p.m. boded ill for her own anticipated labor.

But it wouldn't be Hattie called in to help in Mary Catherine's time of need. Seaborn wanted to do it in private, knowing that she alone understood about Mary Catherine's swooning spells. But a distraught Wolcott sent for their mother, and Catherine Marr came, arriving at close to midnight. Above them the light, reflected off the Fresnel lens, beamed over the waters around the head and the Sheepscot inlet.

In the bedroom, Mary Catherine was conscious enough to feel the spasms of labor tearing through her body, and aware enough to recognize her mother's face hovering above her. Drawn, pale, distressed, yet able to smile. Holding her daughter's hand. Saying something about a woman's time for courage, a woman's time for strength, and that in the future—the exciting new century she and her baby would explore together—she'd never remember this dark pain.

Gilberta was standing at the bedside with a bowl of hot water. Ten years in the future she would be in Normal School and then out on her own, living with a railroad man and his wife, helping him pump the hand-car over the snowy rails to her one-room schoolhouse—a course, a choice Mary Catherine could never have conjured. And yet in this lighthouse, Mary Catherine could have found gratification working as her husband's companion, together keeping the light lit through white blizzards and black storms, maintaining the fog signal's blast through days-on-end when mist obscured the coast, and, if need be, launching the dory to recover survivors dropping from the swaying masts of sinking ships. Perhaps her mother, her namesake Catherine, had felt the same romantic tug—and had been allowed to live it to its zenith, the night she rescued Seaborn—but she then had to relinquish her role when her sons became old enough to take on the duties she, at one time, had assisted in accomplishing. Yet mother-Catherine didn't look back with regret, instead always speaking of the future, an unspecified morrow where there was more than just a birthright. It was all there, whether her mother said it or not, whether Mary Catherine understood or not, it was there in her mother's upside-down smile.

When Sissy saw the quiet reconciliation between nearly estranged mother and daughter, and saw the dark haze come into Mary Catherine's eyes, she took the hot water and asked her adoptive mother to hasten Gilberta from the room. Soon Mary Catherine's body roiled past labor and into a seizure. As usual, Sissy was there to soothe Mary Catherine's torment as best she could. But this time Mary Catherine was too weak to withstand both events, and as her child gushed into Sissy's hands, Mary Catherine never knew the moment, had lost too much blood, her brain strangled of oxygen, and the stillness following the seizure was death.

In an epilogue you find out what became of everybody after the story ends. We all know that Wolcott Garrett Marr served honorably as keeper of Hendricks Head Light for thirty-five years. Just as he'd sought to safeguard Mary Catherine, he loved and protected his family. His guilt over his intervention in Mary Catherine's life led him to permit his eldest daughter to leave the secluded life on Southport when she was 17, to further her education toward a profession, and even to play basketball in a long, dark skirt.

When Wolcott retired, he planned to live in the same house in Cozy Harbor that his own father, Jaruel, had built, and where his parents had gone to live when they'd retired from the lighthouse. But he never retired. He died in 1930 of bleeding stomach ulcers, not yet 65 years old. Like Mary Catherine, her brother Wolcott was born and died in the same room at Hendricks Head. The lighthouse was assigned an unrelated keeper for three years until it was decommissioned in 1933. It was during those three years that the well-dressed lady walked from Boothbay Harbor to Southport Island and drowned off the coast near the Hendricks Head.

Wolcott's eldest daughter, Mabel Gilberta, likely didn't suffer years, months or even weeks of tormented images of the night her aunt Mary Catherine died. If any other distress endured in her imagination during or after the years she grew up, finished school, taught her pupils, and courted her beau, it doesn't show up in the family tree. We know she had to stop teaching when she married and moved to Boston with her dentist husband. Her last child, Emily Marr Irving was born in 1931, the same year the enigmatic lady drowned. While growing up, Emily did not know her great aunts and uncles—her grandfather Wolcott's brothers and sisters, including Seaborn. Wolcott died before Emily was born, and all of Wolcott's other siblings were also dead, except perhaps Lowell, who went on with his life as a tradesman, carpenter, or fisherman, with no awareness that his adoptive sister, the shipwrecked baby Seaborn, had once, for a lingering duration, looked to him with special feeling.

Wolcott's cousin Nahum similarly would have no awareness that Mary Catherine dolefully persisted in clinging to memories of him. He'd ceased thinking back to his time with Mary Catherine with melancholy or remorse. He realized he'd been a boy on Southport and would have remained a boy if his brother hadn't facilitated his passage. Leaving Southport, a bigger, more complex world splashed in his face. Of course he married, and as his family began to grow, he retired from a seaman's life. He may have tried to return as a sailor during the Great War, but would have been in his forties and probably rejected due to old injuries sustained in the previous century on the old wooden sailing vessels. It can be assumed he maintained, or re-established connection with his family—those still living, which may have been only his mother and one sister—so perhaps his children were all that allowed his family tree to grow, but it did grow, written down or not, full of leaves and branches of its own that don't connect with mine, except way back to the grandfather, Thomas Marr, he'd shared with Mary Catherine. The same great great great grandfather that we share.

But there's no connection, no answer in any of these lives, to what became of Seaborn. Moreover, the night Mary Catherine died at the lighthouse, there was a baby. Mary Catherine wouldn't have been irrelevant to a kindred genealogist (one who grew up with her), but she also would not be immaterial to *any* genealogist, if there was a baby.

And Seaborn would have taken the baby. Wrapped her in a sheet stained with Mary Catherine's blood and carried her to the buckboard wagon outside. Without a word to the family gathered in the somber parlor, dimly illuminated only by one kerosene lamp with wick lowered. Seaborn's silent egress with the soiled bundle could mean only one thing to the family. The baby was dead. That's also what Seaborn told the man, now widowed twice, that his baby had died in the throes of the exertion, the struggle that had also killed the mother.

Seaborn took the child to raise. The family, unaware of Seaborn's illicit post, might have never set foot in the tavern in Wiscasset. She'd been hired in the first place because she had neither family nor name. But Seaborn moved on anyway. In Bath, by the shipyards, the underground taverns were plentiful. Here Seaborn could have changed her own name, and named the baby. Cecilia was the name Seaborn might have chosen for herself. So if there ever was another person who became close to her, she could once again be called Sissy, or maybe Ceci, and the baby girl would call her Aunt Ceci. As for the baby, she would know of her mother's life—Seaborn would make sure of that—but there might have been something of herself Seaborn wanted to give the motherless waif, and perhaps it was something she'd kept in secret, close to her body: the locket they'd found in the featherbed bundle when she'd washed to shore in the March blizzard of 1875. What if on the back of that locket, in scrolling script almost too fine to read, her own mother's name had been scribed, and what if that woman's name had been Louise Meade.

In the 20's, when national Prohibition increased the penalties and enforcement, Seaborn's choices would have been few: clean houses, do laundry, or go further underground. And so it seems reasonable she would be involved with rum-runners. Seaborn was familiar with a few places along the coast where boats could come ashore, undetected, at night, to offload illicit cargo. And the baby who Seaborn had raised—when she herself reached her 20's and early 30's, could have also been part of the enterprise. If they think the lady who drowned off Hendricks Head in 1931 was mysterious, unknown, and unclaimed because she was part of an alcohol smuggling ring, that piece of ungrounded hearsay could fit into the story.

In 1931 Seaborn would have been around 56 years old. Mary Catherine's baby would be 32. Either of them could have been the Lady Ghost. Witnesses said the lady was in her 40's, maybe late 40's. With the money to be made in the illegal alcohol trade, they could have dressed in fine clothes from New York. Either way, it would be possible.

But if you don't like this uncertainty, something else could have happened: Back when Wolcott discovered Mary Catherine and Nahum together in the new fog bell house in 1890, perhaps Mary Catherine was either already pregnant, or could have been conceiving that afternoon. Ashamed by the immoral consortium, the two families immediately conspired to send Nahum away, not knowing Mary Catherne's imminent condition. But when it became apparent, the Marrs hid Mary Catherine at the isolated lighthouse, helped her have the baby, then prepared to give it away. And that's when Seaborn left the family, removing Mary Catherine's unwelcome baby with her. They never heard what happened to either of them. *That* baby would be 41 or 42 in December 1931. Mary Catherine, always sickly, conceivably weakened by the 1898 flu epidemic, would have still died in 1899, of course at the lighthouse, perhaps during a subsequent pregnancy after marrying the widower. In this rendition she would be agitated and terrified, because Sissy was not there.

But have you ever considered that, either way, the specter said to be seen at Hendricks Head wasn't ever the drowned Louise Meade, but had been Mary Catherine all along? And, if so, perhaps Louise Meade had come there in 1931 to find her mother, or her family's essence. Her pedigree, her heredity, her inheritance. Something drew her, lured her, impelled her, not knowing what it was, but trusting she would know when she found it. And perhaps anything else that happened to her there, including her death, was beside the point.

Historical Note

Jaruel Marr, keeper of Hendricks Head Light from 1866 to 1895, and his wife Catherine were real people. All of Jaruel's ancestors preceding him in the genealogical list provided in this novel are real names, although a few birthdates were changed. For the writing of this novel, however, I altered *many of the real names and birthdates of Jaruel's children.* [It's important to note that although I did alter the birthdates of the twins, J. Thomas and Mary Catherine Marr, these twins did exist, and the boy did die at 4 years old, the woman in her early 30s.] In the following generation, that of Jaruel Marr's grandchildren, I altered many names and birthdates. The last two generations on the family tree used in the novel, those of descendants my parents' age and descendants my age, have been *completely* fictionalized. For the purpose of this novel, other branches of the Marr family tree, descendants of Jaruel Marr's brothers and sisters, have been liberally changed and fabricated. The personalities and personal life stories—including emotions, anxieties, and fates—of the 19th century Marrs of Hendricks Head, *especially Wolcott Marr Sr. and Mary Catherine Marr,* have all been imagined and fabricated for the creation of this novel. For this novel, the spelling of Jaruel Marr's name has been taken from his headstone. In other reportage, it has had other variations.

The story of Seaborn, who was said to have washed ashore between two featherbed mattresses and to have been rescued by Jaruel and Catherine Marr in 1875, is a well-known Maine legend. Some regional historians have tried to debunk the story although many lighthouse buffs prefer to believe it. While it's fairly certain no such shipwrecked baby was adopted by Jaruel Marr, many in the extended generations of Marr descendants believe the baby did exist, was rescued by Marr, and might have been given to a local doctor who either adopted the baby himself or knew of a family in want of a baby to adopt. This is why descendants of Jaruel Marr who heard about the shipwrecked baby from fathers, mothers, or grandparents knew the story not as a legend but as an event that happened in the family's lighthouse-keeping past. They never wondered what became of the ship- wrecked baby, nor who in the family could have been the baby, because they knew she was never adopted by the family. It appears to have been one such family member, the last living child of Jaruel Marr, who told the story to the *Navy Times* in 1955.

The "Lady Ghost of Hendricks Head" is also a popular legend. The identity of the "Lady Ghost"—a real woman who was found drowned off the coast of Southport in 1931—has never been solved, but to my knowledge, no one (before this novel) has ever tried to link the legend of the shipwrecked baby with the story of the Lady Ghost.

Acknowledgments are made to the following publications and individuals for their research or published accounts that were utilized and/or quotes in the writing of this novel.

Edward Rowe Snow for "The Baby that Washed Ashore" from *Famous Lighthouses of New England*, 1945.

Edward Rowe Snow for "The Beautiful Stranger" from *Parade Magazine*, May 21, 1972.

George W. Grupp for "Lighthouse Attendant Rescues, Adopts, Shipwrecked Baby Girl" from *The Navy Times*, July 16, 1955.

Evelyn Stratton for "Life at Marr's Harbor" (not published). Names from her document have been liberally altered.

Rose O'Brien for "The Lady Ghost of Hendricks Head" from *The Lewiston Journal*, July 14, 1956. Some names from this document have been altered.

Merle Edward Bouges for "The Marr Ancestral Home" and the Marr Family Tree (There is no significance to the similarity of his name and the names of the characters: Marr-Burgess. Some birthdates and names have been altered for use in the novel.).

Lighthouse Digest for miscellaneous information.

And to Ben and Luanne Russell, owners of Hendricks Head Light, who treat the lighthouse, as well as its legends and history, with respect, generosity, and affection.

Credit is also given to the following websites for webpage content found in this novel:

No author. U.S. Coast Guard Historians Office. "Breaking the Barrier: Women Lighthouse Keepers of the U. S. Lighthouse Board / Service." Retrieved April 2003 from *http://www.nightbeacon.com/lighthouseinformation/articles/Women_Lighthouse_Keepers.htm*

Brunelle, Jim (1980). "A Brief History of Maine." excerpted from *Maine Almanac*. Retrieved May 2003 from *http://www.mainehistory.info/history.html*

De Wire, Elinor (2000). "Matinicus Rock's Twin Lights." Retrieved March 2003 from *http://www.sentinelpublications.com/abbie.htm*

Mintz, S. (2003). "The History of Childbirth." *Digital History*. Retrieved January 2003 from *http://www.digitalhistory.uh.edu/historyonline/childbirth.cfm*

Mintz, S. (2003). "Housework in Late 19th c America." *Digital History*. Retrieved January 2003 from *http://www.digitalhistory.uh.edu/historyonline/housework.cfm*

Mintz, S. (2003). "Courtship in Early America." *Digital History*. Retrieved January 2003 from *http://www.digitalhistory.uh.edu/historyonline/uscourt.cfm*

No author. "History of Sexual Harassment." Retrieved March 2003 from http://ww.fredonia.edu/aaoffice/index2.htm, State University of New York, Fredonia.

All other websites were invented by the author

Acknowledgments are made to the following publications in which portions of this novel first appeared:

Denver Quarterly for "Go to Ground"
Aethlon for "Can and Will"
Clackamas Literary Review for "Aura"
Del Sol Magazine for the graveyard excerpt

Printed in the United States
by Baker & Taylor Publisher Services